The Captivity Series Book 1

The Summer Is Ended

Jeremiah 8:20

by
Lynda Moldrem

PUBLISH AMERICA

PublishAmerica
Baltimore

First printing

ISBN: 1-59286-374-4
PUBLISHED BY PUBLISHAMERICA BOOK PUBLISHERS
www.publishamerica.com
Baltimore

Printed in the United States of America

To my loving mother, Mary,
who has supported and encouraged me through
the adventures in my life including this one.

The encouraging words of my friends, my staff and my Sunday
school class were of great value in the process of writing this novel.
Thank you to each of you who made me believe I could actually
write this book, this first novel. To my Lord and Savior, Jesus
Christ, I give honor and glory for all I do.

CHAPTER 1

Babylon, Winter 606 BC

Nebuchadnezzar stood, yelling to all within the sound of his voice, "Are there not any wise men left to serve this kingdom?"

He looked back at the spy who had just brought him unwelcomed news from an area northeast of Egypt.

"You are saying, if I understand correctly, that somehow," he paused here to move closer to the trembling spy, "the fact that Pharaoh Necho is preparing to come to the aid of the Assyrians in Carchemish," and again he paused to get his point across, "just came to your attention." He waited for the affirming nod from the spy cowering in front of him. He continued, "Pharaoh Necho is planning on aiding them in their battle against us this spring and you just found this out, is that right?"

The spy nodded, being very careful about how he responded to Nebuchadnezzar. He did not speak.

Nebuchadnezzar moved behind him, whispering into his ear, "Over a year ago we sent you to get information and you are just now coming to tell us this bad news." He moved around to the front, "Spies are supposed to give us advanced warning so we can prepare for the unknown." He went back to his throne and sat down. "Do you think this is what I considered advanced warning?"

Nebuchadnezzar's mind was on the upcoming battle scheduled to begin in a couple of months for Carchemish. This city controlled the major east-west ford of the Euphrates River for trade. Control of this route was vital to his father's kingdom.

Nebuchadnezzar knew with the Egyptians helping Assyria he might not win the battle for control. He must stop Pharaoh at all costs. His thoughts returned to the matter in front of him, the man who failed to help him reach his goal.

"I paid for your service," Nebuchadnezzar said from his throne, "and I got nothing in return. Ingarri, what do you think?" He addressed his question to one of his officers.

Ingarri stepped forward from his position, responding, "Sire, he has failed his country and you. He deserves no mercy." The spy fell to his knees and began begging for mercy.

"Could you have done his job better? Could you have been a better spy than he was?" the prince asked, still addressing his solider.

Ingarri walked toward the throne and knelt in front Nebuchadnezzar, "I would give my life to serve you in any way. Searching out enemy's secrets would bring me great joy. Please, sire, allow me this privilege?" He waited, head bowed, for his leader's answer.

"You shall go for me, along with many others on whom I can depend." Nebuchadnezzar walked to Ingarri and touched his shoulder, "Stand, my friend, and come along."

They moved toward the poor man, "You didn't keep me informed," complained Nebuchadnezzar. He scowled at the spy, "Then you have the gall to give me this 'wise' counsel," he said mockingly, "'Be prepared,' you say, 'Pharaoh is on the march!' On the march! What kind of warning is that? It is too late to move my men into position to stop him from coming to Carchemish. Many more men will die in this war because of your foolishness!"

Nebuchadnezzar anger exploded. His right fist caught the man on the chin, knocking the spy to the floor. He moved around him kicking him repeatedly. He motioned for Ingarri to join him. The two continued for another minute leaving the spy bleeding and moaning. Nebuchadnezzar calmed slightly when he spoke, "Get the general in here now," he called to his aid.

He walked back to the side table. After a small drink which he finished in a single swallow, he turned and looked at the spy, who was still curled in a fetal position on the stone. He smiled down at him, "You should have known better than to be the bearer of evil tidings to a ruler. But given the fact that you did not know the significance of this news about Pharaoh, I doubt you would have the wits to have foreseen the result of your message," Nebuchadnezzar said, looking to his body guards. He nodded toward the man, "Take him out and behead him." The two guards moved in next to the man and lifted him from the floor. He screamed repeatedly that he did his best and did not deserve death. He could still be heard screaming until the guards left the palace.

Nebuchadnezzar dropped into a nearby seat. He rested his head against the back closing his eyes to block out distractions while he considered his options. Within a quarter hour the army's general, Nebuzaradan, arrived. He could tell when he entered the room that Nebuchadnezzar was not happy.

"Sire, I am here at your request," he said, bowing and remaining in that position until he was recognized.

"I want you to find some reliable spies and dispatch them to the cities between here and Egypt. You can start with sending Ingarri into the field. I just got a report from a spy that made my blood hot. I should have heard this information months ago."

"What report, sire?" asked Zaradan.

Nebuchadnezzar gave his lead general the basics. Zaradan listened intently and then commented, "I have several generals who could send some of their best men. We will put them in cities at your command. When do you want them to leave?"

"Tomorrow."

Zaradan was not going to argue, considering the last man's fate who had displeased the king's son. But he would risk a suggestion, "Could we have two days, sire? I believe we can have all the men ready and informed by day after tomorrow. You and I also need to meet to select cities and discuss better options," he suggested.

Nebuchadnezzar looked at his general, who had served him without error or selfishness. He respected the man. Although he hated to have his word questioned, if anyone could get away with it, Zaradan could.

"Do what you can. The sooner the better. I want men who know how to read the people and understand the politics of the area. I hope you can find a few who are not fools like the man who just left. Tell them I want regular information sent back to us either here or at Carchemish. Let's get busy right now and talk about how Pharaoh's arrival complicated our plans. Meet me in the war room with the other generals in two hours." Nebuchadnezzar rose and walked to the curtain near the throne. He turned back to Zaradan who was still standing where he had been. "Bring your list of suggested spies and the cities they need check out. I will need your years of experience. All of you get to your jobs now until we meet in two hours."

CHAPTER 2

Jerusalem, April 605 B. C.

Jerusalem was hotter than usual on this April morning. Although Dinah had on light-weight fabrics which breathed easily in the humidity, she still felt slightly wilted in the hot sun. She had taken extra care to look her best since she would be at the temple, as well as, running errands and visiting friends today. Her vivid blue sash around her waist looked lovely, she thought, and blended well with a paler blue cotton cloth covering her hair which hung down her back.

She could see the temple wall as she wound her way skillfully through the hilly terrain toward the gate. Today, her first stop was for lunch with her father and brother. She plopped her heavy basket on the threshold at the foot of the gatekeeper.

She was prepared to go in to find her father, when he stopped her. "You know you can't go in. Just leave the basket here and I will have one of the boys take it to your father," he smiled politely at her. She treated him respectfully. Some of the others he dealt with who came to the temple were demanding or rude.

"Sir, I can't leave the whole basket of things I brought. Some of them have to go with me to make another delivery. And Father said he would rather I bring the basket back home than leave it for him to do later," she puffed, still winded from the uphill climb carrying the heavy basket. "I can go to the other gate to get him. He and Azariah can come to the door to see me there, but it's a long way to walk." She paused, hoping he might reconsider making her go to the other door.

He had made up his mind. He seemed to ignore the fact that she was waiting, so she turned to leave. Then reconsidering, she sat the basket down and reached in carefully, (Grandma wouldn't miss a fig, she was sure) and removed a nice, juicy one. Giving him the treat, she said, "Thanks for listening anyway." With that, she turned to walk back down the steps and over to the south entrance.

Turning the large fig over in his hand, he reconsidered, "Wait, Dinah. I will send someone to get your brother."

She thanked him and began setting the lunch out. It would have taken quite a few minutes to have gone around the temple. She knew she was running late, since the sun was directly overhead. It was already time for lunch and her family would be very hungry. She sat down for a few minutes to wait while they called Azariah from his studies with the rabbi. He was in training as an apprentice scribe to be like his father.

They arrived in a few minutes bringing an extra friend along. Azariah said, "I hope mother sent some extra."

Dinah nodded approvingly in answer and gave Daniel a welcoming smile. When they were all comfortable , Dinah unwrapped the food. She laid it on the cloth. It was a beautiful place to eat. From up on this high point you could see all over the western part of Jerusalem and enjoy the flow of people below on the roads.

Azariah took a large hunk of fresh bread and broke off a piece of goat cheese, "Father" he said handing the first part of the meal to him. Then he did the same for Daniel and himself. "...and some lamb?" he asked, offering them a chunk.

"Let's thank our God, first." father stopped to pray for the food and his family, saying "Baruch Atah Ado-noy Elo-heinu Melech haolam, hamotzi lechem min haoretz" ("Blessed are You, G-d, King of the Universe Who brings forth bread from the earth.").

Dinah helped herself to the cheese. She took a piece of bread and dipped it into delicious olive oil. After a skin of wine and apples at the end, Daniel reached over to check the unwrapped package still in the basket.

"Not a bite of those, Daniel" Dinah giggled, slapping at his hand. "You can have some tonight at home. Those go to your grandmother for all the help she was to us when mom was sick. They will bring you pleasure at dinner."

Daniel had always been like another brother to her and had grown up visiting their house often. He was in school some of the same days as Azariah was with the Rabbi. She respected Daniel's for his maturity and loyal friendship to her brother.

Daniel finished and stood to leave, "I need to hurry to the palace. I have tarried too long here, but I enjoyed the time and lunch." He rushed away taking the steps down two at a time.

Hadad said, "Honey, be alert and careful. People are not trustworthy there." As he and Azariah got up, he added, "You are going to the market for mother, aren't you? Where are you going first?"

"I am going to visit Chloe for a few minutes, then Grandma Mary's and lastly, the market. You heard Mom say this morning she wanted me to pick up a couple of things. I will be home well before supper to help, though."

"Sounds like a good afternoon for you. Give Mary my blessing, when you see her." He kissed her forehead and left.

Gathering up the left-overs quickly and she hurried down the steps taking the Tyropean (tI-ROPE-Ean) Valley toward the Ephraim Gate in the upper part of town. This road moved along the side of the west wall and went across the city from the upper gate to the lower city's Fountain Gate. Much of the city's traffic flowed along this path. She turned left on a side path that connected the Tyropean Road to Fish Gate road. She would see Chloe first.

Chloe was a clerk at the Sash Shop owned by Daniel's mother. They met there two years ago and had become close friends since. Dinah crept into the store behind two other ladies so Chloe wouldn't see her. She noticed Chloe was at the back of the store folding shawls.

Walking up behind her, Dinah reached over her shoulders and put her hands over her eyes. "Who do you think it is?" she teased.

Chloe pretended, "I have no eyes in the back of my head, so how could I possibly guess?" She knew exactly who it was. She whirled around, laughing and hugged her, "What are you doing here? I didn't think we would get to visit at all this week since everyone has been so busy."

"Oh, mother needed me to make a delivery and I got permission to make an extra stop here before I went to Daniel's house. Can we sit outside for a while?" asked Dinah.

Chloe disappeared into the back area. She and Meriel, Daniel's mother, returned together. After a hug, Meriel asked, "What brings you to our shop today? Are you buying a new sash?"

"Well, that wasn't part of the plan, but actually, I would love to look at some. Do you have anything in purple? You know how I love that color," Dinah smiled.

Both other ladies laughed, Meriel speaking, "We both know your love for the color purple, your royalness!"

Dinah laughed, too. It had been a joke for years that she was the princess of her family and loved the look of riches and beauty. "Okay, enough said. Show me a sash, if you have one that you think is pretty."

Enjoying their time together they finally did find a beautiful lavender sash that was braided with pale yellow and purple yarn. Meriel agreed to reserve the sash until Dinah could talk to her mother about purchasing it. They had taken longer shopping than Dinah had planned, so she said her goodbyes and went to Mary's.

CHAPTER 3

At Ephraim Gate Road where Gideon's house was located she turned down a small side path. Daniel's family, related to the royal line of Zedekiah, had moved from Beth-Horon to Jerusalem when his father began his position with the King as clerk. Now his father was the chief financial advisor to Jehoiakim.

She spied their house immediately. It was easy to see since it was a two-story home surrounded by single story homes near the Ephraim gate.

She knew that at this time of day probably only grandmother and Salme (SAL-mA), Daniel's 4 year-old little sister, would be home. That was perfect since Mary was the main person to whom she wished to speak. But it would be good to see Salme, the cutest little sprite of a girl with big brown eyes and straight, raven black hair. She had a trusting spirit that endeared her to all who knew her, and her questioning and eagerness made her a great deal of fun to the family.

Within the quarter-hour Dinah was knocking at the courtyard gate. Mary was sitting in the shade by a small pool of water in the stone paved court. The servant working in the garden was a young Moabites in a dark blue rough linen skirt. Dinah noticed she was a tall, healthy girl with brown hair that was pulled back and tied with yarn. She wore a green over-blouse of cotton and a thin sash of twirled green and yellow cloth. Mary waved eagerly when she saw Dinah come through the gate. Dinah crossed to the bench indicated by

Mary.

"Hello, dear girl," she said, hugging her. "It is so good to see you." She continued, "It is a hot day for such a long walk. Follow me to the shade and put the basket down. Cache, please bring her some water," Mary asked. Dinah drank eagerly while Mary continued, "Now, what brings you uptown in the heat of the day?" Mary was slight of frame and about five feet tall. She was tough, wiry and had a quick mind. Her white hair pulled into a knot at the nape of her neck gave her a distinguished appearance. She was dressed in a smooth cotton shift of pale yellow with a sash made by her daughter of yellow and green linen. At fifty-five she still had beautiful smooth, olive skin that made her look years younger.

Daniel's family depended on her to run the home while his mother managed a store selling woven sashes. Some were woven in their home by servants. Others she purchased from local ladies involved in that work in their homes.

"I am on an errand of thankfulness for my family. Last month mother was ill with a sick stomach. Do you remember?"

Before grandma could answer, a raven-haired flash flew into the court with arms flailing and voice screeching, "Don't let him get me, Grandma! He is right behind me."

"What's wrong, Salme? Did someone hurt you?" Mary asked with concern.

Salme looked startled, "Hurt me? Oh, Grandma, no. It is Jothal (JO-thul). He was chasing me from the street where we were playing. It wasn't anyone bad." Turning slightly, suddenly she noticed they had company, "Dinah!" Salme yelled and jumped into her out-stretched arms.

Hugging her tightly, Dinah responded, "Well, it sounds like you were in real danger from that brother of yours. You better hide behind my bench before he gets here. I'll bet he will be at the gate any minute." With that Salme jumped down, squealing again, and slid behind the seat.

And just in time too, because a shadow darkened the courtyard entrance as eight-year-old Jothal stormed into the area. He was slight of frame, but tall for his age, with light brown hair and green eyes. He had his family's good mind. "Where is that little gnat? She took my apple and went fly..." Jothal stopped mid-sentence, when he saw Dinah, whom he always liked. "Hello. I didn't see you when I came in." She had been with the family often enough that they all knew each other as friends.

Dinah hugged him, saying, "I am not surprised you didn't notice me. You were in a big hurry when you came in."

He laughed; putting his hands on his hips, he looked around. He faced the two ladies, "Anyway, did Salme come home?"

"Now let me see," Mary thought out loud with a twinkle in her eye and looked at their guest, "Dinah, didn't we see a girl come through here recently?'

"Hum? I did see this beautiful little, helpless girl," added Dinah, "but surely you couldn't have been referring to her?" she gazed in wonder at Jothal. "Would she take someone's apple?"

At that instant they heard a 'chomp' as Salme took a bite from the apple in question and popped up from behind the bench. Running at her top speed, she fled inside with one of her sandals flying free of her foot. Jothal was not far behind. Cache followed them inside planning to referee the situation.

"I just love them like they were my own brother and sister," Dinah said to Mary. "If you need help with them anytime, please ask me. Now, let me finish with the errand that mother sent me to do. So, do you remember?"

Mary nodded, remembering clearly. "Abigail was in bed for a week and couldn't get up to meet the family's needs. It was such a burden for her. Everyone here was fine, so I was glad I could be there at your house."

"And you were such a great help. Mother appreciated you so much she sent these figs to thank you. She was able to fully recover because she knew you were there. Thank you so much. You demonstrated true giving to our family and this is just a small gift to let you know you are loved," Dinah set the fig bundle on the table and added, changing the subject, "By the way, I saw Daniel at lunch, and he discovered the figs. He will be eager to get home for dessert tonight!" They both laughed as they thought of his sweet tooth.

Mary and Dinah enjoyed an hour together before it was time for Dinah to go to the market and then home. She hated to leave. In the short time they had known Daniel's family, they had become more like family than friends. She kissed Mary and left.

Home was only just over a mile. Her mother asked her to stop at the market, which was not far from Daniel's home.

As she started to close the gate, Mary called, "You keep a careful eye on the vendors in the market. I have been hearing stories about their dishonest scales and unfair prices."

On the way to the market she considered how quickly her parents and Daniel's parents had become close friends even though his parents were a few years younger. Meriel, Mary's daughter, had met Gideon when they were about ten and eleven respectively. Their parents had betrothed them to each other a year later and they were married when Gideon was eighteen and Meriel was seventeen. It had been a good marriage. They had learned to love each other. Eventually, their trust in each other had become complete. Daniel had come along just one year later bringing great joy to them.

His family lineage was filled with leaders in the local villages. His father had been the magistrate of Beth-Horon, the village to the west of Jerusalem from which Gideon's family came. Gideon's quick mind had distinguished him from his siblings. It was one of the things Dinah's father had most enjoyed about his friendship with Gideon. They thought alike on many important issues.

Gideon had been sent to Jerusalem for training in the temple and thrived so well in the educational environment that his teachers recommended that the King consider giving him a job in the area of accounting. He had a way with numbers. Shortly after the recommendation he took a clerk's position and he moved his family to Jerusalem, where he advanced to the position of the city accountant in two years with the responsibility of all of the city's money. He worked directly for the King's 2nd in command, Tigner and advised the King in fiscal matters.

CHAPTER 4

Dinah arrived at the market as it was closing. It was in the upper part of town not far from the Ephraim Gate. This site provided merchants with good commerce because of the movement in and out of Jerusalem through this gate. They could make significant money if their product was good. The market was still busy although some vendors had already closed their booths. Last minute shoppers were still scurrying through the area trying to buy a few more products before the vendors closed. Most ladies had done their shopping early so they could spend the day preparing the food. But her mother only needed olive oil and wheat so purchasing it at an earlier time wasn't important. These were staple items that would be for future use rather than for today's food preparation.

This is the time of day you often saw the "people of the night" shopping, because regular citizens were not there to cast a critical eye toward them. A local prostitute was just down the lane. Everyone knew her, but few spoke to her. As she passed by Dinah she nodded. Dinah spoke, "Hello, Abeetha."

Abeetha was surprised. She looked at Dinah, responding hesitantly, "How is your family?"

"Everyone is fine. And your mother?"

Abeetha continued, "Mother is doing okay."

"I am sorry about the death of your father last year. I know it has been hard for the two of you," Dinah paused. She didn't want to offend Abeetha, but she knew the reason she was in this 'profession' was out of need rather than preference. "I, uh, am sorry life has become so difficult for you."

Abeetha thanked Dinah, "Thank you for speaking to me. Very few acknowledge that I am around. It has been very hard, but we are surviving. I must go, but thanks again for speaking." She moved away.

Dinah had heard stories about Abeetha's choice, but instead of being angry at her, she felt sorry for her. Abeetha only did what she had to do and probably would never have made that choice otherwise.

Dinah got back to her task. Her late arrival made it necessary for Dinah to get her oil from a man that she never had purchased from before. His was filthy with eyes that darted around from side to side.

She stopped at his booth, asking quietly, "Could I buy a log of olive oil, please?"

Without looking directly at her, he commanded, "Away with you, girl. I only deal with customers with money." But actually he was watching her carefully to see if she revealed how much money she was carrying.

Pulling out several coins to purchase the oil, "How much is the oil?" she questioned, trying to sound confident. She had never faced a vendor like him in the past.

Turning around slowly he rubbed his greasy beard, as if reconsidering, "Well, it appears I was mistaken about you. You do have some money," he said, pausing to emphasize his point. "I will deal with you. But be quick. It is the end of the day and I am hot and tired, so no haggling. Five gerahs for the oil and not a fraction less," he barked.

"What? That oil should cost only 1 gerah at the most," she practically shouted. She remembered what Mary had said dishonest merchants cheating their customers, but the ones she usually purchased from were not like this man at all.

He thought he had her over a barrel, "Take it or leave it. It makes no difference to me. I am the only oil vendor still at market, though, so you'll have to wait until tomorrow, if you refuse my offer," he smirked. Turning his back, he began packing up his things, hoping she would think he was closing up shop to increase her feeling of desperateness.

"But, sir, if I buy the oil at that price, I will not have enough money left for the wheat I need," she pleaded. "Please lower your price." She didn't know whether to leave without the oil, then to go home and tell her mother what happened and try again tomorrow, or to pay the price he asked and not get the wheat. She wasn't really sure how urgently her mother needed the oil. Maybe she should have made the purchase earlier in the day, but she didn't want to carry the items all day. Now she wasn't sure she had made a wise decision to wait.

He glanced to the side, watching to see her decision. Although it appeared he was ignoring her request, actually, he was trying to see how desperate she was. There was no question the price was too high and he knew it, but he could use the sale, even at one gerah. If he could squeeze out more, why not? She was young and inexperienced, and he hadn't sold much today, so he figured she was an easy target that would help him make up his loss for the day.

Before either of them had a chance to make a decision, someone called to Dinah from the next vendor's booth. Dinah saw Mishael (ME-shA-el) picking up some leather at the next booth. Most leather goods were sold outside of town, since the tanneries were there. It was a smelly, messy business not welcomed in the market area. However, this vendor usually set up a shop in the local market to sell the finished product.

He gave her a big smile, when he got to the vendor's booth, "I am so glad to see you." He was, since he thought she was one of the prettiest girls in town. Her wavy auburn hair set a frame for her golden-flecked hazel eyes. She had a way about her that made him feel at ease. He liked to share what he was thinking and get her opinion.

Not that many people, especially girls, affected him that way. Girls liked him, though. He was the tall, dark and the mysterious type, some would say.

"Dinah, what are you doing in the market at this time of day?" he questioned as he shifted his package. He noticed she did not seem as carefree and happy as usual. Rather than her usual smile, she looked unsure, so he asked, "What's wrong?"

She was always glad to see him, but today it made her feel helpless to have him there when she was trying to deal with this vendor and getting no where. She tried to make her face look pleasant, "Hello, Mishael, I am glad to see you. I am getting some oil for mom before I go home." She smiled and hoped she looked convincingly happy.

Quickly, she made her decision to do something before he noticed she was having a hard time with the vendor. She took out all the gerahs and laid them down on the counter beside the jar.

Her smile, which usually made his heart flutter, was painted on her face like an artist's portrait. Taking in the situation with the money she had placed on the counter and the jar of oil, Mishael asked, "Is this the jar of oil you are buying, Dinah?"

She knew there were two questions in that one statement. She nodded 'yes' in answer.

The vendor started to slap his hand down quickly on the coins and move away, but Mishael was quicker. He grabbed the vendor's arm with his left hand, laying his right over the coins. His grip was strong and his eyes were flashing, "Sir, I suggest you adjust your price now." He picked up four coins and the jar. "That is a fair market value for the oil with a little extra," Misha warned pointing to the single remaining coin, "and if I find out that you are trying to take advantage of young ladies in this market again, I will find an authority who will take away your space and license to sell. Do you understand?"

The vendor jerked his arm free and picked up the coin, putting it into the ratty money pouch on his belt. He turned without saying a word and moved to the back of his booth leaving from the two teenagers.

Mishael handed Dinah the jar and extra coins. She apologized, "I am so sorry to involve you in this. I really tried to work this out with him, but he was so unreasonable. He made me angry. He just wouldn't come down on his price."

"I am glad I came along when I did. It's sad that our marketplace has become so dishonest that families cannot send their daughters here without worrying about whether they will be mistreated. Do you have any other purchases to make? I could walk with you for a while."

"That would be wonderful," she said. This time her smile was genuine. "Let's see if any vendors remain who have some wheat. I need two omers." Then she switched back to the topic of dishonest merchants, "I know others have dealt with these scoundrels on a daily basis, but not me. Vendors in the past were fair and very helpful," she said, placing the jar in the basket with the linens and balancing it on her head.

They had checked several vendors before Dinah said, "There, I see a wheat vendor." She pointed down to the right. Having Mishael along was fun. They had laughed for the last half an hour. His presence reassured her, too, since she was less likely to be taken advantage of again.

Mishael asked, "How is Azariah? I haven't been to the temple for training for some time." Mishael was known for his strong faith in God and willingness to stand up for what is right when challenged. "You know I have been apprenticing with father as a builder and don't have time to continue at the temple," he explained. His father was teaching him the Jewish life and culture.

But Dinah was not thinking about his question. She was enjoying just looking at him. He was strong which gave her a feeling of safety. He looked like he could handle any situation. But even more than his appearance, he had a confidence in himself and his abilities that made him attractive to her. She could imagine a life together with him. Their son would have thick, curly chocolate-brown hair that was shaggy around his ears like his.

He held his head back and laughed, "What are you looking at? You have that far away, dreamy look you get sometimes."

She just smiled and kept walking. His eyes, vivid and green, were the color of her cat's eyes. Oh, she had noticed those eyes many times before. She could just relax in his gaze when he looked at her. She would like someone like him, or him, to ask father for her hand in marriage.

"Oops, watch your step!" Mishael warned, grabbing her arm to steady her as she stumbled on the stone pathway.

"Thank you," is what she said, but she thought, 'Oh, brother. That's what I get for daydreaming and wondering if he would one day ask my father to marry me. That is just too good to ever happen.' They walked and talked until they were out of the market area.

"I need to get to work. Father and I are still at the palace remodeling. I enjoyed the walk. I wish the circumstances had been better in the market. Please let me know anytime you are going to shop and I will try to meet you, if I'm free. Give your family my greetings," he said with a wave and smile as he turned toward the temple area. His father, Benjamin, was the city planning commissioner for the King.

Dinah hurried to her home in the lower part of town. These homes on the escarpment were interspersed with streets and footpaths. A roof of the lower home might make a courtyard for a higher home. It made the whole area appear to be a gigantic staggered stair-step of roofs, ladders and steps. Most of the homes were single-storied dwellings.

Dinah's home was a two-storied home built along the hillside. The roof of the first story became the courtyard and an entrance to the second story. There was a street-level entrance with a walled courtyard on the lower level. Near their home several scattered streets or pathways wound their way along the hillside. Most were narrow footpaths, but some allowed for carts and small carriages. Her house was about half-way up the hill with a wider street, Essene Way, in front of their home.

It had been a long day. She was eager to share with her mother all that had happened since she left this morning. She never thought that going to the market could be so exhausting. Sitting the basket inside the doorway, "Mother," she called as she entered the living area, "where are you?" Unusual; no answer. She called again, "Mother?" Where could she be"

CHAPTER 5

Daniel hurried to the palace, which wasn't far. He had taken longer at lunch with Azariah's family than he usually did. Today of all days, he should not have been late. The palace staff was already tense and his lateness added to it. Daniel took his work seriously and was not habitually late, but his father would still not be happy. Gideon had earned this position because of his giftedness with numbers and his hard work. Daniel knew being late and not dependable reflected poorly on his father.

He took the palace steps two-by-two and cut through the courtyard toward the offices. As expected, Gideon was reviewing some shipping data with his second in command. He was at his usual post sitting right where he could observe the entrance. Daniel tried to scurry by his father without being noticed.

"Stop, young man," said Gideon. He paused and nodded to his aid that he wanted some time alone. He motioned for Daniel to come near, "You hoped I wouldn't see you, didn't you?"

"Father, I am sorry. Time just passed so quickly at lunch..."

Gideon held up his hand, "Hurrying in to the counting room will not restore the time you have stolen from your employer and fellow clerks. You know this could delay our deadline for this tribute payment."

Daniel knew everyone was edgy since the shipment was due to leave any day. He apologized and started to walk away. His father touched his arm,

"Son, I am sure your reason for being late is excellent, but I cannot excuse you any more than I could other clerks. I want you to plan on staying late this evening until the project is completed. That shipment needs to leave soon."

"I had already planned to see Azariah and we were going to …."

"I want you to do as I asked. I need you for the shipment to be ready."

The tribute payment shipping date was a secret kept quiet until the day it left town, but it was known that it would be soon. The shipment was closely guarded until the actual day arrived.

Daniel was embarrassed for himself and his father. He agreed with a nod and turned to go to the counting chamber with the other clerking staff. He heard a quiet voice as he walked away, "I am still proud of you. I know this is uncomfortable for you when I have to speak to you publicly. I care enough that I cannot ignore the character training that comes with learning from your mistakes." Daniel's humble grin told his father that he was okay.

Daniel hurried around the corner and nodded to the palace guard who opened the counting chamber door. The clerks were busy tabulating the payment to Pharaoh Necho, the king of Egypt, when Daniel arrived. Judah and its king, Jehoiakim, had been vassals of Egypt for many years. The tribute they paid yearly was one talent of gold and one hundred talents of silver along with other goods including wool, spices, cedar, and animal skins. Each payment opened up old wounds and caused discussions about rebelling against Egypt and seeking Judah's independence. If Egypt had been faithful to help Jerusalem when it was requested, there may not have been as many dissenters. Every time a call for help was sent to Pharaoh, it was not clear whether Egypt would come to help or not. On top of that, Pharaoh Necho had killed King Josiah, a beloved king, during a battle. Necho was not a loved man in Jerusalem.

The shipment was to be ready on time or Jehoiakim would be angry. Heads would roll. Maybe literally! A clerk lost his life recently when gold was missing and it could not be accounted for. This king was volatile. Everything was checked and then double-checked.

Although Daniel was from a noble family, he was assigned to be trained and work alongside other clerks until he learned all the processes of governing. He helped in the tabulating the gold and silver as it was packed for shipment and confirming the total with the aid when it was finished. Although Daniel was doing training with an experienced clerk, Ben-Zion, he was still afraid they would make an error. He took this work very seriously.

Ben-Zion was not happy when Daniel arrived. "Where have you been? I have been working non-stop since day-break today. I know you only work after lunch on school days, but you are way overdue. I am hungry, hot and tired and haven't taken a break, because I was covering for you," complained Ben. Stopping mid-fold of one of the cow hides, he challenged, "Well, where HAVE you been?" It was obvious that the answer Daniel would give him of sitting at a leisurely, home-made lunch with friends would not help his fellow clerk or himself.

"Let's just say that I picked a bad day to be late and I am sorry. No explanation would change my negligence or make your lot easier. How about if you take a break and eat something, while I review where we are? I will confirm what you have completed so far."

Ben was jealous of Daniel and his noble position and did not tolerate any slacking from his noble trainee. He left, gladly stopping his tabulation and handing the parchment to Daniel. Ben went to the back of the room to sit and eat a bite and get some much needed water.

Daniel went down to the loading dock. He spoke to the packers, some of whom appeared new to him. He carefully reviewed what had been packed and he checked to see if the gold and silver were distributed evenly in the wagons. The almost four-ton weight of metals was a disadvantage when traveling in sand on the trip to Egypt or if it was necessary to flee from an enemy. Distributing the weight evenly in several wagons was vital to the success of the trip. He quickly confirmed that each of the talent boxes was secure, and then he went back up to the counting area.

"Well, Daniel, is everything in order?" Ben smirked, although he seemed in better spirits returning from his lunch and a rest.

Continuing to review the work, Daniel replied, "Everything checks out. Those boxes are so heavy, even with just a few per unit. It takes two men to handle each." Trying to smooth ruffled feathers, he added, "I know why my father has depended on you for the last two years. This is a delicate operation with potential danger to us and to the caravan. I am grateful to have been trained by you. You are such a careful man." Ben's eyes brightened and he gave a tilt of approval to Daniel, who said, "Let's get back to work and finish as soon as possible."

With that the two men resumed working with the packers who came up to the counting room to get the supplies and returned downstairs to load the tribute in the wagons. If things continued to go well, they would be finished before dark. Daniel wouldn't call Ben a friend, but he was a good trainer. He could tell that Ben was jealous of his position as the son of the chief accountant to the King. For the life of him, Daniel did not know why that was considered an advantage. If anything, being Gideon's son made things harder on him rather than easier. Gideon did not intentionally demand more of him, but in an effort to make Daniel a man of character and a good leader, Gideon watched his son more carefully than the other clerks for an error or for character flaws. Ben had it easier and he should be grateful for that.

They followed careful plans in loading and supplying the caravan wagons. The highways were dangerous places to travel these days. Many robbers made their living from travelers taking those paths. The caravan and guards would travel some of the back roads to Egypt when possible and take the Patriarch's Highway, which went north and south along the mountain ridge, when necessary. No completely safe route existed, so every precaution had been taken to protect the shipment and the men. The metals were concealed under crates of other goods, like standard merchants would carry traveling in a caravan. The guards had been specially trained and were clothed like hired guards rather than soldiers. The caravan was heavily armed and should be prepared for any event. A supply wagon was also prepared for the animals' food and needs. A second wagon with food, bedding and other supplies along with a royal cook was loaded. They should be able to make the trip with minimal problems.

Ben went to Oshiel, Gideon's aid, "I believe we are ready to have you check the shipment, sir."

With that, Oshiel caught Gideon's eye and they followed Ben back to the counting room where Daniel joined them as they went to the back and down the stairs to the loading area. Guards were at the loading dock doors and scattered around the room. They were relaxed, but alert. Although the general public did not know about the times and dates of these shipments, nothing would prevent inside information from leaking out with large number of personnel involved in preparing the caravan. A guard held the door for them as they entered the area. It was at street level and had sufficient space to hold twenty horses, ten wagons and a large staging area for getting supplies ready. There were guard stations, sleeping quarters for servants and guards, and storage bins for supplies and weapons. Today ten wagons were loaded and under guard. The camels and horses were in stalls being readied for the long trip. The supply wagons had been equipped and stood against the far wall.

Gideon walked to the first wagon and was handed the shipping list. He checked each and every item, the packing, the quantities and the concealment. He followed the same process for the next nine wagons. When he was satisfied that everything was correct, he turned to Oshiel, "Let's get word to Tigner that we are ready for a final inspection for this shipment." Oshiel found the King's eunuch and sent him to the palace court with word of their completion of the shipment. "Daniel and Ben, go back to the counting room and finish up with the clean up details and check with the other clerks. They can go home, but you two wait until I return."

Daniel wanted to stay in the loading zone. This was the first time he had been involved personally with the tribute payment shipment and had this close of contact with the King's court. However, it seemed that meeting Tigner and the others would have to wait until another time. But if he couldn't stay there, he would rather have gone home. Obviously, that wasn't an option either, so Ben and Daniel went upstairs. They helped the other clerks as they finished storing all the supplies they had used in processing. Daniel began an inventory and while Ben prepared a list that would help them get ready for the next payment.

Within the hour they heard the voices of Gideon and Oshiel as they approached the top of the stairs, "Sir, I think Tigner was pleased with the way the shipment looked and the preparation of the caravan. It is rare when old eagle-eyes cannot find an error of some sort and tonight he couldn't. Good work was done by all."

Ben and Daniel exchanged glances with raised eyebrows. Those comments, not necessarily intended for their ears, made them both feel proud. They would share that information with the other clerks tomorrow, since they had left earlier.

Gideon spoke as he entered the room, "Daniel; Ben. Well done, boys. The King and Tigner are both pleased that we were able to get everything ready tonight. Good work. We can go home now."

They put out the lamps in the room and exited to the main entrance. Gideon stopped at his desk to put a few items away and then joined the others who were in the courtyard.

"Good-night. Jehovah be with you," he said of the group separated. He and Daniel hurried uptown to their home. They were much later than usual, but Meriel would be ready with a good meal whenever they arrived. Daniel's stomach began to growl thinking of a warm supper and sweet figs.

They talked about their country and the tribute payment. Since Israel and Judah became separate, they had followed varied paths in leadership and in spiritual direction. Israel had been conquered by Assyria's King Sargon II over 117 years earlier and Israel's capital, Samaria, had been inhabited by

Assyrians. The offspring of the intermarriages with the Hebrews and Assyrians were called Samaritans and were rejected by the Jews. Hebrew law about what Israel and Judah would do was clear: they were not to intermarry with other Gentiles.

Judah had been spared when the next king of Assyria, Sennacherib, had set up a siege against the town of Jerusalem. Hezekiah asked God for deliverance and was granted that for his city, however, Sennacherib took an estimated 200, 000 other captives to Nineveh during that campaign. So far Jerusalem had not been totally conquered, but they had been made vassals to several peoples. The city's patriots and loyalists truly believed that because Jerusalem contained the Temple, God would protect the city from being taken. They were confident in their safety. Others, not in their political camps, were not as sure of Jerusalem's guarantee of safety from invasion.

As they left, Daniel mentioned the discussion he overheard today. "Father, I heard rumors today that recent merchants coming from the north had witnessed more war. The same country that conquered Assyria's capital--what is it called?" asking his father.

"Nineveh."

"Well, the country that conquered Nineveh is on the move again. Is it called Babylon or Chaldea? Both have been mentioned as powerful countries with strong rulers, according to the accounts I have been hearing."

"Nabopolassar, from Babylon, is a powerful man who has been campaigning in areas around the north. He is often victorious in battle. We hear of him often in discussions at court. He also sends his son, Nebuchadnezzar, as a battle general on some campaigns and he has been very successful, too. The Chaldeans are a group of people in the Babylonian empire who are considered wise men and leaders. What else are you hearing from the work force?" Gideon asked.

"We all know that Josiah died trying to stop Necho before he got to the north. But the southern merchants say that Pharaoh is again in a campaign in that area. He wants to protect himself and Egypt from this new threat of the Babylonians. The battle could be fought anytime, but Necho is expected to win. Merchants traveling from north to south have been giving us periodic updates." Daniel added.

"Well," commented his father, "rumors do fly around the palace fast. Surprisingly, they are fairly accurate. Necho left Egypt in early spring about four years ago and met our King Josiah. You know Josiah died trying to stop him, but failed. Necho is marching north and will return going through this area later this summer. He is trying to get into the northern Euphrates area to try and settle matters and put down any uprising before this young general, Prince Nebuchadnezzar, does damage to Egyptian territories to the north."

They grew quiet while they finished their walk home. They were several streets from their part of town. As it grew dark, Daniel noticed the city's crowd of evil doers began to appear. Abeetha was in her usual place along the main road which contained many shops, vendors and other offerings. All the vendors were gone, but there was still plenty of foot traffic for her to tempt with her voice and her eyes. She was eighteen now. Her mom, Magdala, and she were left without any means of support. She had turned to the only profession she felt she could learn and be good at. She had become very good at it, if being sought out by many regulars was any indication. Daniel heard her name tossed about among the young men at temple and some of the clerks. She appeared to a very busy girl making a livable income. But the price wayward women paid was high. The King had not encouraged righteousness during his reign, but some still lived godly lives. Magdala would have preferred that they lived like they used to, but they could not survive like that. She tolerated her daughter's life because of the support it provided, but her heart broke to see how her innocent daughter had become a hardened woman of the street.

Gideon and Daniel smelled the Cain's Inn before they turned the corner. Soldiers and merchants who frequented the tavern were not worried about bathing. The smell of wine, roasted meat and sweat wafted across the warm night air. Cain's Inn was very busy tonight. The street tables were full of military men and several merchants with their female escorts. It had been a local landmark for decades.

They hurried by and on toward the upper market area. By this time they were both too hungry to think about politics or the conditions in the city. They just wanted supper.

Entering their own courtyard, they immediately noticed the inviting smell of their supper cooking. What a pleasant contrast to the smells of the city.

"Meriel?" Gideon called. He was standing in the entrance area of their large home. Meriel's face appeared above the stone banister. Her beauty still caused his breath to catch. She waved and headed down. She was getting Salme ready for bed.

Kissing her on the forehead, he begged "My dear, we are so hungry and tired. I am sorry we missed supper, but tonight demanded extra time to finish our work." He did not specify what they were doing. The less she knew, the less she could be responsible for if she were ever captured or put in jeopardy by robbers. He loved her too much to take that chance and she was wise enough not to ask. "What are we having?"

"We had lamb stewed with potatoes, onion and carrots. Cache made bread and Dinah dropped by today with fresh figs."

They talked happily as they followed her into the dining area. The table had been left partially set with utensils, bread, a bowl of figs and a bottle of red wine. She quickly filled brass bowls with stew placing them in front of the men. They stopped to bless the food and hungrily dug in. Talk was minimal until they were on their second bowls of stew. She went back upstairs to finish with Salme.

Daniel finished and reached for the figs. He remembered Dinah's slap as he reached to take a fig at lunch. The thought brought a smile to his lips. "What's so funny, son?" dad wondered.

"Today at lunch," he paused, remembering that is why he had been so late. He decided to continue and explain, "I ate with Hadad and his family on the temple steps. Dinah brought them lunch and they invited me to join them. I wanted the figs then, but she teased me and told me I had to wait until supper," pausing again, "That's why I was late to work. It took me longer than usual to eat and visit with them over the meal. I am sorry, father." He looked up and his dad nodded an acceptance of his apology. "Dinah made me laugh. She actually slapped my hand and remembering that made me smile."

"She is going to be a handful for a husband someday. Are you considering her as a girl you might like for us to arrange to spend time with? We are very close to her family, you know."

"No, father. Although she is wonderful and would make a worthy bride, I don't think she is the one for me. I have noticed Mishael seems to take great notice of her, however. Do you remember my friend? He is the one who is an architect and builder. His father is the city architect and has worked often for the King and the priests. They do excellent work," Daniel added.

Gideon did remember them. Their work had received praise in the palace from the queen and queen mother for remodeling their baths. Ben and Misha's work had pleased them greatly. "They were well received at the palace. I think they may call on their services again when the need arises. It isn't often that quality work is done with honesty. The royal family admired their work ethic and the workmanship. And the price was fair, but not cheap. However, one doesn't mind paying for good work."

Meriel's voice interrupted their conversation, "Gideon, come kiss Salme good-night. She is almost ready to go to sleep and Jothal won't be too far behind her," Meriel called from upstairs.

With the statement about his going to bed soon, Jothal let out a cry of disapproval. He wanted to stay up and spend time playing with his brother. "Mom, please let me stay up for a while to see Daniel and Daddy," Jothal begged. Gideon appeared over her, as she sat on the bed in the room with the two children.

"Salme, my little raven," Gideon said, sweeping her into his lap. "You look so precious with that black hair falling around your face. Talk with me a minute. Jothal, you come too. You are becoming more of a little man every day." They both got up to be near their father, with whom they could never find enough time. Gideon sat on Jothal's bed as he placed his arm around his son and held Salme.

"It is very late. Maybe since tomorrow is the end of the work week, we can find time to do something together as a family. Would you like that?" Both reacted so happily that it made Gideon realized how much he had neglected spending time with them, to his regret. He must plan something with Meriel tonight. "I promise we will plan something before your mother and I go to sleep, okay?"

"Oh, daddy, I love you so much." Jothal hugged his father as tight as he could. He held him as if letting go would change the decision to have a family outing. "Can we fish?"

"Fish?" Gideon thought about all that would entailed, but his son's eagerness overruled his common sense, "Yes, son. I think I can arrange that. Salme, what about you? What would you like to do?"

"Pick flowers and catch butterflies. Aren't butterflies beautiful?" she smiled at him, thinking of their colorful wings shining in the sun. "Is this the time of year, father, when there would be butterflies?"

Mother stepped in at this point, "Yes, dear, this is the right time for butterflies. Daddy and I will talk this out, but both of you hop under the covers and let's get to sleep." They kissed the children and walked to the living area. "Honey, do you really have time to go on an outing this weekend? That would be so refreshing. We haven't done that since last summer." The light of pleasure he saw in her eyes helped him made up his mind that he would make time this weekend. They set down on a small couch and relaxed. Daniel came in to join them. There was an easiness in the family that all enjoyed.

"Let's plan on going to the Kidron Valley and spend time at the water and in the pasture. Have Cache pack a lunch for Sunday. We will leave after breakfast, have a fun afternoon and return by supper. How does that sound, my dear?" Gideon smiled at the thought of some relaxation and getting out of town.

"I'll talk with Cache tomorrow. Can we take the wagon? It would be more comfortable for all of us and give us more time at the river."

"I'll check with a driver tomorrow. I am really looking forward to this."

"I think I missed something. Are we going out for a trip?" Daniel asked.

Dad answered, "We are going to get some much needed time together as a family this Sunday."

"That sounds great. We don't get away often."

CHAPTER 6

Dinah was concerned about where her mother could be. She hurried into her house and looked around the lower level. Finding nobody downstairs, she ran to the upper level. Distant crying could be heard when she entered the courtyard area on the roof, but it wasn't coming from her house. She looked around trying to determine where the sound came from. Well, it wasn't to either side, so she tilted her ear up to see if it was coming from above them. Yes! She sprinted up the side stairs to the pathway winding around the neighborhood. Since her mother wasn't home, she might have followed that same sound. Dinah listened and followed the sound to three houses up the street to the right. The wailing increased to a yell. She arrived at the shabby house that was small and dark. Letting her eyes adjust, she tried to see inside. "Hello?" she called.

"Dinah, hurry. Come inside," her mom answered back immediately. She sounded worried.

"What's wrong? What are you doing here?"

"This young woman is having a baby and it is coming out feet first. I need the mid-wife. Can you run to her home and get her? We don't have much time. We may lose both of them, if something isn't done soon," she whispered most of this to Dinah, although, over the yelling, the mother probably wouldn't have overheard the conversation anyway.

Dinah took off as fast as she as could, continuing down the same foot path to the right that had brought her to the house. It took about five minutes for her to reach Dariann's house. She prayed that the mid-wife was at home. It was supper time and maybe she would be in. Knocking frantically, she yelled, "Dariann, this is Dinah. Abigail's daughter. Mom sent me to get you. Dariann? Are you home?" She continued to knock and yell.

Finally, movement behind the door. Dariann's husband answered the knock, "What on earth is this racket at suppertime? Don't you have any respect for a man and his time with his family?" He opened the door and stood facing Dinah, whom he did not know.

"I am so sorry, sir. We have a woman in birth and we need help. She's in real trouble. Can I speak to your wife?"

Before he could answer, Dariann appeared behind him. Having overheard Dinah's comments, she was already getting her instruments together along with some rags. Touching her husband's arm as she rushed past him carrying her bag, she followed Dinah back up the pathway toward the house. It took twenty valuable minutes, including the time at Dariann's house, for the round trip from the house. During that time Dinah explained to Dariann what she understood about the situation.

As they neared the house, the noise was less. Dinah wasn't sure that was a good sign. Looking up at Dariann she sensed that she was thinking the same thing. Dinah had no idea how long the lady had been in labor.

Stepping inside, Dariann asked, "Abigail, tell me what is happening and how long she has been laboring?"

"I came about three-quarters of an hour ago and I think she had already been struggling for several hours. She seems to be ready to deliver, but I feel the baby's feet instead of the head if I reach up inside the birth canal."

"Let me look. Dinah, can you get a lamp from your house? Abigail, get some water, wet some rags to wash with and light a fire. We will need heat for the baby, I hope. Oh, and find me some fat or grease." Abigail moved, but Dinah was already on her feet looking outside for fire wood. She had a small fire going in the hearth in minutes, then she went to her house for the lamp and some fat. Her mother had prepared wet and dry rags and had those, plus a large bowl of water, sitting beside Dariann.

"When did she become quiet?"

"About ten minutes before you arrived. She almost appears to have lost consciousness."

Dariann rinsed her hands and rubbed some fat over them. She slid one hand inside the woman who moaned slightly, but that was all. Dariann could feel the feet; she tried to push them back inside and turn the baby. That didn't seem to be working. "Abigail, push down on her stomach and toward her feet and try to help me. I am going to try to pull the baby on through the canal." Again, inserting her hand she pulled. "Good! Some movement. Yes...yes. I think the baby is moving out." The mother began to stir when the birth started to progress. She was awake enough to listen. "This is Dariann; I am a mid-wife from this area. Can you hear me?"

"Yes," she answered weakly.

"What is your name?"

"Bethany."

"I want you to push as hard as you can when I tell you. We will help. Do you understand?"

"I can't. I'm too tired. I have been trying to deliver for hours."

"You must try. We will help all we can," said Abigail.

"No, just let us both die. It would probably be better for everyone."

"I hope we're not going to let either of you die today. Now push, young woman," said Dariann with authority.

"I'll try," the moaning began to increase as the urgency to deliver took over again.

"Okay, push now!" With that, the three of them, each doing their part, pushing, pulling and straining to deliver, tried to get the baby to come out. Slowly, the movement increased and then, he was out! He was ghostly pale. It didn't look good for him and Bethany was very quiet, too.

Dariann picked up the baby, while she observed Bethany, she said, "Abigail, take several dry rags and push them against her birth canal very hard. Dinah, message her stomach." She had torn badly from the arms and shoulders of the baby coming out the wrong way. The bleeding was bad and it needed to slow down.

Dariann was working with the boy. He was that ugly gray-blue hue that skin takes on near death. In this kind of birth, Dariann had seen many babies die when she couldn't coax them to breathe. She turned him upside down to drain the fluid out of his lungs. Not a sound from his little body. Dinah couldn't take her eyes off the mid-wife. She had seen birth before, but never with these complications. For an infant or mother to survive, it often depended on the experience of the women helping. Today Bethany was blessed, for in the limited births that Dinah had witnessed, she had never seen any mid-wife so knowledgeable. Dariann turned him over on to her lap face down and massaged his back trying to loosen more fluids and open up his breathing. It was amazing how much drainage there was in such a tiny body.

"How is the bleeding?" She aimed her question toward Abigail. Removing the rags, it did appear that it was slowing, but certainly not stopped. Abigail grimaced and added new dry rags and pressed hard on Bethany again. Dinah continued to massage Bethany's belly. She was in a trance as she watched the event unfold.

Dariann lifted the baby and blew her breath hard across his face, nostrils and mouth trying to stimulate him. He wheezed. "Come on little boy," she coached. "I don't want to lose another one this week." He made a small sound and began little breaths. Dariann blew softly this time across his face. He responded by breathing deeper. She had begun wiping his body with the damp rags and stimulating him any way she could. Once he was cleaned, she swaddled him in a dry rag and held him again upside down on her lap. More drainage, but he was beginning to breathe regularly. Finally, he began to cry. Dariann smiled, rubbing his back, and nodded to Abigail, who smiled back. They may have saved one of them.

When the little cry came out, Bethany looked for the first time toward the baby. She was so weak, but she wanted to hold him. Dariann stood and walked to the new mother, laying the baby in the crook of her arm as she lay on the palette. She believed the baby would survive, but she wasn't sure about the mother.

"Let me look at her again," said Dariann.

Bethany had lost a great deal of blood, but it was finally slowing down. If she could regain her strength, then maybe she would make it. "Let me stitch the tears up. I think the bleeding has stopped. She will bleed slightly for a couple of weeks, which is normal, but I hope she can regain her strength."

"Do you have any family coming home?" Abigail asked.

"No, I live alone," came the answer that Abigail suspected. The poor conditions, no evidence of a man around the house or other family members confirmed her suspicion.

It was now getting very late. What were they going to do? They couldn't leave her here without any help and it didn't appear she had any. Abigail turned to Dinah and said, "Stay here. I will be back within half an hour." Dinah looked panicked. "Don't worry. I think Dariann will stay till I return, won't you?" Dariann agreed.

With that, Abigail returned to her home where she knew things would be in an uproar. Hadad and Azariah had no idea where the two women in their lives were and they were probably very worried.

Entering the upper floor, she called out, "Hadad, where are you?"

"Abigail, what's going on? I was worried sick," he said coming up from the lower floor and taking her by the shoulders. "Where were you and where is Dinah?"

"I have been up the street helping to deliver a baby most of the afternoon. Dinah came to me late in the afternoon. I sent her for the mid-wife and we have just finished helping a new mother deliver her son. They are struggling to survive."

"Well, I am glad you were there to help. Why didn't you bring Dinah back with you?"

Abigail hesitated, "I have a favor to ask of you. This little mother has no family, and I suspect no husband. She is still very weak from the delivery and needs some help to recover. I could go there and help her, but I think it would be easier on me and the family, if I just brought her here to stay with us for a while. Would you be willing for me to do that?"

Hadad looked at his wife in surprise. She was not one to bring home stray animals or people. She was a driven woman with a practical natural. This situation must have really affected her for her to be willing to uproot her routine and minister to this woman. "Abigail, you must feel strongly about this situation to even ask such a thing."

"I do. I just cannot leave her like that. Watching her struggle and seeing that little boy fight to live, I just don't think I could leave them on their own. They already have a rough situation. We can find out later how she got to be in this condition in the first place, but for now I don't want to judge, I just want to help. Is it alright with you?" she asked, tears brimming in her eyes.

Hadad hugged her and called Azariah, "Son, come up here quickly."

Azariah came up the outside steps two at a time stopping when he saw them hugging. He thought maybe they had bad news. Things were certainly not normal at home tonight. His mother and sister were missing and they were all worried. "What happened? Are you okay and where is Dinah?" questions came tumbling out of his mouth before they could tell him their plan.

"I will fill you in later on the events of the afternoon. Your dad and I have agreed to bring home a new mother who will need our care for a few weeks. I need the two of you to help me move her and the baby here right now," Abigail said.

That took Azariah by surprise and he eyed his dad with a question on his face. "It will work out, son. Let's take some blankets and a large basket for the baby. Where in the house do you want to put her? It would be good to get the area prepared before they arrive." Abigail had been thinking about that. They could take one of the rooms in the upper level that served as Hadad's office at home. He could survive for a while without it. Talking out their plan, they moved from the courtyard into his office. They pushed the table against the wall, but left the chair at the table. It would be used for bathing the baby and for a meal table until Bethany felt well enough to join the family at meals. They made an extra wide palette for her and the baby together. They also arranged some soft, unspun wool with blankets over it in a large, wooden box for a baby bed. A second chair was brought in to allow for visitors or family to have a place to sit. They found a rug that had been in the storage area and that filled the center of the room nicely. Reviewing their quick work, they were satisfied.

"Let's hurry. I know Dinah is afraid and that Dariann would like to go back to her family tonight also." Abigail led the way as they rushed along the path. They were there in minutes. When they entered, Dinah let out a sign of relief.

"How are they?" were the first words out of Abigail's mouth to her daughter and Dariann.

"Dinah has been doing very well with them while I cleaned up. I think they will recover with proper care."

"I just wanted to tell you what a wonderful job you did. I have never witnessed anything like that before. I don't know if either of them would have made it, if you hadn't come," Abigail said.

"I agree, Dariann," said Dinah.

Abigail continued, "You have literally saved two lives this evening. What do you usually charge for you services? I am sure we can pay you something for your excellent work." She turned to Hadad, who reached into his tunic for his money bag. He gave Dariann a shekel, which was excellent pay for excellent work. She looked at him with surprise.

"Thank you. This will help with the other times I helped and they are not able to pay anything. I must go and see to my family." With that she took her bag and the messy towels and went home.

Abigail turned to Bethany, kneeling down beside her palette. She spoke softly. Bethany had her eyes closed, "Bethany, are you awake?" Her eyes flickered open and she turned her head slightly toward Abigail. "I have a proposition for you, and please don't say 'no' until you hear my suggestion. You are too weak to take care of yourself or the new baby. We would like to offer you a room in our home until you are able to take care of yourself again.

My daughter and I are willing and able to meet your needs until that time. Please receive our offer freely."

Abigail watched her closely in the shadows of the room as a variety of emotions swept across her face. She could tell Bethany was unsure. Not only was she too weak to think clearly, she must be overwhelmed by the prospect of being a new mother and being alone. Abigail added, "I'll tell you what. Let's take you home tonight and take care of you and the baby. Tomorrow after you have had some rest and some food, we can discuss this further. Is that acceptable?" Thankfully, Bethany agreed.

With that response the room became a bustle of activity. Abigail took the baby away and handed it to Dinah. She placed him in the basket along with a dress and tunic she had noticed on the wall across the room. Nodding to her mother she stepped outside and waited. Very carefully, they rolled Bethany to one side and place two blankets under her, and then they rolled her back on to her other side and on to the blankets. Wrapping her carefully to help cushion her from the movement and to keep her warm as they moved her, Azariah lifted her into his arms. They followed him out the door and walked as a group toward their home. It was a short distance, but Azariah and Bethany were both grateful when they arrived. He carefully placed her on the prepared palette, but even that gentle motion was painful to her. Dinah kept the baby for now, watching him closely.

"Hadad, I would like to feed her and all of you before we go to bed. Could we get her some water and she can rest while I find something for all of us to eat?" Abigail hurried downstairs to the lower level. Dinah tried to make Bethany comfortable, until water had been brought to the room. Azariah returned with a pail of water, a cup and some rags for washing, and discreetly left. Dinah moistened a rag and poured a cup of water which she took over the Bethany.

"Bethany, I think you need to drink something. You lost a lot of blood. That is important. Lift your head and I will give you a few sips."

Bethany did her best. With Dinah's other hand behind her head for support, she was able to drink some. It was so refreshing. She was thirstier than she thought. She lay back down. A hand wiped her face, neck and arms, then her legs and feet. She was so tired. Dinah could see Bethany was drifting to sleep. She knew she needed to get some more water into her.

"Bethany, let's try to drink a little more," Dinah said, lifting her head. She drank even more this time. "Good. It won't be long until mom brings us a snack. If I bring the baby to you, do you think you could nurse him for a while? He is stirring and I know he must be hungry, too."

"I'll try," she answered. Dinah brought the infant over. She loosened his wraps and let him wiggle. He was looking better. With a little movement she was able to remove Bethany's dress. It was in need of laundering anyway. She would get her something else to wear in a few minutes. She covered her with blankets. She rolled another blanket up for a pillow for Bethany, raising her head slightly so she could see and drink better. Dinah then made a long roll and placed the baby in that next to Bethany. The two of them maneuvered until the baby and mother could get comfortable to nurse. It was slow going for a while, but about fifteen minutes of trial and error, finally had him nursing fairly well. Bethany smiled a weak smile up to her helper.

"You are doing a wonderful job. If we can feed him well before they come back, then he will rest for a while."

They continued to work together and managed to feed before they heard movement coming up from the lower level. "I am going to my room to get you a tunic to sleep in before they come." She disappeared, and just as quickly reappeared with a cotton tunic. "Here let me take him." She placed the baby in the basket and returned to help slide the gown over Bethany's head. They got everything in place and had her resting before Abigail and Hadad came in.

Dinah said, "I will hold him if he wakes while you eat."

"Are we doing well up here?" Abigail asked. She noticed that Dinah had helped her change clothes. "I have a good, light meal prepared for both of you: bread, olive oil, yogurt and delicious figs and grape juice to drink." She sat a tray down on the table. She laid some of the food on a plate where Dinah was sitting at the table watching the baby. She took the rest to the palette and sat Bethany up against the wall. With help, she was able to eat bread and oil. She took a few bites of yogurt and drank grape juice. She was too tired to try any more food right now. She just wanted sleep. "Dinah and I will check on you throughout the night. When the baby wakes up, wait until we come to help and carry him to you. You should not lift him; it may start the bleeding again. Do you understand?"

"Yes. Thank you so much for helping. I still do not understand why you are doing this for a woman like me. I have nothing to offer you and can only cause you work and hardship."

"Don't think about that now. We can discuss everything at another time. We will leave the door open so we can hear the baby and you. There will be a lamp lit in the hall to give some light in the room." They said their good nights and left Bethany alone for the first time with her baby, who was sleeping quietly in his bed.

Morning found everyone in better spirits and much more rested. Rising at dawn was a normal pattern of life even after a big day and busy night. Bethany had slept and awakened only when Dinah disturbed her so she could feed the crying baby or to take some fluids for her own needs.

"Mornin', Mother," Dinah said, leaning over to brush a kiss across her mom's brow and handing her the sleeping baby she had carried to the family table. "He is coming along very well. He ate three times last night and seems to be learning to nurse. Bethany is still resting," Dinah informed her mom and helped herself to some hot cereal, honey and goat cream. She had some delicious, strong coffee also doctored with cream and honey.

"What about the other patient? When I looked in on her in the middle of the night, she seemed to be resting well and I didn't notice any excessive blood, just the normal post-delivery bleeding," Abigail asked her tired daughter.

"I noticed she had moved around some in her sleep, but I didn't see any unusual bleeding either. I think she is just going to need time to recover her strength. What are we going to do until then?" The breakfast tasted so good to Dinah. She hadn't realized how hungry she was.

Hadad entered the kitchen, hugging his daughter and kissing is wife. He paused long enough to give the baby a once over and nodded approval to his wife. Helping himself to coffee he sat down on the pillow beside his wife. "How were things through the night?" His wife gave him an update and then repeated Dinah's question about what to do next. "I suggest we take a couple of days to meet her needs and the baby's. When they are healthy enough to go home or to wherever, we can discuss the details. I know both of you may have had other plans, but I think those plans will have to be postponed until she is well. Do you agree?" They agreed.

Dinah finished her breakfast and put the dishes in a wash basin. She prepared a breakfast tray for when Bethany awoke. They had no plans to wake her, since the baby had not shown any signs of being hungry yet. Dinah would serve the food at the last minute before she took the tray upstairs. She cleaned up some of the kitchen leaving the rest until others finished their meal.

It was still quiet upstairs, so Dinah went outside to the cistern in their courtyard. She drew two pitchers of water balancing them on opposite ends of a pole. She began the filling the household barrels. Carefully, sitting the pitchers on the floor, she emptied them one at a time into a big barrel in the kitchen. She then repeated the process until the barrels were refilled. It usually took several trips to replenish the water used the day before. She quickly repeated the process to fill the water barrel in the bathing room upstairs, stored the pitchers and went back inside.

Abigail had bread rising in the kitchen and she had gone upstairs by the time Dinah came in. The baby was awake and hungry. She could hear him crying from Bethany's room. "Mom," she yelled up the stairs, "should I bring up breakfast?"

The two levels were connected inside by a stairway that went from the back of the first story into the middle of the gallery in the second story. There were four bedrooms, two were on either side of the gallery and a small room at the end of the gallery had a bathing basin, a small water barrel, a covered slop pail, a stone wall basin with an outside drain that fed into the street-side sewer through a tile pipe below. Azariah took the human waste in the slop pail down through the Dung Gate into the Hinnon Valley once or twice every day. With all the activity last night, it was not dumped, so he would be making that trip as soon as everyone was up and ready this morning. All of the rooms were whitewashed inside. The doors were of poplar with bronze handles and hinges. The floors were hewn stone of a terra-cotta color, rich and warm. The house was heated by a fireplace at the end of the living area downstairs and a smaller one in the same end but opposite of the bath in the upstairs gallery. A smaller foyer entered between the two front bedrooms allowing access to the upstairs central gallery from the roof-top patio. The front rooms had windows that were tall and narrow and were covered with shutters at night.

"Yes, Dinah. I think she will be ready to eat by the time you arrive," she yelled down the stairs. Bethany was finished feeding the baby and he was asleep again in the basket. "Bethany, would like me to help you to the bath to wash and relieve yourself? I am sure you are miserable and would like to have a chance to clean up," she asked Bethany.

Seeing the eagerness in Bethany's face, she continued, "I will get you a clean tunic and sash and sandals from Dinah's room." With that, Abigail helped her to stand and move to the bath at the end of the hall. Dinah came around the corner.

"Here is the food. Where is she?"

"She is washing. Could you get her a tunic and sash of yours? We will wash today and be able to use her clothes tomorrow. I think she has two tunics, doesn't she?" she said, looking at Dinah, who acknowledged a 'yes',

"Good, then we can help, too, if we have any extras."

Dinah left to go to her room. She walked back down the hall and knocked at the bath, "Bethany, I have laid your clothes on the table in the hall by your door." She then returned to the baby's basket. He was resting peacefully. He was beginning to look better and his color looked rosier. He had a little light brown hair with a slight wave. Turning to her mom, "Bethany needs to give him a name. I wonder if she has been thinking about one?"

"I haven't heard her mention anything, but maybe we just need to ask. I hate to keep calling him 'the baby', don't you?" Looking up, she saw Bethany in the bedroom doorway.

"I feel much better. Thank you for the clothes," said Bethany. "I am still bleeding, but I think it is just normal, right?"

"Yes, dear. Some is normal after a birth," said Abigail.

Dinah helped Bethany to the table to enjoy her breakfast. They watched her eat in silence, wondering if she had heard their conversation, and if she had, why hadn't she commented on the name?

As they were cleaning up the tray, Abigail asked, "Bethany, we would like to call the baby by a name. What name have you chosen?"

A strange expression crossed Bethany's face--a mixture of sorrow and anxiety. She really just didn't know how to answer that simple question. She overheard their comments about naming the baby, but she had hoped, if she pretended she had not heard them, they would forget they had asked. She had no idea what or if she would name the baby. How do you tell this kind family that this baby was not supposed to grow up at all, or to be a child or an adult, so why pick a name?

So she said, "I have no idea. Do you want to suggest a name?" She tried to smile as she asked, but she knew the statement sounded cold and hollow. Well, so be it. She couldn't help the situation and the life that had lead up to it.

Abigail could see there was turmoil in the girl's mind. Avoiding the question and the awkwardness of the moment, she said, "When you have chosen a name that means something to you, we will call him by that, but for now we will call him Mattan for 'gift'."

"That is fine. I am sure we won't be here long enough for you to need to call him by any other name for very long," said Bethany. With that she lay down on the pallet and turned on her side facing the wall. Dinah and Abigail quietly left and closed the door.

When they got out into the gallery, Dinah asked, "I am confused, Mom. It doesn't seem like she is that interested in the baby. It almost like she didn't plan on him living or is not excited about having the baby, don't you think?"

"Honey, sometimes after a birth, a woman is confused and very tired. Let's wait for her to rest more and we will see if her attitude changes," said Abigail.

Azariah and Hadad finished a few chores before they returned to the Temple. They were busy each day with the affairs related to keeping track in writing of daily temple events, sacrifices, gifts and recording visitors. Anything that happened was put down for history. It kept Hadad and Azariah busy from the start of daily business until the temple closed.

As they neared the south wall they saw a crowd gathered in the plaza below the stairs leading to the lower entrance. When they got near enough, they could see that Jeremiah was prophesying concerning something. His warnings stirred some people to fear and others to ire, but almost no one to action. He was in his late thirty's and had been prophesying since his early twenty's. After that many years, as in the case of many prophets, he was often heard, but ignored. Most did not believe there was any truth to his warnings. A familiar face approached them, "Have you been hearing what Jeremiah is saying?" asked Hananiah.

"No, we just arrived. Why don't you fill us in?" answered Hadad.

"He is once again warning of imminent danger from the northern kingdoms. This time he is talking about their chariots, fast horses and them plundering the city. Have you ever heard him speak before? What do you think of his prophecy?" he asked.

"Hananiah, I believe Jeremiah to be a legitimate prophet among many who are dishonest. No man would have chosen to be humiliated and have his life threatened unless he was convinced he had a message from God to deliver. As to what he says, I can only pray God shows us mercy instead of his justice in these matters. It seems impossible to believe that all the destruction he has told us about could happen. Then again, I just said I thought him to be legitimate, so how can I not believe his message. But boys, I would be careful in telling this belief to just anyone. Jeremiah's warnings have made him a danger to himself and others. Those who side with him are taking the risk of being associated with everything negative he has preached," Hadad warned. They listened for several more minutes before entering the temple.

Jeremiah could be heard, saying, "You speak to a tree, saying, 'You are my father,' and to a stone, saying, 'You gave birth to me.' You have turned your back to me in a time of trouble, but in a time of trouble, you will say,

'Arise and save us.' But where are your gods that you have made for yourself. Let them arise, if they can save you...'"

"He is right. You know he is. We have become a country filled with idols that control the lives of our people," Hananiah commented.

Jeremiah again, "Return, backsliding children, and I will heal your backslidings."

"He asks us again to admit to our sins. You know our people do not think they are sinning. They believe it is their choice to worship any way they please."

"It is their right, I agree," says Hadad. "The problem with choice is that the price for choosing wrong has been decided. They are willing to worship themselves and their rights or another false god until it begins to cost them, then they make excuses for what has happened to them. It is the fault of others, but not their fault. God should not judge them, but should judge the world they live in. He had given man many warnings, but each man thinks God is not talking to him personally. 'Surely, I am not sinning,' he says."

"Well, today, Jeremiah is making it clear. God is not giving us any more chances. This is it. Repent or pay the price," says Azariah.

CHAPTER 7

Cain was sweating and his beard was plastered to his neck and face. His filthy, gray woven shirt stuck to his skin. He hated rushing around trying to help with serving. Tonight the crowd was so large, that Moriah, his mistress, could not serve everyone. He was a poor substitute for the quality of waitress Moriah was. She was attractive, quick and the patrons liked her flirtatious attitude, which helped his business. He was slow, gruff and found the clients demanding. No doubt her good work was more beneficial to the success of his tavern than was his. He was glad waiting tables was not his usual job at the inn. Usually, he served drinks at the bar and kept his ears open to the customers' conversations.

His father had operated the inn before him. He had grown up learning everything about tavern work, but he disliked most of it as a child. His father had taught him well, however. When Cain was thirty his father passed away and Cain inherited the business. He surprised even himself by taking over the inn and making it a success. He had been more capable than he thought. The tavern was not only succeeding, but had prospered under his management. Cain's methods were rough, like him.

He knew many secrets because he was a good listener and better eavesdropper. He had once been suspected of killing a man, but it had never been proven. His information had served him well, both in favors and extra income. But the dangerous business of blackmail caused him to be very cautious. His life and the life of others could be easily lost with one careless word.

Cain's provided food, lodging and spirits. More personalized entertainment was available for a price, too. Travelers came into town looking for food and a good time. Cain tried to provide for all their requests and needs. Not that he cared for them personally, but he was practical and fiscally savvy. He knew you could make good money by offering all the services a traveler might want. Some had wants that even surprised him.

The Inn had two stories both made of stone. The ground floor had a stone floor that offered seating at twelve tables with stone tops supported by smoothed-log legs. Benches and stools were used around the room at tables and the serving bar. The second floor included Cain's rooms and lodging for guests.

There was a long, narrow kitchen on the back wall. His cook, Hablin, had an adequate work area with hanging racks for salted meat, copper utensils and pans, a stone-lined storage area dug into the ground to keep food fresh longer because of cooler temperatures, and two large basins on the outside wall allowed for washing utensils and food. Both had drains that ran outside to a collection trough. It was connected to a drainage area heading out of town. Water barrels stood at each end of the counter to aid in food preparing and dishwashing. The dishwasher was able to at least make a good show of cleaning the utensils for the cook and patrons. Other storage barrels containing staples such as flour, salt and olive oil sat around the area. They would serve as tables, when the crowds were heavy. Tonight they were in use. Many baskets also hung from the rafters with fruits and vegetables. The large fireplace with a spit was usually cooking something. Hablin was known for preparing acceptable food with good-sized servings. He was also known for his short temper and a quick knife.

Tonight Hablin demonstrated his temper with the waitress, "Moriah, shut your mouth and get this food out before it gets cold!" he bellowed above the din. "The clients aren't here to look at you or listen to you flirt with them. They are here to eat, so get moving."

She moved to the counter, "Look, you weasel, I am serving double the normal number of people tonight. I am running like a rat, trying to cater to their demands. So, I don't need your attitude.. If you want this food out faster, take it out there yourself." She jerked two plates from the counter, balancing one on her left forearm and holding one in her left hand, she picked up a third plate in her right hand. Moving through the crowd with grace, she arrived at a group of soldiers in the far corner. They weren't any different than hundreds of others she had served in the five years she had worked here.

"Here we go, gentlemen. Stew for you; lamb chops and potatoes for you and the deer for this fine man," she cooed as she placed the meals in front of the men. It never hurt to flirt a little. Sometimes they would leave her a few more coins. She had the looks that made men think thoughts that would have caused Cain to kill them, if he could read minds. She couldn't read minds, but she was a great observer of body language. She could see she had an effect on most men. Her physique was tall and slender, but she had great curves. She made sure her dress showed every one of her assets. Her rich, golden brown hair was braided and wrapped up into a bun at the nape of her neck and her intelligent, brown eyes missed little or nothing that happened around her. She noticed that the table she had just served seemed tense and paid very little attention to her feminine wiles. Something was definitely wrong there with that group. She would alert Cain to them; he was a great one for gossip and information. It might be worth something to them.

"Cain, drop over to the table in the corner. That group has something going on," she tilted her head toward the group. "Could be a new source," she said as she moved away, glancing at him over her shoulder as she walked away.

Cain observed the room. It was beginning to thin out, so he had time to eavesdrop for a minute. He picked up a basket and moved toward the men, clearing the tables near them. They were speaking in Hebrew, which surprised him. He heard and understood several languages, which was helpful in this business. They must be afraid they would be recognized by their speech. They were a careful group.

"Nebuchadnezzar is eager to get set up down here and take this city and country from Egypt. He is looking for an immediate cash flow to fund that move. What's the word in the palace?' Timath asked Zarallon, while a huge bite of lamb and potatoes managed to stay in his mouth.

"Timath, I'm going to cut up your right arm so the scars on it will match the scar on your left arm, if I leave an arm at all. Shut your mouth!" Wakeem spoke through his teeth. "You know better than to speak that name out loud."

Timath was a tall and wiry soldier. He got his scar during a hand-to-hand battle. Although fighting up-close and personal was not his strength, he could shoot an arrow 400 feet and hit a target or a bird in flight. Accuracy like that made hitting a human target in battle a simple feat. Timath was undercover as part of the palace staff that helped supply food for the king's household. It gave him an excuse to be out for days at a time hunting where he could get new information and he would not need an explanation. It was perfect cover. He could still easily manage to come back with a harness filled with pheasant, kite and pigeon or sometimes a deer.

Zarallon jumped into the conversation, hoping to calm Wakeem down, who had no patience. He would just as soon chop off Timath's arm with his always ready sword as look at him. "We loaded the wagons today with the tribute payment and they are due to head out in a few days. I am on duty at daylight and hope to find out for sure what the route will be. It is likely they will take the Patriarch's Highway for at least part of the way, especially in their own territory. Meet me at the west wall mid-morning Monday and I will confirm the route. Eddu, you know that little shop under the wall that serves strong coffee? Good. Wait for me there at lunch."

Eddu-aram was a commander of twenty lancers in Nebuchadnezzar's army, but was undercover working as a carpenter in Jerusalem and camping outside of town. "I'll be there early," Eddu agreed, "and take my time eating. Benjamin can wait for me after lunch. He is the first one I am going to kill when we take this city. I smile at him daily while he is barking orders and think about the privilege of running a spear straight through his heart."

"You better make sure his son is tied up before you try that. He is one tough kid," added Zarallon, who had seen Mishael at work in the palace during the time the remodeling was done for the queen and queen mother.

"Enough!" Wakeem warned. "Where is the best place for an ambush on that highway? If memory serves, there is a narrow pass between here and Adullam. No use letting the caravan roll any further south, when we need to take the goods to the north."

"There are several narrow, lonely stretches of road on both sides of Bethlehem before the city of Hebron," clarified Zarallon, who had been in this area undercover longer than the others. He would not be involved in the raid. They needed his position to continue for information, so if he was involved in the raid, he would give away his true purpose for being here.

"If they are taking that path, we will set up troops on both sides with access routes down to the road. We should be able to take them without much trouble. We are likely to meet resistance heading up the highway for some distance, but with enough men, I think we will be fine. I will send a messenger to Nebuzaradan in Carchemish when the deal is completed," Wakeem said.

Wakeem was a lieutenant of fifty swordsmen with five other divisions under the command Nebuzaradan, the commander of Nebuchadnezzar's army. He thrived in battle, but for now he was out of combat because he had been dispatched as a spy leader to get up-to-date information. When he thought of battle with the power and thrill of racing horses, clattering chariots, the sound of the metal swords as they hit shields, swords and flesh, it made his pulse quicken. Never did he consider he might die. He was too good and sure of himself. At twenty-five, it seemed that life was his for the taking and he planned on taking all he could. For now, he was just another soldier on leave staying at Cain's. Spying for the king was a bore, but at least he could get some added rest.

He had little personal character. Basically whatever appealed to him and could further his own interests were the things he did. If working here in town was good politically, then he would do all he could. Not so much for Nebuchadnezzar, as for himself and how it would improve his career in Babylon. Besides, he needed to get on the leader's good side, in case anything from his past was to come out in the open. In Babylon he had murdered a palace eunuch who caught him 'borrowing' coins from the king's treasury, a penalty worthy of his death. He decided the death of the eunuch was necessary. He was not caught for either crime. He had strong private appetites. He usually had plenty of women around who found him attractive and fulfilled his wishes voluntarily. It didn't matter to him, however, if no volunteers were available and he had to take what he wanted by force.

Cain listened to the men at the table. He could hear some of the conversation over the talk of other patrons. This was a tidy bit of information he had. He moved away before they finished speaking. The tables were cleared and staying longer wasn't necessary. He had what he needed.

"You were right, my dear," he came near her table. "They are spies from up north. You are worth your weight in gold." He took the dishes to the kitchen and set them in the sink, then took a seat in the corner. He had to think and he didn't have much time. This was happening in a day or so. This information was valuable, no doubt, but it was also dangerous to know so much. What he did with the knowledge would not depend on patriotism, but on where he could make the most profit. He saw the little group breaking up. Two were coming his way; his tenants, Wakeem and Zarallon.

Wakeem asked for two lamps, which Cain provided. They both walked out the back door. Zarallon went up the outer stairs, but Wakeem went to the shed off the back alley. On one side it had been equipped with a tub made of stone. There were barrels of water used for cooking, bathing and to fill the tub. Nearby pegs held semi-clean towels hanging on the wall and there were slop pots and a wash basin. On the other side, a laundress's tub and scrubbing board was set up with several lines of rope running between the shed and the limbs of the nearby olive tree. During the day, Levine, the laundress, washed clothes for the tavern and selected guests and she was responsible for making the soap used in the inn. It was made from lye and fat (from the kitchen) in a hanging pot over the fire pit outside for the bathing guests and her wash.

He set the lamp on a wall support and stripped to his waist. He relieved himself in the slop pot, and then washed off some of the dirt from the day. Soldiers seldom had a chance to be in such comfort. They bathed in streams or lakes. He considered a bath, but he had one a couple of weeks ago, and it was too much work to have another until necessary. Before he could redress, the door to the shed opened and Cain stepped inside, closing the door behind him. Wakeem could see this man had some business on his mind and it didn't appear to be bathing. He would watch this innkeeper closely; he looked like he could handle himself.

"I have some business for you, sir," Cain said to Wakeem.

"You and I will never do business," Wakeem replied as he bathed and began to redress.

"Oh, I think you need me and you definitely need my silence."

Wakeem bristled; what had the innkeeper overheard? Cain had been close, but it didn't seem he was that close when they were at the table in the inn.

"Are trying to threaten me, Cain? Yes, I know your name. When I come to town, I check around carefully. What is it you think you know?"

"Rumor is that the King's tribute payment is on the way to Egypt soon. I am thinking you and your friends are looking to redirect the caravan to the north to aid in war plans. Your king may one day come to our fair city, and I want a guarantee of safety for me and Moriah," he paused, and then added, "and I want one talent of silver. You will have a hundred and one won't be missed."

"You are playing a dangerous game, my friend," Wakeem said, tucking in his shirt.

"You need my advice. This is a business deal, such as it is. Let's not pretend any other relationship, so don't call me friend. Tell me about what you need."

"If I agree to this 'arrangement', what kind of guarantee do I get that you will not share your knowledge with anyone else?" Wakeem wondered. He had finished dressing and was giving Cain his full attention.

Cain was confident. He had him where he wanted him. "None, but if you don't work with me, you have a guarantee I will share the information for profit to someone," Cain smirked. Before the smirk faded, he was in a death grip. Wakeem had pinned one of Cain's arms behind his back. Wakeem had his other arm over Cain's shoulder with a knife at his throat.

"I believe there is another option; death. Is that the choice you prefer or can you do better at guaranteeing your silence than you did a second ago?" Wakeem held him tightly and let the knife just take a thin slice in the surface of his skin.

Cain squealed, "Yes, alright, I'll hold my tongue. Let go of me." He pulled against the soldier's strong grip, but was unable to release himself. Gradually, when the soldier had convinced him that he could not have escaped on his own, Wakeem let go.

"I think we have established that you work for me. You will do as I say when I say. Tomorrow, I am going to use the room upstairs to meet my men. I can lay out our plan and work without hindrance. We will eat supper in that room, served by your lovely waitress. Get someone else to fill in downstairs. For tonight, we are through. I am too tired to discuss anything else with you." Wakeem picked up his weapons and cloak. He climbed up the stairs outside which lead up the back way from the kitchen door up to second floor entrance. At the second floor door the stairs took a sharp turn and continued another flight up to the roof.

Cain was faint. Never had he been so totally unable to help himself. He was considered by many to be a very strong man, but he was no match for this man. His breath was still coming in gasps and he was trembling. He hurried inside and straight to the bar. He needed a stiff drink and then another.

He was thinking to himself, 'Okay, that went well. Yeah, right.' It was not even close to what he had imagined. He was in over his head. These men were not your run-of-the-mill soldiers. If the soldiers of this northern king's army were all like the one he had just met, Judah would have no hope, if they were invaded. He was glad he had made an agreement with the would-be invaders. It was safer that way.

CHAPTER 8

Sunday was a beautiful day. And the valley was filled with enough flowers to keep Salme busy for hours. They caught butterflies of varied colors with glistening wings and great beauty. She was so happy and busy that she would have forgotten to eat lunch, if mom hadn't demanded she sit down and eat. "Salme, come here this instant. I have called you three times. Having fun is not an excuse to disobey when you are called."

Salme ran to her mother with a hand full of wild flowers. "Look, mother, Daniel has been teaching me. This is a daisy and this is a lily and this is a ..."

Mother was getting exasperated, "Salme, give me the flowers to hold while you eat. You can give me a run down of what the kinds of flowers are later." Taking the flowers from her daughter, she almost had to force her to concentrate enough to eat some flat bread stuffed with chopped olives, cucumbers, feta cheese and a herb dressing. She gobbled it down, talking constantly about the butterflies that were still out there that she hadn't had time to see. She drank delicious white grape juice from an earthen bowl and ate an apple.

"Now, mama, can I go? I have eaten very much food!"

"Yes, go on and play. I will come see your butterflies in a few minutes."

After Salme left, Meriel laid back on the blanket the family had used as a lunch table and turned to Gideon, resting quietly beside her. "Dear, do you know anything about a war that might be coming our way? The city leaders' wives have been talking about it for weeks. They overheard their husbands in conversations. All of them are very upset. I haven't heard you mention anything about a war. Do you think we are in any danger? You know, they say the prophet, Jeremiah, is preaching the destruction of the city by a northern king. What do you think?"

"You are full of questions today. A little gossip over the gardening?" he said with a light-hearted smile. A restful day like today was likely to turn into one of turmoil, if he explained all he knew to her. She frowned at him, indicating she was not kidding. Trying to play it down, he responded, "There is some truth to what you are hearing. Pharaoh marched to Babylon, a northern country. That is when our former king, Josiah, was killed before the battle was engaged, remember?" looking over to her to see if she was following him and seeing a 'yes' nod, he continued, "Well, Pharaoh is once again in the north set up for battle with his troops, and he is engaging the Babylonians in battle to protect his territories. Most think Necho will win and things will continue as they are now. Jeremiah, however, seems to believe that God has shown him the destruction of the city and the exile of the Hebrews."

Meriel sat bolt upright, "Oh, honey, you are frightening me. You don't believe that, do you? That would be awful. God has protected his people for centuries. Why would he turn against us and give us to a heathen ruler now?"

Oops, he had given too much information, "Honey, let's not talk about this today and ruin the relaxing atmosphere."

"Gideon, I can't rest now with just a partial answer. Those conversations I heard have been stirring around in my mind for weeks now. I haven't had any time alone with you for a long enough period of time to talk. We are always too tired in the evening and so many other days you are working. Please don't deny me this time with you. Help me understand what's happening."

Giving in to the inevitable, "Okay, according to what I have heard Jeremiah say, God is judging us for our sins," said Gideon.

"What sins? Why most of the people I know are kind and upright. They are wonderful. What kind of God would do such a thing? Condemn his own city and people to destruction and death? What an awful thing for him to say. This prophet Jeremiah, have you met him personally?"

Gideon commented, "I heard him a few times outside the temple speaking and met him once. He is a man of about thirty-five with a very ordinary appearance and demeanor. I believe he believes he is truly sent by God and that his messages are true."

"How many messages has he been preaching? I only heard about this recently. Has it been going on for long?"

"He is the son of a priest and has been preaching to the people since his early twenties. His warnings have become more harsh and specific in the last few months. He goes everywhere in the city: in the gates, the market, the temple and the palace. I am surprised you haven't heard him during one of your trips to the market or into the country."

"Do you believe him?" she got up and began pacing back and forth, and then turned to face him, "Please don't say 'yes.' I don't think I could stand it," she pleaded.

He got up and stood behind her, putting his arms around her waist. He pulled her close. "Honey, please don't get so upset. None of us know the future. The best authorities think that the country and the city are safe. Pharaoh is a strong ruler with a mighty army. It is likely he will easily subdue the young general, Nebuchadnezzar."

"Don't patronize me, Gideon. You just said Jeremiah claims to know what God has planned," she said as she pulled away and stared at him. "Let's talk about this as if he might be right. What could we do?"

"If God plans to destroy the city and people, I cannot think of anything we could do to stand against his plan. I would like to say we could run or escape or hide, but the messages I have heard say that none will be spared or escape. I know you think that people here are good, but honey, God does not look at people's good deeds alone. He looks at their hearts, according to King David's psalms. You know our people have continued to worship idols, offer human sacrifices, live immoral lives, divorce their spouses and turn against the God who has protected them, as you said, for centuries. Based on our turning away from Him, does he continue to owe us that protection? Have we shown any loyalty to him?"

This line of conversation about man and sinfulness had been previously discussed in their home. Meriel did not see people as 'sinners'. "You know I believe that God will show us a great deal of grace, since He is a loving God and should not judge."

'She thinks that God would always ignore sin in lives and forgive indefinitely direct disobedience to His will,' thought Gideon. He said, "In real life people don't work like that, but they somehow expected God to. They do not ignore the sins of others when that sin affects them. It is easy to be generous with forgiveness, when someone else's sin does not hurt you or someone you love."

"I am very forgiving of others. I rarely judge," she defended herself.

"But sin hurts someone each time it is commented. If you ever saw someone hurt Salme or Jothal, you would want the ultimate punishment for that person, I think," he said. In Gideon's opinion God is watching over the world to protect it from those whose freedom to sin affects others and hurts them.

She gave that idea some thought. "You are right. When sin gets personal, then I do have different feelings about judging the person."

"Usually, sin ultimately hurts the sinner himself. 'Wine is a mocker,' Solomon says. None know the truth of sin better than a man whose sin is that of drinking. It begins by drinking with a friend occasionally and ends up for some as drunkenness. And that is just one kind of sin. Each has its own ultimate end," said Gideon.

"I thought according to the Law and the Prophets, that God also allowed grace. What happens when men continue to rebel?" she asked.

"Based on history," Gideon answered, "He then sends judgment." If Gideon understood his readings and the prophecies he had heard, he believed that the future for them held judgment rather than grace, but he wasn't sure he wanted to convince Meriel of that. It might mean that everything he had been hearing from Jeremiah was true and judgment was just around the corner.

Meriel broke the silence. "The next time I hear that the prophet is in town, I am going to go to hear him myself. I want to see what kind of man, what kind of crazy person, frightens innocent women and children into thinking they are going to be killed and taken away. Life is hard enough without trying to imagine what it would be like to have soldiers running around and killing and burning and destroying our town...." she burst into tears and crumpled to the ground. She looked up at him, crying, "Oh, Gideon."

He sat beside her and held her. "Honey, we could ask our God, the one we know to be merciful and kind, if he would spare us and our family. That sounds a little selfish, but we have been faithful to him. I cannot speak for the whole city, but I do know that we have not turned from worshiping him to worshiping idols or to illegal or immoral practices in our home or business."

"Pray out loud with just you and me, right now," she asked. She thought about it for a second and then said, "I think this is as good a time as any. It is quiet and we are agreed on what we are asking God to do. I cannot find any peace until I know our family is in his hands and not just the hands of an enemy."

Praying was a comfortable thing for Gideon. He had been in a family that prayed freely and without reserve. They believed God was listening and cared about them as individuals, as much as He cared for all mankind. There were prophecies in Isaiah that said God was sending the Messiah to take away their sins and the sin of the world. Gideon personally believed that and faithfully offered his animal sacrifices at temple until the Messiah came and offered himself as a once and for all sacrifice. Yes, it was easy and enjoyable to Gideon to talk to his God.

"Jehovah, we come in fear and concern to you now. We have heard rumors about a war and death and captivity. We are afraid and we don't know what is going to happen. We have not turned from you as others in our city have and we have not worshiped idols, so please would you give us protection because of our faithfulness to you and because of your grace. I ask first of all that there will not be war, but if you have determined that war is our judgment, then I ask that we will be spared and safe and that you will watch over us, please. One more thing, please give us peace in our hearts now that you have answered us. Thank you our God and provider. Amen." Gideon looked into his wife's eyes. What he saw surprised him, although, he had just prayed for that very thing. He saw what looked like peace and rest and trust. "Honey, what are you thinking?"

"I don't know how to explain it exactly, but I am calm. I believe we will live and be protected whatever happens. Isn't that funny? Just a simple prayer and the world seems like it is a place that once again we can survive and prosper regardless of what comes." She reached over and kissed him. They held each other for a few minutes and rested.

Jothal came running up shortly, "Father, look. I have a big perch. If we keep on fishing today, we can have a good fish supper, right?"

"Absolutely, son. Put it here in this bag. I will go with you right now." He stood and looked at his wife.

"Okay, dear. Let's do what we came here to do. Spend time as a family," she said and got up. "Salme, we are coming to the river to see you and your butterflies," she yelled. They went to the Kidron where the children relaxed and Salme chased each colorful, fleeting butterfly that passed.

CHAPTER 9

Mattan was a joy to be with. They were all falling in love with his precious face and tender cooing when someone held him. All of the family felt the same, that is, all but one. Their guest, Bethany had been there three days and had faithfully fed the baby and done all the right things, but she didn't seem to have that 'motherly instinct.' Bethany was better now physically, but had not returned to the home where the baby was born. She was young and had regained her strength fairly well.

The family was not encouraging them to leave since they loved having Mattan with them. It was likely that it would not be too long before they thought about leaving. Mattan was now like one of them. He had a special place in their hearts right now and for always.

"Mom, why don't you get out of the house and go to the market. Mattan is too small to go, but I will stay with him and Bethany. I don't think she would mind if you went out and left just me here," Dinah suggested.

Mom agreed, "All right. Check with her, and if she is okay with that, I will pick up some fruit and new fabric. And I could also get that new sash you had put away at Meriel's shop."

"That would be wonderful." Dinah ran upstairs to where Bethany was, "It's me, Bethany. Can I come in?"

"Sure," she said, walking back to the chair by the table. She had just laid her son in the basket. "Mattan just went to sleep. It seems like that is all he does is eat and sleep. I don't see what fascinates people about babies. I think they really are rather a lot of work and what do you get for it?" Bethany asked no one in particular.

Dinah didn't know how to respond. She had never heard a woman talk that way about children and especially her newborn baby. "I think they are beautiful. I was the last baby in our house and since I couldn't enjoy being the baby myself, I am glad to have one here that I can hold and love. The reason I came up was to ask if you would mind if my mother leaves to go to the market leaving you and Mattan with just me? The walk will do her good."

"No. Tell her to do as she pleases," Bethany answered as her mind began to turn. This was the first time that only the daughter had been at home with her. There were always so many people in this house that she was afraid of stepping out of her room and getting into someone's way.

In a few minutes, Abigail moved up Essene Way to the lower market. It was on this side of town and easier to reach. She would also go to Meriel's shop to pick up Dinah's sash. Maybe Meriel would be there and they would have a few minutes to catch up on events in town. She was looking forward to getting a few things they needed.

She finished shopping in the lower market and went to the sash shop. "Hello, Meriel," she said as she entered. They did not get to visit often enough. "I came to get the sash that Dinah had you hold for her and maybe pick something up for myself."

"I am so glad to see you. We are still planning on getting together for the Shauvot celebration, right?" asked Meriel.

"Oh, yes. We can't wait. I know Mary will have a lovely meal and the house will be beautiful. We will honor the memory of the gift of God's law to Moses together," she answered.

"Good," she said turning her head and calling to the back of the shop, "Chloe, would you get Dinah's sash I held for her?"

They looked around the shop together. In minutes Chloe came with the lovely sash, giving it to Abigail with a hug.

"This really is pretty. It looks just like my 'princess's' color choice, doesn't it?" said Abigail. They all laughed. "I am glad to see you, too, Chloe. You are welcome to come visit anytime. By the way, we have a guest at our house right now."

"Who is that?" asked Meriel.

Abigail explained the story as they listened in amazement.

"You have been an angel of mercy to them both. May Jehovah reward you for your graciousness," said Meriel.

"We have been absorbed with caring for the girl and her son. She has some problems," Abigail observed. "Her maternal instincts are missing completely. Either she was orphaned very young or had a very poor roll model for a mother. I would like to encourage her and help her with the skills it would take to become a good mother. She would live just up the street, so it would be possible to see them often. Do you have any suggestions?"

The ladies spent an hour discussing things that might help with the situation. Abigail left the shop with two sashes and a lovely scarf. But she also left encouraged in her ability to help the lonely girl in her care. She prayed for Jehovah to bless her indeed.

The house seemed very quiet to Bethany. Dinah was in the kitchen cutting melons to serve at supper, when Bethany walked in. It startled Dinah; Bethany had never been downstairs before.

Bethany was not a big girl; maybe only 100 pounds. Her red hair was hanging down her back loosely. She moved around with ease. It was clear she was feeling much better. Dinah guessed she was probably about eighteen.

"Hello. Would you like something to eat?"

"No. I just thought while all was quiet I might take a tour of the house. It is bigger than I thought. I have only seen the upper level, until now."

"We are very happy in this home and very fortunate."

"Yeah, you are really spoiled. You all have no idea how the rest of us lives."

"I beg your pardon. I am not spoiled," said Dinah, very surprised at the comment.

"Oh, I know you don't think so, but actually, you have everything you need and a lot of things other people want."

Dinah was seething. Bethany was impolite and hateful. Dinah felt like picking an argument with this ungrateful girl, "Well, that is a funny way to look at things. It seems instead of being thankful that we could and did help you and Mattan, you are jealous of what we have and wish it was yours. Do I have the right understanding?"

"You are right on target. I'd love to have your life or even a richer one. I would do whatever it takes to get ahead, to make a success of myself," Bethany said, taking the challenge. She had met many girls just as naïve as Dinah before. She said, "In fact, I have had a life that would be very hard for a girl as protected as you are to even imagine. You might be surprised at the things happening in our sweet little Jerusalem."

"I am shocked at your attitude. I am protected, but sometimes that can be a good thing. It seems your life has had a temporary set back with the birth of your son and you are really being very selfish. What about Mattan? Where does he fit into your plans for this big life?"

"Oh, he is an inconvenience. I am not sure how he will fit in, but I am sure I can work something out," she said, smiling, and walked out into the courtyard.

Dinah could hear Mattan begin to cry upstairs and so could Bethany, but Bethany just ignored it and sat down on a bench in the sun.

Dinah went to him, "There, there, sweetie. Come to me. That's right, you little doll. Let me walk you around the house and we will talk."

Dinah carried Mattan downstairs to the kitchen along with his basket and sat him in it where she could see him and speak to him while she worked on the vegetables for supper. He watched her move and she told him how she was cutting the carrots, onions and the potatoes for the pot. He seemed to listen to the conversation with attention, but in a few minutes the crying returned. She picked him up again and bounced him on her hip which satisfied him for a little while.

When it was clear he was not going to be happy until he was fed, Dinah said, "Ok, little one. Let's go see your mommy. I know it is time to eat again." Dinah walked out to Bethany with the baby. "Here we go, sweetie. Momma is right here, ready with supper."

Bethany looked up at her and took Mattan. "Is it that time again? I just fed him a couple of hours ago. I wish someone else could do this," reluctantly she began feeding him. She was impatient with the time it took to feed him often cutting it short. It seemed he would nurse forever. Didn't he ever get full? And besides, nursing was not comfortable for her.

Abigail came around the corner and into the courtyard, "Hello, Bethany. Look what I brought," Abigail said holding packages in the air. Abigail was pleased to see her downstairs. She thought that might be a good sign.

Dinah came in from the kitchen. The group had moved into the living area. Bethany was sitting with Mattan on the couch which was quite comfortable. It was framed in poplar wood stained with a medium wood wash. The seats were a shade of smooth leather about the color of sand and stuffed with camel hair and wool. The feet were carved lion-paws and the legs were smooth with a nice curve.

"Dinah, this is the sash you were wanting. It really is lovely. I also got this scarf of soft wool for me, and for Mattan, this little gown of fine cotton," said Abigail, handing Dinah her sash. She turned to Bethany with the gown and added, "Bethany, I didn't forget you; here is a pretty blouse." Bethany didn't respond so Abigail laid Mattan's gown in the basket and put the blouse beside her on the couch. Abigail went to the kitchen with the rest of the food items.

Bethany was speechless. Never in her short life had anyone taken care of her. She really didn't know how to receive a gift from someone with no other motive than love. She believed this to be her very first gift of that kind.

Instead of being touched, Bethany became angry. Thinking, 'Well, gifts can't buy me. They are trying to make me into someone I don't want to be-- a good girl. I am and have been since I was a child, a very bad girl and I am rather proud of it. At least I know who I am and know how to live that life well.'

She had enough of this touching scene. Leaving Mattan in Dinah's arms, Bethany escaped upstairs for a nap. She would be able to rest at least an hour before supper in her room. She would not join them for supper, even though she felt well enough to do so. She didn't need to grow any closer to this family.

"Dinah, come in here and let's get supper finished. Dad and Azariah will be home within the hour."

Putting Mattan back in his basket which was still in the kitchen, she and her mother quickly finished the meat; it had been stewing since after lunch. They set the table with plates, forks and cups and put out wooden bowls of cantaloupe and some grapes. Dinah sliced bread putting it in a basket with a towel over it and put a bowl of olive oil out, too. They were ready when the men arrived. Abigail got a tray ready to take up to Bethany, since it appeared she would not be eating with them again.

"Do you think she would like some grapes, too, Dinah?"

Dinah was lost in thought.

"Dinah...?" her mom turned to look at her since she didn't respond.

Noticing her mom's questioning gaze, she said, "Mom, she is the strangest girl I have ever met. I don't know what she would like. This afternoon she came out and talked to me while you were gone. I don't think she cares for anyone but herself. She really doesn't seem to love Mattan, although I don't know how she could help it." Dinah reached over and took his little hand and his fingers curled around hers. He was so wonderful.

"We will keep working on it and maybe in time a motherly love will develop. Anyway, for now, it is enough that we can share him." Abigail picked up the tray and delivered it to Bethany.

It was clear Bethany seemed to have her appetite back and was strong enough to leave. Abigail hoped she would wait for a while. Her concern was not for Bethany's health, but for Mattan's. What would happen to the sweet thing if he was at home alone with a mother who didn't care about him? Tears welled up in her eyes. It just broke her heart to think they might leave and that he would suffer or be unloved. She hurried down to the kitchen, wiping her eyes dry. If Dinah saw her crying, she would burst into tears, too. The men would come home and find two weeping women on their hands. That would never do.

Just minutes after she returned to the kitchen, Hadad and Azariah arrived. Both kissed Abigail and dad hugged Dinah rubbing his face against her hair.

"Let's have supper and we can talk about the day while we eat," he said. He was very hungry. While the food was placed on the table and the family participated in the traditional Jewish blessing. 'Lord, please bless our home and family. Thank you for the provision of this food from your bounty. And bless Bethany and Mattan. Amen.'"

Although Hadad enjoyed the time around the meal and visiting, he was tired. He had a stressful day and was looking forward to a good rest. He took his coffee to the roof courtyard and sat down. Abigail joined him.

"My dear, it is beautiful out this evening," Hadad said. "Look at those stars sparkling. There are so many of them. The moon's little crescent gives just enough light. Here, sit near me." They sat quietly for some time. "Although I love creation; I love the Creator more. It is hard for me to understand how people have gotten so confused and now think that it is the creation that is to be worshiped. There are people on their rooftops tonight offering incense to the Queen of Heaven. How wrong that is."

"I have heard that our neighbor now worships the stars, moon or sun. Those things can't help you when we need it like God can."

"I agree, my dear, but I am too tired to get into a philosophical discussion tonight. Let's go to bed," Hadad said. They got up and went to their room which was behind them in the second level. Dinah's candle was still lit in her room, but Azariah's room was dark, as was Bethany's.

The next morning moved along as usual with preparations for the day. Abigail was at the breakfast table when she heard Mattan begin to cry. 'It was time for his breakfast, too,' she thought. She prepared the breakfast tray for Bethany. Today she would ask her if she wanted to begin joining the family for meals. She seemed to be strong and able to move around okay now. She went upstairs with the tray and knocked at Bethany's door.

"It's Abigail, Bethany. May I come in?" She didn't answer. She looked down gallery at the wash room; the door was standing open and the room was empty. She knocked again.

Mattan was wailing. She was sure Bethany couldn't still be sleeping with that racket. She knocked one more time, before she gently turned the knob. The room was still dim as the sun was barely up. She didn't see her anywhere in the room. Where was that girl?

"Dinah, can you step out here, please?" In a few minutes, Dinah's door opened and she came to her mother's side with her wrap around her shoulders.

"What's wrong? Why is Mattan still crying?" Dinah asked, sleepily.

"I can't find Bethany. She is not in her room and not downstairs. Have you seen her or heard her this morning?"

"No." Dinah lit the candle in Bethany's room and they set the food on the table. Something was wrong. Dinah picked up Mattan and put her little finger in his mouth for him to suckle until he could be fed. Looking around carefully, the tunics and clothes that had been hanging on pegs in the rooms were gone. One blanket was missing and Dinah's sandals. Dinah got an awful feeling in her stomach. She and her mother exchanged a glance with the same fear in their eyes. It appeared Bethany had left in the middle of the night, leaving Mattan without a mother.

Abigail stepped back into the gallery, "Hadad, come quickly. I think we have a problem." Hadad came out of his room with his night tunic flowing round his shins.

"What's happened?" He quickly evaluated the room and saw Dinah holding the crying baby. "Is she gone?"

Abigail and Dinah nodded yes, "Well, that is a problem." Thinking quickly, he said, "First things first. We need to find a way to feed Mattan."

"Dinah, get dressed and go to Dariann to she if she has any suggestions on who would serve as a wet nurse for Mattan. Abigail, try to find something for him to suck that will satisfy him for a few hours, while we search for a help," said Hadad. "I will see if I can find out anything in the city about where his mother went."

Dinah dressed quickly and ran back to the home of Dariann, the mid-wife. If anyone would know of someone who might be available to nurse Mattan, she would know. Within the hour Dinah was home with a name--Lotta.

Dariann recommended her because she was at the end of nursing her son. Dariann said that Lotta moved back with her parents because her husband had been killed in an accident, but she wanted to support herself and her son. This opportunity might allow her some independence and meet the needs of this baby, too.

Abigail had given him a rag to suck soaked in warm milk, but he was not really interested in it. When Dinah returned, they bundled up Mattan, and rushed out. Dinah and Abby walked to Lotta's parents' house about thirty minutes away. Knocking tentatively at the door, Abby waited for a response. Mattan was hungry and crying. He probably hadn't eaten in the night either. It was hard to tell by looking at the room how long Bethany had been gone.

Abby knocked again. She would never have considered going to a stranger's door to ask for this kind of help, if she had any other ideas.

Lotta's father answered the door, "Hello." He looked rather surprised to see two ladies with a crying baby. "May I help you?" He could see and hear that they had a very upset baby with them. The baby didn't appear to be very old, maybe a week or two.

"My name is Abigail and this is my daughter, Dinah. I have a rather unusual request about this baby. Could we come inside and talk about it?"

"Please, I am sorry I didn't offer." Stepping aside, the two ladies went in and sat on a bench in the front room. "My name is Abram and this is my wife, Myra. Is the baby ill? I am sorry I don't know much about babies, except for the experience I have with my year-old grandson, Nathan."

"No, he isn't ill, but he is the reason we came. Dariann, the mid-wife, remembered that your daughter, Lotta gave birth about a year ago and she thought maybe she would be weaning her son and could help us feed this little one. We took in a troubled girl who abandoned him at our house last night. Do you think your daughter could help us? We are desperate to find a way to feed and care for him."

"Let me go get Lotta. I think only she can answer a question as serious as this," said Myra, who left the room and returned with Lotta and Nathan, her son. Myra introduced them, "Lotta, this is Abigail, her daughter, Dinah and a little orphaned one. What is his name?"

Dinah responded, "Mattan."

"Ah, how appropriate—gift," said Abram.

Myra continued, "His mother abandoned him at their home. They have no other choice but to find someone to feed him. They wondered if you would be willing to wet-nurse him?"

Lotta looked surprised, and understandably so. It wasn't often that such an offer was made. Maybe this is how God was answering her prayers. She had been asking to be on her own again. She missed being independent. Her parents were wonderful, but she longed for a home of her own. If she could earn some money, maybe she could save enough to buy her own home.

Thinking quickly, she answered, "How about if we start with me feeding him right now? Let's see if he takes to me and is willing to eat. As hungry as he is, it may just work." She reached for the screaming baby and left for a back room. It wasn't long until the crying stopped and all was quiet. Everyone was relieved and grateful that the child was eating. He was so pitiful.

Lotta returned and handed Mattan to Dinah, "Everything went fine. What are the arrangements that you would like to make?"

Abigail really hadn't thought that far ahead. She just wanted to get food for the baby. She turned to Abram, "Sir, I am so sorry that I didn't have my husband come. I really have not considered how this arrangement might work. Could I have him come and talk with you this evening?"

"That would be fine. Lotta, how about you going to their home for today and taking Nathan with you? You can take care of both boys, and by the end of the day the arrangements can be worked out. Is that acceptable with everyone?"

There were nods all around the room. Dinah gave Mattan to Abby and went with Lotta to help her get some things together. They returned with Dinah carrying fabric bags of items and Lotta carrying Nathan. The three ladies and two boys walked down the street. Abram got directions to where they lived. Abby asked him to come to their home that evening after his supper. She would have Hadad ready and waiting to finish the negotiations.

They moved Lotta and both boys into Bethany's room. The morning and afternoon passed quickly with the ladies getting acquainted. They were so compatible, that it seemed they had known each other before. Nathan was precious and only made the house that much happier.

Mattan was happy and content. That was the most important thing at this point. He quickly adjusted to his new nurse, but he was more comfortable with Abby and Dinah. He seemed to rest better when one of them was holding him.

That evening during dinner Hadad explained his efforts to find Dinah during the day. He had several sources who had looked and some others that were interviewed for information. Bethany had told them nothing about herself or her life, so they had very little to go on to find out where she might have gone. He had given up the search that afternoon. Maybe one day she would turn up, but they would not wait for that time. They would care for Mattan as if he was one of their own family. That decision pleased everyone.

Abram arrived about an hour after supper and the two men went to the roof courtyard to negotiate the arrangement for Lotta and Mattan. They shared a cup of wine and some fig bread while they visited. Within the hour they returned to the waiting families in the living area.

"Lotta, your father has agreed for you to stay with us for a year. Since the baby is a newborn, we will wait to see when he is weaned. In exchange, we will provide you and Nathan with room and board. If you would like to earn some spending money, then you may help Abby with the chores here. Are these arrangements acceptable to you?"

All Lotta could say was, "Yes." She was speechless with excitement. She had asked for independence and had been given that with a safe environment. A chance to be on her own, but still not having endanger herself or Nathan. 'Thank you, God!' she was saying repeatedly to herself.

With the arrangement complete, life returned to a new normal. The addition of Lotta and Nathan to the Hadad family enriched everyone's lives. Bethany seemed to never have existed. Not once had it occurred to the Hadad's to consider giving Mattan away or even to abandoning him on the road, which was a common practice of the day for unwanted children. They had loved him from the first day with his struggle to come into the world and that love had only grown as they watched him grow. He was part of their family now and they loved him.

CHAPTER 10

Freedom! That is all Bethany could think about. Not once did she feel a twinge of guilt as she moved away from the Hadad family. She was free and that was all that mattered.

Leaving Mattan with the Hadads was best for him. He would be safe and loved. It was written across their faces when they talked with him. They looked into his eyes with such love. She was not capable of giving that kind of love to anyone. She hoped they understood that what she had done for him was actually the best for him. Really, they should be grateful to her for not keeping him.

She was grateful he was alive, but glad she didn't have to care for him. The fact that they had both survived the childbirth was a miracle. About half of the children or mothers didn't.

Temple prostitutes' children who died in childbirth were always given to Molech. Some infants who lived were even allowed to die by neglect and then offered in the fires. The temple officials took the position that it was for the best to all concerned. A temple was no place for the children or the infants to live.

Most temple prostitutes were slaves and not free to do what they pleased. Keeping their children to raise them was usually not an option. Bethany was a slave prostitute, but not in the typical sense. Although she served at the temple, she did not worship Molech, the god. She felt no obligation to give her child to the fires. Her debts, due to the lack of a husband to support her and no family to take care of her, caused her to sell herself to the temple for a small income for a period of five years. She still owed them two more years, but she didn't owe them Mattan.

Remembering the discussions around the temple when she was nearing her delivery time made her uneasy. The chief priest had been excited, when she mentioned she was pregnant, "Praise Molech! The god of all gods who has provided for himself a new offering."

A few weeks later, another prostitute asked, "Bethany, when are you due? It must be getting near the time for delivery. It is not that bad; I gave my son last spring, remember?"

She remembered all right. Although, she wasn't attached to the idea of having a child, she was not going to give them her baby no matter what. These comments made her more determined than before that she would try to escape. She had seen many infants burned on the altar. It turned her stomach each time she remembered the smell. They burned incense to cover it up, but it really didn't help much.

She admitted to herself she was bad. In her short eighteen years she had done what she had to for survival, fighting the odds against her. But she was not bad enough to do that to her child, whether he had been born alive or dead. The thought that the child she would bear would face that fate was more than she could stand.

So she began looking for an unused or abandoned home that she could claim when the time came. She found the little room up from the Hadad family about a week before she delivered. She quietly gathered her belongings and disappeared from the temple the same way she had from the Hadad's. She was afraid she might be followed when she left the temple and her baby taken, so she was very careful not to give away her plans or the location of the room she had found. She remained there about a week waiting for the birth. She ate very little since she had little money.

Even though she left abruptly without any thanks, she was grateful for all the Hadad's had done for her and Mattan. The family had kept them both alive and given her son a name. Mattan was as good as any she might have thought up.

The lead prostitute asked, "Would you like for me to aid you in selecting a name to honor our god?" Thinking that would be a good thing for Bethany. Choosing a name for Molech's honor was not really a priority to her. One of the reasons she hadn't thought about naming him before was because she was afraid he would be sacrificed. Thinking about a name for the child would have made it seem like he had a chance of living and not being offered as a sacrifice.

She answered, "You know he is not my god. I simply needed a job and this was safer than the streets."

The lead prostitute did not like her attitude. She was a little unsure about what Bethany was thinking, so she added, "I question your loyalty and dedication to this cause and your employers. If you think you are safer here than on the street, you might consider the fate of the last girl who attempted to escape. She is now deceased. Being here is your job and they will watch you carefully as the time nears for your delivery. Maternal instincts to preserve the life of an unborn child are a common cause for prostitutes trying to flee. Most do not make it. They then lose their life and the life of their child, too. You had better be careful in your plans." She turned and walked away.

For all of these reasons, Bethany had not allowed herself to get too attached to him in case the escape failed. She wasn't sure she would be able to escape in time and find a place to hide when he was born. Her confidence that the whole thing was going to happen at the right time was low. But, fate was on her side, and she was able to move away from one of the temple customers one night when he was in a drunken stupor. They were not watching her, since she was with a temple regular. It was fortunate for her that she knew he loved to drink. She plied him with wine until he was unable to stay awake. Hurrying under the tent flap and to the small hut she had seen several weeks earlier she had made her escape. That is where the Hadads had found her.

She was deep in her thoughts as she came around the corner and saw her destination. It was good she was here, because she was not feeling too well. The long walk was harder than she had planned since she had not fully recovered. She moved quickly toward Cain's Inn. Of course, they wouldn't be open yet, since it was still a couple of hours before noon. That wouldn't stop her, though, because she knew how to get in and where her sister's room was. She had been here many times before.

Her sister would be shocked to see her. Last time they had talked was six months ago when she was a miserable, pregnant temple prostitute. Now, she was not well and in possible danger from temple guards and needed Moriah's help. She couldn't go back to the temple yet, but they would be looking for her until she paid her time. Besides, she reasoned, she was still sore and healing from the delivery and would be of no use to them for a time. She hoped she never went through the birth process again. Shaking her head from side to side, as if to remove a cobweb, she cleared her thoughts. She must forget the past and move ahead. Today was a new beginning and she was a young, single lady with a new start in the world.

Coming to the back of the inn she spied the laundress, Levine, busy at the pots making soap. "Hello, Levine. How have you been?"

"It has been a long time, missy, since I seed you. Looks like you doin' okay."

"Been doing okay. Is Moriah around or Cain?"

"They's havin' a bite inside with Hablin. Kind t'ov a business meetin. Go on in."

Opening the back door, she stepped into the dim room and stopped to let her eyes adjust. In the corner near the front window of the inn she could see the group eating. They had all turned toward the light from the door, when she entered, but had no idea who she was yet. She had the light at her back and her face was in the shadows.

"Hello, everyone. Thought I would come by for a visit. It has been too long," she called to them from the doorway.

Recognizing the voice immediately, Cain grumbled, "Not long enough for me," under his breath. He respected her sister, who was a hard worker with a kind spirit. But Bethany was a no-good, bum with screwed-up morals. Who could work at a place that burned babies? She seemed to use Moriah, coming around only when she wanted something from her older sister. Moriah was always willing to oblige, even to her own hurt because she loved Bethany. The girls were abandoned when they were very young and left to fend for themselves. Moriah, being six years older, had done most of the providing and protecting: stealing to eat, selling herself to men or whatever it took to take care of them. Who they had become was the best they had been able to do for themselves. Cain's focus shifted back to Bethany wondering what she wanted this time.

"Dear sister, it so good to see you," Moriah said, and went to Bethany. Hugging her, and then pushing her out to arms length and looking her over, she said, "And I see you are getting your figure back."

Moriah didn't ask about the baby. She didn't really want to know. How could her own sister sacrifice her baby on a flaming altar? Since Bethany wasn't pregnant anymore, she had to assume the baby had already been born and probably sacrificed. It broke Moriah's heart to think of it, so she put the thought out of her mind.

71

"Hello, dear, I have missed you, too," Bethany said, and broke away from her hold twirling in a circle. "Looking good again, aren't I?" She looked better, but she knew how weak she really was.

"Good as always," Hablin chimed in. He liked Bethany, regardless of how Cain felt. Cain had no room to criticize anyway, with his life style. Hablin looked again at Bethany and smiled. What a beautiful woman. He would do just about anything to see Bethany smile.

"Do we have any lunch to spare, old friend?" Bethany leaned over and kissed the top of Hablin's balding head. "I missed breakfast and am famished."

Getting up quickly, he said, "Coming out to you in just a few minutes. Take a seat and I will get it for you," and he went to the back. Hablin always fawned over her when she came to visit. Her beauty had that affect on men and she used it to her advantage whenever possible.

She sat down carefully. She felt a little light headed. Both Moriah and Cain noticed how pale she looked. She saw them watching her and tried to cover up how she felt. She turned to Cain, "You are being very quiet. Aren't you glad to see me?" she taunted him. She knew he didn't care for her and liked to see him fish for an answer that was not too offensive to her sister.

"Let's just say, if Moriah is happy to see you, then so am I." He gave her a look that warned her not to push it.

"Bethany, you don't look well. What are you doing here in the middle of the day? Isn't the temple open all day?"

"Yes, but I left the temple. That's what I wanted to talk about. I have taken a break from the temple for a while. Is there somewhere here I could stay and maybe work?" she asked. She looked from one to the other as Hablin served her lunch. She ate heartily while looking up at them for an answer.

"How does a slave take a break from her owners? They will be looking for you. I don't want to get in the middle of a battle with them and you," Cain responded looking at Moriah and shaking his head 'no'.

"We have to help her, Cain. She has no where else to turn. Bethany, why are you taking a break? What happened?"

"Moriah, let's just say I needed a change. I know this puts all of you in a hard position. I don't think they will look for me in here, but until things cool down, can't you put me up here? I will work for you for nothing but my room and board?"

Moriah begged, "Cain, I know how you feel about Bethany and so does she, so let's get it all on the table. I doubt that they will look for her in this part of town, so it should be okay. Just a couple of days ago 'our guest' said he wanted me to serve his men, so you have been working double duty to try and do all the work. The serving down here needs to be done by someone. How about if we let that someone be Bethany?"

Cain thought about the suggestion. The price was certainly right. He had no idea what kind of waitress she could be or if she was a hard worker. He had his doubts, based on her history, but he did need help tonight.

"Let's try it for lunch and tonight. We will discuss how she did later tonight. If she is able to do the work, then I will consider it. She can stay with you in your room and we will decide tomorrow if it is going to work out. Who knows, maybe she can't do the work."

Bethany gave him a haughty look. Of course she could do the work, if she wanted to. With that resolved the sisters settled into a long-overdue conversation for the rest of lunch. Bethany knew it was obvious that she had had the baby, but she wasn't going to tell them anything, if she could help it. That topic of conversation never came up.

Lunch was busy. It would have been overwhelming for any new waitress, but her problem was she was so weak, too. She managed to get food to the guests without spilling it and to make sure they paid before leaving. She was much slower than Moriah and couldn't begin to meet the guests other demands. She was working as hard as she could to make sure they got the right plates before the food was too cold.

"You idiot! Take that away and bring me the lamb stew I ordered. What's wrong with you? And where is Moriah? Why would they hire you to replace such a good waitress?" fussed a disgruntled regular that ate here often when he was traveling from Petra.

"Sorry, I will get it right now." She took the plate away and gave it to the man waving at the next table indicating that plate was his. She returned to the counter to get the stew and some bread.

Returning with the correct food, the patron added, "Better. Much better. You may make it as a waitress yet." The merchant acknowledging that she got it right this time.

Bethany had to agree. She was no replacement for her sister's experienced service to these men, but maybe she could learn. She actually liked this okay. At least it was better than the temple. She noticed about half-way through lunch, however, that she was beginning to wear out and to hurt. It was clear to her she was not very strong and would have a hard time keeping up this pace for long. She definitely needed more rest for a while and wouldn't be able to return to the temple until she was better, if she decided to return at all. She might make this her new profession, if they could keep her on and if she was worth it to them. She wondered how much help she would be able to be here for a while, since she was still so weak.

Upstairs, Moriah was busy with Wakeem and his men serving their lunch and taking care of his room. Cain's arrangement with Wakeem included room and board and whatever he required for meetings with his men while they were spying out the city for Nebuchadnezzar. In exchange, Cain and Moriah would be guaranteed safety, if the city was conquered. Moriah didn't like the arrangement and being a traitor to this country. But what could she do but go along with the arrangement. She had no other place to stay and she was making a good enough living.

"Get us some more stew and bread. Bring the whole skin of wine, not just a cup. That will never be enough," Wakeem barked.

She went downstairs and came back with his food. Wakeem, Timath, Zarallon, and Eddu-aran were finalizing the raid plans for the tribute caravan. She laid everything on the table and cleaned up from the last meal, overhearing most of the conversation. They did not seem to mind her presence in the room, since they believed Cain and his mistress were under their control.

Wakeem began, "Zarallon, according to your report we will need to be in place tomorrow at mid-morning. The caravan will leave at dawn and arrive in Bethlehem about noon, correct?"

"Right. From our best information it takes about that long to get there. You should be fine if everyone is in place early tomorrow," Zarallon confirmed.

"Timath, your archers should be spread along the side of the Patriarch's Highway to the east and hit the caravan when they are through the city of Bethlehem moving toward Hebron. That area is hillier and should give a better view. The path narrows for several miles there just outside of the Bethlehem. You should be able to hit the targets easily."

"Eddu, hide your lancers in the rocks to the west. After the archers begin their attack and the guards are seeking shelter, you come down from your side behind them. They will have their backs to you. I will gather my men from their caves in Adullam and wait just ahead. We will come in to join you and finish the battle. It should be over quickly," Wakeem finished his instruction.

Eddu commented, "I will leave my job today and gather my men for tomorrow. We can camp in the area tonight and be in place before dawn."

"When we finish meeting today, I will go out to the campsite for my men in Jericho and plan on being in place at dawn also," added Timath.

"After we take the wagons we will return to the caves at Adullam and hide, sorting the things we want to take. It is about fifteen miles, but we ought to be able to make that by nightfall. If any of their men escape, they will not be able to get back to town and rally the soldiers before we can be out of the area. We will unload the gold and silver, distributing the weight among the camels and horses of all the men and ride toward the west to Gaza, then Ashkelon. We should be able to make it in one long day, if all does well. Once we are out of their territory, we will sell or board the horses and camels, and leave a few men behind to stay with our other supplies. We will have the metals boxed while we get passage on a boat. The rest of men will go by boat up the coast to Ugarit where we can unload and hire camels for the trip across land to the Euphrates. We should be able to avoid any search parties completely. Let's finish eating and get to our men to bring them up-to-date. Tomorrow looks like the big day."

The group finished eating and separated. Wakeem, loaded his few belongings and adjusted the bag over his shoulder as he came downstairs to find Cain, "I am leaving for a while. I may be back, so be prepared to have a place for me." With that word, he left to find his troops outside Jerusalem. He took all of his things from Cain's for now. He might be back later, but was not sure when. He would make the trip north with the group. They would get the next plans from the military men working with Nebuzaradan and bring them back when they returned.

Hurrying to the stable, he paid his fee and readied his Arabian horse, for the twelve mile ride to the caves south of Jerusalem where his men were camped. He left them there a week earlier with a sergeant who could keep the lid on them. They had plenty of water and supplies and could hunt for meat.

Wakeem had been in town for a week. Inn rooms were smelly and close. He liked the openness of camping and being out in nature. Entering the stables, he spoke, "Ibbisin, I am here to let you go." His Arabian whinnied back his response in eagerness. He took out the apple and some dates he had taken from the inn. "Here you are, boy. These will make up for leaving you here so long without riding you. Let's get out of here. You and I need to be moving, not tied in a stall." He saddled his stallion and trotted out of town.

Ibbisin, King of the south wind, got his name from an old, Arabian fable about the horse. "God regarded the south wind with pleasure and decided to make of it a creature. 'Condense,' He said to the wind, and the first horse sped over the earth." Arabians were not tall horses, but they could drink the wind. They had a sturdiness and endurance that made them ideal for the harshness of the barren deserts and plains. He took his time riding out of town until he was in open terrain, then he rode hard for most of the distance toward Adullam. During the ride there Ibbisin's tail was arched high in the air and his nostrils were flared as he enjoyed the run. Wakeem held his head as high as the head of the horse he rode. His horse was just like him: loved to run and loved to fight.

CHAPTER 11

The palace was bustling with activity. Today the tribute payment was leaving for Egypt. The sun was barely up, but everywhere you looked in the palace work areas, people were busy with last minute details. The loading dock was filled with clerks and officials as they did a final once-over. Daniel was downstairs, too, with Oshiel, doing a final check on the wagons and their loads, supplies and tribute metals. The shipment had been delayed with a broken axle which had taken three days to repair including the unloading, repair and reloading of the goods. Gideon came into the dock area with Tigner. It was the first time Daniel was with the King's second in command, Tigner. Even though he had checked and rechecked the cargos, it made him a little uneasy. He hoped they hadn't missed any details.

"Gideon, these wagons should be rolling in half an hour. Baileen, tell Garridon to ready his men and horses. Get the supply wagon and all the drivers down here. They are all being fed breakfast in the upper hall in the back. Tell them to push the food in and get down here quickly. Gideon, give me an update," said Tigner.

"Sir, the wagons are ready. Oshiel and Daniel have confirmed that everything is in place," he said, confirming that again with a nod. "Would you like to look at the list once again?"

"Yes. I see the silver and gold listed and the grains, the skins and general supplies for the trip." He paused and looked over the list carefully, approving,

"Okay. Good. Let's get the commander here to review the route and safety precautions. The drivers can meet with you, Gideon, to answer any questions about the route, loads and supplies."

With that, everyone split up to meet with the different groups of people. The men came down from breakfast and gathered around. After the instructions were given to Garridon, the second in command of the King's guard, he gathered the soldiers and they saddled their horses and rode out into the streets outside the exit gate of the palace. They did a quick check around the area for any would-be dangers, and re-gathered around in the street near the exit to wait for the wagons. In ten minutes the first wagon rolled out with the cook and travel supplies, followed by eight more wagons each with two drivers each carrying the tribute. A supply wagon was last followed by horses carrying the one emissary, one ambassador and two servants. Traveling with the group were two emissaries who were King Jehoiakim's representatives to Pharaoh Necho. All together fifty men and soldiers left just after dawn for Bethlehem.

Everyone in the palace breathed a sigh of relief. The caravan got off without a hitch. All hoped the rest of the trip went as smoothly.

The morning was slow and uneventful. Near noon, Garridon stopped the caravan and came back to the emissary, "Sir, we are about to enter Bethlehem. Let me scout ahead to find a place to leave the wagons and see if there is an inn for a meal for you and the ambassador."

On the north side of town was a large field for the wagons to camp. Once in town he asked a few people if there was a place to eat. They suggested he stop at the tavern just ahead.

"Hello," Garridon called. "Anybody here?" He stepped off his horse and into the dimly lit room.

A woman came from the back, "Can I help you, sir?"

"Yes. I will be bringing five men here in about half an hour for lunch. Can you be ready for us with a good meal? Are you prepared to handle a group like that on short notice?"

"Yes, sir. We will have everything ready. May I ask who is coming?"

"No, you may not. These men are on a business trip. That should be enough information. Here is a shekel for our payment." With that he stepped back outside, mounted his horse and went quickly back to the wagons.

They moved the caravan to the field and he had the wagons line up 2-by-2 putting ten of the guards on watch. The wagoneers hopped down and unloaded supplies. Two of them doubled as cooks. He left the men to prepare their lunch and watch the wagons. They quickly had a fire going and a stew of cabbage, sausage and corn, pita bread and wine.

"Sirs, if you will come with me, we will ride to the tavern." The dignitaries and their servants followed him into town, dismounting and taking a seat at the table just inside the door. The tavern was acceptable and since the proprietress had been forewarned, she was able to set a good table of food. She had cleaned up a nice table and seats, and put some wild flowers in a pot. The daughter quickly brought all the men wine.

"Surprisingly good wine, for a tavern of this caliber," commented Caramoth, the official ambassador to Egypt. He had only been to Egypt once before by a different route than they were using this time. The meal was quickly served. Tasting the fresh lamb chops and potatoes, "Well, I am pleased. This was worth the stop." Both men were soft in body, but they had good political experience and quick minds, which was why the king asked them to go. They knew little of travel and its hardships, but were good politicians and could speak to Pharaoh's court with intelligence. They knew Pharaoh would not be in Alexandria, since he was on a campaign to the north of Israel. It was likely they would be speaking to some underling or they would have to stay in Egypt until Pharaoh returned.

Donolly, the emissary agreed, "The food is acceptable, but not comparable to the excellent dining at the palace. I am still surprised that the King asked us to go, to leave our homes and travel so far on a horse is really asking too much. I am not happy about this trip at all." He turned to see if Caramoth was agreeing with him. Seeing that he was, he continued, "I hate to travel by horse and carriage isn't significantly better. Both are so hard on the body. I am not accustomed to the saddle and the constant jostling." Turning to his servant, he said, "Get us some water for washing up after the meal."

Garridon ate quickly and excused himself. While they finished eating, he went back to the wagons. He found soldiers and wagoneers ready for travel with their fires extinguished and supplies reloaded. Coming to attention when he arrived, he ordered them to roll-out and move the wagons through town. Within thirty minutes they were at the tavern where the dignitaries were waiting and ready. The group remounted and the caravan moved south for the next stage of the trip. This evening they would camp near Hebron. It would be a long day, but they could make it well before dark. The elite and servants would rest in town while the others did guard duty.

It was a very quiet afternoon and enjoyed by most of the men, excluding the honored guests. They complained first about one thing and then another.

They really were wearing on the nerves of the men. But otherwise, the trip was going along well. However, Garridon was uneasy. He had that feeling that comes with years of experience in battle, the sense of tension in the air. You know that feeling that makes your skin itch, and then you hunch your shoulders and try and shake it off. Nothing was noticeably wrong, but there was something that was making him wary. They had been on the road about an hour and everything was quiet. It was too quiet! That was what was bothering him. No birds or animal sounds. Now he knew there was a problem, but what?

Then he heard it on his left—not a bird or animal—but the zing of a bow string! And then, more bow strings! He heard the knowing 'thuds' of the arrows hitting their marks. Spinning his mount quickly to the right away from the attackers, he dove for shelter. Just as he turned, an arrow whizzed past his head, just grazing his cheek. He dropped to the ground and ran for cover, pulling his horse behind him. When he was behind the rocks, he turned toward the west bank and pulled his sword. Five of his men had fallen and two drivers were hit. The rest were quickly running for the rocks near him. The other two drivers were trying to pull the wagons to the side of the road and get behind them. They managed to get down and out of site before they were hit.

Both dignitaries were just sitting in the saddle starring. Fools! He crouched and ran toward them as fast as he could staying behind cover. He saw an arrow hit Caramoth before he could reach him. The man made a guttural sound and fell backwards out of the saddle hitting the ground a dead man, an arrow piercing his throat. Garridon had seen the look Donolly had on his face before; the look of a man facing death all around him for the first time in his life.

Garridon stood and grabbed Donolly's horse pulling it off the road. He jerked the man by the fabric of his shirt lifting him out of the saddle and into the rocks in a single motion. "Stay down, sir, and cover your head. Don't get up until you hear me say it is safe," Garridon whispered to the emissary. The man was shaking violently, but nodded that he was listening and understood.

Garridon looked to see where his men were. There appeared to be ten or more soldiers he could see, six drivers and two servants. Only the guards and drivers were armed. In a hand-to-hand battle, the drivers would be useless. They were untrained for battle. He stopped with that thought. What was that? Looking behind him again he saw it. A movement caught his eye. What was ....?

He motioned to three of his men to watch their backs. They turned just in time to see several lancers with red shields come from the rocks twenty yards behind them with lances at the ready. This was an ambush! Someone had advanced knowledge. They had to have had time to have put their men in place on both sides of the road. The palace definitely had a spy inside working within a sensitive area. The three soldiers rushed toward the spear men, swords drawn. More lancers appeared and all of rest of his men engaged in the fight. Gratefully, the archers were not shooting now. They would not shot into the fray since they might hit their own men. His men were out-numbered two-to-one, but they were holding their own. Three more of his men had fallen along with five of the lancers. His men were doing well and he was about to join them, thinking that the archers didn't appear to be coming from their hiding places to join the battle on this side of the road.

Then, he heard new, fresh voices yelling from the south of his location. He saw the flash of steel waving in the air. Men came running on foot from the south around the curve on the road. A feeling of doom washed over him. There was little hope any of his caravan would survive. There were just too many of the enemy's men.

He prepared to defend the innocents that were with them. Swinging his sword toward the first group that reached him, he took out a young soldier and quickly pierced through a second, before he moved back. He slipped behind a rock and saw another coming his way, rushing toward the emissary. Garridon waited until he came near, then he swung his sword starting at waist height and swinging in an upward direction. From behind his hiding place, he stepped out just in time to see the whites of the surprised soldier's eyes before his head was severed from his body. Another was right behind him. Using the momentum of that first swing, Garridon pivoted in the direction of the swing and jumped on top of the rock. He continued his pivot and swung the sword around cutting the next man wide open across the chest. From behind him he could hear the yells of men dying and others begging for mercy.

To his dismay he noticed that the archers were once again shooting. Before his sword could take another enemy soldier an arrow caught him in the shoulder and he fell into the rocks, hitting his head and knocking himself unconscious.

He began to stir. How much time had passed since he had fallen? He had no idea. When he woke, though, it was quiet again, just like before...before when? He knew he had been thinking about the quietness, when something happened. What was it? He tried to move, but he couldn't. He was in terrible pain and seemed to be stuck between some rocks. He couldn't really remember what had happened. Why was he lying in the rocks and what was wrong with his arm? Oh, his head hurt every time he tried to lift it to see where he was. He began to fade dropping again into unconsciousness.

He awoke with a stab of pain, "Don't move me!" he yelled. "Keep your foul hands off of me." But the hands continued to lift him out of the rocks and placed him on a wagon. Where was he? He still couldn't remember, but he was too weak to argue or stay focused.

Someone leaned over the wagon side, saying, "Garridon, my friend. You have survived a horrible battle. We will get that arrow out of your shoulder soon and then you can take some time and heal. Can you give us any details of what happened? The caravan appears to have been ambushed," asked his commander general, Robron. "We got word a few hours ago that there were many dead and wounded men on the Patriarch's Highway coming out of Bethlehem. We rushed here with a full garrison, assuming that the caravan had been hit. We appear to be right, but can you give us some details?"

"I am sorry, sir. I am kind of confused. I only remember it was so quiet, so unusually quiet, and then I go blank. Maybe it will come to me when I get better," he apologized and faded into unconsciousness. Thinking before he faded, he really had no idea who this man was. Obviously, the man knew him, but Garridon really was not sure what was going on.

"Okay, men. Let's load the wounded into the wagon here with Garridon."

His sergeant came to him with a report on the wounded, "Donolly is unconscious, but alive. One driver survived, but is in poor shape. Probably won't live through the trip back. And we have two soldiers to get from the field. Their wounds appear minor. The dead have been loaded into the other wagon we brought."

"Okay, men, let's finish up here and get back to Bethlehem, as quickly as possible. We will stay there tonight. There may be someone there who can dress the wounds and help the injured men."

The rescue mission camped just outside of Bethlehem that night. A local woman came to the camp and removed the arrow from Garridon's shoulder, dressed other wounds, giving the wounded some herbs to help with the pain. She applied several poultices to the injured. The most serious risk to the injured was getting a running wound or gangrene. Time would tell, if they would live or die. All that could be done had been. They would wait now to see how they healed.

The rescued caravan finished the trip back to Jerusalem Wednesday morning. All of the families of the dead were notified and the bodies were picked up in the shipping dock area. The ill were sent home to recover. Garridon had no family, so he was cared for in the barracks by one of the staff at the palace. His memory still was foggy.

On Thursday Garridon had a raging fever and terrible pain. The servants gave him herb tea and broth. He laid under covers to sweat out the fever most of the day. On Friday the fever broke and he rested quietly. By Saturday he was able to sit up and eat. His commander returned, "Well, son, you are looking like you might make it. How do you feel?"

"My pain is better and I feel a small amount of strength returning each day. The memory seems to be returning. Would you like to talk for a while about the ambush?"

"Fill me in on the details as you remember then," Robron said.

Garridon repeated the story as he remembered it up to the point where he lost consciousness. He had no idea what had happened after that. At this point, Robron added the missing pieces to what happened.

"The wagons were taken to Adullam, stripped of all valuables and abandoned. They had a large number of men, camels and horses. They loaded the camels and horses with the tribute and headed west, probably to a port city with their booty. We have spies in Ashkelon and Joppa now trying to find out if any group of soldiers shipped out in the last days headed north. We think they are part of Nebuchadnezzar's group. Locals have seen soldiers who looked like Chaldeans in the area recently."

"What are you planning to do next?"

"I doubt we will ever catch them. They have too much of a start on us and too many options about where they might have gone. The King is furious, but is trying to work out the details of getting another shipment together. In the mean time, he will send another group of emissaries without tribute to meet with Pharaoh's leaders. He hopes they can work out a time-delayed payment."

"I am sorry, sir. I did all I could, as did my men, but we were so outnumbered. We lost most of them, didn't we? They were outnumbered at least 3-1 and had no chance at all. By the way, have you considered that this was an ambush with advanced planning? That means there is someone inside who is a spy."

Robron said, "We are watching several staff members very closely. It is clear we have a problem. When you are better, we can talk about any ideas you may have on who that would be. Get some rest now." With that, Robron left the room without mentioning how many of the men had died in the battle. Garridon fell back on his bed and slept fitfully.

CHAPTER 12

Many of the city families were in mourning. They had lost good fathers, sons, husbands and brothers last week in the ambush. Daniel's friend had lost his father and his neighbor's husband had died. Daniel came home very upset the day of the ambush. He was glad to be in his home with his family all together and intact, but felt guilty to have been so blessed as to not have lost someone he loved. It was so hard to see all the people in pain. He and his father had been to temple. Hadad said it had been busy all the days since the attack because people were offering sacrifices and others just seeking God during this hard time. Some were asking why God would allow his people to be killed like that.

After dinner, Gideon and Daniel went to the roof to relax and drink coffee. In Daniel's few years he had learned a great deal from his father and the teachings of the rabbis in the temple. He truly believed that God was sovereign and in control. He said as much to his father, "Sir, I have heard so many discussions about why God didn't protect us during this ambush. You don't believe that He is going to let us be conquered and taken away, do you?"

"Our God, son, has been faithful to His people for centuries. Regardless of what happens to us, I trust God to still be working in our lives and in our country. Whether or not He protects us or keeps us from soldiers on the highway or conquerors in our land does not change His loyalty to us. Maybe we need to do something or learn something we have been unable to learn any other way than by being under attack or by being conquered. We are God's to do with as He pleases for His honor and for His glory. All else is insignificant compared to His will. Our well being or lack of it may not accomplish His plan for our nation and people."

"Some believe the men were killed by soldiers from Nebuchadnezzar's army. Could he really have sent spies here and been that close to us and we not know it?" asked Daniel.

"Oh, yes, those men and others are here in our town, and some maybe our neighbors. It is hard to detect a spy. That is why they are so good at being spies. They can hide in plain sight."

Daniel added, "If you believe Jeremiah that is exactly what God has planned. He says God will let us be taken captive, because He says we are living sinful lives. Father, I am not aware of any godless acts in my life currently, so what is the meaning of Jeremiah's warning?"

Gideon looked carefully at his son, "What you recognize as sin and what God sees as sin may not always be the same. I would like to claim I was without sin, but I believe we all sin daily. When Jeremiah speaks, however, of sins of the country, he is speaking of our people as a whole and the majority of individuals who have made sinful choices. For instance, we have many who worship the Queen of Heaven each night on their roofs, offering incense to the stars instead of worshiping Him as He has repeatedly commanded. They believe the Queen will look into their future and give them insight into their life's direction. We have some in Hinnon Valley sacrificing children in the fires of Molech. He has told us many times that we are to worship only Him, not idols. He certainly also values human life and is sickened by the offering of humans to anyone, including any so-called god. Some of His people are dishonest in business or disloyal to their wives or husbands. God's judgment, as Jeremiah has reminded us, is directed toward His whole people collectively this time. We have turned away from Him and do not want His will in our country or lifestyle. Do you understand?"

"I do. But what about individual responsibility? Why should I pay for other's who are wrong if I am innocent?"

"You are responsible for your own sins. The blood of sin offerings that we sacrifice represents our Messiah who will come someday. He will pay for our sins once and for all with His own sacrifice. Until then, we will continue to offer the blood of animals as a substitute. That is your individual responsibility. We all will answer to Him someday for our lives individually. But there is a national responsibility as well. That is what Jeremiah is warning us about so consistently. We have sinned nationally and may have to pay with some sort of conquest. I don't understand how or all that is involved in the prophecies that Jeremiah has made. I only know that I believe him. This little battle that happened to the men on the road to Egypt is small compared to what it sounds like God is going to bring our way, if we as a country don't turn around."

"I think most would disagree with you. They don't believe in individual or national sin and they don't believe Jeremiah. What if we are wrong?"

"If there is no God and no sin, then you and I have lived a good life and have not suffered any harm by living with a moral code. We will die with a personal peace and go back to the dust from which we came. We lived with a clear conscience and lived well and will have lost nothing."

"And if we are right?"

Gideon sighed, "But if we are right and they are wrong, they will die in their sins and go to God to be judged for their sin without any payment. They will not have an excuse. They are taking a great risk and are too proud to admit it. I would much prefer to trust what laws and prophecies God has given us than to guess about the future. So, son, I am not too concerned about what others think about my belief in God, are you?"

"I am, but I am trying to be more like you. I do believe I belong to God and that I will answer to Him. I am working on the kind of trust you have."

"I know you are seeking God in your life and He will not let you go from Him if your heart's desire is to be near," he stood. "I am tired, son. The day was long and tomorrow promises to be the same. Let's go to bed," Gideon said and laid his hand on Daniel's shoulder, and then he turned and went inside.

Daniel sat quietly enjoying the solitude and quiet for a moment longer. There were others he could see still on their house-tops. A little fire burned on the roof two homes away. The lady was bending and swaying with some herbs in her hand. He just could hear a soft, chanting sound. She must be one of those who worship the stars or the Queen of Heaven. He had really never seen anyone actually performing the ritual. It seemed odd to worship a star or group of stars. They are just bits of light. What could they do to help these people? He did not understand any type of idol worship, even an idol located across the heavens. He got up and went inside.

Thursday morning it was poring rain. The streets stood inches deep in running water. Jerusalem had some paved main roads, but the side streets were unpaved and mud was everywhere. Father and son hurried to the palace trying to miss the deep mud and stay as dry as possible. The rain only added to the atmosphere which had been tense at the palace since the raid. The second set of emissaries had not returned from Pharaoh's court, so there was no idea what the outcome of their request would be. The men might not be sent back. They could be kept there until payment was made or they could be killed. Whatever the answer, the King still had to get things back to order. He probably needed a new tribute payment and that was a lot of money. He would have to add a tax to someone or something in order to bring in the revenue.

When people began to arrive at the palace, they could see that Jehoiakim was not in a good mood and he was hopping mad about the messy court area, "Get some rugs and put them at the doors. The court is getting tramped full of mud. Everyone who comes in leaves a mess behind them. Tigner, get someone to clean up the mud that is already spread around. Why didn't one of the staff think of putting rugs out? Do I have to think of everything around here?"

That got the staff up and moving quickly. Rugs were gathered and placed at the different entrances. The staff was posted at doors to help the different court members who came in dripping wet, some were muddy and most were generally disheveled. Things became more orderly after a time and the morning began to take on a semblance of propriety that the King preferred. Gideon arrived just in time to have Baileen help him get dried off and cleaned up, for which he was grateful, before entering the court. He headed toward the accounting table set up at the side of the court. He worked there with clerks who kept track of business in the court each day. Several clerks were used to record payments, offerings, tribute and other gifts that came in. They also were responsible for recommending expenditures or other payments based on previous records or contracts.

"The King would like to add a tax to something to make up for the lost tribute payment. What do you recommend?" asked Tigner, who had approached the two men at the accounting table as soon as they were seated.

"Oh, sir, that would be a true hardship to the people. They already have given a great deal for the first payment. I am not sure what to recommend that would not cause anger and an uprising," said Gideon.

"We are not concerned about attitudes or hardships. We are concerned over the much larger issue of our lives and our freedom. Get busy thinking about your options, because he will be asking you for suggestions shortly," commented Tigner as he moved back to the side of the King.

But before Tigner arrived at the King's side and before the King could query Gideon about new taxes, just when the day's events were coming together and court was about to begin, a voice from the doorway of the palace, just outside on the steps, is heard. "Set up your standard toward Zion. Take refuge! Do not delay! For I will bring disaster from the north, and great destruction. The lion has come up from his thicket, and the destroyer of nations is on his way."

'Oh my,' thought Gideon. He looked at Daniel, who was working with him today. Daniel appeared genuinely afraid. What was going to happen? Jeremiah was yelling so everyone, including the King, could hear. That had not happened before. Jeremiah had preached around town in the streets and gates, but he had never come to the palace. The court all turned to the King with apprehension, to see how he would react.

"Get him out of here. Now!" Jehoiakim said with fury.

"'And it shall come to pass in that day,' says the Lord, 'That the heart of the king shall perish, and the heart of the princes; the priests shall be astonished, and the prophets shall wonder,'" Jeremiah continued. "A dry wind of the desolate heights blows in the wilderness toward the daughter of My people...Behold, he shall come up like clouds and his chariots like a whirlwind. His horses are swifter than eagles, woe to us, for we are plundered." With those words, Jeremiah was removed to a spot far from the palace where he could no longer be heard. Jeremiah decided to seek a crowd at the temple mount and turned in that direction.

Jeremiah was gone from the court, but it was too late. Everyone had heard the message of dread and could think of nothing else. The King said quietly to Tigner, "Get Pashhur from the temple right away." The court whispered quietly. He said nothing to them, but watched Tigner dispatch someone and then return to his side. "How did he get that near? Why didn't a guard stop him? He has disrupted the flow of things for the whole morning, now. People will be discussing this at every free minute. What a fool he is."

The King sat quietly and discussed business for the morning with Tigner, including tax options. The aid walked across the divide from the palace to the temple. As he neared the temple Jeremiah could be heard, continuing his message, to be heard by all inside. The aid ignored Jeremiah and moved around to his side and explained to Pashhur that the King needed him immediately. They returned to the palace with the aid and bowed, waiting to be spoken to.

"Did you hear about Jeremiah?" asked the King. When Pashhur nodded he had, the King continued, "Is there anything we can do to stop this prophet?" the King was steaming mad. "He is stirring up strife in the city. What kind of religion encourages dissidents to speak against their king?"

"Oh, King, please do not assume that this man speaks for the temple or our religion. We have had him speak against us, too. He is at the temple even now while I am speaking to you. He is railing against us in his own religion. We feel as you do, that he is a nuisance and should be quieted," Pashhur said, very concerned. How could the king assume they approved of Jeremiah?

"At your next opportunity, I want you to do something to get his attention and stop his preaching. Do you understand?" Jehoiakim said with an implied threat.

"Yes, King. We will do something at the next opportunity," Pashhur said as he was lead away from the King's presence. He returned to the temple. What would he do? He was not sure, but they would discuss options with the other priests. They need some options that might work for any future times when Jeremiah appeared at the temple.

The King said to the court, "Listen carefully to me, people. This man, Jeremiah, will be dealt with soon, and if he continues preaching these threats against the city and his people, it will be harsh dealings. I want any discussions about him to end in this court now. We have much business to finish today." The court became quiet and the first business began. Thoughts quickly moved from Jeremiah to the day's work. When lulls came, minds wandered to the warnings that Jeremiah had yelled out this morning. Things were so busy, however, that little time was available to evaluate what he really said.

"Do any of the officials have any suggestions about a new tax? We must recoup the tribute monies for Pharaoh and we do not have enough in the coffers to pay that much without a new tax, so let me hear your ideas," said Jehoiakim.

Muttering in the court could be heard, but no individual spoke up. It seemed they were all short of ideas. The King spoke, "Gideon, let's start with your ideas."

Gideon stepped out from behind the table to the center of the court, "Sire, Tigner mentioned that you might be thinking about a new tax just before Je.., I mean, before the recent interruption. I really have not had time to develop any ideas."

This was not the answer the King was looking for. There was a lengthy pause, "I will pretend I didn't hear that answer to my question. So, Gideon, I want you to 'think' out loud so we all can hear." The King smiled his wry smile at the man and waited.

Gideon was on the spot. He had voiced his opinion to Tigner, but he could not say that to the king. So he said, "I believe that any tax will cause a reaction from the people, so we need to choose carefully. They know we lost the money, but they are not considering the seriousness of the situation and the possible outcome of not paying the money to Pharaoh. Whichever tax we choose, we need a campaign to sell the people on the need for it and the reason. I think you could choose just about any tax, if you have the right campaign of information preceding it."

The King liked his way of thinking. So this might work without an uproar, if they sold it right. "So, Gideon, choose the tax that you think might work best with the least reaction." Again they waited.

Gideon hated to be the center of attention and to be put on the spot without a chance to think through all the possible outcomes. Lack of planning always allows for greater probability for error. Gideon hated any error, but especially ones that might have been avoided with a little thought. The King was waiting on him to answer, so taking time was not an option. He needed a suggestion, "Sire, how about a tax on luxury items--leather goods, house decorative items, fancy tunics, big pieces of furniture and additions to homes?"

That caused a stir in the court. It would hit the wealthier citizens much more than the average citizen. Gideon thought to himself, 'Well, they were the ones that could spare the money the most.' He simply waited.

"I like it. So be it. Write up the new tax and assign some court members to begin selling the idea to the citizens. The tax will begin in two weeks. Excellent work, Gideon. You may return to your desk."

Gideon gladly returned to his quiet desk in the back. He hoped he would not be called on for things like this again any time soon. He looked at Daniel, who spoke, "Father, I was terrified. How could you speak up like that with such confidence and such good ideas? I was so proud of you."

"Son, did you hear the King give me any other options? I was not confident. I was desperate both for my job and for my life. I am glad that God gave me an idea the King liked. It could have gone the other way very easily."

The temple was in heavy debate over what to do with Jeremiah. They had spies out looking for ways to catch him and deal with him. Their opportunity came later that week when Jeremiah came back from the Valley of the Son of

Hinnon where he had been prophesying. "Behold, I will bring such a catastrophe to this place, that whoever hears of it, his ears will tingle. They have filled this place with the blood of innocents. They have also built the high places of Baal to burn their sons and daughters. Behold, the days are coming when this place will not be called Tophet, but the Valley of Slaughter." This is the place where Bethany had served in her temple.

The prophets and worshipers of Baal and Molech could hear his curse. They laughed at him. This place had been used for decades for idol worship and was going to continue being used, if they had anything to do with it.

At God's direction, he had visited a potter earlier that day and purchased a vase. He paused and threw the vase against the stones at his feet, shattering it. He continued his words after breaking a pottery vase he had just purchase, "Even so I will break this people and this city, as one breaks a potter's vessel, which cannot be made whole again; and they shall bury them in Tophet till there is no place to bury." When he finished, he returned to the upper part of the city to the court of the temple on the mount and continued preaching.

"Thus says the Lord, 'Behold, I will bring on this city and on all her towns the doom I have pronounced against it."

Pashhur was sitting in the court when Jeremiah arrived. He was personally facing Jeremiah and not far away. The prophesy was the last straw. When was he going to be quiet? Pashhur looked around at the people and they were listening. They were curious about what Jeremiah was saying and that angered him more. Pashhur was being watched by some to see what he would do. Most of them knew, except Jeremiah, what had been discussed with the King and what the decision was. When Jeremiah finished, Pashhur got up and faced him. Jeremiah waited expecting a discussion; instead Pashhur struck him as hard as he could in the face, knocking him to the ground. The temple guards stood Jeremiah on his feet, but held him firmly.

"We are not interested in anything you have to say, Jeremiah. You are embarrassing your family, your temple and yourself. The people of your city would like to see you dead, as well. Your family and their fathers have been priests who served God faithfully. You should have been a priest, but it is too late. You have lost all respect of the people and have defiled yourself beyond God's use. Stop prophesying these detestable things in the name of God. God has not spoken through you. Our prophets are telling us that you are lying and God has told them we will be saved from conquest."

"Your prophets are all liars."

Pashhur struck him again. "Guards, take him to the Benjamin Gate and put him in stocks." They half carried, half drug him to the area just north of the city. A crowd followed to enjoy the spectacle. They were sick of his negative prophesying and eagerly awaited a chance to let him know how they felt. A prophet that had followed from the temple hit him with a couple of rotten eggs he had picked up during the walk just for this purpose. He was instructed by the temple leaders, "Stir up a small riot to let everyone know where Jeremiah stands in our eyes."

"Tell us, Jeremiah, what is God telling you now? Can you hear him when you smell of rotten eggs?" Someone found spoiled tomatoes to hit him with, and then a rock caught him in the forehead.

This continued until the crowd became bored and gradually broke up. Jeremiah was left alone and miserable. It was early afternoon when he was placed in the stocks. Hours had passed and darkness had fallen. His ankles were raw from the rough wood and he was hungry and thirsty. Why was God allowing him to be treated this way? God had promised to take care of him, but this seemed like God had forgotten him.

It grew cool. As he grew tired he had a hard time resting with his feet in the wooden stocks. He changed his positions often to try to be more comfortable. About midnight, when all was quiet, he heard someone coming toward him. Who would be out at this hour? Was he in danger? He was certainly helpless to any attacker.

A quiet voice, "I know you must be hungry and thirsty. If you do not mind taking this from woman like me, I will help you," Abeetha whispered as she appeared from behind him. She knew she could be in danger, if anyone found out she had helped the prophet.

"Come close, so I can see you," Jeremiah asked. "Abeetha, is that you? Oh, child, don't do this. You'll be in danger if anyone finds out. Don't help me. I wouldn't want you to be harmed."

"Jeremiah, I have heard you speak many times, usually from the shadows where I hide. I think I believe that what you say is true. I don't understand all that you say, but I know enough to be afraid. I think that they are treating you this way because they are afraid, too. If you are the man of God speaking to us now, then I would rather be on your side than on their side." She came near him and lifted a jug of wine to his lips. He drank small amounts several times, which refreshed him. She gave him bread in small pieces and then cheese. He could not have been more grateful. She took a few minutes to help him wipe the egg and tomatoe from his face.

"Abeetha, I thank you with my whole heart. But I cannot encourage you in this gift, that it will give you any value to God. I appreciate it, but God does not just notice good deeds. The life you live does not please God, you know that?"

"I do know that, but I have no other options. Would you pray to God for me for a deliverer from this life and from His coming destruction?"

"I tell you now that God is sending you safety and deliverance more than you can imagine. Trust him. It will not be long," he smiled at her in the dim light. "Thank you again. The next time I prophesy, do not hide. I will consider you a friend. Now slip away before you are seen, quickly."

"Pray for me now, before I leave," she begged.

"Our father, gracious God, I come before you now for Abeetha and her acts of kindness. She knows her life is not pleasing to you. I pray that in a way that is known only to you, you will protect her and her mother and meet their needs in a miraculous way. Bless them now," he finished and spoke her name. No answer. Without a word, she was gone into the shadows of the night where she lived.

Morning brought the jeers from workers as they passed and the laughter of children. Children are sometimes the harshest to people who are hurt or weak. Some had heard from their parents who he was, "Hey, you, prophet, do you know my name? What a fool you are talking against Jerusalem, God's city. Our father says God will not let His city be destroyed."

Others added, "You are a stinking egg and your words stink in our noses. Our fathers laugh at you."

Jeremiah thought, 'Someday, and likely soon, children and fathers will see that God has kept His word and my prophecies were true.' He said nothing.

Mid-morning a priest arrived to loose the bonds. "You are to come with me to Pashhur."

'Good,' thought Jeremiah, 'I would like a word with him, too.' He gladly went back up to the temple. When they were facing each other, Jeremiah said, "The Lord has a new name for you--Magor-Missabib--Fear on Every Side. All who live in your house along with you will go into captivity. You and your friends shall die in Babylon."

Pashhur was furious. He had already punished Jeremiah, but that did not stop his prophesying. What would the king do? What else could the temple priests do? "You are not to prophecy any more! Do you understand me? The King and I have given you your warning. Mark my words; you will be in grave

94

danger, if you continue with these supposed 'words from God.'"

"If I do not continue, the danger that would be greatest to me would be in not following my God. I hear you, but I have a higher calling to fulfill and cannot be stopped by man's warnings." For now, Jeremiah was released with a stern warning to stop preaching, and he left the priests to think about their next course of action.

CHAPTER 13

The Cedar King Shipping Line, based in Tyre, worked the coast of the Mediterranean moving from northern Egypt to the coast of Israel and to cities in the Hittite area. When *The Goliath* arrived from Ashkelon, it was loaded with a variety of beautiful woods like cedar and poplar, a pile of fresh cotton, light and airy, from Gaza. The ship had stopped for freshly tanned hides in Joppa. Locals all turned their noses up when a tanner was around. It was dirty and smelly work and not recognized as a clean profession by the Hebrews, but they loved the gorgeous hides that made their sandals and covered their chairs.

The Goliath was a smooth sailing bireme ninety by twelve feet. Its double bank of staggered oars allowed it to move along at a good eight knots when its large square sail on the central mast wasn't enough. Rowers rested under the deck and on it. The deck often housed both cargo and passengers. There was also a good sized cargo hold. These ships were the major cargo moving vessels in the Mediterranean and some ventured into the Atlantic through the straits between Europe and northern Egypt. Some ships, as did this one, had a pointed ram at the bowline allowing them to ram other ships, if under attack from pirates. It also carried passengers and on this trip that included twenty soldiers sailed north to Ugarit. They had not disclosed their destination after they reached the port or their cargo.

As the crew loaded the soldiers' shipment they were speculating about the heavier than usual boxes. They weighed 300 lbs. each, if they weighed a pound. The soldiers who came aboard in Ashkelon guarded them carefully during the loading. Since they doubted it was rocks, the only other heavier items had to be metals. Some of the crew felt it might be worth the risk to take a look and help themselves to a little treasure, depending on how the metals were cast, whether in bars or coins.

Wednesday evening when passengers were sleeping two crew members decide the time was right to open a box and see what treasures were inside. Phinehas said, "I will bring a bar to open a box. Meet me in the hold on the third watch tonight." They both knew the risk, but were willing to take a chance to maybe live for a lifetime on the booty.

Raja, the Egyptian cook, agreed, "I will be there waiting ahead of time and watch to make sure we are alone when we enter the hold."

They moved quietly to the hold in the aft of the ship. Raja left a flask of ale in the area near the patrol path of the guard, hoping he would notice it and take advantage of the opportunity. Raja was not disappointed. The guard had been drinking for over an hour and was very sleepy. They watched quietly until he nodded off to sleep.

They slid the hold cover to the side and dropped into the hold, Raja carrying a heavy sack. "Get the top box there marked with their sign, the Red Sabre, and open it," said Phin. Raja tried to lift it, but it was too heavy.

"Help me. These weigh a lot," he said to Phin, who came over to help. The two of them placed it carefully on the floor and quietly worked the plank in the center so that the right end popped up. Phin took the bar and removed the nail on the other end. That gave them enough room to get a hand down inside.

"Move the lamp closer, boy," commanded the older helmsman, Phin. "Let's see if we found a treasure." Reaching inside the first thing he found was a skin of a leopard, beautifully tanned. When removed, he noticed it was lovely, but of little value compared to the gold he hoped to find. He continued down further into the box. He found packing straw and silver utensils of excellent quality. Still no gold. Time was not on their side. He had to hurry so he would have time to get the box back to normal. The night watch would make rounds in this area soon and see the hold was open. One more try was all he had time for. Reaching into the box almost up to his elbow, he felt something icy cold—metal and large. He dug around in the box. Near the bottom of the larger box were two bars. He pulled one out.

"Shine the lamp right on my hand, Raja," he whispered. Both men groaned, for in Phinehas' hand was a shiny silver bar. "We've done it, son.

Hold this and let me get the other one. If we stick to two and replace them with the stones, I don't think anyone will notice that some are missing." He reached in and took the other bar, handing it to Raja, too. Then he put in several heavy stones, replaced the silver utensils and straw and smoothed the leopard skin back into place, so it wouldn't appear that anything had been removed. He muffled the hammering the nails back into the boards with a canvas sail lying near where they were sitting. They carefully replaced the Sabre box.

Raja had never seen a silver bar this size personally in his whole life. It was rare to have jewelry of your own in silver, but a whole bar of it. Each was worth a life-time's worth of money, depending on what country's coinage was in use where the ship stopped. "We each get to keep one, right Phin?" he asked.

"I think the wise thing to do is to hide them somewhere in the ship, then we can take one into town somewhere when we dock in a harbor. We will get cash for one and spend it carefully. The other crew could get suspicious if we suddenly seem to be spending too much money every time we are in town. Any ideas as to where we could put these where others won't look or won't see when we take one?"

"I have a perfect place. The galley is only used by me. Rarely do any of the men come in since it is so small and so hot. How about hiding them there?" Raja suggested.

"Yes, you have a good idea. Let's go leave them behind a barrel until tomorrow and hide them when you go to cook in the morning, yes?"

"Yes!" Phin pulled himself up with the help of Raja and then handed him first one bar, then the other. Phin then pulled Raja out. They replaced the hold cover and went to the galley and their quarters. Raja lay down in his hammock. Tomorrow at breakfast he would hide them where only he could find them. If Phin treated him well, he would share his hiding place with him later. If Phin was harsh, well, Raj would hold his secret. He went to sleep with a smile.

Morning began quietly with the ship leaving port and sailing the last leg of the trip for Wakeem and his men. They would be in Ugarit in late afternoon. At sea the men finished cleaning up after breakfast and the life on ship was normal. Wakeem sent Timath into the hold to check on the cargo and ready it for disembarking this afternoon.

He looked over each box, checking it for secure positioning in the hold and for good secure top planks. He didn't want any of the contents to spill out or accidentally be dumped if a plank came loose. He was checking the top boxes when a plank came free in his hand. He yelled, "Eddu, get down here," who dropped immediately into the hold. They moved that box to the floor. Timath yelled out the hole in the ceiling, "Someone bring another lamp and come down here."

A third soldier came down with a lamp. When they were all there and the area was lit, he examined the box. The plank seemed undamaged, except for the slightly bent nail in the end. He looked at the box itself. It was in good shape, so why did the plank come free? He noticed some of the wood was slightly lighter in color, like it had been scraped and another area was a little indented. He began to remove the contents, which appeared normal. "Get the roster of contents from Wakeem," he said to the other soldier.

Returning shortly, he gave the list to Eddu who gave it to Timath. Eddu didn't read and Timath was only slightly better. Timath watched as he checked the top layers. Everything was good until they neared the bottom.

Timath reached down and took out, not a single bar of silver, but a large rock! "Rocks," he kept reaching inside pulling out six more rocks. "According to the manifest, this box has two bars," he said placing the rock on the floor. "What the fricken demon are these rocks doing inside?" he swore.

"How could that happen?" asked Eddu. "The box and hold had been under guard since they had left Ashkelon. We had better get Wakeem to come to the hold opening."

Eddu climbed out of the hold and found Wakeem, who leaned over the opening, "What's going on, Timath?"

"Two silver bars are missing from one of the boxes, sir. They are worth several years' wages each."

Wakeem was livid, "Bring the box out and I will get the captain."

Eddu leaned over and passed a rope into the hold. Timath quickly secured the box. Eddu and the other soldier hauled it out and it was quickly followed up by Timath himself.

The captain arrived and was brought up to date on the situation. They searched both of Wakeem's men to make sure they had not personally taken the silver. They were clean. The hold was searched to see if the bars were hidden anywhere down there. They emptied the box and compared the contents to the bill of lading. There was no doubt about it. The bars had somehow been removed during the trip. It was up to the ship's crew, and Wakeem and his men to find out who took the silver before the ship docked this afternoon.

While all of this was taking place, Raja was at work in the galley preparing lunch. He had not heard anything until the door opened a crack and Phin's familiar voice spoke a warning, "I don't know where you hid the bars, but I think someone has found out they are missing. There is a big stir on deck."

"How do you think they found out? We were very careful," asked Raja. "What should we do?"

"I have no idea, but I did see soldiers checking the hold. They must have noticed something odd and looked in the box. Let's throw them overboard," Phin said.

"Are you crazy? It's too much money."

"We won't have a life to live to spend them, if they find out we took them. Throw them over!" said Phin and with that he moved away quietly.

'Now what should I do?' thought Raja. 'This is my big opportunity. I'm taking a chance with both of our lives, I know, but they will never find them here where I hid them. I really doubted that anyone would even consider me as the thief.' His decision was made and he went on with lunch preparation.

The crew was already involved in a search of each of the ship's areas, systematically working their way through, when Phin went out on deck. Late in the morning nothing new was known. No clues had been revealed and it seemed the crew had seen nothing unusual since the beginning of the trip.

Lunch was served and Raja got an update, asking, "Any news, Phin?"

"Naw, they haven't found anything. Did you do what I said?"

"I have everything under control," Raja responded.

Phin got angry, "Did you or did you not toss them?"

"Not!"

Phin' skin turned a gray color and just as quickly, it turned beet red. "You have just killed us both, if they are found," he said

After lunch the search continued. By late afternoon Wakeem was getting desperate. Only if the captain was willing could they hold everyone on ship once they reached the port. If the captain decided against that decision, it was likely the thief would escape as either a passenger or crew member. Wakeem decided he would demand that action, if the captain didn't cooperate. He would wait to make that decision when all other options were exhausted, since he preferred not to draw added attention to his group and their cargo.

The crew and some of the soldiers had finished searching the officers' areas, crew quarters and command areas, and had reached the work areas which included the galley. Phin was sweating and pacing on the upper deck.

Why hadn't Raja followed his direction? The boy was foolish. Watching the searchers, he realized that the galley was the room next in the sequence.

The door to the galley came open and in stepped a soldier and one of the crew, "Raj, you will need to clear out. We are checking the ship for some stolen items from one of our passengers. I have already checked the crew quarters and you are cleared. We are finishing up the work areas. Just leave what you are working on and step into the hallway until we finish the inspection," said Kalath who was with a fellow crew member on the ship.

Raja began to shake, "Well, I certainly will not quit what I am doing just to give you time to look around this tiny hole. I wouldn't have room in here to hide a grain of rice."

Kalath grabbed Raja's arm and pulled him out into the hall, "This is not a request; it is an order," snapped Wakeem's man. With Raj out of the way they began the search in the obvious places in the room; barrels, cabinets, drawers, boxes of utensils and under loose boards on the wall or floor. They lifted barrels to check the bottom for any hiding place and moved the food all around to see if the bar might be mixed in with cabbage or carrots. They were finished and nothing had been found.

Raja sat quietly on a barrel in the hall. They left the galley and slowly walked past him and turned to go up the stairs. Kalath paused and looked back at Raja, who smiled. Kalath was missing something and this kid was part of the theft, he just knew it. Maybe it was the barrel? Coming back down the hall, he pushed Raj off the barrel and opened the lid. He brought a lamp over to see to the bottom. It was empty. How could that be? He thought he'd found the silver. He stood still and surveyed the area. What was the cook hiding? Everything had been opened, moved and inspected.

Kalath stood in the galley door and looked around. He was at a loss for ideas. His mind drifted and he rubbed his beard as he rocked back and forth in place. He noticed the bright sky out the porthole. It would have been a lovely day, if not for this foolishness.

Raja spoke, "You have tried everywhere. I told you you're wasting your time. Now move on so I can finish the clean up in here." Raja stepped around Kalath and into the galley. He busied himself as if getting ready for dinner. He wanted to sound convincing, because the soldier was getting too close.

Kalath stood right behind him. He watched the cook nervously kneading the bread dough at the counter in front of the port hole. He continued surveying the room. Was that a wire on the edge of the port hole? Raj moved to get more flour blocking Kalath's view of the hole.

Kalath had found his mark, he was sure. He stepped forward, pushing Raj to his left and out of his way, saying "One more place just came to mind, kid," smirked Kalath. He sensed he was on the right track. Another soldier stood beside the jittery cook.

"With a mind like yours, I am sure you have the wrong idea," said Raj.

His smart answer only confirmed to Kalath that he was headed in the right direction. He crawled on the counter and stuck his head out the hole. He had found the silver. Hanging from two separate wire baskets attached to the porthole were two bars of silver.

Raj tried to run, but his crew mate held him. Kalath pulled the bars inside one at a time. He turned to the crew man who held Raja. He laid them on a towel to wipe them dry.

"Well, kid, for a short time you were a wealthy man. Now you'll be a very dead man. Take the boy to the ship's brig or whatever you have that can hold a prisoner," said Kalath.

Raja was in shock and barely able to move. He was going to die. He stumbled along beside the man taking him to the hold. He really thought they would never find out his secret hiding place and they almost didn't. As he thought about that idea a little bit more, what he almost did, he began to feel a little smug. He almost got away with it. He stole a great deal of silver and just about fooled the soldiers and crew. Some thought he was stupid, well, this would show them he was smarter than they thought. The two of them reached the storage area. The soldier pushed him into room and locked the door.

Kalath hurried to the deck carrying one wired silver bar followed by the crew man with the other bar. He found Wakeem in deep conversation with the captain, trying to see if he would hold the passengers on ship, if the bars weren't found. Kalath moved in close, whispering, "Sir, I found the bars." He didn't wait for the men to acknowledge him or to stop their conversation. He just butted in. He figured that the news was worthy of being in danger of insubordination. He laid his silver bar in front of the two men.

Wakeem was very excited as was Kalath. Relief washed over his countenance. Wakeem looked at Kalath and slapped his shoulder, "Good work, soldier. When we get to port, I will give you leave for the evening." Then he called, "Timath, come here at once." While they waited for Timath, he asked Kalath for the facts which revealed the identity of the thief. When it was revealed that it was the cook, the captain was upset. He hated to see such a young man die, but that would be the only outcome possible. What a fool!

Phinehas was frantic. He had been watching the group with the soldier and the other men, and came to the quick conclusion the bars had been found. That meant that Raja had been captured and would soon be put to death. It didn't appear they had talked with him yet, so he still had a chance. No one had considered that more than one person was involved. He had to do something and do it quick

He went downstairs and looked around. He guessed they would keep Raj in the store room area. When he saw the crew member outside the storeroom, he knew he was on target, "Hajeeg, I am here to take over your duty." He slapped the man's shoulder, encouraging him to hurry away. The guard took the hint, which left Phinehas alone to speak to Raja.

His plan was clear in his mind almost immediately after he realized Raj was captured. He opened the storeroom door shutting it quietly behind him. He spoke, "Raj that was a stupid. What were you thinking?"

Raja came up to him, smiling, "I guess that is a matter of your opinion against my opinion. I'm sorry we were caught and won't have any of the money from the bars."

"You know Raja, WE weren't caught," said Phin. He wanted Raj to think about what he was saying. He wanted him to understand that he had no intension of being caught, too. He continued, "You were! I am not worried about the money, I am just glad that I won't be dying with you."

"Who said you won't? I have no plan on dying without your company. It is a lonely thing to die without your partner who was such a big help, don't you think?" He laughed.

Phinehas laughed too, just before he struck him in the face with his fist, knocking him to the floor. Raj was stunned. Phin followed up with a kick to his side, several times. It took a couple more slugs before Raj quit struggling. Phin put a rope around the boy's neck and tossed the other end over a rafter. He pulled it up until Raj's feet were off the floor and tied it to a pole. The boy did struggle slightly, but not for long.

Finding a box, he placed it nearby so that it would look like he had stepped off the box to his death, committing suicide. He carefully adjusted the distance between Raj's feet and the top of the box. Everything looked right.

He reviewed what he saw and knew it was convincing. He had never killed a man outright, just when he was in a war. It made him queasy, but the other option was his own death. He rushed back outside to his post and stood there until the next guard relieved him. He didn't know how he had become a man who would steal and murder. But, when the choice was to die or to kill to protect yourself, well, it was an obvious choice. He had a twinge of conscience, when he remember what he had once heard a religious man say, 'Vengeance was the Lord's and he would pay back.' or something like that. He just hoped that man had been wrong.

No one found Raj until about an hour later. The captain came down and wanted to question the boy. When the door was opened, he was greeted with the site of the dead cook.

The captain turned to Phin, "How sad to have come to this state. I am, however, grateful that I didn't have to make a decision about the boy's death and how to execute him. The boy did it to himself. Probably couldn't stand the waiting and wondering."

Phinehas nodded in sad agreement, saying only, "Yes, sir."

In late afternoon the ship pulled into port. Wakeem left the ship immediately to find a storage room to rent for a couple of days. They needed an area to wait while they found a caravan driving toward Carchemish which was about 150 miles east on the west bank of the Euphrates. Nebuchadnezzar was in a campaign there with the Assyrians and was waiting for the arrival of the Egyptians. The money would be of great value. The men helped unload the cargo and stayed with it, while Kalath with a couple of other soldiers went to town to buy supplies. They would work out the details of their trip to Babylon as quickly as they could.

When Wakeem got back, the men were moody and seemed edgy. "What's eating you, Timath? The men seem on edge."

"While you were gone, the ship's crew unloaded the cargo."

"Yeah, and?"

"A crew member who I met and talked to some on ship was on the dock pulling a rope to direct a wenched-up cargo box. It was lifted about twenty feet in the air over him, when the ropes holding it broke and it came smashing down on him. It crushed part him to mush but left him alive and screaming forever, it seemed. It turned my stomach."

"You see death in war all the time. Why did this one bother you?"

"Oh, you know, in a peaceful setting, it just is out of place to see that kind of death. I really didn't know him well, but just knowing his name was Phinehas and that he was alive a couple hours ago bothers me."

"I see," he said and thought, 'Death was never easy.' He understood how this event upset the men. Changing the subject, "I have made arrangements for tonight. Get the men together and put the boxes on the wagon. We will move them to the store room and sleep there. The men can go to town in shifts for dinner and Kalath can have the full evening off until breakfast in the morning. Tell him he is free to go at his leisure." With those instructions the action on the dock picked up again. It had been rather quiet after the body and mess had been cleaned up when Phin had died. All were glad to have a useful distraction.

The wagons rolled through town to a room where the cargo was stored for the evening. All the men were grateful to get on solid ground again. Many soldiers did not find sea travel pleasant often suffering sea sickness for a portion of the trip. Tonight they looked forward to the rest with fresh air not the dank ship's quarters. Half of them left immediately after the goods were stored and walked to the local tavern. They would ask around to help determine if any caravans were moving east soon and would have a couple of hours before the watch changed.

Wakeem went with them. He was hoping to have his men and cargo underway tomorrow for Carchemish and his general, Nebuzaradan. He was traveling with the army serving the prince, Nebuchadnezzar, who was also in the campaign in place of his father because his father was not feeling well and stayed in Babylon. Nebuchadnezzar was an effective leader and respected by the soldiers.

The meal was poor and none of them enjoyed it. But it was filling and the information in the tavern proved helpful. Wakeem noticed a trader that he had seen in Babylon in past years. He stopped at his table, "Sir, I am looking to hire a caravan to transport some men and cargo. Are you available for hire or do you know who might be?" He stood beside the table waiting for a response.

A smirk crossed Abdullah's hairy face and he grinned through two missing front teeth. He thought he might have a novice that he could swindle, saying, "I might be and I might not be available depending on who's asking?" He peered over his shoulder to see a man in scarlet uniform that did not look like a mark at all.

Wakeem was not in the mood to argue. He wanted services and upsetting this caravan owner would be futile. Wakeem turned to Vicken, speaking in Chaldean, so others wouldn't understand, "This man is a slug, but from what I have heard he is the only one in town that might be moving in our direction who has enough camels for our load." Abdullah was not Babylonian, so Wakeem assumed his little aside to Vicken about the man was a safe comment.

Speaking many languages, including Chaldean, was an advantage to a merchant. His frequent travels allowed him to be in many countries and stay long enough to become adequate in their language. Abdullah spent many months moving around the middle east. He understood Wakeem's comments clearly. "What are you looking to move and to where?" he asked, without revealing what he knew what had been said.

"We want to send the men and their cargo to the area of Carchemish starting tomorrow. Our commander is camped somewhere in the vicinity. Are you up to that on such short notice?"

"I am if you can pay the price. I am not sure you can afford a 'slug', however. We are very expensive," his eyes shifted toward Wakeem with a knowing look and waited for a response.

'Well, well, the man knew Chaldean,' thought Wakeem, 'Since I have offended the man, the price will be outrageous.' He would have to pay whatever was the asking price. Why couldn't he learn to keep his thoughts to himself? He said out loud, "What are you asking?" He already knew what to expect: twenty gold shekels for the men and twenty more for the cargo. He was right. That price was high, but manageable. "I will be here at sunrise tomorrow to pay you. Will you be ready by then?"

"I am ready now. Will you be going or can I expect a more cordial leader?"

Wakeem's face hardened. He looked at Abdullah carefully and leaned in close to his foul-smelling body, "I will not be going, because I prefer to travel with men not animals." He turned to Vicken, "This soldier will handle the travel from here to the camp. I expect the trip and travel to run smoothly. If any ...." he paused here to make himself understood, "events seem to be questionable or any unnecessary dangers arise, I will find you personally and squash you under my boot. Do I make myself understood?"

Abdullah decided this was not a man to tangle with, and besides, Wakeem was a paying client. Abdullah stood and faced Wakeem, bowing his head slightly, "Sir, I understand you perfectly. My humblest apologies for offending you. I will transport your men and cargo in the finest of fashion. My camels are excellent and my handlers the most experienced. We will be within the camp in about a week and a half from tomorrow morning. We move very well and can cover at least twenty-five miles a day. Before April is half through, your men will be back in the service of their king." He bowed again, more deeply this time, and held that position for a few seconds.

"Excellent. We truly understand each other. Tomorrow, then, at one hour after sunrise we will meet here in the street outside the tavern. We will bring our wagons. Our load is heavy. What number of camels will you have with you?"

"I have forty fine camels for travel. They are strong and quick. Should that be enough?"

"I think each will be needed for our large cargo and men. Here is enough for supplies," Wakeem gave the merchant five shekels. "You will have the other thirty-five soon, but these should give you a start." Wakeem turned and left with the rest of his men. They returned to the warehouse and relieved the remaining soldiers who walked into town. They remained at the store room and prepared to rest.

Wakeem was waiting passage back down the coast of Palestine. Two days ago the caravan left for Carchemish. The men were not looking forward to the trip, but were glad to be returning to see some friends for a short time. Wakeem stayed behind without his men. He would rejoin the ones that had remained with their horses and other stuff in Ashkelon. Getting back to Jerusalem was his priority. He needed to continue gathering information in the event the general decide to come to this country in his conquests. Nebuzaradan had discussed that possibility in one of their meetings several months earlier. That Pharaoh was marching north to do battle with Nebuchadnezzar was definite. Since that was true and assuming the battle was won by Nebuchadnezzar, then Pharaoh would try to escape to Egypt passing through or near this country of Palestine. If that happened, the intelligence he could gather might aid in the capture of not only one country, Egypt, but two or three more, including Israel.

CHAPTER 14

It had taken Vicken and the men eight days to arrive at Nebuchadnezzar's camp near Carchemish. The trip had been uneventful. The men would be happy, however, to have no need for further dealings with the camels and their owner. After eight days with Abdullah, the title 'slug' seemed to be a step up on the animal ladder for him.

It had not been hard to find the camp. Every shepherd and merchant along the way had bits of information about its location and size. The caravan moved around the recently conquered city of Carchemish. The camp spread over many acres south of town where soldiers were bivouacked in their specialized battalions. They had been camped outside of town for a month in preparation for the battle. Last week Nebuchadnezzar had taken the city from the Assyrians and it was under his command. The battle had been heated for several days, but Nebuchadnezzar's army was prepared, well-equipped and in good condition and had quickly overpowered the Assyrians. The Assyrians had hoped their allies from Egypt would arrive in time to come to their aid, but that didn't happen. The Egyptian army had still not arrived at the city, but intelligence reports indicated that they were in route.

When the caravan arrived at camp, they were stopped by guards with questions before letting them pass. A guard accompanied them to Nebuzaradan's tent, the commander of Nebuchadnezzar's army. An appointment time would be set up directly with Nebuchadnezzar, if the commander deemed it appropriate and necessary.

In the center of camp, the caravan stopped near the main tents, the guard saying, "This is as far as you go. We will have the camels unloaded, watered, and fed, and take care of the men and soldiers." He turned toward Vicken, "You, come with me to see Nebuzaradan." Other guards came to join them from the commander's tent and took over the care of their visitors. They took care of everyone else, while Vicken went with the first guard.

He and the guard entered the tent and stood at attention waiting for the commander to finish his conversation with another man. They waited to be recognized.

"What is it, soldier?" asked (Nebu)Zaradan.

"I have a soldier here from a campaign in the south who has a message for you. Would you speak with him?"

Looking up at the guard, Zaradan could see the man at attention behind him. The only southern campaign that Zaradan was aware of involved the spies in Jerusalem. "I will speak with him. Leave us alone." He waited until the tent was cleared and then asked Vicken to step forward, "What is your name and what is your business with me?"

"I am Vicken, one of the soldiers serving with Wakeem, son of Jabed, who is a spy in Jerusalem for his majesty, Nebuchadnezzar. I have a payment to bring to the King's son from the raid in Jerusalem."

"Tell me more," he said. His interest was peaked.

"In recent weeks we captured a tribute payment from Jerusalem intended for our enemy, Pharaoh Necho of Egypt. We have brought that gold and silver to Nebuchadnezzar for his use as he sees fit."

"Excellent! Wait here," he said and left for a few minutes. When he returned, he said, "We will go to see the prince. Where is your payment now?"

"It is with my men in the area just near here," answered Vicken

"Take about one-half an hour to get cleaned up and ready to see the prince. Get several of your men to bring the tribute and meet me outside at that time. I have arranged for you bring the money to the prince and tell your story. Hurry now. You are dismissed," Zaradan stood and moved to the back and began getting ready.

Vicken left and got cleaned up and presentable. They were all soldiers and had seen each other in horrible conditions and filth. But outside of battle, it was still expected that a soldier be attired appropriately and that he be reasonably clean. The men also got ready. The cargo had been unloaded and placed in small chests with four bars each. Each bar weighted about ninety pounds, so the chests had to be carried on a palate with polls by four men. They moved one to the designated area. At the right time they met Zaradan outside the prince's tent to wait for permission to enter and speak to him. He was the king-to-be and everyone knew it. Etiquette was even more rigorous than would have been used the leader of an army only, because he was not just a military leader but a king.

"You may come in," said the servant. Nebuchadnezzar looked up from his report to see his general. Nebuchadnezzar was a strong leader and highly respected. Several years of soldiering made him physically fit. He had an excellent mind for strategy and good people skills. The tent was richly furnished with rugs, gilt tent poles and a sturdy throne, also gilt.

"Sire, I have several men who have news and a message for you from Jerusalem," he said.

Nebuchadnezzar nodded to him and said, "Bring me your message, sirs."

Vicken said, "Sire, we are just arrived from Jerusalem and have brought a captured tribute payment with us. With great skill and cunning your servant Wakeem and our men ravaged the emissaries to the Pharaoh Necho of Egypt and the soldiers and took all that was destined to him. We are pleased to bring it to you today," Vicken bowed his face to the floor and backed away while the men brought the silver chest forward and opened it. The money was worth millions of shekels. None of them looked up again until the prince asked them to stand. He had servants bring the chest closer to be examined.

"By the God Marduk, you have all done well," Nebuchadnezzar was very pleased. He moved around the chest and circled the small group. "How many more chests are there?"

"Twenty-five, sire," Vicken answered, still in a kneeling position.

"Stand up, men. Excellent," the prince said. "Have a drink to celebrate with me. Zaradan, pour all some wine." They waited until each had a glass, then the prince said, "To the success of Babylon!" and held his glass in the air.

The men followed his lead; "To the success of Babylon!" they said and held their glasses up. Then they watched and followed as the prince lowered his glass and drank the small drink.

Nebuchadnezzar spoke after a few seconds, "This money will buy us many additional men and tools for fighting against our enemies. Even now we can use this to prepare for the upcoming battles." He was indeed pleased and he rewarded the men, "Zaradan, give each man a gold coin and two days of leave." Nebuchadnezzar motioned to Zaradan, who spoke to the men and paid them. They were dismissed, bowing and backing out of the tent

Vicken and his men were gone, but Zaradan was asked to remain. When the room was clear, the formalities were dropped and the two men sat together in discussion about the battle of Carchemish and likely upcoming battle with Pharaoh's army. Zaradan spoke, "This money will help keep the mercenaries happy while we wait for the armies of Pharaoh. It could be a week or more of just waiting," he paused, remembering the recent take-over battle. "We still have many men recovering from their battle injuries, so the extra time for them will be a good thing. There are still weapons to repair and arrows to make. They need the time for work and for the rest. I think they will just need to be patient after they finish their work."

"My scouts tell me that Pharaoh is not too far south of us. He is coming this way through northern Syria and will be crossing into this area in days. He brought mercenary armies with him, but the scouts say they have had problems."

Speaking from experience, Zaradan interrupted, "Well, it is no wonder with the great distance they have traveled from Egypt that there have been problems. The soldiers are probably exhausted. You know food can be hard to supply on a long march. Not getting enough rest because they are pushing to arrive at their destination and hunger can make for unhappy, uncooperative men. Pharaoh has been pushing them hoping to get here in time to help the Assyrians save one of Egypt's last strong holds in the north. He thinks that by hurrying his men, he might be able to make it in time. By now, word should be trickling back to him that Carchemish has already fallen."

"Let's see if that changes his mind. I doubt that it will. He is stubborn and desperate to hang on to his few remaining northern areas. Well, he is too late," bragged Nebuchadnezzar. "The scouts said his army is scattered over many miles, with stragglers camping in separate areas. They aren't working together at all. I am confident that this battle, if he shows up, will be won by us."

"The intelligence I have received says he has the Ethiopians and some Libyans with him. They are excellent with the spear and shield. The best bow men are the Lydians and I hear some of them have also joined his ranks," added Zaradan.

"True, but with their problems of the army being disassociated from each other and with their exhaustion, I still think we have the upper hand. I have heard of another group that has me more concerned than anyone you have mentioned so far. The Naharin, that elite archery detachment of about 200 troops, are said to be traveling with him. If they are healthy and in the advanced group who arrive, we could loose a great number of men to their arrows."

"I will brief my lieutenants about them and see if we can devise a plan in advance to take them into account. I want to avoid as much loss of life as possible. We will be ready for anything he does, if he comes."

"I know Necho will come. He desperately wants to control this city in the center of the trade route. He knows that whoever holds it has the power to control the Babylonian area's trade and is strategic to keep our area submissive. He is too late! He will have to take the city from us and he has tried before. I think we have the victory already wrapped up," Nebuchadnezzar was speaking to himself more than anyone in particular.

"I agree. From everything I have heard and seen, we have the upper hand. I am very confident in our supremacy and in your leadership. You have proven yourself to be a valuable leader to your father and to your country. The next question," said Zaradan, "is what would you like to do with the soldiers from Jerusalem? I will take care of their current needs, but after that, what?"

"Send them back to Wakeem. Tell them that if the battle here takes place and we are the winners, which I expect to be, then we might be chasing Pharaoh home to Egypt. I plan on taking or destroying everything between here and there. I want nothing left for him to reclaim. Anything I spare will only be by mercy or something I think may be to our advantage in the future."

Zaradan added, "Jerusalem will be directly in the path of that trek back to Egypt. The whole land, though of no significant political value or military strength, is a valuable passageway to all points in the middle east. It would be a military and economic advantage to hold the cities on any direct land routes."

"Lay out a plan for me that would include any cities that you would consider worth saving, rather than destroying," said the prince. "When we move south, we will have everything we need to know before the battle begins. We will meet again when you have your recommendations," Nebuchadnezzar said and stood dismissing Zaradan.

Vicken told his men they would be returning to Ugarit in three days to sail back to Ashkelon and bring battle information back to Wakeem. It appeared that very soon the Babylonian army would be here. It would take several weeks to move through the cities and to the south, but by the end of summer his people would be in Jerusalem. That thought brought great happiness to him and the men. They had been waiting for a long time to see that day.

They worked out another agreement to make the return trip to Ugarit with their favorite caravan owner. In the next few days, they spent time resting, preparing for the return trip and visiting Carchemish. The city was on the west bank of the Euphrates. It controlled a major ford for eastward-moving caravans from the Mediterranean. From the southern gate, they walked toward a beautiful temple they could see ahead toward the center of town. Along the way they passed the markets where a wide variety of wares from many countries were exhibited. The streets were well patrolled with their Babylonian army, keeping a tight lid on activities and movement. When they arrived at the temple, it was Hittite in style with a wide complex of temple service buildings. The walls that surrounded the city had several towers with numerous gates. There was a nice citadel, also walled, with two more gates. They purchased supplies and stayed in an inn for two days before returning to camp. The break was enjoyed by all the men.

On their return to camp they learned that Pharaoh was camped only two day's journey south of town. They would get on the road early tomorrow for Ugarit. Wakeem needed their information so they wanted to get away before the battle was engaged. After packing and preparing for the trip, they left at sunrise the next day.

CHAPTER 15

Pharaoh was not happy with the current situation. All his troops had not arrived at the final camp location SE of the city. They were due to arrive a day ago. The Lydians and the Ethiopians were still not in camp and he needed them to strengthen his fight against the strong armies of the Babylonians. When he last met the Babylonians in battle, he was not able to defeat them and had no intention of repeating that defeat, losing valuable territory. He had every intention of making this battle come out in his favor. The Lydians and the Naharin would soften up the Babylonians from a safe distance with their arrows as the chariots and infantry advanced behind them. The archers would destroy as many of Nebuchadnezzar's men as they could and then the chariots with spear men and swordsmen would follow up.

"Call Jamemar (JA-me-mar)in to give me an update," he called to his servant concerning his general. "I cannot wait indefinitely for the others to arrive. Is there any word on their current location?"

Jamemar came in from a briefing with his scouts. "Sir, they have not been seen since noon yesterday. We think they might be together and about a day or more away."

"Noon yesterday? By the rays of Re! How did they get so far behind? Weren't some of our men with them working to keep things moving?"

Jamemar knew Necho would be angry and rightly so. He was paying these armies to be ready for battle and they were not here when he needed them.

This was an expensive undertaking that had taken months in the planning; now it was falling apart.

Pharaoh received word a month ago about the tribute payment raid and loss. The lack of tribute payment from Judah was not going to stop the battle, but it had added fuel to Pharaoh's angry fire for conquest of this usurper of his power in the north. This son of a king was taking all of Egypt's territory.

Jamemar finally answered, "Sir, I wish I could explain or excuse them, but we did have men with them and we sent others to encourage them to catch up. If they do come, we may already be in battle. Should we send a group of soldiers to find them?" he paused to consider, "And tell them what?"

"Send a small detachment to find them. If they are not here by tomorrow evening, we will leave without them and they will not be paid the rest of their agreed upon sum. The pittance they already received won't cover the days of travel. Do this quickly. Have the detachment leave within the morning. Send me Makat. Go now and get them ready, then return quickly. I want to review the attack with him and you."

Jamemar found Makat, a lieutenant in the officers' tent, "Lieutenant, go see the Pharaoh immediately. I will return to join you to review plans for the upcoming battle. Where is Denlin? I am sending his detachment to encourage the mercenaries to get here quickly. Have any of them shown up yet?"

"Denlin is on guard duty at the south edge of camp up toward the west side. I will send Damac to replace him on duty, if you need Denlin. As far as the other armies, I saw the Ethiopians coming toward camp on the west plain about one hour ago. Reports have not mentioned the Lydians yet. They must not be near."

"Good. Send Damac immediately at a rush and tell Denlin to come to me as soon as he arrives. You hurry to Pharaoh once you have talked to Damac. Hurry. You know that Pharaoh is impatient."

Makat left the tent and went to the soldiers' encampment. He found Damac, sending him on horseback to guard duty and to get the message to Denlin.

Within fifteen minutes Denlin had returned at a full gallop to meet with Jamemar in his tent. Winded from the hard ride, "Denlin reporting, sir," he said.

"Good. I would like you to choose twenty men to leave with you immediately for the south to find the Naharin and the Lydians. The Naharin have been seen near, but the Lydians have not been seen recently. Necho would like them to be here by tomorrow night. They cannot be far, yet it may take some searching to find them. Get them up and moving. I want them here or I wouldn't want to hear what else Pharaoh might do except not pay them."

"Yes, sir, I remember when they were last seen. I will start that direction and hope to cross their path soon."

"It is their lives, I am sure, after Pharaoh finishes this battle, if they do not get here in time. Hopefully, it will not require a threat to get these men to come quickly. They want the money. I am not at all worried about loyalty. No mercenary is loyal to any cause except his own money bag. You must be gone before noon, so hurry. The sooner the better."

Denlin rushed away to his errand. Jamemar went back to Pharaoh's tent. He joined Pharaoh and one of his lieutenants who were deep in review when he arrived. "Join us, Memar. We have much to do before we head north." The men reviewed each detail in earnest. They stopped for lunch and continued into the afternoon. By supper time they had finished their attack plan.

A meeting with the generals was called by trumpet an hour after sundown. It was sure that the men would have eaten by that time. If the Lydian and Ethiopian generals had arrived, they would attend as well. If not, they would be briefed tomorrow.

Jamemar spoke, "Tonight we will review our attack plan against the interlopers of our city, Carchemish. Tomorrow we will move into position and be ready for attack. I want the Naharin or Lydians to soften up the front line and sides of the city with a borage of arrows. Chariot divisions of lancers and swordsmen will follow directly behind each group of archers. Along with the Pharaoh's body guard, the Thebes Elite, let's send the Green Division of the Lancers and the Swords of the Nile Division to the south. The Wargod Infantry and the Sacred Spear Divisions with the Ethiopians will attack from the East. The Swords of Re and the Red Lancers will advance from the west. Reinforcement in the south will be the Swears of Nubis Division and the Sphinx Swords. Assign your men according to these plans. The Memphis Guards and the Slayers of Evil will enter the city followed by infantry. Any escaped Assyrians will join our forces during the battle. I will keep five other divisions with me at the back to reinforce the front lines. You can spend tomorrow adjusting your plans within your divisions. The northern and western divisions will need to move into position late tomorrow. When you hear the trumpet blast to advance, begin your attack against the walls and gates near your areas. The Western and Northern divisions will chase any stray soldiers from the Babylonian army, but don't go more than one day's journey. We need you here. Re-gather at this location. But if Re is with us, as we know he will be, then we will meet at the palace in the center of the city for a victory celebration." With that last statement, the group erupted in a roar and stood to their feet ranting and yelling. "We will leave at dawn in two days and Re be with us."

The group disbanded to meet with their troops and lay out the plans within their divisions.

In Carchemish Nebuchadnezzar listened carefully to the spy's report. "Sir, his troops are in place. Some of the stragglers to their camp have now arrived, but the Lydians are still out. From what we hear he plans on beginning the attack in the morning day after tomorrow. They have the Naharin with them and they will surely be in the first line of attack. It looks like the size of the army would be around 50, 000 troops."

"It sounds like everything we had already planned is right on target. Let's proceed as it has been laid out. Make sure everyone is in place by evening tomorrow," said Nebuchadnezzar.

Zaradan nodded. "We will be ready. The Naharin cannot shoot through shields. They are already stationed around the city and on the city wall. We have our own archers, who are at least as efficient as the Naharin, in place outside the city who will pick off the enemy, including the Naharin. Other troops are camped around the city at strategic areas and they will attack from all directions once the battle is engaged."

"Excellent. I am ready to resolve this issue for this city. We will route the enemy and follow them home to Egypt taking every village, city and farm between here and there. We will ravage the countryside of all living beings and animals and we will scorch the earth so it will not sustain any living thing for years. Any survivors in the countries will have no food from which to live. Locals, who would seem to be of value to us or, if left in their countries, could provide leadership to rebuild, will become captives." Nebuchadnezzar was in his glory, raving about his kingdom and battle prowess, "They will become our willing slaves or they will die. The future for Babylon looks very bright. Victory is ours, but the weak Egyptians do not know it yet."

"We are ready and eager. Let them come. Babylon's army is stronger, quicker and we will be victorious. Sire, I will be moving around the city tomorrow. If you need me, please send someone to the headquarters in the lower palace. They will know where to find me," said Zaradan. "Your location here will see little battle. They will never take the city."

"I welcome the battle, even hand-to-hand combat would be a treat," he stood and walked around the room. "I want to win this badly. I will not give Pharaoh one inch of territory. Not one inch!"

"We will not give up, I promise," said Zaradan. "Anything else?"

"No. Tomorrow is a big day," he said. Then he walked over and poured the two of them a drink. Handing it to Zaradan and held up his cup, "To victory!"

CHAPTER 16

The noise from the battle was deafening. Zaradan could see the chariots whirling passed him at break-neck speed going in every direction around the city. Nebuchadnezzar's scarlet chariots were easy to pick out from his vantage point on the city wall. They appeared to be on fire in the sun. The yelling and screaming added to the din and the clang of metal against metal. He could hear behind him the frightful sound of flesh being pierced and breaking bones. War was anything but quiet.

The sounds were overwhelming, but all the senses were assailed with the smells, feel and sights of war. He could even taste the battle. It involved the whole man; his whole spirit. Maybe that is why men are fulfilled and thrive in a war situation. It makes use of the total man.

The smell of dust stirred up by the chariots as they spun around filled the air. The odor of human and horse sweat mingled with the distinct smell of the blood of both. The fragrance of fear filled his nostrils. True fear that those who faced life and death know, emits a fragrance that one never forgets.

He remembered the feel of cold steel as the blade of the enemy grazed his skin. The feel of a rushing chariot pounding across the rough terrain barely missing him, and the hand-to-hand combat with muscles straining to gain the advantage made his pulse pound. The feel of power as you toss a javelin into the enemy.

He remembered the shock of watching his first kill die in battle, a sight not easily forgotten. Seeing his first friend fall to the enemy, never to rise, was gut-wrenching. Dead and dying, mangled bodies and the gruesomeness of war was a horror to behold.

He could taste his own sweat as he fought with the enemy and the blood running down his face from the wound on his brow. He knew the taste of fear in mouths of young recruits as they awaited the signal to advance toward the soldier just across the gully. With the senses on overload a man must try to concentrate on the matters at hand. Mortal combat. For failure to maintain self-control one could pay the ultimate price, death.

The sound of the chariot wheels snapped Zaradan back to this battle and this moment. He could see the charioteers were doing well. The men who wielded their hand-held weapons from the chariot were more effective than foot soldiers. The drivers would effectively use their only weapon, the chariot itself, by running down and crushing escaping enemies or cutting them to ribbons with the chariot wheel spikes. Chariots would battle each other like wild animals. The strongest and most experience charioteer and chariot would emerge victorious leaving the loser in heap of tattered leather, shattered wood and bleeding flesh with a loose wheel spinning beside his wreck. The soldier riding along used his sword or spear to hack away at bystanders or to pierce them as they whizzed passed. It didn't matter the age or the gender of the enemy. All were fair game when it came to the heat of battle.

Zaradan was in his glory. He wanted to be in the thick of the battle, driving wildly around outside Carchemish in his chariot, but for now he was on the south wall watching the battle play out. He heard his lieutenant calling, "Sir, I have a battle update," said Makat.

"I see from here we seem to be battling well in this area. How fares the rest of the skirmishes?"

"On the west the Naharin have been split and a quarter of their men are dead. The Lydians still have not reported to the camp, so Nebuchadnezzar is short one of his elite groups of archers. The Swords of Re have been routed by our men. What few remain have scattered or joined their other troops. We are still fighting with the Red Lancers."

Zaradan said, "And on the East?"

"The Wargods Infantry has been cut in half and is in disarray. Their general, Galam, was killed and they are lacking someone to lead. The Sacred Spears are nearly wiped out. The Ethiopians are still fighting hard and it will be some time before the outcome of those battles will be known."

"They appear to be holding on toward the south. Is that the reality on the ground?"

"Yes. About the time one group is subdued reinforcements come to their rescue. It will be an extended battle in that area. When the east and west are more under control, we can send troops around the flanks and come in on the edges of the southern battles."

"I will update the Prince. Keep up the good work and report again in a few hours. Dismissed."

The troops withdrew for the evening. Effective fighting was impossible and more dangerous when one would not see their foe. Pharaoh met with his men, "What is the update? How many men did we loose?"

Memar was hesitant. He hated to give Pharaoh the update. It was not good. "Sir, we are doing well in the south. We have not lost any ground and only fifty of our men have been listed as dead."

"Fifty? Fifty! You say that like it is a good number. That is too high," Pharaoh paused to move to the table. He poured himself a drink, "I noticed you only mentioned the south. If things were going well, you would have included the west and east. Tell me all the report, not just your selected portion. And do so quickly." He downed the rest of the drink.

The generals were squeamish. They had lost one of their own and many of their other men. Necho turned from gazing out the tent door and faced the men, looking into their individual faces. He turned to Memar, "There is something else, isn't there? What has happened?"

"Galam is dead. The battle to the east is not going well. The Wargod Infantry is in disarray and needs a new general. Their lieutenant is capable. We should talk with him and let the men know he is in charge for the morning. Many of the men have died and others have scattered, but with the Ethiopians, I think they can hold on. The battle on the west is in chaos. We need to send reinforcements in the morning."

"Nebuchadnezzar has overcome us in the west and the Swords of Sphinx have been lost completely. Nebuchadnezzar's men have taken up that location and are moving in on our west flank. The east is still holding, but just barely. They need reinforcement. Who can you spare?"

Pharaoh had already sent in his last division of reinforcements. The only group left was his Thebes' Elite Body Guard. He looked over at his general, Nubecca. "What do you think? Can we spare part of this division?"

Nubecca nodded from his chariot, "Sire, it would be our privilege to fight for you in the east. I will go with the men and leave a platoon here with you, for you to command."

"Nubecca, do not loose all your men. If the battle is not going well, fall back to me and we will regroup. Do you understand? I need you for later, so I cannot afford to loose all of you."

"I understand. We will fight hard, but we will be careful. By your leave, sire." Nubecca took 400 of his men leaving 100 behind and they raced away with Jamemar.

Pharaoh was silent. He hoped this would go their way easily, but it appeared it would be an extended battle. "What number are missing in battle?"

"Over 3, 000. It was a hard fought day and I am proud of the way the men worked, but they were outnumbered. Tomorrow I hope we will see more success."

"Tomorrow, see me at noon to report on the way the day is going. Let's get some rest, sirs. You may go," Pharaoh dismissed them, but it was clear he was upset. Far too many men had already died. Tomorrow must be a better day.

Nebuchadnezzar and Zaradan enjoyed a quick bite of meat and bread for supper and strong coffee. They were pleased with the way the battl was going.

"We have lost about 500 men total, but sir, the enemy has lost m   I believe four divisions have been eliminated and at least some of the o   have had their effectiveness destroyed. Tomorrow will be the final day of battle here at Carchemish, if I am not miscalculating."

"Prepare any divisions that we can spare to be ready to follow Pharaoh and his army toward the south. If they retreat, they will likely go through Syria into the valley of Megiddo. Logic would say they would take the shortest route toward Egypt which would be through Israel. We will follow them all the way to Egypt. We will not let this man come to us again and challenge our control of these territories."

"We will get ready to move. I think we can get all the generals ready, even those who are in battle. The men want to finish the job. We will leave a division here to maintain control and a regiment of doctors to help with any wounded who cannot travel. We will prepare all of the others to travel. Thank you for the meal. I will see you tomorrow on the battlefield," Zaradan said as he left to join his generals in a planned early evening meeting.

After he had met with the generals and relayed the information, they rested. Tomorrow was going to be a busy day.

Tomorrow faired no better for Pharaoh. Nebuchadnezzar's men advanced from the west and the east. Those areas were nearly completely in their control. Pharaoh's guard had returned in part to him and they were fleeing south. The battle in the south had turned in Nebuchadnezzar's favor and Pharaoh had called his troops back. They were retreating back to the west side of the Orontes River.

"Memar, have the Naharin hold the line for as long as is possible. If they can give us a few hours, we can put a few miles between us and Nebuchadnezzar's army, since I think they will follow. We will move everyone else we can spare with us and move as fast as possible."

With those instructions, Necho and the Thebes Elite and other remaining men rode their chariots at full speed toward the ford of the Orontes being followed by a ragtag group of lancers, swordsmen and foot soldiers. They would keep riding until nightfall and camp, waiting for others to join them as they could. This was not cowardice on the part of Pharaoh. It was survival of the country. The loss of the Pharaoh in a battle would have meant sure defeat of all the remaining army and possibly the country of Egypt itself. He must be protected at all cost.

CHAPTER 17

Necho and his men had been on the run for two weeks. Scouts were concerned because Nebuchadnezzar's army was gaining ground on them daily. If they continued to advance faster than Pharaoh could move, then there would be a second confrontation and Pharaoh knew his troops could not win in any battle right now. They were hungry, tired and battle weary. They also were discouraged because they had not been victorious. They were not used to being defeated. Getting home alive was their only interest now. None wanted to face Nebuchadnezzar again.

Jamemar came to the tent, "Sire, I have a recent report from the few remaining Naharin. The twenty survivors finally arrived to join our camp last night. Some are wounded and they all are weak. They did hold the army back well so we could escape, but little real progress was made in slowing down Nebuchadnezzar's army. I thought you might like to consider a bonus for their excellent work, when we get back to Egypt and an award for valor. On their way here they could see the enemy advancing as they moved passed them quietly. Nebuchadnezzar is camped just twenty miles north of us."

Necho was pacing the tent. He knew they needed to make better time, but his army was already being pushed to their limits. He was amazed at the speed of Nebuchadnezzar's travel. The Babylonians were conquering or raiding every village or city that they passed. Some were being burned to the ground. Nebuchadnezzar had set up a captives camp, according to the spies, to hold some of the prisoners he had already taken from these cities. He would pick them up again when he came back this way. Pharaoh didn't know how the Babylonians could travel that fast and also do all they were doing in the cities in Syria.

He stopped to face Memar, "I agree with you about the Naharins. I will have the staff arrange for an award to be presented with some silver included, if we get home with survivors, which sounds more doubtful than ever with Nebuchadnezzar getting this close." He paused and looked at Memar for agreement, "I really believe a second battle may be imminent. Tell the generals to have the men up and on the road one hour before dawn. We can get several hours of space between us before they are up and have broken camp. We will camp at Hamath tomorrow night at the latest possible time."

"I wish the situation was different, sir, but I do agree that a second battle is not out of the question. I will have everyone going early tomorrow. Anything else?"

"No."

Things did not go well the next day for the Egyptian army. The men were even slower than in the past. The injured had to be carried and the ones doing the carrying were the walking wounded, too. Morale was at an all-time low.

Food had to be scavenged from the surrounding communities. There was very little food left in camp and it was given to Pharaoh. Trying to find food made travel even slower. They did reach Hamath, but it was well after dark. Most of the men simply did their best to get comfortable with only a basic camp set up. Guards were put on duty, but they could not be depended upon in their state of exhaustion. The situation was very serious indeed.

At sun-up the first flurry of arrows took out the guards and fifteen soldiers camped near the perimeter. The second round took out the men who sat up from their sleep to see what was happening. Then twenty-five chariots moving five abreast pounded into camp. Soldiers in the chariots carrying double-edged swords went through the unprotected edge of camp and directly into the center. They were followed by units of twenty chariots and men with spears who came into the north and south edges of Pharaoh's camp. A third of the infantry followed each chariot group wiping out the unarmed men. By the time Nebuchadnezzar's army reached the center of camp, the Egyptian army was fully awake and the survivors were armed and ready for battle.

Nebuchadnezzar was in his chariot at the back of the center advance. He raced at full speed toward what he and his men thought would be the tent of the Pharaoh. He was slashing everything within the reach of his sword. He was not going to be stopped in any way from reaching his target—the Pharaoh's tent.

When he reached the tent, he and his body guard jumped out of their chariots and invaded the tents in the center of camp. Fully armed as they went and prepared to kill or capture anyone alive inside, they systematically worked their way through the tents.

"No one is here! How could they have gotten away? This should have taken them totally off guard. But obviously, we were wrong about our intelligence," Nebuchadnezzar said to Zaradan.

Nebuchadnezzar was trashing everything in site. He was angry, "I really thought we had him, finally. How could they have known? There is no way he could have escaped without advanced notice. We were too quick."

"The last time they knew we were camped behind them by twenty miles. There is no way they could have known we had traveled all night to make up the time and were right behind them all the way here," said Zaradan. He continued to look around, then a thought that seemed obvious came to him, "Could we have a spy in the camp giving information to the enemy?" he asked.

Nebuchadnezzar gave that some thought. That was certainly possible, but hard to imagine. Who among the men he knew would have done something like that? "Yes," he said, "that is possible. Any ideas who it could be or how to determine who that someone is?" He turned and watched his men at work around him. Which of them was a traitor? He hated that thought, but if one of them was a spy, Nebuchadnezzar would make sure he wouldn't live long enough to have the enemy kill him.

"Sir, I will begin an investigation. We will find out if anyone was alone for a long period of time last night. Maybe one of the men's tent-mates disappeared for a while. We will have to wait until we bivouac for the day."

"Alright. We will start the investigation when we camp," Nebuchadnezzar said, still upset about Necho. He spoke about it again, "Pharaoh is probably on the run with his body guard. It is obvious that he was informed and we have missed him completely." He was quiet for a minute, staring at the battle, "Let's take our time and try to find out who our enemy is in the camp before we chase Pharaoh. That is the most important thing. We can go to Egypt slowly and take the land in-between and captives as we go.

When we finally get to Egypt, we will find Pharaoh and take care of him. For now, let's finish up here and find a place for tonight. I want to deal with this spy first and foremost." Nebuchadnezzar left the area and got into his chariot. He rode around the camp to see how the battle was going. It was nearly over before it had begun. It didn't seem fair. The Egyptians were so weak and exhausted; it really wasn't much of a fight.

He saw that most of the survivors had surrendered and were being taken to a holding area. The camp was looted, but nothing much of value was found. The Babylonian army regrouped and relocated to the south to a good camp area. They set up camp and marched the men and animals to the nearby river. They washed the weapons, men and horses. After the meal at noon, they began the process of trying to find out who was their spy.

Zaradan met with his generals for a briefing. They were to find out which of their troops might have had an opportunity to sneak away and whether any of them were gone for a length of time last night. Since they were really camped very close to Necho, it would not have taken very long to sneak out and go to the other camp.

"So men, I want to know by tomorrow morning if you have any men who were gone for, say, a couple of hours last night. It doesn't matter who it is, I want their names. Tomorrow, I will meet with all of those men. You are welcomed to join us while we talk, if you would like."

"Sir, none of my men would ever have done something like that. They are completely loyal to the King and Babylon," said Pescal, who was the general with the archers.

Zaradan agreed, "Yes, we all want to believe that. What makes someone a good spy is the ability to fit in and appear like one of the group. But someone must have given Pharaoh information for him to have escaped. We need to know if we have a spy. Let's begin immediately."

His generals were busy for that day and through part of the next before he received any names that were even remotely possible suspects. Each man met with Zaradan and his general along with a couple other lieutenants beginning the third morning after the battle. Most of them were legitimately absent—on guard duty, ill, on a drinking binge in the woods, but a couple were very thin on excuses.

"So you say you just took a walk. Where did you go? I would think that after walking all day—," he turned to Mongin, general to the infantry, "What's his name? Ingarri. So, Ingarri, weren't you just too tired to walk another pace?" Zaradan got in his face.

127

"I just had cramps in my legs and needed to walk them out. I came back in an hour or so," he said, with a slight tremble in his voice. He seemed fidgety and unable to look Zaradan in the eye. He glanced around to the other men in the room. "Lieutenant, you have known me for a year. Have I ever done anything to make you question my loyalty? I volunteered to come with you, remember?"

The more he tried to explain himself, the more his sincerity was in question. Zaradan said to the lieutenant, "Take him into the next tent and stay with him. We will talk with him again later." The two men left. Zaradan spoke to his servant, "Bring in the other soldier."

Feshdalla came in with his lieutenant and Pescal. "Zaradan, this is Feshdalla. He was out of his tent last night and we have not been able to account for his actions. I understand you would like to ask him some questions," Pescal turned to Feshdalla. "Be seated on that box, soldier."

Feshdalla sat down. He was frightened, but he was a tough man. He was not going to be intimidated by this investigation. He looked the general in the eyes.

Zaradan liked this man. He had courage. He hoped he was not a spy, but asked, "Tell us of your actions last night?"

"I was out at the camp fire. After a long day, I need to spend some time alone and unwind. I just sat there and stared into the fire and then I went back to the tent and to sleep." He looked at the men with an innocent face, "What's the problem? Why are you wondering?"

"What we are doing is none of your business," said Pescal.

"Did anyone see you at the fire that can verify your presence there?"

"Yes. A couple of men, Okono and Ubuli, were at the fire also. Ask them."

"Oh, we will, you can be sure," said Zaradan. "We will also inspect your tent and your personal items. Take him to the next tent down and wait until we get back with you." The three men left and went to the other tent beside where the two men waited.

Zaradan sent several soldiers to inspect the tents of Ingarri and Feshdalla. They came back with some surprising items for a soldier. Feshdalla seemed to have no incriminating items, but Ingarri had a stash of money, way beyond the wages of a soldier. It looked like they might have their man.

They brought Ingarri back in to Zaradan who held out the coins in front of the man's face after he was seated, "Can you explain these coins?"

Ingarri turned green. He began sweating and his throat went dry. He really couldn't speak. He simply shook his head. Zaradan hit him in the stomach knocking him backwards off the box. He just laid there catching his breath, and then he crawled back into the corner, holding his side and whimpering. "Get back over on this box, man," commanded Zaradan.

Ingarri did not move. Two other soldiers jerked him up and plopped him down on the box. They stood behind him with their arms crossed, but ready for action.

"I need to know about this money," Zaradan said again.

"I found them, sir," came his feeble response. That amount of money he had could not have been found in a raid or several raids. Someone had paid him the money and they all believe that someone was Pharaoh.

"We also found an amulet of the god Re. That seems like an odd token for a Babylonian soldier, since they worship Marduk," said the soldier who went to the tent.

"I found it in battle. It was on an Egyptian man's neck. I tore it free," Ingarri said eagerly.

"Tore it free? Let's see," said Zaradan examining the leather trace that supposedly came from around a man's neck to see if it was damaged. "Do you see anything wrong with the leather? Any damage or tearing?" All agreed that the leather was perfect and undamaged. It was also not dirty, sweaty or bloody, any of which would have been likely for a soldier in the heat of battle. However, for an amulet stored away safely and one that could never be worn it looked perfect.

"Not a person in this room believes you found this or the coins. Unless I am really off my guess," he looked around the room, "we have found our informant." He had the other soldier take him back to the tent and stand guard. He would be taken to Nebuchadnezzar for final judgment before the day was over.

Zaradan went to see Nebuchadnezzar and give him the facts in the story. Within the hour Ingarri was standing before the future King of Babylon. "Based on the facts of this story I believe that you betrayed both Babylon and me. I do not know if you are truly Babylonian, but if you are, then you need to pray to Marduk to give your soul his forgiveness for this vicious betrayal. You are condemned to die by beheading at noon today."

Ingarri began to scream. The two soldiers who had been watching him dragged him from the tent and back to the holding tent to await execution. He had never been a brave man and had only volunteered to be in this army because he was commanded to do so in order to save his life. The Pharaoh of Egypt had caught him stealing when he was conscripted into Egypt's army.

They gave him the choice of becoming a spy or of death. At the time, spying seemed to be a better idea than death. Now he was going to die anyway.

The men were called to the center of camp for the execution. At noon sharp the general of the infantry and two of his men brought out Ingarri and made him kneel with his hands tied behind his back. They forced his head down on the tree stump and the soldiers held him there. The general had the unhappy duty of beheading his man, but it was also counted a privilege to rid the county of a mortal enemy. After a brief explanation to the assembled men, the general brought the sword down hard on the neck of Ingarri, severing the head cleanly from the body. He would have to be more careful about the men with whom he worked.

The assembly was quiet and then Nebuchadnezzar spoke, "I am grateful to Marduk that he has revealed to us the offender of our people and the traitor to our country. He has paid the price for informing Pharaoh about our activities. Take warning from this execution that I will not tolerate any disloyalty or insubordination from those who claim to serve me." He turned and went back inside. The assembled men quietly dispersed.

Pescal had been standing in the nearby tent door with Feshdalla. Pescal told him that he was free to go since the spy had been captured. After they witnessed the execution Feshdalla returned to his tent. He began to shake and collapsed on his bedroll. It had been a close call. Last night he had sent Ingarri to the Pharaoh after they had talked just outside the fire's light. He was the controller for Ingarri and had been spying for Pharaoh for five years.

CHAPTER 18

It was hard to believe that there were enemy soldiers that close to Jerusalem. It had been over a month since the raid and families were still in mourning.

Dinah picked up Mattan. He probably wanted a snack and Lotta was out on errands. She had also left Nathan, but he was playing well on the floor right now. Dinah went to Mattan picked him up. They had given him some honey water the other day when Lotta was away and that had worked well. Dinah mixed a spoon of honey in a cup of warm water. Someone said it was better for the baby to have warm water like the temperature of mother's milk. Then she dipped a cloth into the water and let him suck on the damp end of the cloth, re-dipping it, occasionally.

"Here you go, sweetie. How does that taste?" He sucked it hard. He would be happy for a while with the substitute for his nurse. "You are the most precious little one. I am so glad God gave you to us. We all love you," she leaned down and kissed his face and ran her finger along his cheek while he sucked. Nathan came over to see what Mattan was eating and to get a little of that sweet talk that Dinah had given to Mattan. She kissed his face and offered Nathan the water, which he didn't care for, but she did offer him a small, torn piece of dried pita bread spread with some olive oil. That seemed to satisfy him.

While they ate, she thought again of soldiers being that close to town. It made her afraid to go far from the city. It was not likely they were near anymore, but you never did know about soldiers. If Jeremiah was right, there are likely spies here, too, from that northern king. Some even thought the palace had a spy. Daniel had been talking to Azariah and her last night about that possibility. His family had joined hers to have dinner.

"The king has been investigating several different people. We have not been told who, because they are afraid it will leak out. They don't want the people being investigated to run away or to suspect they are being watched," Daniel told them.

"That is so unbelievable. A spy in our very city. Do you think there is one, really?" Dinah asked him, with her brother looking at her and rolling his eyes, like she was stupid for asking.

"Dinah, of course he believes that. It had to be someone inside who was helping the soldiers with information for the soldiers to know which road was being taken by the wagons for the tribute. They were in exactly the right location for the ambush," Azariah said.

"I do believe that," said Daniel. "I think someone in the warehouse-loading dock area is involved. There are new people hired down there often. It would be easy to get inside. There is not much clearance needed to get a job there. It is considered a 'low risk' area for information. But if you listen well, you can hear a great deal about what is going on in the palace from the workers."

"Who do you suspect?" Azariah asked.

"There are a couple of new men. One is snoopy and has a strange accent. He is not from this area and I do not recognize the accent. I don't think I have ever heard it before. He always moves around and stands near other people when they are talking. He appears to be working, but I wonder if he is. Maybe he is from that northern kingdom that Jeremiah mentioned. Father calls it Babylon," said Daniel.

"Are they investigating him?" Dinah wondered.

"I really don't know, but I did tell the King's eunuch, Baileen, about him. He seemed interested in my information."

Azariah agreed, "I think it sounds like you are right on target. He sounds very suspect in his actions. Where does he go when he is not working and where does he live?"

Daniel continued, "I work with a clerk called Ben. He has seen Zarallon, that's his name, at Cain's Inn talking with several men and with Cain. We don't know where he lives. Ben said Zarallon has a girlfriend. She is a new waitress at Cain's. He thinks her name is Bethany. Ben and I watch him a lot and talk about our suspicions often. Ben has made it his project to find out more about Zarallon after work. Ben saw another man watching Zarallon at the market last week. That man works for the King. We have seen him at other times in the palace, but never in the dock area. Zarallon wouldn't have seen him."

'What will happen to the man, if he is the spy?" Dinah asked.

"If he is captured, then he will be probed for information. When they have all the information from him that they can get, he will be killed," Daniel said.

"Oh! Killed? I guess I had never considered what you would do with a spy, but couldn't they send him back to his country?"

"Two things are important to remember here, Dinah," Daniel added, "they will not try to catch him for a while. Watching him will tell them more about what's happening in the city and about who might be involved. In fact, they may let him continue to work and feed him false information. If that works and they can set a trap for the men he is working with, maybe they can catch the group who stole the tribute payment in the raid. Secondly, when they do catch a spy, letting him go home would never be possible. He would know too much about what is going on in town and could help them against us if a war broke out."

"I see. That makes sense," she said. She was lost in thought about their conversation. She suddenly turned to Daniel, "Wait, go back to what you said a few minutes ago. What was the spy's girlfriend's name?"

"Bethany."

Azariah and Dinah looked at each other. "Do you suppose it could be the 'Bethany' who is Mattan's mother? Surely, she wouldn't be friends with someone who would betray her country. What do you think, brother?" Dinah asked.

Azariah was sure she would betray her country and probably more, if it meant something good for herself. "I think it is a possibility she is our Bethany. I am glad she left Mattan here if she is going to be a waitress. I wonder how she ended up at Cain's? Knowing what is going on with her might add more information to the King's research into Zarallon. Daniel, maybe we can help find out more about what is going on by working through Bethany using Mattan as bait."

That idea had Dinah on her feet, "What! You will not endanger that baby with one of your hair-brained schemes. Anyway, maybe I can help and we can leave Mattan safely at home."

"How, in the name of all that is holy, could you help? You would be in the way and have us watching you to keep you safe," Azariah chided her.

"Well, you never know how helpful a girl can be. I might be able to find out something without your help," she smiled at the two guys and sauntered out of the room.

"Whenever she gets something into her mind, she gets dangerous. We had better keep an eye on her," Azariah said to Daniel, who nodded in agreement.

She remembered this conversation with the boys, while she was laying Mattan down for a nap. Maybe she could pay Bethany a visit and pretend it was about letting Bethany know they knew where she was and thought maybe she wanted to know about her baby. Of course, it would be risky and she would have to deceive her parents about why she was going to town. She would make up a partial truth about shopping for something, but would add a visit to Cain's, as a little side trip. 'It is for a good cause,' she said to herself, 'so a little white lie is allowed.'

Lotta came back about that time. "How are my babies?" she called, entering the kitchen where Dinah was sitting. Nathan came tottering to his momma. "Can you believe how much he has learned to walk in just one week?" Lotta said to no one in particular. Picking him up, she kissed him and cradled on against her hip, "Dinah, what is Mattan doing? Do you think he is hungry?"

"No, I gave him honey water and that settled him down. He is sleeping upstairs."

"Wonderful. I'll take Nathan up for a nap now, too, and maybe lay down for a while with them, okay?"

"That would be great. I have a couple of errands I could run, if that is okay with you. I should be back by suppertime."

"Go ahead. I will help your mom with dinner, when she returns from her visit to her sister."

Dinah grabbed her hair cloth and hurried uptown, toward Cain's. She had to talk to Bethany. She was so curious about what happened when she left. She thought she might see the spy or something else just as exciting. This was so really going to be fun. Adventure always excited her.

She was outside of Cain's, but she couldn't go inside. Ladies did not go to inns alone very often. They always went with a male family member. So if she couldn't go in, maybe she could look through the window lattice to see something.

She walked to the side of the window and looked around the edge. She could barely see through the cobwebs. It would be hard to tell anything about what was happening inside through this window. Her eyes adjusted to the darkness inside after watching for a short time and she did see a waitress. Yes, that was her. Bethany, Mattan's mother, was indeed the waitress that had been seen with the suspected spy. Well, that was one question answered.

She could see the room was not very full. It was well after lunch and a slow time in serving. She decided to take a chance. Dinah stood between the door and side of the window, watching for the next time that Bethany was near the front door. Dinah saw her stop at a table right by the window and beside the door. She opened the door and stepped inside. Naturally, Bethany turned to see who had entered behind her.

Shock! Utter, panicked shock was the look on Bethany's face, "What are you doing here?" she whispered.

Dinah took her arm and pulled her into the street. "I am looking for you. Someone said a new waitress was at Cain's by the name of 'Bethany.' I just had to see if it was the mother who left her son alone. And it is you! How could you do that?"

"I don't have time to talk now," she jerked her arm free and glared at Dinah, "Come around to the back of the inn and I will meet you in the alley in a few minutes. Cain will give me a short break, since we aren't busy right now." She stepped back inside and disappeared.

Dinah walked to the side street and to the back alleyway. With each step she was more afraid. She had never been alone in an area of town like this. She looked around carefully and watched every shadow to see if it moved. She was on pins and needles by the time Bethany came out of the back door.

"What took you so long? It is scary back here," said Dinah.

"You are fine. Come with me," Bethany lead her to the back stairs to the second floor.

"I don't like this. Where are you taking me?"

"To my sister's room. I don't want others watching us and to see me talking to a girl who obviously is not from around this neighborhood," she laughed as she as the fear in Dinah's eyes. "You look like a frightened fawn in the woods. I told you you were spoiled."

"Stop belittling me. Besides, you have a lot of room to criticize. At least I didn't abandon my newborn and run away. Some mother you are," Dinah shot back.

"Oh, be quiet. If they see you, they will wonder how I could know someone like you. It is obvious we didn't meet at the temple. It would start them asking questions. I can't afford any questions right now."

They were in the hall and at the door to Moriah's room, when suddenly, another door opened and a young man, half-dressed, stepped out, startling them both. "Bethany, I thought I heard your voice in the hall. Why are you up here?" Zarallon was curious as to why she was not working.

"Go back inside. I will see you in a few minutes," she said. She started to go into Moriah's room.

"Who is your friend?" he asked. "She doesn't look like your typical tavern girl." Dinah noticed he had a strong, unrecognizable accent. He was tall, swarthy and somewhat frightening to Dinah. She stepped behind Bethany trying to step out of his sight line.

"Well, well, I have finally found something that frightens Dinah," laughed Bethany. "Zarallon, it seems she thinks you are someone to be feared."

He reached around Bethany and took Dinah by the arm, trying to get a better look at her. He pulled her toward the room where the light from the window was better. The lighting in the hall was very dim from just a couple of lamps on stands.

She started screaming. Zarallon put his hand over her mouth and his other arm around her pulling her into his room. Bethany came in quickly and closed the door.

He jerked her up tight against him, "Shut up and listen to me, little thing," Zarallon whispered in her ear. He could feel her heart beating wildly. "I am going to release you. When I do, I want you to sit down over there and be quiet. One more sound and I will knock you unconscious. Do you understand?" She nodded her head.

He let her go and she just stood still, trembling like a leaf. He pushed her toward the chair, which she fell into and sat quietly.

"Who is she, Bethany? What does she want?"

"I have no idea what she wants. I had a little problem a couple of months ago and she helped me solve it," explained Bethany.

"What kind of problem could she possibly solve? She can't even take care of herself. How could she help you?"

"Well, I had an unfortunate pregnancy and she and her family agreed to keep the baby."

"We didn't agree to keep Mattan. You just abandoned him with us without any warning," Dinah finally found her voice.

"Shut up," Bethany walked over and slapped her across the face. "I did the best I could," yelled Bethany.

"Stop it. Now! Both of you. Do you want people to hear you?" Zarallon jerked Bethany away from the girl. "What do you want, Dinah? That is your name, isn't it?"

She nodded yes. She was shaking so hard, it was hard to control the tone of her voice and her movements, "I heard a girl named Bethany worked here and I came to see if it was Mattan's mother. I wanted to talk to her and see if she cared at all about her son and how he was doing."

"Well, now you know," Bethany said, "and tell me, how is my son?"

"Just fine, as if you cared. It was the best thing you could have done for him," Dinah was angry with her.

"Thanks. Now you have told me he is fine, just get out of here and leave me alone. Don't ever come again, do you understand? As far as I am concerned, that boy died to me and he is yours," Bethany grabbed Dinah's arm and jerked her to her feet to lead her into the hallway. Before they moved far, Zarallon stopped them.

He took both of Dinah's arms and held her right in front of him, rigidly. His voice got quiet and his eyes bored into hers, "Dinah, you had better forget ever being here this afternoon. No mention of me or of Bethany. If you do, you and your family will be in great danger. This is your warning. I will find out from Bethany after you leave where you and your family live. If there is any hint that you have betrayed us, someone will tell me, do you understand?"

Tears were streaming down her face. She understood all right. She would sign a death sentence for her family and friends if she talked about meeting Bethany or Zarallon. She still didn't know who he was, but there was no doubt he wasn't kidding. He was a dangerous man.

"I understand," she whispered. He released her and she quickly stepped into the hallway, running quietly to the stairs, opening the door carefully. She was hurrying down the stairs and not paying attention to what was in front of her. She ran right into a man getting ready to go upstairs. She tried not to look to conspicuous and excused herself, passing on around him. Looking back, she noticed his piercing eyes were watching her. He looked like Zarallon, and if it was possible, even more dangerous. She turned quickly away and ran down the alley.

She looked around carefully to see if she was being followed. No, it looked clear. There really was no need for them to follow since Bethany already knew where the Hadads lived. Dinah found a place to sit down in the square. She was still shaking and didn't trust herself to walk right now. If she went home in her current state, she would have to explain why she was so upset. Any explanation would mean endangering those she loved. They must never know what had happened today.

What would she tell them if they had asked what happened? Her goal of finding Bethany had been accomplished and her answer was clear. Bethany was through with Mattan and no longer wanted anything to do with him. Well, that suited Dinah just fine. The Hadads had taken to him and wouldn't dream of letting anyone have him, unless Bethany demanded her rights as his mother. That seemed very unlikely after her comments.

She had rested long enough. Her shaking had stopped and her breath was coming normally. She needed to start home right now, or they would worry and come looking for her. She stopped in the market and got some cloth at a vendor where her family had credit. That would give her a reason for being in town and cover up the event at the Inn.

Thinking more about what had happened as she walked, why had Zarallon been so worried about her talking? What secret did he and Bethany have? He seemed to be an ordinary foreigner staying in Cain's Inn. Many passed through Cain's place, according to her brother. Maybe since he was from another country, he was just worried about getting in trouble for frightening her and pulling her into his room. But his warnings seemed to be an overreaction to her, for something as simple as frightening her.

Deciding that it was something else, she thought about their conversation. It was obvious that this was Bethany's friend and if that was true, then he was the suspected spy. That might be important. But nothing else was said to give away any information. So she decided maybe it was what she saw in the room and tried to see the room in her mind.

The typical wooden bed, small table, several chairs and wash stand were the only furniture. A uniform jacket was lying on the bed and a shirt was draped over a fabric bag. Zarallon must be a soldier in someone's army, even though he was working in a palace loading dock. Zarallon had been bare-chested and in his stocking feet with his boots standing beside the bed. Some sort of leather satchel was in the corner along with a sword and dagger. A drawing lay on parchment on the table near the chair she had been pushed into and it had some words in a language she didn't know.

Oh my, that was it! It was what she had seen. She knew he was more than a worker and probably a soldier. And it was the drawing. She recognized the design based on the discussions she and Azariah had about the palace.

Zarallon had a drawing of the floor plan of the palace. That wouldn't be easy for him, even though he worked there. He would have had to be snooping around to get the detail the drawing had of the other floors of the palace. That kind of information could be used by a thief, murderer or the enemy of the country to assassinate the royal family.

Now her tremors had returned, but for different reason. She began to walk faster trying to run away from her thoughts. What was she going to do? How could she keep this quiet? But if she told, they might kill all of her family. Zarallon meant to give the drawing to someone else. But who? It wouldn't be valuable to Bethany, so she wasn't involved in that. It was for someone else.

Then it hit her. More than the two of them were involved and her bet was on that other man that looked like Zarallon. Really it didn't matter who it was, but no doubt harm was meant to the palace or the royal family. She was really in trouble. What if she didn't tell someone and the royal family was murdered? How could she live with that?

Any other thoughts would have to wait. She was home. Lotta was in the kitchen and whispered pointedly, "Where have you been? I had no idea you would be gone this long. Help me finish up the meal and set everything on the table. Your family is upstairs and will be down shortly."

"I'm sorry. It just took me longer than I had planned to run my errands."

"You don't have any package or items. Where did you go?" Lotta asked as she placed the dish of boiled carrots and pita bread basket on the table.

Following her with the fish and corn, Dinah was vague, "I do have some fabric, see. I know it took too long. I didn't find what I thought I might." That was a true statement.

Azariah came down with his father and mother was just behind him with the boys, "Well, we are all finally here," Hadad said. "Dinah, you were very late in coming home and Lotta was working all alone. Where did you go?" He took his place on the cushion at the head of the low table.

"Sir, I went to run an errand and it just took much longer than I had planned," Dinah offered, hoping that would satisfy him. She added, "I did find some lovely fabric for a new tunic. It is on the chair over there, see?"

Hadad was a shrewd man, "Yes, I see. What part of town were you in for your errand?" He began to fill his plate and kept a semi-interested look on his face, "Were you looking for just fabric or something in the market area?"

"No, sir. I was more in the main part of town and I found not one thing I cared for at all," she tried to act as casual as he appeared to be, also putting food on her plate and helping to serve Nathan's plate. All of this was true, so far. It was just a lie of omission. If he kept pressing her, she would have to decide whether to tell it all or to keep the secret to protect her family from being hurt.

"Azariah, weren't you in the main area of town today? I am surprised that you two didn't run into each other. Did you see your sister in town?"

Azariah was really enjoying this, like a typical brother when his sister was squirming to get out of a full explanation to her father, "Yes, sir, I was on an errand today for the priest. Dinah, exactly what street were you on? We might have passed on opposite sides," he said, pushing her even further into a corner.

"I think I was on Fish Street," she said in an outright lie. Changing the subject quickly, "Nathan is getting bigger each day, isn't he Lotta? I enjoy seeing his personality develop and he is walking so well."

Lotta jumped in to help save the girl and flashed a triumphant smile at Azariah for coming to the girls' aid. Women had to stick together. "I am so proud of him. I hope he continues to develop into a fine man. He has wonderful examples in this family," she said and changed the direction of conversation, "But I do want him to get acquainted with his real grandfather. Hadad, could I have a few days to go home and spend with my family. I would like to take Mattan with me and continue his care."

Hadad ignored Lotta's efforts to change the subject and asked, "Dinah, you think you were on Fish Street or you were on Fish Street? Which was it?" he took a bite of bread.

"Oh, I was definitely on Fish Street, but I was probably in a shop when Azariah came by," she smiled at him sweetly, but with an edge in her eye that said, 'You better watch it!'

Hadad looked at Abigail and they agreed silently to let the issue drop about what Dinah had been doing, but each knew they would talk later about where she had been this afternoon. It was not a small matter that she had been gone and no one seemed to know where. Her hesitancy to talk made the issue even more of a concern for both parents. They would get to the bottom of the issue, but it may not be tonight.

Hadad, instead, responded to Lotta question, "Lotta, please take a couple of weeks to see your family. When would you like to go? I will have Azariah take you home."

"I would like to leave on Friday before the Sabbath so I can spend a full two week's time with my parents. I can return two Fridays later before Sabbath begins. Thank you for this time away. I really miss my family."

"Good, you may leave anytime after breakfast in two days. That will give you a great time, too."

Supper finished quietly. Dinah grabbed a lamp and went to the door to call Hagi. She found her sleek, black female cat in the garden. Dinah picked her up and moved upstairs to the bedroom, undressing hurriedly for bed. Hagi curled up at the foot of the bed waiting for her to get in so she could curl up next to her master. Dinah slipped under the covers and blew out the lamp. She was comforted by the contented purring as they lay in the bed, but was still having a hard time going to sleep, thinking about what had happened today. She really didn't want to lie or deceive her parents, but she was afraid. It seemed the right thing to do to not reveal what she found out today for their safety. Finally, she turned over and dozed off.

CHAPTER 19

"Who, in Marduk's name, was that? Was she in this room?" Wakeem was back and he was worried.

"I don't think she will be a problem. She came upstairs with Bethany and we talked for a couple of minutes. I made it very clear to her that she was to keep quiet," Zarallon said.

Wakeem struck the man across the face, knocking him across the room into the wall. Wakeem followed him and punched him in the stomach, collapsing Zarallon to the floor.

Bethany was screaming, "Stop it, please."

Wakeem said, "Be quiet! Get out and stay away from Zarallon. He is my soldier and works for me. As long as you are here, he is not effective and you distract him from his duty. If you cause any more problems, I will kill you."

Zarallon was watching her face. He knew she was frightened, but she stood her ground, "I am in love with him. I promise I will not get in your way again, I just want to be with him. Maybe I can help."

Deep laughter peeled from his throat, "You, a help? In what way?"

"I could continue serving downstairs and listen for information. I will be glad to do that, if you will let me stay with him."

Wakeem considered the offer, "I will let you do as you suggested, as long as you do not cause Zarallon any problems. I do not want you around me, but you may give any information to Zarallon. If he believes it valuable, he can share it with me." He looked over his shoulder to where she stood near the door. "One wrong step and you will be dead. Are you willing to risk death to be with him?" He looked down at Zarallon.

Bethany came across the room, avoiding Wakeem and knelt to help Zarallon to his feet, "Yes," she said.

"Take him out of here."

They went to Moriah's room. They were glad to get away from Wakeem. He was a hard man and they both feared him. "Are you okay?" Bethany asked as Zarallon sat down on the bed.

He was angrier than he was hurt, "If it wasn't for your foolishness, none of this would have happened," he looked at her. "Now we have to keep a close eye on that girl to make sure she keeps quiet. We have to keep him happy. Get ready and take me to her house so I can find out where she lives and arrange to watch her." He stood up and walked back to his room to dress.

He was back in just minutes at Moriah's door. He opened it and looked in, "Let's go. We have to get you back soon for the evening meal so I want to move out of here now."

She was ready. Once outside they worked their way across the city to the lower part of town where the Hadads lived. It was suppertime and the family sat around the dinner table. They could see through the window and watched quietly as the meal progressed. They had the right house. Zarallon and Bethany watched Dinah, while Bethany filled him in on the layout inside the house. Bethany confirmed that the whole family was at the meal. Since the family was at the meal, they took this time to walk around to the upper part of the house and looked around on the upper courtyard area. They peeked inside at the upstairs rooms and then went back out to the street. Bethany pointed out Dinah's room and the room of the parents.

"Go on back to the inn. I am going to stay here and watch for a while. I will see you later tonight," with that Zarallon moved to the front of the house to see if he could hear the family and to get closer for a better view. Bethany watched for a minute, and then she turned into the night and rushed back to serve the supper meal at the inn. Cain would not like it that she had been away this long.

Zarallon could see that dinner was finishing. Dinah hurried out of sight and a light appeared upstairs. He continued to watch for half an hour and the house gradually became quiet. He moved across the hill and up the outside stairs to the entrance on the upper courtyard and listened. No sounds were heard. He would not do anything tonight, but soon he would remind her of her promise to not tell anyone. He slipped back into the night quietly.

Morning began normally. Hadad left early for a palace meeting. After breakfast Azariah had planned to go to the temple for school and then to work after lunch. Before he left, however, he and Lotta were left at the table alone. Azariah said, "You seemed to enjoy helping Dinah out of a tough situation last night. Do you know where she was?"

"I have no idea and if I did, I would still keep her confidence. We women need to stick together," she smiled at him and picked up Mattan. "All right you precious one, how about some time to wiggle around on the rug for a few minutes?" She laid him on his stomach on the kitchen rug. He happily kicked and squirmed in his freedom on the floor.

Azariah really was concerned about his sister's whereabouts, but right now his mind was on Lotta. He watched her gentle movements around the kitchen. He liked the way her pale brown hair fell out of the knot at the back of her neck. Her hair had streaks of color that were several shades of brown and it framed her face in damp strands as she worked to clear the table. She was a very attractive girl. More importantly, she had a strong spirit that he loved. She shared her love so freely with this little boy that was not her own and he admired that. He would miss her when she went home tomorrow. More than missing her gentleness, he would miss her company. They had spent many hours together and he was wondering if maybe she might like him. He couldn't admit to himself that he might like her, too. "I will be glad to help you tomorrow to get to your father's house. When do you want to leave?"

She knew he was watching her. She looked up to catch his beautiful, amber brown eyes when he spoke. "Your father said I could leave after breakfast. If you don't mind waiting, I would like to leave as soon as I can get the boys ready. We should be able to be at my home in less than an hour. Could you find someone to take that message to my parents about our arrival?" He nodded affirmatively. "You are very kind to help. I couldn't do this alone."

"Anything I can do to help you and the boys is my pleasure. When I go to temple today, I will find a runner to deliver a message to your family about tomorrow. I will check with you later tonight to see what needs to be gathered together to take by bags to your parents' home. We will hire a donkey to carry everything and Nathan can ride while we carry Mattan. Do you need any bags for packing?"

"I have everything I need for my items, but I could use two bags for the boys and their items."

"Let Dinah know or mother. They will get the bags today for you."

He stood and faced her. Azariah was a strong and handsome young man. His close presence to Lotta made her heart beat wildly. Her breath came a more little quickly as he stood near her. Neither of them moved. They were each lost in thought about how they were feeling.

"Mommy!" At this moment Nathan let out a scream that startled them back to the present. Lotta ran toward the sound and found him in the garden crying. He held a smashed lily in his hand. She picked him up to comfort him and noticed around the other lilies there were active bees. When he calmed down, she examined his hand, finding just what she expected. A large welt was swelling up in the area of the bee sting. She kissed his hand and wiped his tears. Azariah had followed her and was relieved to see that the cause of the cry was not serious. She smiled up at him as they all went inside.

Minutes later, Azariah left for the temple. On a nearby street when he walked by he noticed a man standing against the community cistern. He had not seen him in this area before. Azariah paid little attention, but wondered if they had any new families moving in. He had not heard any comments from the women about a change in their community. The women usually were the first to know since they worked in the home and knew what was happening in other families and homes in their area. He would ask his mother tonight.

"I really do love you, Zarallon. I love being yours more than anything," she whispered to him while she was sitting in his lap. They made a likely couple which included their selfish interests.

"And I love that you are mine," he tipped his face down to kiss the top of her head. "What happened at lunch today? Any news worth sharing?"

"Two palace guards were here. They have been hearing rumors about your king and his son. They also said that Pharaoh has been in the area with his men. It seems he is camping just over the Jordan in Moab. They are not sure where he is heading, but their spies hear he is might be going south to his territory running from your king's son."

"What else?"

"The king's wife and mother are remodeling the palace. The workers are the men that Eddu works for—Mishael and Benjamin. Isn't that their names?"

"Yes, and if Eddu continues to work with them, he will give us an inside track to what is happening. Great work!" He kissed her again, this time on the lips, and got up, "I will see you this evening. I need to see Wakeem." He stomped his feet into his boots. "See you later." He rustled her hair and stepped out into the hall.

"Come in," Wakeem answered the knock.

"Sir, some news from Bethany. Pharaoh is running south to his territory running from Nebuchadnezzar. Two palace guards said as much at lunch and they volunteered that the palace is being remodeled. What is Eddu involved in? Is he still helping the man, Benjamin, and son?"

"The information confirms what I have heard as well," said Wakeem, pausing to consider. "Eddu has pretended to be sick for a while. I doubt that they will have him back, but tomorrow I will have him wait outside the palace and beg to be taken back. A real sad story about his family or something."

Zarallon laughed, "Oh, begging will really upset him. You know how he feels about this man and his son."

"Yes, I know," Wakeem had a grin that made his tough features almost pleasant. "It will help keep him humble." He looked up at Zarallon, "Anything else?"

"No sir."

Zarallon left and went across town to the Hadad's house. He sat and watched for a while. It was late afternoon and very quiet. He didn't see any movement at all. He came into the garden and listened at the door. He could hear humming and peered around the edge of the window. A young woman sat holding a baby and singing, but it wasn't Dinah. He moved around the house and up the side stairs. Before he got to the top of the stair he could hear sounds in the courtyard. Edging his head slowly up to eye level, he looked over the edge of the short wall. Sitting alone with a lyre, there was Dinah. She was singing a song about her people and county.

Zarallon whispered just loud enough for her to hear, "Very lovely, young lady. You must be quite relaxed to be singing."

Dinah jumped to her feet, dropping the lyre and shattering it. She whirled around toward the sound of the voice. Just at the edge of the wall she could see his face and his evil eyes. "What do you want?" she spoke, barely able to breathe.

Looking around to confirm they were alone, he took another step up and rested his arms on the wall. She involuntarily backed up a step. He said, "I came to remind you of your promise to keep quiet about our meeting and what you saw. I was concerned that you might forget. Are you about to forget or is

146

your mind clear about what you need to do?"

"You have no worries. I have kept my promise and do not plan on telling anyone about what happened or about you. Now get out of here before I start screaming. You are in my territory now, sir." She smiled at him in confidence, maybe a little too confidently. He vaulted over the wall in a single smooth motion grabbing both of her wrists with such force that it pulled her forward and down, bucking her knees. She dropped to the ground and screamed as loud as she could.

"I will do as I please in any territory. Don't try to intimidate me again." Letting go, he ran across the courtyard, jumped over the wall and rolled to the ground. He was gone and out of sight when Lotta came up the inside stairwell.

"Dinah, are you alright? I thought I heard you yelling," Lotta called.

Dinah looked down at the lyre and at the place where Zarallon stood, "I am okay. I am down here picking up the pieces to my lyre, which I just broke. Sorry about scaring you." She twisted the truth again. This was getting to be a habit. 'Oh God, please forgive me. I am doing this to protect my family,' she prayed. "I'll be down to help you prepare dinner in just a few minutes. Let me pick up the pieces before I do."

Zarallon was about five streets away and moving quickly. He was trying to maintain a normal pace, but not waste any time. He looked around as he moved, making sure he was not followed and that he was not drawing attention. He walked fast to the loading docks at the palace. There was always work to do. He would get a lecture from the dock manager because he had not been there all day, but his explanation that he had been taking care of his sick mother should calm him down.

Azariah was going home when he saw that same man again. This time he was moving toward town at a good pace and he acted funny. He looked over his shoulder and then all around him like he was afraid he was being watched. This man was in trouble of some kind. Azariah needed to find out from his mother or the girls if he was a new neighbor. If he wasn't, why is he in the area so much?

He entered the kitchen and asked his mother right away about any new neighbors. "Honey, to the best of my understanding, all of our neighbors are here and no one new has moved in. Why do you ask?"

"I noticed a man today that I have never seen before. I saw him again just minutes ago."

Dinah came around the corner into the kitchen in time to hear just the part about 'seeing him again.' "Who are we seeing again?" she wondered out loud.

Azariah said, "I noticed a strange man, kind of foreign looking. He was at the cistern this morning and walking quickly toward uptown this afternoon. Have you heard about any new neighbors recently?" He looked her way.

She became pale and wavered slightly. Azariah reached over and took her arm. "Are you okay? Sit down before you faint. What's wrong with you? You've acted funny since that day you disappeared all afternoon."

"I am fine, just need some supper," she sat beside him on a cushion. Glad to be seated, she took a grape from the bowl on the table and regained her composure. "You know, mom, there is a new family two streets up on the right. Remember meeting her in the market?" This was true, thankfully. Maybe that would satisfy them.

"You're right, dear. They have been here about one month. I didn't think they looked foreign, however. I guess that is a matter of opinion."

Azariah dropped the conversation, but he would talk to Dinah later. He knew for sure she was hiding something and it was not a small matter. It was obvious she was worried.

"Lotta is leaving in the morning. Has she said anything today?" he asked.

"She has finished packing and I believe she is waiting to hear from you about the donkey and whether you got the message to her parents," his mom said.

"Oh, no! I was so busy and distracted that I forget to send her parents a message, but I do have a donkey that will be brought here about 9 AM. I hope the family is home when we arrive."

He left, looking for Lotta, to help get everything ready for loading tomorrow. Dinah watched him go. She knew he was not buying her story. She would need to be very careful to not react so violently next time.

CHAPTER 20

Morning was Mishael's favorite time of day. He and his father were enjoying the air and the breaking dawn while they prepared to begin retiling an upstairs bathroom. Just minutes after they had started, they noticed a man standing beside the wall watching them, as if he was trying to decide whether he wanted to come over and talk to them.

A few minutes more and he was standing beside Mishael, "Could you use some help today?" he asked.

Mishael stopped opening the box that contained the new tile, and looked more carefully at the man, "Didn't you work for us before, like a month or so ago?" He removed the board continuing to work.

Eddu shuffled his feet, trying to appear humble and answered, "Yeah. I had a little family trouble and was out of circulation. But I am back now and could sure use the work."

Misha looked at man in front of him and then tossed a look over his shoulder to his dad, saying, "You will have to talk him in to taking you back. He does the hiring." Misha raised his brow in a question, and left to take the opened box upstairs to the bathroom.

He had spent yesterday hauling tile out of the upstairs bathroom suite in the palace. They would finish that job today and get ready to add new tile. Yesterday his dad had tried to talk the Queen Mother, Zebudah, out of doing the project, "Queen Mother, the tile in the bath is really in good shape," his

149

father had tried to argue, politely with her. "It may need to be cleaned and have a few improvements. We could do some updates," but before he finished, she stopped him.

"What I would like," she turned her crimson-colored face him, "is for the workers here in the palace to do what I say without arguing. Not another word. Replace the tile and do the work ordered."

That was the end of the conversation. She had the same wicked deposition as her son. When Benjamin asked her a question about why she wanted new tile, it didn't go well. She would have her way regardless of the reasoning behind her choice. Some of her decorating choices were cause for complaints in the palace staff. She was extravagant and refused to consider other options. Pulling out that perfectly good tile was one of those poor choices.

He was remembering that conversation, as he came back down from the bathroom with some rubble. Mishael said, "That was the last load of tile."

Benjamin nodded toward Eddu, who was working on a new box of tile, taking off the top boards. "He is back with us, at least until this job is completed. After that, we will see if he is worth keeping employed."

They worked through the morning without event. Eddu was sweeping the small debris and preparing the surface for re-tiling. He had gone from the room, presumably to take down the waste.

Mishael said, "This new Assyrian tile is beautiful, isn't it? The cobalt blue with the geometric pattern is amazing. But I sure hated to break up the gorgeous stone that was here before."

"We just need to move ahead with our work. We don't make the decisions; we simply follow the plans that were given to us. Let Eddu finish up while you to go down and mix the first batch of adhesive for laying the tile. When that is ready, bring it here to begin. I will measure the space and mark for the layout. We will move from the center of the room, as usual, and can mud it tomorrow."

Misha looked for Eddu. He went down the hallway to the left toward the back stairway and around in the hall outside the bath and found no sign of him. Turning back around he glanced around to the right. Not there either. Misha turned back to the left and walked to the back stair. For claiming to want the job so badly, Eddu was sure making himself scarce. Mishael went down the back hall past the bedrooms and noticed a door was ajar to one room. He thought he saw movement. What caught his eye next surprised him!

There stood Eddu at the Queen mother's desk. He was examining the drawer contents and stacks of parchments. Mishael stepped out of sight and watched as Eddu made his way around the room looking expertly in every space. He didn't appear to be taking anything and he left the place exactly as he had found it. When Eddu turned to exit, Mishael took cover quickly behind a hall chest. Eddu was careful. He looked left and right to be sure it was clear, stepped into the hall and walked back to the bathroom area. Mishael managed to stay out of his sight until he was in the room.

He sat back against the wall and exhaled slowly. 'I think I just saw a spy in action,' he thought. He had suspected that there were spies in the palace and had discussed it with his friends. Was Eddu working here alone as the only spy? He doubted it. Mishael had heard about a guy in the loading dock that might be a spy, too. They could be working together. This was some story. He had to talk to someone about what had happened, but who?

He jumped up and went outside to mix the adhesive. When he returned to the bathroom, he said, "I was looking for you to help bringing up more adhesive."

It was obvious that while he had been outside, Eddu had finished the clean up and was helping Benjamin with the layout plan. Mishael said as he picked up tile to begin working, "Where were you?"

"Oh, I just had to step outside to empty my last load of dust and fragments."

Calm, cool and collected and a liar, too. Misha picked up tile and began working, "I see we are ready. You can bring up some more adhesive."

"Do you want me to get some now?" Eddu asked.

"No, we will go down together later when the next batch is needed. Let's just get to work." Eddu began spreading adhesive ahead of Misha. Mishael tipped his head in a questioning fashion toward his dad who agreed with a raised brow. Misha worked his mind as hard as his body that afternoon. He grew more concerned and decided he would talk to Daniel. He had seen Daniel at the palace that afternoon so maybe he could catch him after work to get his opinion of the news. They had talked before about the palace gossip that there might be spies. He knew his other friend, Azariah, believed there was a spy in the palace, too. Now, Mishael had seen with his own eyes that the rumors were true. He needed to share that with his friends and get their ideas about what should happen next.

It seemed to Mishael that the work-day would never end. He needed to find Daniel and talk with him about what he saw, so he left Eddu finishing up one side of the room and went outside where his father was cleaning up tools coated with adhesive, "Father, I know we are just about done. Could I leave you with Eddu to finish? I really need to talk with someone before they leave the palace."

His dad tossed his head, "I will see you at supper time." And he turned back to cleaning the tools from the day in one of the troughs behind the palace.

Misha went inside to the central meeting room. He saw Daniel and Gideon were still working, but it appeared they were closing up the day. He stopped at their table, "Good afternoon, friends," he smiled and noticed their work. "Are you about to finish up your work today?"

Gideon said, "Hello, young man. It is good to see you. Our day is about done. Are you and your father working in the palace today?"

"Yes, sir. We are on a remodeling job for the Queen Mother." Moving quickly to his reason for his visit, "I wondered if I could take Daniel a little early? I would like to spend a few minutes with him to discuss some things."

"Son, how much do you have left to finish?"

"I believe I am good for today. It would be good to talk to Mishael for a while before supper, if I can."

"Alright, boys, go ahead. I will see you later," with that Gideon dismissed the two.

As they walked out of the palace, Daniel asked, "What's going on, Misha? You never ask to take me from my work." Daniel wondered.

"Let's cross over to the temple and get Azariah, if we can. I would like to discuss something with the two of you."

"This must be serious, if you need to see both of us. I am very curious," added Daniel.

They walked across the shallow depression and were there in about five minutes. They found Azariah in court area transcribing records from today's business.

He turned on his stool. His two very best friends were talking as they came toward him. He stood and greeted them, "Hi, brothers. What is the occasion to bring both of you here this time of day?"

"Azariah, we are here to get permission for you to leave. Can you leave now?"

"Now? Maybe. Let me check to see. Father, you remember Daniel and Mishael?" Hadad acknowledged the boys. "Could I call it a day and go with them for a short time before the evening sets in?"

Gideon agreed and the three guys went down the steps from the temple. They took the lower exit and stopped at a vendor under the temple mount walkway to buy some strong coffee and a bun. They sat outside the vendor's area.

As they walked to their seats Mishael began his story, "You know those conversations we have had about spies in the palace?" They nodded, but didn't speak. They were enjoying to food too much to talk. "Well, today I saw one in action."

They were walking away from the temple mount in the Tyropean Valley. Azariah froze, choking on his dry bun and went into a coughing fit. It took a few seconds to catch his breath. Daniel was walking slightly ahead of the others and splashed his coffee as he spun around to face Misha.

"Are you kidding? What did you see exactly? Did you know the person?" he shot questions at Misha like kids throwing rotten eggs. He was really excited. An actual spy!

"You know that man who worked for us for a while and then disappeared?" he waited to see if his two friends remember. "This morning he showed up with a sad story about a family member being ill and not being able to work. He has been gone for over a month. He wanted his job back."

"Misha, get to the point. I am interested in your business, but I am more interested in the spy. Tell me the other story about this man later," Daniel was getting impatient. He was ever the practical one.

"I AM telling you about the spy! He is the man we hired back!"

"Unbelievable! You have a spy working for you? Did you tell your dad?" Azariah asked, finally being able to breathe again.

"No. We didn't have much time alone and I wanted to talk to you both first. I may tell him tonight. Today I couldn't find Eddu, that's his name, when I needed him to do a job. I thought it was strange for a man desperate for work who had just been rehired to not do everything to show his dedication. When I went to look for him, I passed a room with the ...." and Misha continued the story up to the point where Eddu lied to him. "Well, what do you think? Does that sound like a spy?"

"Absolutely. I can't imagine a more convincing set of circumstances. You must tell your dad tonight. He needs to tell the palace guards so they can pick him up and then your dad needs to fire him. If you aren't careful, they might think Gideon is part of the plot," Azariah said adamantly.

Daniel shook his head 'no' He wasn't as sure, "It might be wise to keep him employed and watch his actions."

They talked about it for a few minutes and Azariah decided, "Daniel is probably right, but I still think they might think you were part of the group spying if you don't let someone official know."

"That is a frightening thought," Misha commented. "I think that father should talk to the officials right away, but if he fires Eddu he'll know that he has been found out and will escape. Besides that, the guards will loose the chance to follow him and see if there are more spies. I think we should keep him working for a while, too, and see if we can find out more. I have to admit that it would be hard working next to him knowing that he is betraying everything and everyone we love," Misha stopped and looked into the distance. "I don't know if I am a good enough actor to cover my feelings that well."

They were sitting in a small square by the vendor's place, Azariah said, "I believe you are very capable of covering your feelings." Azariah smiled at him. In a sudden change in the conversation, he added, "Aren't you doing that right now concerning my sister?"

His two friends laughed and Daniel slapped Misha on the back. Azariah couldn't have surprise Mishael more with that comment than if he had hit him. He simply looked at them. He didn't know what to answer. Some friends they were sitting there laughing at his discomfort. He was not someone who talked about his feelings, "I don't want to talk about girls; I want to discuss spies!"

Azariah continued, "You know we have been friends since we were young boys. I know you and how you think. I have watched you with many girls, but my sister is special to you, and don't deny it. You go out of your way to see her or do things with her, don't you?" Azariah challenged him.

It was silent while they sat for a minute. Daniel looked at Azariah, thinking maybe they had stepped over the line in asking that question. Mishael did not like to reveal his feelings, but they were his best friends. He finally spoke, "I suppose you could be right, but I think you are overstating the facts. I have simply helped her a few times. Besides, you are one to talk. You're crazy about that girl who is living with your family. You usually talk about her each time we're together. She is gone now, isn't she? Do you miss her?"

This time it was Azariah who was uncomfortable. He knew Misha was trying to change the subject and get the focus off himself, "Okay, you are right. We ARE getting too personal, aren't we? And don't try to switch the subject again. We are talking about you and my sister right now. I think you ought to consider Dinah as a good wife candidate. She would be a handful to deal with, but she has a heart of gold and a good mind. And you know she also sings and plays the lyre. Do you ever consider her as a possible mate? I know I sound like a matchmaker, don't I, but I do love my sister. Nothing would make me happier than for one of my best friends to also be my brother-in-law," Azariah smiled a sincere smile at his friend.

Daniel chimed in, "I said that very thing recently to someone about Dinah being a handful to manage, but Mishael would more than qualified for that job," he said that as a compliment.

Azariah laughed and agreed, "He could handle almost anyone."

Mishael ignored him, "Okay. You have both made your point. I do like her. But I want to get back to my question, 'Do you miss her? That girl who lives with you, Azariah?'"

"Yes, I do miss her and I am surprised about how much. We are getting closer. I hope she is thinking about me, but it is hard to tell with girls," he looked intently at Misha, "Alright, you have my answer, now, what about Dinah?"

"Since you have been open, I will tell you both that I think about Dinah as more than a friend. I know she is young, but not too young to be considered a possibility. I wonder what she thinks about me? I get so few opportunities to see her. Does she ever mention me?"

Daniel and Azariah exchanged knowing glances. They had been around many times when he came up in her conversations. Misha questioning sounded as unsure as a little girl, "Yes, my dear friend, yes," said Daniel. "She often asks me how you are and what you are doing. She wonders if you have a girl that you like or if you are serious about someone else. She respects you a great deal," he smiled at Misha, who looked truly pleased. "But, we aren't going to brag about you for her. If you want to know how she feels, you talk to her."

"I will talk to her. Maybe I can arrange something with your father soon. I am humbled and thankful she likes me. I had no idea she was that interested. Unless we happened to see each other, we have had little private contact. It is always easy to talk to her and we seem to have much in common," he looked at Azariah. "You said she was musical, didn't you? I would love to hear her play the lyre and sing, if she would," he paused, as if he could imagine her sweet voice. "Do you think Hadad would allow us to spend time together?"

"My father thinks highly of you, but you would have to ask him yourself. I cannot speak for him. I would hope he would be pleased you're interested. As far as what Dinah might do if you asked her to play and sing, I really don't know. She surprises me more often than not."

"Okay, friends, can we talk about something not so painful for men; something exciting, like spies?" Mishael asked. They laughed and sat back and relaxed. It would only be a few more minutes till they needed to go their separate ways. After the coffee and buns were finished, he continued, "You think I should tell dad tonight?" Their questioning looks made him laugh, "About the spies I mean?" he looked at them with a twinkle in his eye.

Azariah raised his eyebrows and chuckled, "Yes, for now tell him about JUST the spies and save the romantic interests until later. Right after supper would be good, so he has time to consider his options."

Daniel stood up, "Tomorrow I will find you upstairs, right?" Misha nodded he would be there. "Good. Bring your lunch and I will come to get you to eat with me. It will give us a chance to watch and talk. I am going home. See you then." He put his cup with theirs, hoping one of them would return them all, and went home. He picked up his pace as he walked away from the park.

Azariah stood and so did Misha, saying, "Tomorrow, then. Can you join us in the palace at lunchtime?"

"I doubt I can get away, but I could meet you here on the way home for a brief update. Would that work?" Then he picked up their three cups, "I'll return these."

"Sure, see you tomorrow right here after work. If something happens, don't wait longer than half an hour or so. We can try again the next day." They shook hands and went to their homes.

The next day Mishael was eager to see Daniel for lunch. He hoped that Azariah might surprise him and show up. He had told his dad last night about what all had happened. His father was so wise. They decided to inform the palace guards. His dad was meeting early with Robron to explain the situation and what had been observed. While his father was away in the morning, he kept a close eye on their hired man.

Benjamin stood in the loading dock until he spied Robron, "Sir, I have important news to speak with you about. Could we meet privately?"

The commander snapped to attention, "Sir, I am at your service." He pointed to the office just a few feet behind him, "Would this office be acceptable? It is quite private." It was the commander's office which was located in that area.

"Yes, this is quite fine."

They stepped inside closing the door behind them, "Please be seated," encouraged Robron.

"You know my son and I are currently remodeling the bath suite for the Queen Mother, Zebudah?" Ben paused to wait for Robron's acknowledgment that he knew who they were. "We have a hired hand, Eddu-aran, a foreign man of unknown origin. Yesterday began queerly with Eddu returning after one month's absence and requesting his old job again. We were very skeptical about his absence, but really could use the extra man-power, so we took him back. His sad story was that his mother was ill and he had stayed out with her." He paused here to see if Robron was keeping up with the story and understanding.

"Go ahead, sir, I am interested. Any idea of his country or accent?"

"No, his accent is strong, but he speaks Hebrew well. It is not an accent from any area around us or from an Egyptian area. Maybe it could be from a northern country," Benjamin proposed.

"Possibly. Please complete your account," Robron encouraged him.

"I sent my son to find him in early afternoon, because he had disappeared. We thought that strange, since he seemed so eager to go back to work. He should have desired to make a good impression, but he was not bothering to do so. While Mishael was looking for him, he passed Zebudah's room. The door was ajar and someone was inside. Mishael paused to see who it was. He was shocked to see Eddu rummaging around the desk and other storage areas in the room. He completed his foray and came back to the bath, not knowing he had been seen. When asked later by my son where he had been, he lied. I believe he is possibly a spy and up to no good, sir," Benjamin was not surprised that Robron was excited. That had been his exact reaction last night when Mishael shared the story with him. Benjamin explained Mishael's discussion with his two friends and the advice they gave him at this point.

"No doubt you are right, sir. We have suspected spies were here, but have only followed one and have yet to catch him in any questionable actions. But this account is absolutely one of intrigue and guile. If you don't mind, it would be of great help if you continued to employ him and let us watch for other odd behavior or other contacts he may have. Would you agree to that? I know it will be hard for you maintain normal behavior. I know that is asking a great deal, but the information we could gather might be vital to national security," he waited for Benjamin's response, thinking all along that this could be very dangerous to the man and his son, if the spies found out that they knew and had revealed the secret.

"It would be my pleasure and privilege. I would love to aid in any way to reveal the cowards who would spy on Israel to seek harm to our great country and holy city. My son is in total agreement. We discussed that very possibility last night. I understand, as does he, that this may be dangerous. We will try not to reveal that we know his secret at any time," he stood and shook hands with the commander. "If we need to contact you again, would it be advisable to come here or do you think we need to make different plans?"

"I believe that we might be observed talking at any moment in this area. The man we have followed works the docks behind you. He has not come in yet today, so I think we are safe this time. In the future, you cannot come here without possibly being seen. If you have any message, send Mishael to the outer court area. You said that Daniel knows about this, so let's use him. Find Daniel and have him explain to his father, then they can work with us. When they can arrange it, they will get word to one of the guards using varied methods."

"Concerning your man, I would like for you to point him out to me so I can recognize him by sight. I will also try to show you who the other suspected spy is. If at any time you were to see them talking, that might be a clue of their working together," Robron waited. "I have one other question. When did Eddu disappear from your service? Was it near the date for the raid on the tribute payment?"

After a moment of consideration, he said, "Yes, it was, almost exactly that date. Why is that important?"

"If he is involved with Zarallon, the other suspected spy that is the same time that he took a leave to deal with a personal problem. He returned about a week later. Maybe they were involved in the raid. I would think some of the robbers had to travel with the money, so maybe your man was out of the area longer. I do have one soldier who saw some of the men in the raid. I will put him to work to investigate. He might recognize some of the people they would be in contact with."

"I can see you are a man with a good mind for this work. This situation gets more suspicious with each bit of information," Benjamin commented and then stepped toward the door to leave, "I will follow your suggestions if any new information comes to light." They shook hands again and Ben opened the door to go out of the office into the dock area.

Robron took his arm before he stepped out the door, "After you exit keep walking as if I was just walking behind you, but we were not together. Slow down near the wagon and I will point out Zarallon to you."

Benjamin walked ahead casually looking at supplies in the wagon. As Robron passed him, he slowed up and said, "See the man coming across the floor. The one in the center is the suspected spy." He did not stop and in a couple of seconds Benjamin went up the stairs. He had seen the other spy clearly. He would be careful to note if they had any contact.

When Ben entered the bath area, Eddu and Daniel were mudding the walls in the bathing area and around the flat sink. The commode's wooden frame was also tile-covered and mudded. Eddu did nice work. He must have had a profession at one time related to a field of carpentry. Too bad he was a spy now.

They both noted his arrival, "Good morning. Sorry I am late. Is everything going as planned?"

"It's fine and we're moving along well. Are you planning on joining us or are you going on to do something else, father?"

"I have a short meeting with Zebudah for her to review our plans. If that goes well, we will be finishing this job tomorrow."

Ben left and the two men continued, "So, how is your mother now, Eddu? I know you just returned from caring for her and I hope she continues to improve," Mishael bated him.

"She is well," Eddu did not break his motion in mudding at all.

"Does she live in the area?" Mishael said, but he thought, 'I can play his game.' He hoped his conversation sounded natural. He also scooped up some specially mixed mud and angled it across the wall.

"No."

"Did you have to travel far to take care of her? Some travel can be so hard in this terrain," Misha moved the mud around wiping off the excess. He kept working and talking as if it was all part of chit-chat among fellow laborers.

"My travel was of no hardship to me," Eddu hated to be cornered and considered how far to carry his lie. It was clear Misha had some questions about his absence and was fishing for information. "I prefer not talking about my personal life," he turned with a glance that said, 'Drop it!', but said out loud, "I am a private man." With that comment he moved away to mud across the room from Misha.

Misha was pleased. He had gotten all the answer he needed. If Eddu could have answered, he would have. His irritation indicated his unwillingness to give an answer. Oh, the plot was thickening with each passing day.

At lunch Misha and Daniel met at the top of the steps in their hallway which lead down to the first floor kitchens. As they ate they kept one eye on the bath in case Eddu left. They had just about finished when they heard a quiet sound. Looking toward the bath Daniel saw Eddu, for the first time, in motion moving across the hall into an alcove. What was he doing? Maybe someone was waiting there.

He stepped into the hall and in the next step he was out of sight. Men could be heard talking, but not well enough to understand their words. Misha moved closer to listen while Daniel watched the hall right behind him.

"I was able to verify where each family member lives in the house and to draw a rough plan on this parchment that I took from one of the rooms. I think this finishes the floor layout for the whole palace. That builder's son, Misha, was asking questions about my absence this morning. Wanted to know about my 'mother,'" whispered Eddu to someone out of sight, "but I gave him a simple answer and moved away. Do you think someone is on to us?"

"He is just curious. We have been very careful so I doubt anyone knows what is happening," commented the unseen voice. "You are to stay here until further notice to gather any bits of information possible." Misha didn't recognize the other man's voice.

"All right."

Zarallon added, "I'm going out on a mission from the boss. He has been on edge since that snoopy girl came to see Bethany about her baby the other afternoon. I'm going to her home to give her a little incentive to remain quiet and stay away from us. I will check in with you in a few days; sooner, if needed." It grew very quiet except footsteps were heard moving away. Misha and Daniel took two steps back down the hall and then began walking toward the bathroom, as if they had just come up the stairs together. There just wasn't time to hide. Maybe Eddu would believe this ploy.

As Eddu stepped out of the alcove, Daniel appeared to turn his head from a conversation with Misha, "So how much longer will your project take?"

"I don't know. Dad went to find that out this morning and I haven't..." They both stopped and looked at Eddu. He nodded and went back into the bath area.

Misha whispered, "Well, we have confirmed there is another spy in the palace. I wish we could have seen that guy's face."

"We also know there is a third man, 'the boss', who is staying somewhere else and that he is worried about a girl," said Daniel as he tried to recall the rest of the conversation. "Did he say the name 'Bethany' as well?"

"Yes, he did. We need to follow up on that. I will meet with Azariah on the way home and give him the details. Can you join us?" asked Misha.

"I don't need to see Azariah and you can just tell him we will talk when he comes to my house. We have a special family dinner tonight and the Hadad family is our guest. We will have a good long time to visit then," Daniel's family often shared time with the Hadad's. Tonight was the beginning of the celebrating of two weeks called Shavuot.

They stayed in the hall for a minute, and then Mishael said, "That was close. We had better move apart and not arouse any questions. See you later." Daniel went down the central stairs that had just been vacated by the unseen voice.

With that settled they both returned to their jobs and finished the day. Benjamin was at work already with Eddu when Mishael came back. They finished their work and discussed the plans for the bath that had been modified somewhat when Ben came back from his meeting with Zebudah. It would be several more days before all the remodeling was completed.

Misha met with Azariah later that afternoon and told him the event of the day. He also told him that Daniel said the two of them could talk more tonight.

CHAPTER 21

The evening was a success for Mary and Meriel. They had the house beautifully decorated for Shauvot which recalls the lovely green of Mt. Sinai when Moses received the Ten Commandments. They brought in several potted palm trees in the dining area that were lovely. Around the room many flowers had been added, both those that were cut and those brought in for the occasion in pots. The room and house smelled like a garden and the food only added a more festive feel and smell.

Before the meal the traditional blessing was given, but they also added the reading of the Ten Commandments. They had asked Daniel to read them this night. He said, "I am reading from Shemot, chapter 20 and verses 2-14 from the Holy Law of God—

1.   "I am Hashem, your G-d, Who has taken you out of the land of Egypt, from the house of slavery. You shall not recognize the gods of others in My presence."

2.   "You shall not make a carved image nor any likeness of that which is in the heavens above or on the earth below or in the water beneath the earth. You shall not prostrate yourself before them nor worship them, for I am Hashem your G-d - a jealous G-d, Who visits the sin of fathers on children to the third and fourth generations, for My enemies; but Who shows kindness for thousands [of generations] to those who love Me and observe My commandments."

3. "You shall not take the name of Hashem, your G-d, in vain, for Hashem will not absolve anyone who takes His Name in vain."

4. "Remember the Day of Shabbat to sanctify it. Six days shall you work and accomplish all your work; but the seventh day is Shabbat to Hashem, your G-d; you shall not do any work - you, your son, your daughter, your slave, your maidservant, your animal, and your convert within your gates - for in six days Hashem made the heavens and the earth, the sea and all that is in them, and He rested on the seventh day. Therefore, Hashem blessed the Day of Shabbat and sanctified it."

He paused here and looked at the two little ones, "Jothal, you must know the next one. Please quote it for me."

Jothal stood and in a confident voice, quoted, "Honor your father and your mother, so that your days will be lengthened upon the land that Hashem, your G-d, gives you."

"Excellent, son," said Gideon to his younger boy. "I would hope you could say them all, but the next five would be good."

Jothal continued his quoting of God's Law,

6. "You shall not murder!"
7. "You shall not commit adultery!"
8. "You shall not steal!"
9. "You shall not bear false witness against your fellow!"
10. "You shall not covet your fellow's house. You shall not covet your fellow's wife, his manservant, his maidservant, his ox, his donkey, nor anything that belongs to your fellow!"

When he finished, all of the family bowed for God's blessing as Gideon washed his hands, prayed over the bread and the meal.

The food was superb with the combination of milk and meat foods carefully prepared to keep them from mixing. They had a cream of asparagus soup and crusty flat bread with heavy creamed goat's milk spread on it. The ladies cleaned up the areas changing the dishes and table linens while the family retired to wait the customary hour before the meat course. It was not good to mix the milk with the meat course from God's command to not cook the lamb in the mother's milk. Time was necessary to clear the milk course, and let the body and mouth clear of any dairy foods. They continued with roast chicken, yams with crushed figs, lentils, green beans and a loaf of soft round bread with olive oil.

This First Fruits Feast always brought great joy to all. Of course, many visitors were in Jerusalem to worship at the temple during this time. It was one of the required visits in the Hebrew faith. The temple mount was crowded the last few days with pilgrims coming to worship. Some would stay for the full two weeks in the city and in tents around the area.

The evening had been a blessing and the conversation was pleasant. Most important, Salme and Jothal had behaved themselves, talking with the adults politely and with good sense. Everyone settled into a quiet time of visiting before dessert and asked Dinah to play her lyre and sing one of her many songs:

We celebrate our Feast of Weeks
We bring to you, our God, this gift.
Our harvest of first fruits, of barley and wheat
And to you our praises now we lift.
We remember Moses when he received your Law
We remember the mountain so lovely and lush
Accept our praise as to you we bow
And humble ourselves with reverent hush.

Praise Jehovah! All glory to him.
We lift our voices in holy praise.
Praise Jehovah! With joy we sing.
Our anthem, now, to him we raise.

Hadad stood and went to his daughter. He kissed her cheek, "Dinah, my sweet one, that was lovely. You truly have a gift with music."

"Thank you, father. It is my joy and my best method of honoring our God. He deserves better than I can ever give to him," she said, laying the lyre beside the stool.

Cache entered the room and nodded to Meriel, who stood, "We will have coffee and cake for all who wish. Children, right after the dessert, Cache will take you upstairs. The day is getting late." Meriel invited everyone back into the dining area where Cache had prepared everything to be ready to serve. They enjoyed what Mary had baked. It was a wonderful spice cake with flour, meal, ground almonds, crushed dates, cinnamon, cloves, honey and eggs. The coffee was strong and black. It was a fabulous way to end the meal. Praises abounded to all the ladies for their excellent services and food.

Right after dessert, Daniel asked to be excused. He and his friends went to the roof. "Dinah, bring your lyre so we can enjoy more of your music," requested Daniel as he left to go up the outside stairs. Dinah got the lyre and followed the boys outside.

When Azariah and Daniel got to the courtyard, they had a surprise waiting. Misha was seated on the wall enjoying the quiet.

"Friend, what are you doing here? You should have been with us for dinner. It was great," said Azariah.

"When Daniel told me about the 'party' tonight, I just couldn't resist joining you all for part of it." He leaned close to them, "Besides, it is a chance for me to see the girl who just came up those stairs over there." They turned to see Dinah approach with her lyre.

"Misha, what a lovely surprise. How did you know about this dinner party?"

"Today Daniel and I ate together and I also talked with Azariah after work. It was just too good a visit to miss. Besides, I heard you are a great musician. I was hoping that I would get to hear you play and sing," he looked up at Dinah with a lost puppy look in his eyes.

"Oh, don't be silly. I am just making joyful noise to the Lord. I am not convinced that others find the music that great," she loved his compliment, but wanted to sound humble. "Besides, what would I sing for you?"

Big brother helped her along, "How about that song about Jerusalem? It fits this time well." They all encouraged her.

"Okay. Give me a couple of minutes to think it through before I sing. You all talk."

The guys rehashed the day's events and talked about a couple of issues until she was ready.

"Here is my song to our city..."

Look at her walls so tall and strong, her gates that bar the way
To travelers and tyrants. She stops those who betray.
Secure and happy, here we dwell. Protected from all harm.
No enemy shall conquer her. No need for the trumpet's alarm.

Jerusalem, Jerusalem. You've stood the test of time.
Prophets, priests and kings of old have walked your streets sublime.
Homes of stone and marble, palms and olive trees,
This city of hills and valleys will always be home to me.

On a mountain high and rocky, stands the temple to our God.
The center of our city, its beauty we applaud.
There we recall his loving ways and look to him for grace.
One day in heaven's glory we will see our father's face

"Dinah, that was unbelievable. You wrote that, words and music, yourself? I am truly impressed," said Mishael.

"That's enough. You will give her a swelled head. She will think she is really talented," said her ever loving brother. They all laughed.

"This was a beautiful night and the food was delicious. Your family prepared an excellent celebration, Daniel," Dinah praised him. He returned a smile to her for the praise.

Azariah agreed, "This was just a wonderful celebration and time with your family only made it more blessed." Again the nod of thankfulness from Daniel.

"Daniel, do you think your mom would share some of her cake with Misha?" she asked.

"You can be sure she would. If you are going to get some, also tell them about our surprise visitor. They will be happy to know he is here," said Daniel.

Dinah left the boys to their conversation. She returned shortly with the cake and coffee, "Everyone downstairs wishes you well, Misha. They said you are welcome at any celebration." She handed him his food and sat beside him on this spring evening, "The weather is mild, without a cloud to cover the moon. I love to be outside on nights like this." Dinah was speaking to herself, mostly. She got in these romantic moods often. Spring always affected her this way. Once the weather warmed up and the flowers began to bloom, she began to daydream about her future husband and family, her home and her perfectly dreamy life.

Azariah teased her, "Yes, isn't life just so perfect without a care in the world?" The men laughed as she came over to her brother and swung at his arm. He quickly caught her hand and pulled her to his side on the roof wall. "My dear sister, you have the heart of a romantic and musician. I hope someday you have all your dreams fulfilled," he hugged her shoulders, then he moved to the other wall were Daniel was seated.

"Fill me in on what happened in the palace today. Any new information gathered about our spies?" he asked Daniel as he sat down. Misha came over to join them. He wanted to know everything they thought.

Dinah really could not hear their conversation, but they were intent on whatever was being discussed. She really hated to be left out of anything. They seemed to be carrying on about some issue that was taking far too long, as far as she was concerned.

She thought to herself, 'If they had just talked for a few minutes, I would be content, but they just seem to go on without end. This is really rude of them to sit and whisper. It is not fun sitting on the roof with other people who are not including you in what is happening. They were not visiting with me at all. I was hoping Misha came to see me, but I guess he came to see the boys.'

She finally got up and moved near enough to hear them, acting nonchalant, so that she hoped they think she was just strolling around the rooftop on this lovely evening. She picked up on the conversation at this point.

"Eddu talked with this guy that we couldn't see, in the alcove of the stairwell. He said the 'boss' was upset about some girl and about another girl named 'Bethany.' They are watching this other girl's home and using intimidation to keep her quiet about something she knows or saw," said Azariah to his friends.

She had moved close enough to hear that last statement and it took her breath away. Her whole body froze in panic. They were talking about Zarallon, Bethany and her. The guys were discussing the details of her 'secret' and must have known much of the story already. They didn't know she was the one being spied on. She couldn't move and she couldn't breathe.

She just had to breathe, but her mind didn't seem to be able to force her lungs to work. Gathering all her strength, she took a breath. Instead of sounding normal, it came in a set of broken, panicked gasps. However, it was not enough to prevent her from becoming faint and crumbling into a heap.

Her gasp caused the men to turn toward her, just as she crumpled. Misha picked her up and took her to a bench on the roof. He put her head in his lap and patted her hand.

Azariah sat down by her feet. When she was breathing at a more normal rate, he asked, "Dinah, are you all right? You fainted. You sounded like you were holding your breath. You used to do that when you were a little girl and you were frightened." She still couldn't speak

"She is trembling violently," said Misha.

He looked at Daniel, who shrugged. Azariah continued, "Dinah, I am more concerned than ever about what's going on. The last time you acted this way was in the kitchen when I told mom that someone stranger was in our neighborhood," he looked at his friends and explained, "I had seen him snooping around twice. I told her I thought he had something to do with...," Azariah stopped mid-sentence and stared at his sister. The light was dawning in his mind. "Oh, Dinah. No wonder you are frightened. Oh my goodness!"

His friends just looked at each other and then at him, Daniel said, "What are talking about now? Did something come to you?"

Azariah explained, "The spies and Bethany and 'the girl'...she is the one they were talking about intimidating, the girl who had been to see Bethany. Oh, my dear sister, it was you! You were the one who saw something about our Bethany and these spies." He looked up at Daniel who was hovering above them, "The last time we met, Daniel, you remember she overheard our conversation about the spies and wanted to act on it then. I believe that is exactly what she did."

Dinah began crying now. Azariah motioned for Misha to change places with him which he did. Azariah just held her and waited until she grew calm again. He was still looking up at Daniel who was nodding in agreement.

She was so relieved to finally have the secret out and to have someone she could talk with about what happened. She had been terrified. She still wasn't sure her decision to keep quiet was the best choice, but it was the only one at the time that made sense.

When she was calm enough, she sat up and rubbed her eyes, "I am glad you figured this out, brother. I have been so afraid and I didn't know what to do."

"Tell me everything that happened when you met Bethany," Daniel said, sitting down on the stone pavement lining the roof, listening to her every word. Misha sat on the bench. The men felt both amazement and fear. It was more serious than they could have believed. The family was in definite danger from these spies. But the greatest awe they experienced was for Dinah's courage and her foolhardiness.

"Her story matches perfectly with Eddu and the other spy's conversation," said Daniel. "She is definitely the one who has caused such concern for the 'boss.' Dinah, who did you see in that room?"

She said, "Describe the spy, Eddu, for me."

Misha chimed in, "He is tall, muscular and wears an eye patch. He is foreign, maybe Oriental mix."

"That is not Zarallon. He is average height, maybe 5' 9", but very strong. He has brown hair and a sharp, pointed nose. He also has a small round beard."

Daniel asked, "Did you see anyone else, besides Bethany and the inn patrons?"

"No. I raced out of the room toward home as soon as he released me."

"What do you mean 'released' you?" Azariah questioned.

Now she had revealed unnecessary facts. This would add anger to the mix of other emotions her brother had shown. She hesitated.

"I want to know two things; what do you mean 'released' you and how do you know he is so strong?" Azariah was on his feet facing the bench.

"Well...I...he..." she hated to tell him this part.

"Dinah, I want the whole truth and I want it now," he practically yelled. "This is not a game and we could all be in danger. It is vital that we understand who we are dealing with. Now out with it!" Azariah was angry.

"Take it easy on her, Azariah. She is trying to tell us," said Misha protectively.

"I got scared when I saw him in the hall. My panic worried him, so he forced me into his room. I started to scream. He grabbed me and held his hand over my mouth until I promised to be quiet, then he threw me into a chair, asking all kinds of questions. He was mad at Bethany for having the baby. It had caused them to be involved in her mess when she left him behind. And he was mad that her act brought me to the inn. Then later, he held me very tight and threatened me telling me to remain quiet about what I had seen. He is really very strong," she looked at them shaking her head up and down for added effect, like they might not believe her.

Azariah spun away from her and slammed his fists down on the retaining wall again and again. Daniel got up and stood beside him talking calmly. He understood the fear Azariah was feeling for Dinah and what could have happened.

Azariah was thinking, 'That man was and still is frightening my sister on a regular basis, and he dared to touch her. He had no right.' The more Azariah thought about them in that room, the more his anger burned. 'And she was such a fool.' He was also genuinely concerned for everyone's safety.

"Azariah, I understand," Daniel whispered to him quietly. "I am sure she fails to see the gravity of the situation like we do."

She heard Daniel, "Stop talking about me as if I am not here. I know exactly how much danger I am in. I am the one he threatened, grabbed and followed. That is why I've not told this to anyone, to protect them. I was the one in the room and on the roof when he threatened me."

Azariah stood up straight and blinked several times, as if it would clear his mind of her most recent admission. He looked at Daniel and then turned around slowly this time, not sure he had heard her correctly. He said calmly, "On what roof?"

Why, oh, why didn't she learn to keep quiet? He was even angrier now. What would happen when he knew Zarallon was at their home and on their roof? She wasn't sure she wanted to see him any angrier than he had been when he was hitting the wall. If he hated her now or was afraid for her, she really wasn't sure, then this new information might put him over the edge. She looked at Misha for reassurance.

He gave his approval, so she was about to continue when Azariah yelled, "WHAT ROOF?"

"Ours!" she yelled back.

He sat down on the wall and just stared into the night. Daniel walked over and sat with Dinah, "Tell me what happened at your house."

She related the story and included that Zarallon grabbed her again and pushed her to her knees. She figured all the harm had been done that could be and she may as well finish with whole story.

Daniel put his arm around her shoulders and pulled her to him. It was somewhat easier to be neutral when it wasn't your home and your sister. "Dinah, you have been very brave and very foolish. You could have been killed or worse. Your family is still in danger because of what you know."

"I know, but I cannot go back to before and not 'see' what I have already seen. What are we going to do?" She began to cry again. Azariah was quiet. She wished he would yell at her again or just speak to her. He still sat staring into the night as if he wasn't listening or even interested in what was happening. She left Daniel and Misha and walked over to Azariah.

"Dear brother, I am so sorry. I was only trying to help with Bethany, Mattan and the spies. Please don't be angry with me," she begged through her tears.

He reached over and took her hand. For the first time she could see tears in his eyes. She came closer and sat on his lap. She wrapped her arms around his neck and they wept together. She kept saying, "I am sorry. I am so sorry."

"I am not angry with you. I am afraid for you and for us, and I am furious that any man would lay a hand on you, other than a hand of gentleness."

"I am so worried. They have a map of the palace and now they know what rooms contain the royal family. What do we do next?" she whispered.

"Dinah, have you not learned your lesson?" asked Azariah, standing up and practically dropping her on the pavement as he began pacing the roof's perimeter. "We, meaning Daniel, Mishael and I, will handle this. You are to stay inside and at home. Speaking of home," he stopped pacing and faced her, "what did you tell Lotta that day you were late?"

"She knows I went to town, I was late and I wasn't shopping. That is all she knows."

"Good. I am glad that is all she knows," Azariah didn't want to be worried that someone might also be after the girl he was in love with. Thinking about the events of recent weeks, it was clear to him that he did, indeed, love Lotta. Her absence from their home seemed far longer than two weeks to him. He would talk with her father to ask for her hand in marriage very soon, he decided.

Daniel spoke, snapping Azariah's thoughts back to the present, "Let's summarize what we know. Bethany is staying at Cain's Inn. She likes a man named Zarallon, a spy also living there. He probably knows the other spy named Eddu who works in the palace with Ben and Misha. There is a third spy, the boss, who knows about Bethany and Dinah and he has floor plans to the palace and rooms for the royal family. Zarallon is spying on our home and Dinah because the boss is worried about Dinah and what she might know. I believe that is everything."

Dinah spoke up, hesitantly, "Well, do you remember asking me if I saw anyone else? I did see another man carrying a bag. He was on the inn stairway coming up to the second floor. He was taller than Zarallon, built like a bear; foreign looking and he had a look in his eyes that sent terror through me. I passed him as I was going out of the inn and turning into the alley."

They all knew they had just heard a description of 'the boss', and now they knew he lived at the inn, too. No wonder he was worried. If they all lived in the inn, then it were likely the inn's owner also involved. Dinah was indeed a danger to his gang of spies and she knew his location. She was in grave danger and so was the family.

"I just thought of one more thing," said Dinah. "Do you remember I told you that Bethany took me upstairs to a room? She said it belonged to Moriah, her sister. She has a sister working as a waitress in the inn, too."

CHAPTER 22

Garridon sat in a corner at a small table. He was not a soldier today; he was a spy for his country. His clothing was that of an Egyptian merchant which was an easy cover for him, since he was fluent in the language. His mission was to try to spot anyone in the inn from the tribute raiding party.

The waitress appeared and he asked, "You have beef?" hoping they didn't. He could claim to need more time, allowing him a legitimate reason to wait. He spoke to the waitress with a heavy accent. When she responded in the negative, he asked, "Wine, cheese and bread for now, and let me think about what to order." He continued to review the room.

Several men were at the bar and the tables were busy with lunch patrons. None caught his eye as having been part of the raid. The waitress, he assumed her to be Moriah, returned with his appetizer and he nodded his thanks. He cut a large wedge of cheese and tore off a hunk of flat bread. At least the food was good in this den of spies.

His eyes drifted toward the movement at the back of the inn. He could just see a man in the kitchen area talking with the cook, but his face wasn't clear. Garridon got up and moved that direction maneuvering between the tables. At the back he pretended he was going to the outhouse. As he passed, he got a good look at the face. It was a man from the raid. He went on to the outhouse, so he wouldn't draw suspicion. It gave him a few minutes to try to remember the face and its involvement in the raid. He knew the descriptions of Zarallon and Eddu and the man at the back of the inn was not one of those two. He was shorter than Garridon and more barrel-chested with the look of a man with experience--tough and fit, set jaw line, hardened eyes. In the raid he was at the front of the group that used swords.

Garridon opened the door and peeked around the corner. He saw the man come out the back door and go upstairs. Waiting until he was inside, Garridon bounded up the stairs. He opened the door carefully looking to make sure all was clear. He poked his head inside, then moved down the entry hall and looked down the hall to his right. He saw the hall door two doors down on the left close. Finally, he had a location to search. He was making progress. He went back into the inn.

The waitress returned to his table and he ordered that lamb with vegetables and a large flask of red wine. He could enjoy his meal now. He and some others would stake out the back of the inn and look for an opportunity to get into the room.

This Sunday morning the first floor of the palace was quieter than usual, but upstairs Zebudah's bed chamber was active with renovation. Eddu was washing the walls with a beautiful shade of vermilion while seamstresses in the workrooms were finishing new drapes and bed covers in red and gold. 'What extravagance!' Eddu thought! Each swipe of his brush brought greater anger. He couldn't wait until his opportunity came to wreak havoc with the royal family, and the haughty builder and his son. Every day he worked for them ate at his control. He yearned to take revenge and he hoped that day could be soon.

Since Misha was out this afternoon buying supplies and the father was ill, he could search freely. Moving to the king's room, he made his way around and through the furniture. Nothing caught his eye. The King's valuable papers must be in a secure location in the palace. He left and went down the back way to the main floor. He passed quietly into the servants' area and to the loading dock stairs. He moved to the end step and looked around the room. It was empty. He crossed the dock to the door and exited. Zarallon was just outside.

"Any news from the boss? You said last week that Nebuchadnezzar is running from Pharaoh and I wondered if you had an update," Eddu asked.

"Pharaoh's army was defeated at Carchemish and he fled, heading south, probably to this area. Nebuchadnezzar is following him. Pharaoh doesn't have a chance. His men are too battle weary to put up a fight, if caught."

"What about Syria? If Nebuchadnezzar follows his typical pattern, nothing will be left by broken bodies and rubble after he passes through."

"I would agree. He is probably taking control of everything he passes during the pursuit. I think it is just a short time until he reaches us here in Jerusalem. This king is a fool. He believes his city is invincible because of his God. Well, no god can stand up to the great Nebuchadnezzar," Zarallon tilted his chin up and raised his face in defiance. Turning the Eddu, "What's new in the palace?"

"It is quiet, except for that prophet that keeps spreading bad news about this kingdom. All you hear from the leaders is that he will be dead, if he keeps on talking. They have another prophet that is saying the exact opposite of him. It is easier for them to believe the prophet of good news than the prophet of bad. The good-news-prophet has their respect and he is trying to talk the leaders into jailing the other prophet. What's his name? Jeremiah, isn't it?" He looked at Zarallon who agreed to that name. "Interesting, looking at it from our side. We already know that we, 'the power from the north', are likely to be coming this way soon. If I had to vote on the true prophet, I would choose Jeremiah, the one they want to put in jail. His words seem to be true."

"I agree. Good for us that they aren't that smart," they laughed quietly. Zarallon stood and walked a few steps. Turning back, he added, "Okay. Stay alert and I will see you later this week." Zarallon faded away into the shadows. Eddu walked around to the kitchen servant's entrance and went back to work.

Misha had been at the door just inside the dock area. He hadn't been away buying anything, but he assigned himself the duty of following Eddu wherever he went. The idea the spies knew about their prophets and religion was a revelation. He really didn't think they were that aware of what went on in this community. What a strange business this was! This meeting with Zarallon now confirmed that at least three spies were at work in the city.

Zarallon went to Hadad's house to keep watch. Everything appeared normal, and it was very quiet. He couldn't see inside, but none of the ladies appeared outside which was good. Dinah was too afraid to come outside and that was exactly what he wanted. He went back to the inn.

Standing in the shadows was one of Garridon's men who had followed Zarallon since he came out of the inn this morning. Had there been any danger, the soldier would have broken his cover to protect this family. They had been brave to come forward with this information to help their country. He would count it a privilege to eliminate one of the spies himself to protect this loyal family and his country. However, right now, that would not be necessary.

Zarallon arrived at his room and sat down to eat. Moriah laid out the table with food for their supper, so he ate to his fill. He was famished. 'It had been a good day,' he thought as he lay back on the floor palate. 'That girl was behaving and the spy game was working like it should.'

Wakeem was asleep on the bed. He had evidently been drinking, which happened often and made him very sleepy. It was not often that a soldier had such an easy life of being fed in an inn and sleeping in a bed. Zarallon drifted off to sleep thinking how much he enjoyed the extra rest and this quiet lifestyle.

Wakeem awoke with a bad headache the next day. Too much wine last night. He could see that food had been eaten. Zarallon had obviously come in and eaten last night and now was asleep on the floor. But the problem was Wakeem hadn't heard a thing, which was very dangerous for a soldier. Sleep too soundly and your throat could be cut, even by your own man.

Dressing quickly, he went downstairs to get some breakfast. He had been here long enough that he knew his way around. Hablin had made coffee, and bread and cheese was on the counter. As he ate he thought through the today ahead.

Cain came in the back door and got his food. He sat with Wakeem, asking, "What is your next move?"

"I was just thinking about that. It's what I am NOT hearing that has me worried. Something is not right. Have you noticed how quiet it is? No free flowing talk or dropped information?" Wakeem thought out loud, downing his cup of coffee and going back to the kitchen for more. He leaned on the counter and asked Cain, "Have you seen any strangers in the area or has anyone been asking questions in the dining room?"

"No," trying to remember if anything seemed out of order. "We have had travelers, merchants and soldiers, but none have been curious or asked questions. Business is as usual. Why are you suspicious?"

He rubbed his beard and considered, "We should be hearing more general rumors. All the conversation contains nothing of value to us. It is like the well has run dry. In a town this size that usually means someone is up to no good, or maybe someone knows we are here," he explained.

Cain thought, 'Yeah, we are the ones up to no good!' But Cain could see Wakeem's point. Thinking about the conversations he usually heard at the bar, he had to agree that this was not normal for the rumors to run dry. He said as much, "Wakeem, you could be on to something. When conversations don't include politics and palace gossip, which means that all of the people in power are guarding what they say. The gossip has been stopped like a cork in a bottle." Cain was thinking back to the lack of information he had heard. Wakeem was definitely right. It was too quiet.

They finished breakfast in silence. Wakeem went out back to the wash room, cleaned up, and went back into the inn. He wanted to talk to the girls. Maybe they had heard something. They were eating with Cain when he returned. He sat back down to ask them the same question that he asked Cain.

Moriah responded, "I have seen many of the regulars with a scattering of newcomers. No one stood out." Bethany nodded agreement to her sister's comments as she listened.

"What kind of newcomers?"

"Merchants and a few travelers, but no soldiers. The patrons all ate their meals and left as usual. Really, nothing was unusual. We have some new people, but we get travelers all the time."

"Doesn't the inn usually serve a lot of soldiers?" Wakeem asked.

Moriah considered the question and agreed that it was normal to have soldiers now and then. She said as much, "I guess you are right, but I hadn't noticed they were missing until you asked. Do you think that's a problem?"

"Maybe, maybe not. Be alert. I sense something is wrong, but I am not sure which of our covers might have been breached," he left and went to wake Zarallon. They would go to the caves today to talk to the men for an update on what was happening in the northern campaign and what plans were being made to join up with Nebuchadnezzar. Some of the men had just returned a couple of days earlier. They had delivered the tribute money safely to Carchemish and would have current news and instructions. He was eager to get on the road. This town was stifling him.

When he entered the room, he went over to his sleeping roommate and kicked him in the thigh. Zarallon woke with a start and jumped up ready for a fight. "Calm down, boy. It's me. Now get ready. We are riding to the caves in Adullam today for news."

Wakeem packed his bags, since they might be gone several days. The soldiers were staying in Adullam again, but not in the same cave area as the previous visit.

Zarallon dressed and went down to eat quickly. He told the group of their plans and that they would be gone several days. When he finished out back, he rushed to the room to get ready. In another half an hour they were both at the stables outside of town saddling their horses. Within the hour they were on the road to Adullam.

Garridon was at the palace. His man had reported that the two spies were on the move. They went down the same path they had used for the tribute payment raid. He guessed they would be using the caves again, just different ones. He remembered that road and the raid. He was looking forward to the day he could get his hands on the men who had killed so many of his soldiers. His men were quietly following the other two spies. They would give a full report of what they learned later. He was sure they would catch them all soon. They were waiting for the Hebrew government to give clearance to take the spies into custody. It was important to have all the information about who was truly involved in the espionage before the capture.

Garridon went to the alley behind the inn. He found what he expected to find; one of the young men who had originally caught the spy was watching the back door. He moved in behind him and spoke quietly, so as not to scare him too much, "Mishael, what are you doing here?"

Misha jumped up from his hiding place in the shed, hitting his head on a ledge. "Who are you?" he asked, rubbing his head. He just knew it was another spy who had found him out.

"I am one of the palace soldiers who survived the raid. They sent me to see if I recognized anyone. My commander pointed you and your dad out to me. He told me about how you caught the first spy. That was excellent work. Have you found out anything while you have been watching the inn?" Garridon asked.

Still rubbing his head he returned to his position to watch, and said, "As a matter of fact, I saw the man I believe is the 'boss' yesterday. He looked like a man described by a girl who has seen him. I saw which room he is using," Misha waited for a response.

"I think I know which room, too, but show me the room you believe to be involved. My men saw the two spies in the inn leaving town this morning. I think I can safely inspect the room without any fear of being seen."

Misha stood and looked him over carefully. Nothing about him seemed to cause concern or a question to Misha, although he wasn't dress like a soldier. He decided to believe his story. The two of them climbed up the back stair and down the right hall to the door on the left. Garridon cautiously opened the door to find the room empty and dark. He and Misha stepped in quickly, closing the room door behind them.

Lighting the lamps they moved in opposite directions around the small space. It appeared that the men had taken most of their things with them. Little was left in the room. As Garridon looked under the bed, however, he noticed a glint of light. Reaching under the bed near the wall by the headboard, he discovered a knife partially in its scabbard. It had a curved blade with an ornate handle; inset was a large green stone and an inlay of mother-of-pearl. The leather sheath definitely looked foreign to him. It might have been made of a cow's hide. He put it inside his coat. They were disappointed at how empty the room was. Maybe the knife would reveal some clues. They put the lamps back where they had been and left as they had come.

"I am going to the palace to show the knife around. Do not reveal that you know me, if we should meet. At least, not until this spy issue is resolved," with those words, Garridon disappeared behind the shed. Misha just stood there staring at the place where he had been. That was some meeting. A stranger drops into his hiding place and back out again just a quickly.

Well, no use wasting the rest of the day. These two spies were gone. He wanted to see if Eddu was there working. Maybe he had gone with them. If he was still working, Mishael could find out more by working with him. He returned to the palace after making several quick purchases of supplies. Buying supplies was a good excuse to be gone during the day but it wouldn't do to return empty handed.

Eddu and Misha worked together without conversation throughout the morning. Benjamin was in and out working and having meetings. The painting would be completed by the end of the day. They were doing the trim in a pale cream wash that would blend with the new bedding colors well.

At lunch Misha and his father went down to one of the food vendors in the Tyropean Valley below. After they ordered the lunch special, pita bread with a cheese and vegetable filling and ale, Misha asked, "Dad, what have you been up to all day? You went in and out several times."

"I was meeting with Robron in the kitchen. He is planning on taking Eddu while the other spies are out of town. If they can keep the capture quiet, then maybe the other spies will return and think he ran out on them or just disappeared."

"How are they planning on taking him?"

"Tomorrow when Eddu comes to work, I will send him down through the back stairs through the kitchen to the outside to get some supplies. When he is on the back stairs, Garridon will be the top and Robron will come from the bottom and trap him between them, hopefully, taking him quietly. They have a hidden room to use to interrogate him and keep him separate from other people. If they are successful, they won't alarm the other spies."

"Sounds like it might work. Quick and quiet with a minimum of danger to others. I will be on the top of the stairs as back-up behind Garridon. They probably are trying to do this alone and not tell any other soldiers to avoid the word leaking out. I can help them, in case it doesn't go as well or smoothly as they are hoping."

"They don't need your help. I think the two of them could handle most any situation. Let's get busy and finish this painting project today," he said. They finished eating and went back to the palace.

Morning found Misha and Benjamin working bright and early. They completed the painting yesterday, but they touching up the trim and cleaning up today until Eddu arrived and was sent on his errand. They had been working an hour and were wondering where Eddu was. He usually came on time.

After two more hours of waiting they decided that something had happened. The four men met in the back hall. Robron spoke, "Where is he? I thought you were going to send him down first thing this morning when he arrived?"

"He never arrived this morning. Could he have found out somehow?" said Ben.

"I don't know how he could have known anything. We were very careful."

"Yesterday when we were meeting in the kitchen, did you notice anyone else around who might have heard our conversation?" Ben continued.

Robron thought back. He did hear the outer kitchen door close, but didn't see anyone come in. He said as much to Ben.

They went to the kitchen and talked to some of the staff. Maybe it would reveal who would have been coming in at that time that could have heard their plan. It would also allow them to make sure it was not one of the kitchen staff that had revealed their plan.

After an hour of interviewing anyone who was there yesterday, they determined that none of the kitchen staff had heard anything. They did find a lead, however, "So this man hunts for you and comes in a few times a week to bring in his game. Was he in yesterday when we would have been here?" Robron asked the chef.

"Yes, sir. He came in with several pheasants and a large number of rabbits. He had delivered those items and gone to his mule to bring in other game—a beautiful, big deer—when you came down for your talk with Ben. He may have opened the door and stopped when he heard you talking. You were standing in that area weren't you? Near the door?" explained the man.

Robron nodded, "Where is this man now and what is his name?"

"Timath is a hunter. I am not sure he has any particular place in town. I have seen him eating in the kitchen a couple of times with that man who works for you, Ben. Maybe that man could tell you where to find him," said the chef.

They were all stunned. They had missed one of the spies. That explained why Eddu hadn't shown up for work today; he had been warned about the trap by his friend and, probably, fellow spy. Anger bubbled over between them casting blame wherever they could, but ultimately deciding they were out maneuvered by the spies. There had been a fourth man that they hadn't known about and that gave the spies the upper hand.

Getting back on keel, Robron asked Ben, "Do you have any idea where Eddu lives?"

Ben looked toward Mishael with the question in his eyes, "Dad, I have no idea where he lives. The other spies were at Cain's Inn, but I never saw Eddu there."

Robron made his decision, "We will bring Cain in and ask him some questions. He appears to be our only contact with the spies. The other men have escaped, for now, but we will eventually catch them. If we can find Eddu and Timath before they leave town, we can capture them before they inform the others who left yesterday. Let's work quickly and without anyone knowing, if possible." Robron took the kitchen staff aside to warn them about not discussing anything about what had been discussed with them. He made it clear that if they wanted to keep their jobs, they would keep their mouths tightly closed.

The people who had the most knowledge about the inn were standing in front of him. He turned to Garridon, "It is still early enough that the lunch is just beginning. You and Mishael go to the inn. Mishael, you go inside to eat and Garridon, you wait in the back for a chance to grab Cain when he comes outside. If we can get him away without incident, maybe we can salvage this mess." It was clear that Robron was still angry. This had better work this time.

Mishael had just about finished his meal and was looking for a way to get

Cain outside without drawing attention to himself, when he heard some commotion at the back and saw Hablin come in from outside. Hablin motioned for Cain to move toward the back door. Mishael dropped some coins on the table and went around to the back by way of the alley. When he got there he saw Garridon, dress again as the Egyptian merchant, in a heated argument with Levine, the laundress.

"Sir, I did not wash your clothes. Are you a guest here in the inn?" Levine asked.

"Of course I am, you fool. Why do you think I am asking you about my clothes? Would a total stranger come up and ask you for their laundry?" he was playing the part of a drunken tenant well. His yelling had drawn out the cook, who in turn got Cain to come out.

"What's the meaning of this? Stop harassing my laundress," Cain yelled. He looked the merchant over from head to toe, "I do not know you and have not seen you in the Inn as a guest. I think you are mistaken about where you are staying and who would be doing your clothes." Cain made the situation clear to Garridon.

Garridon appeared to quiet down. He shook his head from side-to-side, as if trying to clear the cobwebs, "I guess I could be confused. Maybe I had a little too much wine with lunch." He continued to speak a little slurred and his quietness caused the crowd to lose interest and go inside. Levine left and moved around the shed to her wash pots. Garridon was alone with Cain, who was about to give him the 'boot.' Garridon walked unsteadily to his left down the alley even further away from the inn, with Cain close behind.

Cain wanted to be sure the man left the area, "You come back again and I will beat you even more senseless than you are now," he said to Garridon.

Cain had just passed the stairs. Mishael decided that this was the right moment to draw his attention away. He stepped out from the other end of the away from Garridon, "I heard a commotion. Everyone okay back here?" Mishael came from the other end of the alley. Cain's attention was distracted toward Misha and he turned to see who was asking that question. That gave Garridon his chance.

Garridon made his move quickly. He pivoted, losing all appearance of drunkenness. Cain was a big, strong man and an error in judgment might make this a long battle for Garridon. When Cain turned his back toward Mishael, Garridon jumped on him. He wrapped one arm around Cain's neck and the other around his side. Garridon collapsed Cain's knees with his, knocking him down. Garridon stayed on top of him, while Cain was thrashing around. Garridon leaned forward putting his right forearm on Cain's neck and grabbing his free arm, Garridon pulled it behind Cain's back, and surrounded Cain with his legs.

Cain was stunned. This drunk was suddenly very sober and very dangerous. He struggled to turned over and get his arms freed. He tried to pivot and bring his legs up under him to get some leverage. But Garridon was experienced and none of Cain's moves were working.

Garridon kept his knee in the middle of Cain's back and had both of Cain's arms pulled up tight and high behind him in a couple of minutes. He said, "Mishael, get the rope from the shed and tie his wrists." Misha worked quickly. While Cain's hands were being tied, Garridon took the fabric piece from his pocket and tied it around Cain's mouth to keep him silent.

It was over in just minutes. They jerked Cain to his feet and went down the alley. At the end of the area was a wagon where several men appeared to be loading supplies from a nearby store. They tossed Cain into the back and covered him with a tarp. Misha and Garridon jumped in and the wagon moved down the street. Only a total of ten minutes had passed. They had managed to keep the event quiet.

During the day, Cain revealed all he knew with the 'persuasion' of the soldiers. Robron was disappointed in the amount he knew, but at least they had a picture of what was happening. Cain did not know where Eddu lived and he had only met Timath once or twice. As far as he knew, Timath didn't live in town. It looked like the spies had gotten away, this time.

The advantage for Jerusalem was that the leaders knew the spies by name and by sight. They also knew the spies had a palace map and that their security was breached. They had shut down the spy ring and stopped the information flow. Wakeem and his men would need to move on or get information from another source. The palace leaders and security personnel had made alternate plans.

Wakeem was surprised to see Eddu and Timath ride into camp. But after spending an hour with them he was even more surprised at their near capture. They had been very lucky not to be caught. It was obvious to him that their usefulness here was finished. It was time to return to Nebuchadnezzar, if they could find out where he might be.

Wakeem knew the palace would make changes in some security plans and some room locations, but the floor plan was still the same. The leaders of the city and the layout of the city were familiar to them. Whatever Nebuzaradan needed, if he came to take the city, they could now supply. Come morning, the base camp would be empty and they would go to meet their general.

CHAPTER 23

Azariah was very nervous and his palms were sweating as he waited with his father to talk with Abram. A few days after Lotta had returned from visiting her parents, he had told her of his love.

He said, "During the last two weeks lots of things have changed. We found out about Dinah and the spies, we confronted Bethany and we faced the fear of being hurt by enemies of our country. These events have given me a new perspective on my life and on the lives of those I care for. When I heard about a spy coming to our house, after my concern for Dinah, my first thoughts were of you. I wanted to make sure you would be safe.

"Thank you for caring. That means a great deal to hear you say that."

Azariah added, "One afternoon my friends asked me about how I felt about you. I had a hard time admitting that I had feelings for you, but I finally realized I did."

"And how do you feel?"

"I'm getting to that. I noticed that your absence left me feeling lonely and missing our times of conversation."

"You could get that feeling from Daniel leaving, too. Do you care about him?"

Azariah sighed. She was not going to left him get by with suggesting how he felt. She wanted him to come right out and say it. "With all that has happened about the spies and Dinah's involvement, I was afraid for her life.

The night she told us about what happened I realized that the other fear I was feeling was for you and the boys. It was then that I realized that I was falling in love with you," he said watching her face carefully. "I don't know how you feel, but I hope you are at least interested enough to give our relationship a chance." There. He had finally said it.

She just smiled and then she kissed his cheek and said, "Oh, Azariah, I have been praying to God that you would feel for me what I have been feeling for you. I do love you, too. I had a wonderful husband who gave me this precious son, Nathan," she looked down at her son asleep on her knee. "Now God has blessed me with the love of another wonderful man. The preciousness of God's love to me sometimes overwhelms me. He has taken care of me like a kind husband until he sent you along. You are strong and kind, and I know you love the two boys I am raising."

She responded to him as he leaned down to kiss her. "Lotta, I would like to ask your father to marry you. Would you be willing to be my wife?" He was still standing above her looking into her face.

"You will make a wonderful father. It would be my privilege to be your wife, if father would agree." They kissed again, and then she asked, "When are you and your father going to see him?"

This conversation was a while ago and tonight was that night. He was sitting beside his own father on Abram's roof awaiting for him to join them. It took several days to arrange a time together.

Finally, he heard Abram on the steps and stood waiting impatiently. "Good evening, gentlemen. It is beautiful tonight with a warm gentle breeze and great to be alive at this time of year," Abram said, making small talk to cover the silence. He already knew why Azariah and his father were here. Every father who loves his daughter knows when she is in love. He had just spent two weeks with her. She once again loved a man. This was a good man with fine character and he was faithful to the God of their fathers. He would make an excellent husband. However, as much as Abram liked him, he wasn't going to let him know that. That would be too easy. A gentle smirk played across his face thinking of the fun this would be. A couple of hours of bantering back and forth was valuable practice for a Jewish soul. Yes, tonight would be an excellent night.

"Yes, sir, it is lovely," responded Azariah. "I love this time of evening with my father at the end of the day. We often sit together and just relax in the silence of each other's company." Azariah talked freely about his father, even in his presence. That was easy. It was this other thing they had to arrange, that was so hard to do. "Sir, I wondered if we could talk about Lotta for a few minutes."

"Slow down, my boy. We have all evening. Let's just enjoy visiting a while and get better acquainted," suggested Abram.

"I agree, son. There's no rush," Hadad smiled as he considered how this old man wasn't going to let Azariah have such an easy time asking for Lotta's hand in marriage. Good for him. Hadad remembered the night he had met with Abigail's father. He chuckled to himself because he had used the same irritatingly slow method of drawing out the inevitable question. This would indeed be a fun evening for the two men as they watched the young man struggle to be cordial and wait for the right time to ask. He leaned back against the cushions on the bench and relaxed. 'May as well get comfortable. It was still early and the evening was going to be long,' he thought.

"Hadad, I understand from Lotta, that the two of you work in the temple and keep the books," stated Abram. "Have you ever been there when the prophet Jeremiah was around? I find some of his prophecies extremely interesting and somewhat fearful."

"Yes, we have both heard him speak on more than a single occasion. He was warned to stay away from the temple and the palace, but I believe he is answering to God and does not care about men's warnings. Recently we heard him in the Zion gate when we were near. He was saying that the men who 'trust in man shall not see when good comes... but shall inhabit parched places.'"

"That is a pretty somber statement," said Abram.

Then Hadad added, "'Blessed is the man who trusts in the Lord and whose hope is in the Lord. He will be like a healthy tree.' Now how can a man speaking with such a Godly message be telling a lie? I truly believe his message, and that frightens me. His prophecies carry dangerous and fearful warnings of destruction and loss of our country and city."

"I, too, have heard about things he has been saying. Although his warnings are hard to accept, I cannot allow myself to not believe him. With the sad things he has told us will come to pass, I would prefer not to believe him. It is not what I would choose to believe will happen to us and our fair city, but I can not choose to believe only one prophecy and disbelieve another. So, I agree. I think him to be true and a man of God," Abram said.

In the presence of elders, younger men were to remain quiet and listen unless spoken to. Azariah agreed with what he had heard. He would voice only those opinions he was asked for.

"Azariah, what do you think about Jeremiah? Is he a true prophet or a liar?" asked Abram.

"Sir, my father and I have been sure he is true. Although in the temple we hear many others, claiming to be prophets, who disagree with his foretelling of doom. They say that God has always protected his temple and He will not abandon it to foreigners now. But I heard Jeremiah say that the people have done their abominations in 'the house that is called by my name.' I think we have desecrated His house already and he will not protect us just because it is here in Mt. Zion," he said, thinking he answered well and hoped Abram thought so, too.

Hadad smiled at Azariah and then spoke, "We pray to God for his protection for our families and for our people. If indeed God is intent on this course, then only he can spare our lives from the destroyers, whoever they are. It does sound like they are from a northern kingdom, probably Babylon. You deal with many merchants at your shops. What do you hear from them as they travel in the surrounding areas?"

Abram thought often about what he had been hearing. It caused great concern on his part. His shops specialized in decorative wares for the home, especially rugs. Vendors came from all areas marketing their wares to him. He responded, "I have heard things that made my ears ring. From the north there are fierce battles being waged for territories. After Nineveh fell in Assyria, I know Babylon came into power. They are an awesome and violent people when they are in battle. If they are the future conquerors for our city, then we are undone. They will not spare the people or the property, and they take many captives." At this point Abram stood and walked away from the father and son.

It was obvious that these thoughts had already been on his mind before and he was not happy, "I believe we will be in a battle for our lives and our fair city soon. I keep hearing that the conquerors are moving more in a southerly direction. Vendors from Syria have said the Chaldeans have conquered many cities in their area already."

"Whew, that is really much closer than I ever imagined," said Hadad. Now his mind was also racing. The prophecies were becoming more real by the minute. He and Abram grew quiet and contemplated what that might mean for Jerusalem and its people.

Azariah was more concerned than ever about his city. With this flow of the conversation, he wasn't sure that tonight was the right time to ask for Lotta's hand in marriage. It seemed to be too selfish a matter in light of what events might unfold in the near future for Jerusalem. Azariah was weighing the idea of postponing the question until a more appropriate time, when Abram turned to him, "Son, I believe you came to talk with me tonight about something important. What was on your mind?"

Now what? If he did ask, the father might think he was insensitive to the political situation and not grant his approval, because Azariah was so brash. If he didn't ask, then he might be thought of as weak-willed. He looked at his father, who nodded his approval.

Azariah looked back to Abram, still hesitant.

"Son, I have known my daughter's ways since early childhood. I have seen her grew into a fine wife and mother. When she was home in the last weeks, I saw in Lotta a peace and radiance that is evident in all women when they are in love with a man. It may be a time of great unrest, but life does go on. We cannot stop and assume anything ill of our heavenly father until the time he brings it to pass, so talk to me about your heart."

What a great man Lotta's father was! No wonder she was such a fine woman. "Sir, since Lotta has come to stay with our family, I have seen her open her heart to a young boy who is not her own and to love him freely. He clings to her as a natural child to its mother. God has blessed him to not know his true mother, for she is unworthy and unwilling to raise him. Lotta has become one of us, but instead of loving her as a sister, I have grown to love her as a woman. I cannot imagine my life without her being part of it daily. I love her laughter and her gentleness. I love the comfort of spending time with her. I love looking at her and having our eyes meet," he stood, "I would count it a privilege if you would allow me to marry your daughter?" It was said, finally.

"That is a noble request, Azariah. How would you support her and the boys?"

"I am working now as apprentice to my father. I believe I am ready to earn a fine living in the field of a scribe. As far as living locations, I would be glad to remain with my father's house, or we could build, if you would prefer," answered Azariah.

"When a couple begins life together, it is usually just two people. You will be providing for four people and you will need all the help you can get to aid in raising the children. I admire you, my son, for your courage and selflessness. It takes great love and confidence to take a woman to your heart, but it takes even greater strength of will to take in a complete family. You love a woman who has a child of her own already. And then another child who does not belong to either of you has been added to the scale of responsibility. Do you have any concerns about these issues?" asked Abram.

"Yes, sir. I have many concerns about providing and being a good husband and father. But I have not a single worry about having enough love for those three you have just mentioned. I could not love either boy more if they were issued from my own blood line. Mattan is our gift and Nathan our precious boy. Life would be a struggle to live without these dear ones." It grew quiet. He was so tense. Was Abram considering his answer? Azariah hoped it would not be that difficult a decision for the father. His pause made Azariah worry.

Azariah waited for someone, anyone, to speak. With all the talking that had taken place earlier, why were they so quiet now? Had he said something wrong?

Hadad came to his side, for he was still standing, "Son, let's sit down for a minute. Abram, are there any questions you have for me?" He guided the young man to the bench where he had been sitting and sat down beside him.

"No, friend. I believe I have an answer right now. It would be my pleasure to grant the hand of my daughter to your son in marriage," he stood and crossed over to the father and son sitting across from him. He shook both their hands, and then said, "Please tell her for me when you return home how happy I am for her. We will arrange the details for the wedding and living arrangements at a more convenient time. You know, gentlemen, the time is getting late and you have a distance to go to your home. I will bid you good-night and we will talk again soon." They said their good-byes and Azariah and Hadad walked toward the stairs. They would be home within the hour and still have time for a good night's rest.

"Well, young man. You are soon to be a husband and father. Congratulations," said Hadad, once they were on the road.

"I think I am still stunned. It seemed like he would wait forever and then all of a sudden he says 'yes' and calls it an evening. I wanted to talk about the details. I feel like we left too many things open-ended," Azariah said.

"I promise we will organize things soon. Don't worry. We will work out the bride price and the house arrangement. I think you should build. Four people need a house to call their own. That is a full-sized family."

"I agree, dad. I will talk with Mishael and Benjamin. We can draw up some house plans. Do you think I could take off time to help the building go faster?

"I am sure that would be fine. Now let's hurry. The ladies will be on pins and needles awaiting our return with an answer. If we had tarried longer to talk, it would be too late to have any time with the family. Now, wouldn't you rather be with Lotta than talking about her?" Hadad asked with a grin. He put his arm around his son's shoulders and they finished the walk home in silence.

As predicted, the ladies were in the living area working on various projects. Lotta was mending Nathan's shirt, Dinah was folding clothes and mother was shucking corn for tomorrow's meals. They stopped what they were doing and looked up as if someone had attached all their heads to a single set of strings, pulling them up like a puppet.

The men smiled and sat down, removing their tunics and dusting themselves off. They took off their sandals and were about to leave to wash their feet. The ladies looked at each other with disgust. What were they waiting for? They just kept piddling around.

"Oh, Hadad. Really. This is no time to wash your feet. You know we are dying to know what happened," said Abigail to her husband.

Finally, Hadad spoke, "We had a good visit with your father tonight. The discussion was edifying. We all decided that we agree that the prophet Jeremiah is a true prophet and we should believe what he is saying," he said all of this casually while he put away his sandals.

Azariah was smiling, but did not make eye contact with anyone. The ladies were unhappy. They were not interested in any information, no matter how significant, unless it dealt with the question on all their minds. Lotta looked at Azariah, but he was looking at his sandals. She was furious. She stood and stomped into the kitchen, expecting someone to follow and explain. Nothing happened, so she returned and stood in the doorway, fidgeting with her sash.

"Father, we cannot stand it any longer. What did Abram say about Lotta and Azariah?" Dinah ran over the Lotta to stand with her.

"Oh, that. Why, of course, he said 'yes,'" said Hadad.

"Yes. Thank the Lord," said Abigail.

"Yes! I am so happy. Finally, I have a sister," said Dinah, hugging Lotta's neck.

Azariah stood and walked toward Lotta. She moved away from the door and ran into his arms. They just held each other, while Dinah danced around them. Lotta wept with glee and with relief. She would have been broken hearted if the answer had been anything else.

"Did you work out any of the details for the wedding? The date? The place we would live? Tell me everything," said Lotta to Azariah, whom she was now holding at arm's length.

"Hold on, dear one. Your father felt it best to continue the conversation later, since it was getting so late. We will answer those questions at another time," he answered her. "And besides, like father said coming home, I would rather spend time WITH you and than talking ABOUT you."

"Well, I for one agree," said Abigail, standing. "It is late. I am so happy for both of you, but tomorrow is another day and we will have hours to discuss wedding plans. I will see all of you tomorrow." Abigail put the corn in the kitchen, then came back to picked up the folded clothing. She and Hadad went toward the stairs. She turned, "Dinah, come with us. It is time for you to be in bed, too."

"Mom, I want to visit with them more about...."

"Dinah! Now, please. Give them some time alone," Hadad commanded.

Dinah followed them up reluctantly. She glanced over her shoulder to see Azariah and Lotta hold each other closely and kiss sweetly. They were standing just as they had been when she danced around them.

CHAPTER 24

Weeping could still be heard in Panias. The moans of the dying pierced the afternoon air. Small groups of people stood around the picturesque village while Nebuchadnezzar's army took stock of the spoil they had collected in this unwalled village near Dan. This area had the distinct disadvantage of being farthest north in Israel, which meant it was a target of frequent raids from northern invaders. Most of the inhabitants were defenseless farmers. None had weapons or training for war. The battle had been short and many dead or dying were strewn around village. The Chaldeans gave no advanced warning. They had ridden at night and raided early in the morning.

At the same time other bands of Nebuchadnezzar's men were raiding nearby villages and cities. Dan, their neighboring walled city, was under attack and it was rumored it would fall soon.

"Mother, what is going to happen to us?" asked a young woman. She wept each time she saw the image of her brother pierced with a sword. They had not seen their father at all and had no idea what had become of him. The men had tried to defend their families and property and most had died in the effort.

The same question her daughter had just voiced came to the mom's mind earlier. She was too frightened by the answer she was thinking to tell her daughter, "Stop crying," was all she said. "We need to be alert and I cannot think with you out of control." Mom did not want to tell her daughter all she expected would happen. She refused to admit it. Saying it out loud made it seem like a fact. It was too much to comprehend right now.

Vicken came up on horseback to that little group of women, "All of you standing by that cistern move over there with the group near the stone embankment." He waited while they moved. Any officer who spoke the language was used to handle captives. It made things easier than motioning.

He followed the group as they joined their neighbors, saying, "We will stay here tonight and move to join the large camp of captives in the valley tomorrow. For now, get comfortable where you are." He left his soldiers guarding the group of 200 old men, women and children. Most of them would make worthy slaves. Farmers were usually more fit than city-dwellers.

By noon the next day they had moved into the valley at the main camp. Vicken's small contingent brought the total number of captives to over 1, 000. They had captured many villages in northern Israel already. There was also a camp in Syria that held captives from their campaigns in that area. Soldiers would move the Syrian captives to Babylon next week. These Israel captives would likely be moved from this area before the full campaign was completed. Vicken left his small group with the guards and rode to the center of camp.

"What's the word on the battle at Dan?" Vicken asked Zarallon as he dismounted by the fire.

"Going well. They have climbed over the wall and are eliminating the inhabitants in fine fashion," said his friend, handing him some coffee.

They settled down on a rock near the fire. Vicken asked, "What is the next city we're going after? I want to join the battle. Yesterday was so easy I could almost have conquered the village by myself." They both laughed, but Vicken was serious. The villages were really not a battle; they were more like a massacre. He enjoyed the fight with an opponent. Killing was no joy when no personal victory gained.

"Most of the troops are going to Megiddo tomorrow. It is a large city on a high hill and controls everything coming from the north. It has good access to the Intercoastal Highway which will help us control what is allowed to move through this trade route."

"Will we go there directly?"

Zarallon answered, "No, we will take our time and capture other cities on the way. It will take several days."

"Have we found out where Necho is?"

Zarallon nodded, "Yes, he was seen with his small band of men in

Megiddo about five days ago. Looks like he has managed to stay far enough head of us that he will make it home without us catching him. However, we will continue moving through this area and toward Egypt. Eventually, we can defeat him on his own land."

"So Zaradan and Nebuchadnezzar will continue the campaign even if we do not catch him? That is not a surprise, I guess. Nebuchadnezzar wants to insure Necho does not come back to the north in a few years for another battle. If he takes everything between Egypt and Babylon, Necho will have no territories that are his own. He would have to fight his way all the way to the north, city by city. Nebuchadnezzar wants to end this man's power in his territories," said Vicken. "Where is Wakeem?" he stood and waited for his answer.

"He is in Dan with Zaradan. Hopefully, we will see them tomorrow with their captives."

A week later Nebuchadnezzar's troops were camped in Megiddo. This city above the valley, by the same name, was strategic. It had taken a week to work their way down to this location. The valley would make an excellent holding area for the captives from this territory until they took them north. But first, they had to take the city from the Hebrews.

The climb to this city was steep. It was at a vantage point 700 feet above the valley. They would be able to send 5,000 men up from the valley on the south while 5,000 troops moved in from the northeast

The wall could be scaled; however, the gate was a challenge. It was 3-chambered which meant they would have to fight their way through each chamber, which zigzagged from side to side. Spies thought this city could be a challenge and that a siege was not a good idea. A quick conquest was more advisable because they had unlimited water from concealed tunnel and good food storage.

Early the next morning the battle was engaged. Vicken got his wish. He led the southward advancing troops. They had the easiest climb since Mount Carmel grew out of the valley toward the northwest and became increasingly steep. Wakeem was with Zaradan coming up from the northeast with as much protection as they could manage.

Megiddo was not like the villages they had taken before. This was an army post with men and weapons. No quick victory was expected here. Time was not an issue. They knew they had the man-power and greater numbers of weapons, but should see victory in a few days.

"Wakeem, take your battalion and Timath's and examine to the back wall of the city. See if you can find a way over. I will take my men and two other battalions and we will take the western portion of the wall. The other men can back us up and act as patrols. I saw a signal from Vicken that his men were in place in the south. Send Eddu to them with his battalion and tell them to attack the gate on the south and the eastern wall. We will advance at noon."

A base camp had been established in the valley below with guards for the captives already taken and the spoils of war. They had moved into place under the cover of darkness. Coming up a mountain allowed very little concealment. Night was their greatest advantage. It was now just after breakfast and they had been on top of the mountain for several hour of sleep before they ate.

With those instructions, Zaradan dispatched his commanders. They moved quickly to talk with their troops and move from the rough campsite. Eddu took his men behind the ridge and moved to the south, keeping a low profile from the town above.

Wakeem and Timath moved behind cover to the north walls. When they got near, Wakeem told the men, "Hold up here. Timath, take a couple of your men to the upper area of the wall moving further north then work your way toward the center. My men and I will work from the lower edge toward the center. If you find a good access area, send a runner to us and we will do the same if we find something."

The small parties separated and advanced. Timath and two soldiers were able to slowly work their way to the northernmost corner. As they crept along they kept their eyes open for any weak points in the wall's defense.

"Sir, look there at the wall just behind that pine. It appears that the ground is higher there than in some of the areas. Maybe we could build a ramp of earth," suggested one of his men.

"It is a possibility, but let's keep looking. Ramp building might be used as a last resort."

They were near the farthest corner when they noticed a large set of boulders near the wall. The wall was nearing the side of the mountain and seemed to be built into some of the stone. The ground rose making the wall appear shorted and the rocks narrowed the climb over the wall even more. They had found their spot. Timath turned to the first man, "Go to Wakeem and tell him of our find. See if he will join us or whether we should bring our men and move over the wall at noon."

Wakeem had also found an area on the south he thought could be weakness. There was a city gate that looked less than sturdy. They were in the process of making a battering ram when Timath's man arrived, "Sir, we have found an area we believe will allow us to scale the wall with a minimum of problem. What would you like for us to do?"

"Take your battalion and one more with you. Go ahead at noon and begin your accent. We will make our efforts here at this door and work our way toward the center of town at the palace, if one exists inside. If no victory is gained, then retreat to the night camp we established for further instructions." The soldier disappeared back into the woods to gather the rest of the troops and move them to the far corner.

Wakeem was so glad to be back in his element and not stuck in town. He felt revived. He looked at his men who had jest felled a tree and were trimming the branches. It would be ready by noon. His eyes were analyzing the wall and other areas that might be good vantage points for his foes to kill his men. The wall did appear substantial, but it did not have any towers. It was likely that they had been seen already, so theirs would not be a surprise attack. He was ready for business.

Everyone was in place and when the sun was directly overhead the attack began. Wakeem had a barrage of arrows flying as his men advanced toward the small gate. They set up a line of men with shields as the archers above them unloaded their quivers. His other men came behind advancing as quickly as they could with the battering ram. He lost two of the carriers when they were hit by enemy arrows. They were replaced and the battering ram moved forward.

They were in place, "Hit is as hard as you can repeatedly. Go, men, go," yelled Wakeem. The ram pounded once, twice and three times. It seemed the door was holding. They repositioned the ram to hit near the door latch. Three times more and the latch cracked and dropped off.

"Keep using the ram. Knock the gate as hard as you can. Try to send it back hard and far. Then follow it in and knock as many soldiers down as possible with the ram. Use its momentum. Drop the ram to the side and we will pile in behind you using our swords," Wakeem continued to call out.

The men set up the ram while the rest of the battalion drew their weapons. They hit the gate and knocked it back, slamming three enemy soldiers into the wall. The rammers ran ahead carrying the pine poll. They took out two more men and then pushed the ram ahead of them as they moved under the wall. Swords and spears were doing the follow-up work behind the ram.

At the front gate, Vicken was also using two rams. He used the poll inside the gate also, but it was also a barrier holding the men inside the first chamber. Vicken followed the rammers to the first chamber along with three of his men. The rest of the battalion moved to the second chamber which was on the right. Vicken and his men kept control of the group in chamber one, who were trapped by the ram across their entrance. The men at the second chamber were clearing the way and several had moved to the last chamber which was on the left as well. Within half an hour they were inside. Across town to the back of the city, a tower could be seen. He assumed that to be the area the men would work their way to reach. It looked imposing, like another wall and tower, protecting someone or something.

Timath and his men had been able to scale the wall with ease, but were confronted with the palace guard. Their area entered directly into the palace grounds which were well protected. Several of them were shot when their heads popped over the wall. Others were cut to pieces the moment they hit the ground. Some managed to make it over and were in a heated battle. Timath was standing on the wall using his arrows to do as much damage as possible in the crowd below. His quiver was nearly empty when he was shot in the hip. He fell to the ground hard, knocking the wind out of him. Before he could get his composure, the palace guard who had shot him was at his side.

"You are mine. Your arrows will not kill any more of us today or ever again," he ran his sword through Timath's body.

Wakeem's men had done better and were winning. They were inside and had moved along the wall to their right. On their left they saw large buildings and a tower. Ahead they saw a market and homes on the far side of town. They decided to work around the wall and then work in toward the center. The rest of the city was in turmoil, but from appearances, they had the upper hand. By evening they should have the victory.

CHAPTER 25

"We cannot continue like this. The inn is losing customers. I am sick of listening to Hablin telling us what a good job he is doing and how grateful we should be that he is helping while Cain is away," said Moriah to Bethany as they passed each other at the bar.

"I am so tired. We need more help," said Bethany. She continued, "I don't care what Hablin does as long as we can keep our jobs and the money comes in to keep the inn alive," she called over her shoulder as she walked toward her customers.

Moriah had seen the money that was coming in and she knew the Hablin had been 'helping' himself to more than his share. He loved the added authority and he tended to push it on others too often. He offended customers rather than attracting them to come in. She had tried to tell him, "Hablin, this is a service business. If we keep making people mad and not meeting their requests, we will be put out of business. The other day when you told that merchant, 'You will eat the lamb as I have cooked it, or you can throw it out. It makes no difference to me.' Do you know that comments like that will spread to others and they will not come back and neither will their friends?"

"Shut up, Moriah. Just because you slept with Cain does not mean you were as smart as he was. You didn't run the inn; he did. I have watched him and worked with him for many years longer than you have. I know more than you do, so leave me alone." He turned and walked out the back door, leaving his assistant cook to try to keep up with the lunch orders.

Business was still good, but there was no telling how long that would continue. Moriah stopped at her table, "Here you are, sir. I have your lunch." She moved to the next table to pick up the dishes, overhearing their conversation.

"I was just in Shechem. I heard that Nebuchadnezzar is near Megiddo. He took the city in two days. They must be some kind of warriors. That city was well protected and had a great wall. They are taking every strong man who survives captive and many women, too. All the livestock and food along the way has been consumed by the troops. If he continues along this path, he will reach Jerusalem in the next month," said a northern merchant.

Moriah was hearing conversations like this daily, now. She was sure the palace was aware of how serious the situation was becoming.

"Moriah, how about some more ale?" yelled one of the palace guards.

"Sure, Marold. Be right with you." When she returned with the ale, she asked, "How is the palace gossip leaning about what will happen with Nebuchadnezzar?" she filled his cup and waited. He was a regular and often shared information with her. While she was talking with him, she would try to find out if he knew anything about Cain.

"Everyone is being 'hush-hush.' about the situation. I think they are all afraid. It seems that the prophet that everyone hates, might be telling the truth after all, huh?"

She had to agree, from what she had heard that the prophet seemed to be on target with what he had said, "Well, I have only heard about him, but he seems to be closer to the truth than any others I have heard about." She puttered around the table near him, clearing dishes, and then she turned around to him and leaned in close, "I want to ask you a personal question, for me. I wondered if you know anything about what might have happened to Cain. He disappeared a few weeks ago and we haven't heard anything. I am really worried," she said, looking inquiringly into his face. He was not the first person to whom she had posed this question and he would not be the last, until she had an answer. She watched a strange haze pass over his eyes.

He turned away putting his hand on his forehead and leaning over his food. He cleared his throat and began to eat. This was a curious reaction. She knew he had heard her question. Why was he acting so peculiar?

"Marold, tell me what you know. I can tell by your reaction that you know something. Please, I am worried sick," she sat down beside him.

He looked from side to side and then away again. He really should not talk about this to anyone, but to be the one to break this to her... Well, he didn't want to do it. He stood up, dropping a coin on the table, and walked out of the inn toward the palace.

Moriah was not going to let him get away that easily. She ran out of the inn behind him and down the street. He was much taller and had longer legs. He covered ground quickly, but she was able to run to catch up with him. She grabbed his arm and held on with all her might, yelling, "Tell me, please, tell me. I have been trying to find out something for weeks and I know you can help. Please tell me." Now she was crying.

Marold stopped, but did not turn around. He said, still facing away from her, "He is dead."

All sound stopped and her hands dropped from his arm. Still not hearing anything, he turned around to see if she had left. There on the stone street, Moriah lay in a heap. Obviously, what he had said, she had never considered might happen. He picked her up and sat her down against a tree and waited. In a few minutes, she regained strength and began to sob. He waited until she was able to listen, "Moriah, Cain was captured by the palace guard and interrogated. When it was determined that he was a traitor, he was hanged. Everything was kept quiet so that the spies would not find out that we knew about them and the inn. Since they are gone, I guess it is okay that you know what happened to Cain."

"Thank you," she said through her tears. "I must get back to the inn, but knowing what has happened is better than wondering." She got up shakily and moved away slowly. Marold watched her walk back to the inn.

"Where did you go? You just disappeared during lunch. What are...," Bethany was on a tirade, until she noticed Moriah was crying. "What happened? Are you alright?" She took Moriah's arm and they sat down. The lunch rush was over and they had a minute or two to talk.

Moriah looked at her sister, "Cain is dead," and she burst into a fresh stream of tears. Bethany held her close and let her cry. 'What on earth happened?' she thought, but only held her. The questions could come later.

Hablin came over. "Now what? You are always telling me that service is what counts and you sit here together while customers are waiting." He looked at the two girls. Neither one told him about Cain.

Bethany said, "Moriah, you go upstairs and rest for a while. I will finish up here and then we can talk. Maybe you could sleep for a while." Moriah wondered off in a daze and Bethany finished up the serving and cleaning.

When Bethany came upstairs later, they spent an hour discussing what might happen to them and what options they had. With Cain dead the inn might naturally go to her, since everyone knew they were living together and he had no other relatives. But since Hablin had been running the inn, he might think he had a right to everything. This could be a problem. They decided to keep on going just like they had been and try to deal with situations as they came up. They would give the situation some time and try to decide what would be best.

Later that week at dinner one of the patrons was eating with several guests. He was giving Bethany a hard time, "This food is not fit for swine. I have had better quail cooked over a camp fire. Tell the cook I want to see him."

Bethany went to the kitchen, "Hablin, the man over at the central table, is complaining about the quail. He said it is tough and has no flavor and would like to talk with you," she smiled, having to agree with the customer. It really was terrible quail. Since Cain was not here to check for quality, Hablin had tried to but corners to save money.

Hablin went to the table with his naturally offensive attitude. Before the man even had time to speak, Hablin started, "Look, you big bear, if you can find better food in town, then go to their inn. Otherwise, eat it or leave. I do not care." He turned and went back into the kitchen.

They lost a good sum of money on that dinner, even if the quail wasn't worth eating. The man left, taking his guests along and he did not pay. "You will regret this," the man said as he was leaving. That comment didn't bother Hablin at all. He had heard it many times.

Moriah and Bethany finished serving the dinners. They were glad that the rest of the evening was not eventful. After cleanup they left Hablin cleaning in the kitchen and rested upstairs.

"Do you think we should leave the inn and go somewhere for a while? We might be in danger of being caught as spies, too," asked Bethany.

"Two things are stopping me from running away. One is the inn. I think we can make a go of it, if we don't have a battle with Hablin. I don't want to leave a good profession with a steady income. Not many women have a business dropped into their laps like I just did."

"And the other thing?" continued Bethany.

"I think we are facing war soon. I heard the other day, the day I found out about Cain, that the king from the north, Nebu—something, is the one that Wakeem and his men were working for. The king and army are in our country and coming south. Some think he will be here in a month. Remember that I helped the spies while they were here. They made a promise to keep Cain and me safe. I think I would be safe and could make a go of it after the war. I am not afraid to be here, if we have a war."

"What about me? Do you think that, since Zarallon and I were friends and Cain isn't here now, that they might take care of me, too, in case there was a war?"

Moriah considered the question, "I think it is likely that you have a good chance of being very safe, as well, in the event of war. Let's just keep on doing what we have been for weeks and see what happens." They agreed that would be their course of action, for now.

Early the next morning Moriah went down to get something to eat. It was quiet. Obviously, Hablin hadn't come to work yet. He was getting lazier and coming in later, since he considered himself the boss. She lit a lamp and walked into the kitchen, stumbling over something on the floor. Holding the lamp near the floor, she saw some fabric and a sandal. Looking more carefully, she realized it was a man. He was probably drunk. She moved the light toward his face and recognized it was Hablin. Well, he was a drinker, but usually didn't get drunk like this. She was about to shake him when she noticed the knife. She began to scream when she realized he might be dead. One of his kitchen knifes was sticking out of his back. What should she do? This was really out of her experience.

A couple of minutes later, Bethany came running in, "Was that you I heard screaming? You scared me to death." Bethany looked at Moriah's eyes and then followed her glance down to the floor. Now it was Bethany's turn to scream. Hablin was a mess and blood was everywhere. It was obvious from looking around that there had been a fight of some sort. They just stared at each other for a minute. Now what?

"Let's sit down. I am too shaky to move far." They sat at the nearest table. "Who do you think did this?" Bethany continued.

"I don't have any idea. Why would anyone care enough about Hablin to kill him? It doesn't make any since." They sat for a few minutes thinking in silence. "Who should we contact about this?" said Moriah. "Do you think we should send word to the palace guard. Maybe Marold would know what to do." They decided that would be the wise thing to do. About one hour later, Hablin's assistant arrived and they sent him to the palace. They locked the inn door and did not open up for lunch that day.

Marold and two other men arrived to investigate what had happened. After interviewing both girls and the assistant, he decided that Hablin was killed by someone else. "Who were his enemies?" he asked them.

Bethany responded, "He only has us and the customers. He has no family. I guess the only person I can think of might have been someone we didn't know or an angry customer."

Moriah said, "Recently, a man left the table angry after Hablin had embarrassed him in front of his guests. He said Hablin would 'regret this' as he was leaving. Maybe he had something to do with it. Then again, Hablin has offended many customers and he has never been attacked before."

"It only takes one," said Marold. "We will follow up on this man, if you can identify him." They finished the interview and left.

CHAPTER 26

Dinah had just sat down after cleaning up from breakfast. She was holding Hagi, her cat, who was purring her very best purr. Hagi loved it when she sat still long enough for her to jump in her lap. She soaked up the attention. "You love this, don't you, sweet girl?" she asked her.

"Well, let me tell you what I am thinking, since you are my captive audience at the moment. It seems some of our neighbors have left on extended vacations to the other side of the Jordan. They are worried about rumors of a pending war with an enemy king."

Hagi responded to her with a roll over on her lap to expose her stomach, which Dinah obligingly scratched. "I am proud of our family. They are sticking it out here at home, no matter what the outcome might be. We still believed God will protect his city and us as he has for generations."

Hagi had enough of the stomach scratching and stood up to rub her face against Dinah's chin. "I know, girl. We are very afraid, too. I will try to take good care of you, too. You knew about the prophet. It seems some people are putting more stock in what he had been saying, now. Our family feels he was a true man, but that doesn't mean God would abandon us, does it? Well, in my mind, it doesn't." She hugged her one more time and placed her on the floor.

"Lotta, do you need any help getting the boys ready for their visit?" she asked her soon-to-be sister-in-law.

"No, thanks. We are just finishing up. You can come up and visit before we leave," Lotta called to Dinah.

She bounded upstairs and sat on the rug in Lotta's room. "Are you staying tonight with your mom and dad, or will be back for supper? I miss all of you so much, when you stay away. Tell your mom and dad hello from me, okay?"

Lotta leaned over to kiss her younger 'sister's' hair, "I am so glad God has given me a sister like you. Mom and dad love you, too. I will tell them for you, but they already know it. Now, take Mattan and I will take Nathan. Let's go down the outside stairs. Azariah will walk me home and then he is going back to the temple. I will see you after supper tonight. We are going to eat with my parents before coming back here later."

Azariah came part of the way up the stairs and took Mattan from his sister. "Are you all ready to go?" he asked.

"All ready. See you later, Dinah." Lotta, Azariah and the boys moved up the lane toward the top of the escarpment. They would be at her parent's house within the hour. Azariah would be at work a little late, but his father was aware he was coming after he left Lotta at her home.

"I am looking forward to dinner tonight with your family. We have such a good time and great fellowship," Azariah commented.

"They are your family, too, now. I cannot wait to have some time to talk about our plans for the wedding. It seems we do not see them enough to get all the decisions made that I would like," she smiled up at him.

They continued the chatting until they reached the house, "Hello, mom, I am home," called Lotta as she entered the living space on the lower floor.

"We are coming, honey. You had better have our grandsons with you?" finishing that last statement as she rounded the corner from the kitchen, Myra went straight to her daughter. They kissed and she took Nathan from her arms and laughed as she tossed him over her head and caught him. It was so good to have him home for the day. She put him on the floor and turned to Azariah, "Hello, dear," Myra said, kissing both her son-in-law to be and Mattan. "Let me have that other precious one," Mattan was kicking his little legs in excitement. He had already learned to love his other grandmother. They had a special bond.

Azariah spent a few more minutes visiting, and then he excused himself. Kissing Lotta, he said, "Goodbye, honey. I will see you this evening for dinner. I love you," he turned toward the boys and said, "I love you two, too." He exited the door, waving as he went into the street.

The new taxes were doing the trick. They would have enough money for the tribute payment to Egypt in a few more months. "Daniel, see these numbers," said Gideon. "We are doing very well with the new tax. I cannot wait to inform Tigner so he can tell the King. I think he will be pleased."

"I thought your plan was excellent, but you seem surprised that it is working out. Didn't you think it would work?" his son asked.

"You never know about a plan. I was under pressure and had no time to prepare any other ideas. But it is working, and that is all that matters now," he motioned to Tigner who came to his side.

"What is it, Gideon? I hope it is good news. Jehoiakim is not in any mood to handle more bad news. Did you hear that our intelligence reports say that Nebuchadnezzar may come this way soon? He is a couple of days north," asked Tigner.

"No, I had not heard that at all. That is very frightening," he looked over at Daniel who was obviously upset. "Well, the news I have is good." He showed the numbers to Tigner.

"Excellent. He will be very pleased. At least, one thing is going well."

"Tigner, what plans has the king put in place to deal with a attack, in the event that Nebuchadnezzar does come?" asked Gideon.

"Of course, his prophets are telling him not to worry. The city will be safe. He has ignored the spies' reports and is denying any imminent danger. I pray he is right," Tigner walked back to the king and updated him on tax totals.

"Gideon, come forward," said the king.

Gideon had not expected to again be in the center of the court with all the attention on him. He really disliked this attention. Regardless of his preference, his king had called and he must obey. He came to the main area and moved toward the throne, bowing low and staying there.

"You may rise. I am pleased with the numbers I am seeing. It appears the tax recommendation you made earlier has been very effective. What is your prediction for the date that the new tribute payment will be ready?"

"Sire, I believe by the beginning of this fall we will be ready to send another payment to Egypt."

"That would be perfect. Make plans along those lines, Tigner. You are a credit to your profession, Gideon. Well done, sir," the king nodded toward Gideon, dismissing him to return to his table.

Gideon gladly sat down and tried to calm his nerves. Each time you stood before the king, you took your life in your hands, even if it was at his command. One wrong move or untimely word might cost you your life.

Benjamin came to the table and lean near to Gideon, "I was standing in the back talking to a tile merchant when the King called you forward. You did very well, Gideon."

"Thank you for the encouragement. Are you still working on remodeling the palace or do you have another project going on?" asked Gideon.

Daniel added, "Is Misha with you today?"

Benjamin answered, "No, Misha is at the lumber market while I draw up plans to make the state dining area more 'attractive.' It is lovely now, but they seem to enjoy spending money making cosmetic changes. Although, I like working, I would rather do something not wasteful or cosmetic. I must get busy, but thought I would speak before I moved on," Benjamin patted his shoulder and laid his other hand on Daniel's neck, giving it a squeeze. "I will tell Misha you asked about him," he said and moved into the back hall.

Life at the inn has fallen into a comfortable pattern. The cook's assistant was working into an excellent chef and the patrons were once again coming to eat. Moriah was the unchallenged owner and manager and Bethany had become the head waitress. They had hired two other ladies to serve from lunch through supper.

"I am so pleased to see several new customers. Several have been back more than once. I believe not only will we make it, but the gradual growth will be sufficient to keep us comfortable for many years," Moriah told Bethany over breakfast.

They opened up for lunch at about an hour before noon. It was a quiet beginning for the usually busy lunch hour. Two of the new customers returned and took their preferred table near the front door.

Bethany came to them, asking, "Sirs, it is good to see you again. Are you ready to order lunch or would you rather wait and have some ale?"

The bigger man said, "Is it really good to see us again?"

She thought that was a strange question. Her comment was a cordial greeting not intended to be familiar. "I am sorry. I don't understand," she said seeking an explanation.

"This is our third time to eat here. Have you noticed us before?"

"Why of course I have. It is a compliment to have customers return to eat with us. I saw you the first time you came," she answered. She still had no idea where this conversation was headed, but she would go along with them for a while. Maybe she could gather what it was they wanted.

"We have not come here because of the food," said the tall, thin man, "We are here because of you."

"Me? Well, thank you. Although, I hope you find the food pleasing."

"The food is adequate, but you... you are our prize," said the big man again.

"Sirs, you have me totally confused. I appreciate you coming here for me, but I am no one's prize," she was getting angry. Who did they think they were, talking to her like this?

While this discussion was going on, several more tables had filled up. The other girls were helping them.

"Let me try to make myself clearer. I would never want you to be confused," the tall man went to the front door. He opened it and stepped outside.

'Boy,' she thought, 'this man is a little off center.'

The door opened again and he stepped aside, waving his hand to indicate someone would follow. Around the corner came four temple guards from the Valley of Tophet dressed in vivid blue. Bethany began to scream and ran toward the back of the inn.

Moriah looked up to see what was causing the ruckus. She could see the guards and then it dawned on her these men were here to take Bethany back to finish her two years as a temple prostitute. She owed them. Moriah began to panic, too. Maybe she could buy them off? She would certainly try.

Bethany was captured at the back of the inn by guards waiting in the alley. They held her in the alley until the rest of the men joined them. The tall man said, "Now, by the god Baal, I hope my statements are clear to you. You belong to us for two more years. We will add another six months that you have stolen away when you left. You also took a baby away that belonged to our god. You owe us for it. That will add another six months to your duty," he said and slapped her as hard as he could, knocking her to the dirt.

Moriah came outside in time to hear his comments and see him hit her. She was sick inside. "Sir, could I speak with you privately?" she said to the tall man.

"I have no need to hear anything you have to say. You aided her in hiding from us and we cannot trust you. You would be wasting your breath."

"Sir, I ask for only two minutes," she repeated her request.

He looked at her for a moment and stepped in her direction, "What is your question?"

"Could you be persuaded to sell Bethany's time to me? What amount of money would it take to purchase her away from you?"

He smiled and then laughed out loud, "You could not begin to have enough money to buy her from us. Do you know how much a woman like her can bring to the temple of her god? She can earn from ten gerahs to one or two shekels for each 'worshipper' she serves. That adds up to 2500 shekels a year. Do you have that kind of money?" he asked.

Moriah was overwhelmed. She had no idea that a prostitute could bring in such large amounts of cash. No wonder the leaders thought 'worshippers' should use this method of admiration for their god.

"No, I do not. Can't I do something, anything? I need her here in the inn. Please, I beg you," Moriah began to cry. She bent down to reach over and help Bethany to her feet. The guard shoved her into the stairwell causing her to sit down on a step hard.

"Moriah, don't worry. I have done this for years. Three more will go by very quickly." The men took her under her arms and stood her to her feet. They moved down the alley and out of sight. Both girls were crying. Bethany stared over her shoulder until she was out of sight of her older sister.

CHAPTER 27

The king was still in his chambers when there was a knock at his door. Baileen answered the knock and returned to tell the King, "Sire, Robron is asking to speak with you. It is urgent." The tone of Baileen's voice caused the King to agree to this most unusual meeting. He was not one to be overly concerned about the condition of his people or his city, especially before sunrise. He was concerned for himself and his well being, however, and the tone seemed somewhat fearful.

"Bring my cape and tell him to come in," Jehoiakim sat up in his bed. One of his mistresses had been with him last night. "Baileen, before you bring him in, help her to the next room and shut the door."

Gelina stirred when the King sat up and said, "Get up and out of here now. I have business to conduct." She move slightly and looked at him. Baileen jerked the covers back and pulled her to her feet. He handed Jehoiakim his cape, then turned and ushered her away physically to the other room.

Within moments Robron stepped into the room. His face was pale and apprehensive, "Sire, I am sorry to disturb you, but this matter is urgent involving the country's security and our lives, as well. We told you Nebuchadnezzar was close, but he was nearer than we thought. Smoke is rising from Bethany, from Gibeah and from beyond the Mount of Olives. Shepherds and others have been observed fleeing along the roads to the mountains and the Jordan. Many other small villages have been destroyed, according to reports. His army is on the move and will be here within the hour. I have posted sentinels around the city wall and in the towers, closed the gate and secured the temple and the palace. Sire, I think we need to take you to our secure area in the lower palace and hide you, for now."

Jehoiakim was visibly shaking. He did not move and was afraid to speak. His thoughts fleeted back to Jeremiah whom he believed to be wrong, betting his life on it. Well, it was evident he had bet wrong and that irked him. He motioned for Baileen to bring him some water. Taking a drink, he paused to think. He really was not sure what the next move should be. Finally he said, "You have made wise choices, Robron. Go to the palace guard and check on the weapons. I will dress and meet you at the main court in half an hour." The king got up while Baileen laid out his attire.

Robron spoke, "Hurry, sire. They will be here very soon." He left and went to the loading dock. He assigned Garridon this area to protect along with fifty men. He went back to the palace front and made sure all were ready with their weapons. Tigner was there with Marold and his soldiers, "Is he coming down soon? We have much to discuss," asked Tigner.

"He will be here in minutes. When he comes, please move to the chamber in the back of the loading dock and use the concealed door," said Robron. The king appeared with Baileen. "Sire, I think we should sound the alarm and let the people know that we are under attack. It will give them time to prepare and seek a safe place. The trumpeter is ready downstairs."

"No. I do not want to frighten the people. Maybe he will pass by us and head strait to Egypt. We have known for months that he has been chasing Necho in this direction. He may just continue on down the road in his pursuit," Jehoiakim could not admit, even to them, that he had been wrong about Jerusalem being conquered. If Nebuchadnezzar did attack the city, the outcome of the northern king winning would be inevitable. The Hebrews were no match militarily for Nebuchadnezzar.

"Sire, I must summon the soldiers to the palace. Without sounding the alarm, they will not know to come," stated Robron.

"Are you questioning my decision during a time of military action? I hope I misunderstood what you said, for that would be an act of treason," said Jehoiakim pausing to watch Robron's reaction. It was obvious that Robron was not intimidated by the statement, even though it was true. It was highly unlikely he would be disciplined, since Jehoiakim needed him more now than ever. The king continued, "Let the soldiers fight from their current locations. Take Donolly with you to help with any messages that need to be delivered to me." Jehoiakim had thought through several possible scenarios, but the most important one involved not summoning the army. If they were conquered, he could blame the military for not being prepared and ready for battle. To sound the alarm would defeat his plan to protect himself.

Robron was livid, "Sire, I will send word to you, if something happens. Donolly will not be of any value on the wall." He would be too busy defending the city to care for this helpless emissary. He was worried enough about how he could defend a city without his men. Donolly would be in the way.

Jehoiakim could see that Robron was weighing the options and the king was not willing to wait or argue. He said to Robron, "That is a command, general." Robron nodded yes, but his eyes conveyed his contempt. He turned to leave.

"Wait a minute," said Jehoiakim. The King was savvy enough to read the message in his glance. He couldn't afford to lose his commander. "It is obvious by your face that you do not agree with my decision. Donolly has had experience in negotiations and working with dignitaries and you have not. You may need him to give input. Concerning the warning signal, do you want people screaming and running around the city while you are trying to defend it? You would not be able to move. The soldiers are armed and are spread throughout the city anyway. Cannot they just battle in the areas that they live in?" he asked, trying to placate his commander.

"Yes, sire. If those are your wishes that is what will be done. Please move down to the hidden room and have Garridon close the door and make sure it is well hidden," he turned and went outside. It took all of his control just to maintain himself in the King's presence long enough to escape. He would do what he could without sounding the alarm, but he thought the King was making a grave error.

"Donolly, go to the main gate and let them know I am coming. I am going to check the temple first." As Robron reentered the city heading across the ravine, he could see that word was spreading throughout the city anyway about some immediate danger. Those who live on the perimeter of the city and in the walls were the first to suspect trouble and see smoke. Smoke alone is not an omen of war, but rumors had spread about cities to the north being destroyed by a foreign power. Those who saw the smoke made some quick and accurate assumptions of real danger. Some decided to try to escape by the smaller, out of the way gates. The large city gates were not opened that morning and they should have been an hour ago. That is usually a sign in the city that there is trouble somewhere. That started people talking, especially merchants and farmers. It was apparent some residents believed they would be safer in the mountains, no matter what situation was brewing.

A sergeant and Pashhur met Robron at the Temple, "What is going on? Why has the alarm not been sounded?" asked Pashhur.

"Our king does not want to 'frighten' the residents. He wants us to do the best we can without it. Use all the temple guards and protect yourselves here. I will take the rest of the men to the main gate. I am guessing we will be hearing from Nebuchadnezzar's army at any moment. I want to be on watch at the main gate to meet any emissaries sent from him."

"The King's decision seems unwise and dangerous for all. Did you try to talk him out of it?" asked Pashhur

"Of course, up to a point. But you know the King when his mind is made up. There is little that changes it. I will be at the gate. Use all the resources at your disposal to protect the temple and all inside." Robron hurried out and toward the west.

"You sent for me?" Wakeem asked as his chariot pulled up beside Zaradan's on the road from Gibeah toward Jerusalem, which was just over a mile north. "Are you going to give them a chance to surrender? I would love for you to just send us in there and let me and my men have at it!"

Zaradan nodded at him, "Yes, that would suit your hot-headed group well, but I am sending two representatives to the west gate in five minutes. Ride along with them and act as a translator. You know this language, right?" he said.

"Yes," so he did ride along. When they arrived at the gate, he did his part in translating.

Mongin, another lesser general spoke, "You up there. We are here on behalf of Nebuchadnezzar, the great general of the Babylonian kingdom, to request your immediate surrender. Our spies have visited your city and your palace. We are prepared to burn the city and all inside to the ground. Our armies are with us and will surround your city and destroy it. We will expect your answer within half an hour or all who are in it will die. We know you will be wise and open the gates, indicating your submission to our great leader, Nebuchadnezzar." After each sentence, Wakeem translated into Hebrew what was said. They waited for a few seconds and then the group spun their chariots around and with a war whop and sped away. They would be back and they expected the gate to be open.

On the wall, Robron had listened without comment. He turned to Donolly, who was at his side, but out of reach of any danger. Robron spoke, "You heard everything, didn't you?

"I heard."

"What do you think?"

"The king will not surrender. He is convinced that God will protect his city. He thinks God will protect it not because he is personally a believer in God, but because God loves the temple and Jerusalem, his holy city. Jehoiakim is banking on those beliefs. Let' go to tell him what happened. I will recommend surrender, but I doubt he will listen," said Donolly.

They hurried or rather, plodded, toward the palace loading dock and entered the secret rooms. The King was in deep conversation with Tigner, "Well, what is the word from the wall, Donolly?" asked Tigner. The King remained quiet, but seemed confident.

"Sire, three emissaries came to the gate and demanded our surrender within half an hour or they would destroy the city and all inside. We are to open the gates and let them in when they return. I think we should listen to them."

Tigner and Jehoiakim talked for a minute and then Tigner answered, "If they return, fight them."

Robron was unsure how to react. They had an army, but not one like what he had heard about Nebuchadnezzar's. He was willing to fight, but he would need to prepare. It was not likely the King would want to sound the alarm, but he asked anyway, "And can we sound the alarm now?"

"Yes, so ahead. The enemy is at the gate." Finally, the king agreed.

Robron went out into the dock and found the trumpeter. They moved to the top of the palace along the highest area open to the outside. The trumpet blast could be heard around the city. He played the same warning to the four directions of the wind.

Robron was running. Very little time remained now. When he returned to the gate and mounted the steps, he was awestruck by the sight before him. Spread like a layer of invading locusts as far as he could see, to the west, north and south, lay the army of Nebuchadnezzar. They were dressed in scarlet with touches of blazing gold. Their helmets' designs and decorations and breastplates were distinctive to their divisions, the colors were all the same. Banners fluttered in the light breeze. Chariots sparkled in the morning sun. The glint of metal was seen like the glitter of sun on a rippling lake. The emissaries waited for the answer at the gate.

"We await your decision," they called once again to those on the wall. Their horses pranced left and right sensing the tension.

Robron turned to his men lining the wall and filling the towers. He knew they were ready and that this fight would be to the death for many. They were vastly outnumbered. He gave the signal to shoot. Arrows flew in every direction, but several were aimed toward the enemy's chariots at the gate. One man fell, but Wakeem and Mongin managed to escape. They drove quickly to the south. Layers of soldiers and chariots peeled away from the front of the gate like a stone breaking the water's smooth surface.

The northern group of soldiers came against the Ephraim and Sheep gate. Those gates did not open easily. Ephraim Gate was a primary entrance into town opening on to the Tyropean Road.

"Take that ram and see how solid that gate is," said Eddu-aran to his men. He was in charge of the group that was attacking the Ephraim Gate. Ten of his men had already died here. To the archers he said, "Give them good cover as they move the ram forward." It was going to take time to get in. Shield bearers protected the archers while they shot up to the wall. This kept the men trying to open the gate somewhat free to maneuver. The archers on the wall were busy protecting themselves. The door did not budge.

"Retreat!" he called to his men with the ram. They fell back. "Hurry up that wagon coming down the road," he yelled to the chariot drivers who went of escort the wagon. "Tell them to watch that lamp oil barrel carefully. It almost fell. Okay, steady ahead, we will give you cover." The drivers were protected by large flap of leather slung above the seat and the horses were draped with shields of thick leather on their bodies and heads. When the wagon reached the gate, the drivers spun the wagon hard to the left causing the barrel to tip over spilling it contents close to the gate, slashing some on the wood and the rest was spilled on the pavement and ran under the gate. A torch flew from the chariot passenger to the pavement and lighting the oil. "Back off, men." The wagon was already retreating. In the next hour, without any more effort the Ephraim gate began to burn and collapse.

Within minutes after the collapse, the army moved forward clearing a path through the ashes as they went. "The city is yours. Move into the homes and market area and then toward the temple. Advance!" yelled Eddu. The northern army divisions charged through the gate. Rattling chariots came in first making a commotion that was unmistakable. The sound of the hooves on the stones was so loud that communication was impossible. The men were on their own. The ability to hear their leaders was out of the question. They began to work their way around the city.

The Tyropean and Carpo Roads were paved and gave excellent access to the city from the north to the south. Some of the road was made of steps in the lower parts of the city which slowed the forward progress of the charioteers.

Meriel and Chloe were in their shop when they heard the warning trumpet sound. They were afraid to try and make it to their homes, so they hid in the shop. The chariots and horse hooves made horrendous racket on the stones in the street. People could be heard screaming and crying. The sounds grew louder.

"I am so frightened," Chloe whispered. "I hope they pass us by."

Meriel nodded in agreement. "We will just have to pray they do. Look, I can see a chariot across the road from us. It just stopped." Her heart rate increased dramatically. It was so loud she was sure it could be heard.

They could see the soldiers moving from store to store outside the shop. The commotion and noise was unbearable. You couldn't hear them coming, but you could see them working their way through the shops across the road.

No one could possibly have heard someone speaking in a normal voice, but Chloe whispered anyway, "Oh, Meriel, that big man with the eye-patch is coming toward the entrance." She began to whimper.

"Quiet. Not a sound. He is coming in." Meriel pulled the canvas over the two of them. They were lying well concealed in the back room among the stacks of sash fabrics and supplies.

Eddu moved around the room quickly. There wasn't time to search every dwelling with care. It was just mid-morning and many shop owners were still at home. This shop appeared to be filled with ladies' items. He moved to the back and glanced around. Seeing nothing, he returned to the street.

For several more minutes the ladies did not move. They eventually heard the clatter of horses and chariots. The noise became more distant. Meriel moved a few inches, still covered by the canvas and peeked around the corner of the counter. Everything in the room was still and the street was empty. She got up and moved around the edge of the room to look outside. It was clear.

"Chloe, I think it is safe to come out. Everyone is gone. We must wait here until things calm down, then I think we can try to go home after dark, maybe. It may be several hours yet, but we will wait until the noise stops and the sound of chariots and horses cannot be heard, then we will sneak home through the back streets."

Chloe had not moved. She was weak with fear. She might never leave her safe spot. She stayed there until Meriel came back and sat down beside her,

"I guess staying where you are is just as good as anything else right now. Rest for a while and I will watch." They both sat quietly in their own world wondering about what was going to happen.

Hours later, when it was nearing dark, they both ventured into the streets. Having said their good-byes inside, they moved into the shadows and down separate alleys trying to make it to their homes.

Chloe went north working her way through the side streets. Her family had a tent outside the northern city wall. She exited the sheep gate and moved to the east along the wall, staying low behind rocks and plants. She could see the area where the tent was. There were soldiers patrolling, but none were around where she was standing now. It was dark and she could not be seen easily, so she ran to the tent and ducked inside. It was quiet and dark.

She was afraid to light a lamp. She tucked the flap of the tent back instead to let in some natural light and waited for her eyes to adjust. Before she could see, she could smell, however. It was not a common smell; it was one that did not belong in her family tent. She had smelled it before in the market. It was blood. Oh no, that was it! Blood! She began to tremble. Her eyes looked into the shadows afraid of what she would see.

The tent was in shambles. It had been looted. And, yes, there along the back edge of the tent were her sister and mother. She moved near them. It was too dark to see how badly they were wounded. She leaned over them, placing her ear against their chests, first her mother and then her sister. Neither one was breathing. She sat back on her heels and held her breathe. Afraid to take in one more because with it came reality and the sting of death. They were gone. She didn't see anyone else inside. She wanted to look more carefully outside the tent. She had no time to mourn. There would be time for that when she was safe.

Moving to the open flap she tried to see if any soldiers were near. When it looked clear, she crawled to the nearest rock and looked back into the area around the tent. Everything looked normal. She worked her way to the back of the tent. She found there what she had been hoping she would not see. Her big brother was leaning against a large boulder, probably dead, too. Her father had probably sent him from the grain fields where they worked to defend the family. Crawling among the bushes, she made her way to him.

"Ezekiel. Can you hear me?" she whispered. He did not stir. She touched his cheek and began to weep softly. "Please don't be dead, too. I cannot stand to see another dead person. Please, oh, please, hear me. Lord, I need him. Please help him," she prayed. She tried to see where he was wounded, but it was just too dark. She leaned around the rock, trying to stay concealed and put her ear against his chest. He was alive. 'Thank you God, he is alive.' She breathed a prayer of thanks.

Looking around her, she could see there was a large pile of boulders just a few feet from them. Maybe she could pull him to the rocks and then she could minister to his wounds. It would give them both better cover from the enemy. She grabbed his tunic by the shoulders and twisted him to the left, laying him down flat. He moaned each time she moved him, but did not regain consciousness.

Chloe watched while the patrol passed her area heading around the wall toward the west. When it was clear, she stood up and took the tunic fabric in both of her hands and began to pull. At first, she could only move him a few inches, but she eventually got into the swinging gate that moved him back a little each time she pulled. She dropped to the ground when another soldier passed heading to the Ephraim gate from the fields, then she resumed her pulling. She was so proud of herself when she reached the boulders. At least they would have a chance here.

Chloe rolled him against the rocks and laid brush against him, concealing him. Then she took dried brush and went back to the tent. She was able to gather several items that they could use and some food, water and blankets. As she returned to the boulders she brushed the dried plants over the drag path and over her steps to erase the path to their hiding place.

When she got to the rocks, Ezekiel was coming around, "Where am I?" He tried to sit up, but pain racked his left side.

"Stay quiet and be still. You were wounded by the enemy soldiers. I pulled you to some rocks, but we are not really safe here. It is just the best I could do for now. Where are you hurt? Can you tell?" Chloe asked her brother.

"My left side is really hurting and my head."

"We will have to wait until morning to see what damage was done. I have some water and bread. Could you eat?" He eagerly took the water first and then the bread. "I think if you are well enough and we are not caught, that we need to try to escape over the Jordan. Mom and Jezreel are dead," she added at the end.

"I know. It was awful. After they were killed, I tried to escape and help father, but I only made it to the outside of the tent. I think soldiers hit me with a mace on the side and on the head. I may have a broken rib, but my head got a less hard hit. It knocked me out, but it only cut the surface without breaking my skull. I think I will be sore, but tomorrow, we will go to the river. Lie down beside me and pull the blanket over us." Chloe welcomed the closeness of her brother and his protection. She was overwhelmed with the events of the day. She pulled all the brush against them and they fell into a hard sleep. Tomorrow they would escape.

Meriel reached her house without event. It appeared to be completely empty. Her heart sank. Watching carefully, she came into the courtyard and looked inside. It was very quiet. She was getting more panicky with each moment of silence. Her home would not be this quiet, if the children were here. Walking from room to room, she found no one. No servants, children or mother. In the far back walkway of the courtyard she spied a splash of color looking more like a pile of rags than a person. But as she approached, she realized it was a person she cared for dearly, her mother. She appeared to be unconscious.

"Mother," she cried, kneeling beside her. Shaking her gently, she tried to wake her, "Mother. Can you speak to me?" A slight moan escaped from her. Mary moved and leaned on one elbow, trying to find a comfortable position. Meriel helped her to a sitting position and leaned her against the wall.

"Mother, what happened? Are you hurt? Where are the children?" Meriel was frantic.

Mary was bruised on her face and some blood was on her hands and knees. Otherwise, she did not appear to have other injuries. Mary looked up into Meriel's face, but said nothing. That look from one mother to another, nearly tore Meriel's heart from her chest. "Mother, no!" she began to wail, rocking back and forth on her knees. Her hands were hiding her face.

"Meriel, the soldiers took them both as captives. I do not think they were going to kill them. At least, they were alive when they left here." When Mary spoke the words 'kill them' the wailing began again. Meriel rolled into a ball beside her mother and just wept. She did not move again for a couple of hours. There was no need. What was there to do or what was there to live for.

Early in the evening, Mary spoke to her, "Meriel. Get up. We have to think of what we can do. Have you seen Gideon or Daniel?" Meriel did not answer. "Well, I haven't. I don't think that is good. They were at the temple when the warning trumpet sounded."

Meriel didn't care. They were all gone now. All gone

Earlier that day divisions were moving around the city entering from several locations. Some moved toward the main gates of the city near the palace. Nebuchadnezzar stood in his gold and scarlet chariot watching from outside the main gate. His men advanced toward the gate from the outside trying to avoid the three towers near that entrance. They did not try to break the gate down; they simply returned fire toward the wall and towers.

This location would be conquered from the inside. The gate was opened about two hours after the attacks began. One of his groups finally battled their way from the south to the main gate and opened it. Nebuchadnezzar followed his troops inside and his men joined the fray. The towers had been under attack for hours and were still holding, but progress was being made.

The southern group, lead by Wakeem, went down through the valley of Tophet. They took the Dung Gate off its hinges with just a small effort and the Fountain Gate didn't take much more time to open. They were in and moving up the escarpment. The angle of incline was so steep that it was hard for the chariots to climb. Chariots on the main road from the Fountain Gate were able to continue. Some left their chariots near the bottom and moved through the streets and pathways on foot.

"Vicken, take over for me. I will meet you later at the top of the theatre where they plan on holding the captives. Work your way through this hovel taking captives. Kill those who get in your way. Take as much spoil as possible," said Wakeem.

"Yes, sir. Where is the theatre? What about the livestock?" asked Vicken.

"Take the people to the upper city not far from the palace. Move the livestock into the sheep market outside the wall to the north of the temple. If you don't see me at the top of the escarpment, then I will meet up with you at the theatre," Wakeem said and left down a footpath.

He found what he was looking for in just minutes. Entering the house through the front courtyard, he walked through the living area and into the kitchen. No one was there. He moved into the back area and still didn't see anyone. Taking the steps two at a time, he went to the left down the hall of the second story, opening doors as he passed them. He turned to the right and walked down through the gallery toward the other end. He found no one in the house.

He paused and listened. The men were probably at work and the ladies must be at the market, but he would find her. He had a very special plan for her. As he turned to leave the bedroom, a tiny scraping sound from the roof above was heard. He bounded outside and pulled himself up and over the eave of the second story. All he saw was some grain and straw. He was sure he heard a sound. Then he saw what he was looking for. The straw had a splash of purple fabric peeking out from the heap. There was someone hiding inside.

He took his time looking around the roof, pretending not to notice. He passed the straw pile then he turned around sharply and thrust his hand deep inside. He grabbed the first thing he touched that wasn't straw and pulled hard.

"Let go of me, you beast," came the screaming response. Out of the straw came the clawing, angry girl who had just about cause the death of some of his best men, not to mention destroying his business in Jerusalem. She was only half-way on her feet when her face turned up to see who was attached to the arm that grabbed her.

Her own screaming racked her body and complete panic overcame Dinah. She was not as confident or proud as she had been seconds ago when she came out of the straw. She was terrified. The 'boss' had her. Of all of the soldiers in the army, he would have to be the one she dreaded the most. His look was one of triumph and joy as he held her by the shoulders, then shoved her into the straw.

In his accented Hebrew, he said, "You have almost caused my men to be killed. You were the cause of two of them nearly being captured. You caused the death of Cain the innkeeper and you ruined my plans in this city. I will show you what I do to women who poke around in my business," he said as he took off his breast plate, helmet and his sword, throwing them to the end of the pile of straw.

The screaming stopped. Dinah just looked at him. He was unbuttoning his pants. She knew what he was going to do. He was standing above her while she lay in the straw. She rolled over and lunged for the wall, hoping she could swing herself over the edge. Wakeem's experience kicked in before she had moved two feet. He jerked her by her feet pulling her back into the straw and then he hit her in the face with his fist, knocking her senseless. He jumped on the straw and grabbed her and kissed her. Then he tore away her clothes and enjoyed the view.

For the next few minutes Dinah was not aware of much of what happened. She knew he was on top of her and she knew he was hurting her, but she was just not alert enough to care what was happening or to fight back. She could hear him laughing and saying things she did not understand. In a few minutes, he rolled over and lay back on the straw, still half naked.

When she came to completely, she saw him lying beside her. He was watching her carefully. Gradually, her senses were alert. Her clothes were torn and she was bruised and bleeding. She covered herself with the dress, which he promptly jerked away from her, leaving her bare. She began to think about what had happened and started whimpering.

But in just seconds, she stopped crying. She was not going to give him the satisfaction of upsetting her. He had done his worst and she was not going to increase his pleasure by crying. He could not hurt more than he already had. Death from him would be a welcomed release from guilt.

"You sleep too long," he said leaning on his elbow, referring to her half-conscious state. He smiled at her again, noticing she had stopped crying, "No tears. You are so tough, huh? I fixed you good. You will not be any man's wife now. No one will want you after I finished."

To her he seemed to be relaxing like he had nothing to do and there wasn't a war going on in her city. She was still woozy and not clear, but she understood what he meant. She would like to have moved away, but was afraid to move again, since he hit her. He just lay there gloating and laughing at her.

He was chattering on about his life and what hers would be like as a captive. "You will be someone's slave and will not have any freedom. I will make sure your new master is as hard as I," he said proudly. "You will not have this easy life you had here, protected by your family." He waved his arm indicating her home and things she was used to.

Suddenly, he got up and started to dress. He motioned for her to do the same. She was glad to obey that request. "We are going to the theatre. I will be watching you so you better do what is right." After they were dressed, he took her by the arm and dropped her over the roof edge to the court below. He followed right behind her taking her up the street toward the top of the incline.

Within half an hour, they were at the theatre. Wakeem spoke to another soldier, who looked her over from head to foot and laughed. "She will not be so proud and so nosey in Babylon. I have put her in her place. Watch her carefully," Wakeem instructed Vicken. Wakeem left to go toward the palace.

It was nearly noon and many had died on the roads and in the market according to the reports given to Jehoiakim from around the area. He knew that they were not going to win. It looked like they would need to negotiate, if they were going to preserve any of the inhabitants. He said, "Tigner, run the surrender flag up on the top of the castle and sound the trumpet for retreat. There is no use in continuing this chaos."

"Sire, are you sure? I know the battle is not going our way now, but maybe the tide will change," asked Tigner.

"I am sure. I do not wish to see everything and everyone destroyed. Do it quickly." Tigner moved away to give the command to a servant in the courtyard. Within five minutes the surrender signal had been sent.

"Send the trumpeter to the roof to signal retreat." Tigner returned when the trumpeter had come back downstairs.

Nebuchadnezzar was waiting near the palace. He was too close to see the flag that had been hoisted over the palace, but he heard their trumpet. He rightly concluded that they were surrendering and would wait until things were under control before he went to the palace.

Dinah sat down right where they had left her. She did not walk or move one inch. Her body ached and she was trembling all over. When she had gained control of her weeping and shaking, she lifted her head and looked around her at her surroundings. Surely, in this group of people she could find a friendly person or family member. It seemed that some people were moving around, so she stood and walked to the wall. She leaned against the wall and looked for someone, anyone she might know.

There in the back, little children were playing. She watched them distractedly. Then one caught her attention. It looked like—yes, it was Nathan. She wanted to just run to them as fast as she could, but instead she looked casually around and moved a few steps that direction gradually. It wasn't long before she was standing beside them.

She sat down next to the three of them, "Hello, dear ones," she said quietly.

Lotta jumped she was so shocked by her just showing up like that. She hugged her, "Dinah, oh, Dinah. I have been so lonely and afraid. How glad I am to see you." They hugged each other again. Mattan was cooing gently at his mother.

Just then, she noticed that sitting over a little ways from them, was her mother. Dinah crawled toward her, laying her head in her mom's lap and crying. They stayed together for a few minutes. Nathan came over and jumped on Dinah's lap.

"Ninah," he said in his baby talk, "have party" he said, innocently.

"I have been busy and now I am here. Where have you been?"

"Here," he said, "and moldiers, too."

"I have been with soldiers, too. It is very exciting and very frightening," she replied.

Lotta asked, "What happened to you to bring you here?"

"Let's talk about all of you first," she replied. At all costs, she would avoid telling them the whole truth. It was much too painful for her right now. She couldn't stand to talk about what had happened. She would tell them the other parts of the story, but not about Wakeem. The stories began to unfold and were for the most part the whole truth with Dinah's one exception.

CHAPTER 28

The inn had finally reopened after two weeks of trying to find new staff. When the battle began Moriah's people all ran, as did the patrons at the sound of the warning trumpet. She had gone upstairs to begin packing some items for the move to Babylon. She hoped someone would arrive soon rather than her being found by an uninformed soldier. She was relieved to find that they had remembered their promise.

Two soldiers dressed in scarlet had come upstairs. She had no idea if they were looking for her or were part of the general conquest group. She sat on her bed and waited until they opened her door. They stood in front of her without speaking and then motioned for her to come with them. She obliged, taking the leather bag with her few things. A few minutes later she was outside the palace where the Babylonian leaders were gathered. Wakeem saw her arrive.

"Look, the traitor arrives," he bowed in mock admiration. "I honor our promise and you are welcomed for the help you provided. I hear your man is dead."

"He was captured by palace guards and hung recently," she choked slightly on the words.

Wakeem smiled, "Good enough. Follow this man to the camp and he will provide you with a tent and take care of your needs," he said.

He spoke in Babylonian to other man in the group, "He will take your things."

She was about to leave, "Wakeem, would you do a favor for me?"

"We have already kept our bargain. I owe you nothing else," he replied and walked away from her.

She followed him, touching his arm, "I agree, but since Cain is dead, I was wondering if I could replace him with my sister. You remember, she served in the inn when you were there. She spent time with Zarallon," she continued, hoping that remembering her beauty might touch a selfish cord in him.

"I remember her well. She was a thorn in my flesh and kept my man in turmoil," he said, but giving it thought, he added, "Yes. She would be an improvement in our arrangement. Where is she?"

"Have you seen the temple of Baal to the south of town?" she asked.

"I passed there when we broke through the southern gate."

"She is a temple slave. He captors took her back last week. Can you free her to come with us?"

He looked at her with disdain, "Free her? With no effort. We will bring her to you before we leave Jerusalem. Now, go with him. You have taken too much of my time." She followed the soldier who was making his way outside the walls to the Babylonian campground a couple of miles from town.

Bethany was back in the swing of serving a different kind of patron. Today was different since everyone was busy defending their lives and families. She didn't worry, she simple sat and waited. She was dressed for work in a white linen, sleeveless flowing dress with a fancy braided gold and red sash. She had gold dangle earrings that hung down an inch or two, a gift from a patron, and her hair was free flowing down her back. She was truly lovely and ready for work, but she was still sitting alone.

Nothing for her to do. She was in no danger. The soldiers were not interested in the temple, other than for booty, and prostitutes were always needed by an army. However, thinking about the booty, she took her earrings off and put them inside the sash.

Two soldiers approached her on horseback. One looked somewhat familiar. As they drew nearer she could see it was Eddu. She hopped off the stone porch and walked toward him. He stopped and gave her a searching look. She spoke, "What? Do I look that different than when you knew me in the inn?" She twirled around in her customary fashion. This was the girl he was looking for.

He liked how she looked. At the inn she had been plainly dressed, but here in this attire she looked regal and desirable. He stuck to his business, however, and spoke, "Your sister has requested that we take you with us in place of that inn owner. Wakeem has agreed. Please come with me."

'Well,' she thought, 'I will gladly come. When the crisis is over, I will not have to worry about being a slave any longer. It will be good to have a new city with a new beginning.' Eddu reached down taking her forearm and swung her behind him on the horse. They traveled around the city about half way between Jerusalem and Gibeah to Nebuchadnezzar's camp. He took her to her sister's tent. It was with other 'business' girls' tents who sometimes camped near where with the soldiers were.

The campground was huge. If Eddu had not directed her to the correct tent, she might never have found her sister. He nodded toward the tent and dropped her on the sand. He went back to the main city gate. She called after him, "Don't you want to come in and see Moriah? I am sure she would be very grateful," Bethany laughed.

"I have much to do in the city. We will meet again." He rode toward the Ephraim gate.

Bethany pulled back the tent flap to see her sister relaxing on a rug with a pillow. "Sister!" Moriah cried. She was on her feet meeting Bethany at the entrance. "Welcome to your new home. I have missed you these two weeks, but I am glad we are together again."

Bethany hugged her and moved away, "Well, thanks for thinking about me. I would have been okay, but it is nice to know you were so concerned. And best of all, I will be free. I am rather excited to have a new beginning." She faced her sister, "And just think about the adventure we will have. We are going to a big, fancy city. Jerusalem is a walled village with old-fashioned morals. I will be glad to be rid of her."

Moriah sat back on the rug evaluating her sister carefully, "I think you have a 'romantic' view of what life may be like for us. I am not sure it will be an improvement, but it will surely be different."

"Well, different is good, too. Who have you seen? Eddu brought me here, but he said he would see you later. Have you seen Zarallon?" Bethany asked.

"I have not. I don't think he is here. Wakeem met me at the palace and sent me here. He looks the same. He seemed pleased that I asked to have you as a replacement for Cain," she smiled at Bethany.

"I should hope he would think I was quite an improvement," she laughed. "Have you done any snooping around? I want to see the camp. Let's go out and look." She took Moriah's hand and pulled her outside. They spent the afternoon touring their temporary home.

Mishael was in the market when the attack began. He took an ax from a nearby chopping block at the meat vendor and attacked the first soldier who approached. He took off the man's hand holding the sword. Misha took the sword along, too. He was not interested in killing any soldiers, but he was determined to work his way to the palace where his father was working.

He ran down the nearest alley and up the next street. He attacked two soldiers on foot. The first one who attacked him was not very experienced. Misha ran him through with the sword in just a few minutes. The second man approached. Misha swung the ax with his left hand in huge, arching motions. This delayed his attack until the first soldier was down. By that time the second soldier was occupied with another attacker, so Misha ran.

He moved carefully to the edge of a building and peeked around the corner. The palace had divisions of soldiers on the north side on main street from the Jaffa Gate. He took a back route, avoiding that area. He carefully came up behind the palace toward the servant's entrance.

He couldn't see anyone, so he moved out from his hiding place and approached the door. A horseman came around the corner just after Misha appeared in the clearing. Their eyes met.

"Aaghh!" yelled Eddu, as he spurred his horse forward, drawing his sword.

Misha was more comfortable using the ax than the sword, so he dropped the sword. He raised the ax with both hands preparing to swing it with his full strength toward the man.

Eddu hit Misha with the side of his horse, knocking him to the ground. He spun the horse and came back trying to trample Misha, but he was able to roll toward the wall near the garden. He scrambled to his feet. He couldn't reach his ax, which he dropped when he fell. He ran the other direction from Eddu and tried to climb the steps into the kitchen. Eddu dismounted on a run and reached Misha in three strides.

"Oh, no, you aren't escaping me," Eddu said, grabbing Misha by the legs and toppling him into a bush beside the steps. Misha and Eddu pounded each other with hard blows to the head and stomach. Over and over they hit and smashed and kicked each other. Misha was very strong and he tried everything he knew, but Eddu's advantage was years of soldiering. Misha could not match his wresting moves or his street-wise ways. Both were bruised and battered, but Eddu pinned Misha to the ground and held him. Then he beat him in the back and along the side of the head and neck. He continued to hit him until Wakeem showed up on his horse.

"Someone you know, Eddu?" he said, watching the beating. "This seems personal rather than professional."

"This," Eddu punched him, "is," and another punch, "the man I worked with and his father. It brings me great joy to kill him."

Wakeem dismounted and pulled Eddu away, holding him. He looked down at the battered man. "Don't you think you would enjoy seeing him become a slave to someone and watching him work the fields? He looks very fit."

Eddu relaxed, "I believe that would also bring me joy. Maybe more than killing him right now. I could watch him suffer for a long time." He reached down and picked Mishael up, throwing him over his shoulder. He took him to his horse tossing him over the back. They moved back to the front and joined the main group. He plopped Misha in a group of other men being held in that area.

He rode over to Zaradan and dismounted, standing in the group. Zaradan spoke, "I want to set up Nebuchadnezzar's traveling throne here by the main gate. We will make decisions from this point until we occupy the castle." He dispatched the men to get the temporary site ready.

By mid-afternoon the king was on his throne and they were ready to do business. "Zaradan, go with Wakeem and Eddu as translators. Meet the people in the palace to negotiate the surrender from the king and his leaders. I want to have this settled before dark," Nebuchadnezzar said.

Jehoiakim sat with Tigner in the throne room. Zaradan entered in his gold breast plate, black leather sandals laced up his calf, scarlet tunic with gold braid and his blazing gold helmet with a crest of short black feathers down the middle paraded forward, his hand on his sword's hilt, ready for action. He stopped ten feet short of the throne. He reviewed the room before he spoke, "Nebuchadnezzar awaits your arrival at his throne outside the palace. You will come to him with your leaders and nobles. There has been a stop in the battle, but it will resume within one hour unless you meet him." He did not need translation. He spoke excellent Hebrew.

Tigner, Donolly and Jehoiakim talked quietly. Donolly spoke, "We agree to your terms with one stipulation—you will spare our lives and the lives of our leaders. Are we in agreement?"

"Do you think Nebuchadnezzar will agree to spare their lives?" Wakeem and Zaradan talked.

"Agreed." He turned and left, taking his men along.

They reported to Nebuchadnezzar. "Excellent. While we are waiting, finish the clean up of captives and prepare a separate holding area for the nobles and leaders."

Zaradan left with his men, "Wakeem, what other area would be good for holding the nobles?"

"Let's use the temple. It is walled and will contain them well until we leave."

A few minutes later small groups of nobles accompanied by two guards began to leave the palace by the front doors.

Daniel whispered to his father, "Where are they taking us?"

"I heard the temple, but I am not sure. It seems they are still working out details. I hope and pray that Meriel and the children and grandma are safe at home and not captured. I wonder where they are taking other captives?" said Gideon.

They would stand and wait for enemy soldiers to move them, all the while wondering about what was going to happen. In a few minutes they all walked across the ravine and up the steps to the temple mount. The temple had surrendered about noon time. The priests had eventually opened the doors when the surrender flag was raised at the palace. None were killed and it was relatively peaceful, though occupied by the enemy.

Daniel and Gideon looked around to see who was there. They looked first for Hadad and Azariah. The group was moved under Solomon's porch and told to sit down.

"Dad, did you see Hadad or Azariah anywhere? I know they were working today."

A guard walked by and stood in front of them. They were all afraid to speak when the guards were near. A few minutes passed and he moved on.

"I saw Hadad with the priests on the steps to the men's quarter. Azariah was not around, that I saw. Anyone else you noticed?" answered Gideon.

"I saw Hananiah and the prophet Jeremiah is seated with us at the far end of the porch. Isn't that ironic? I imagine he was prophesying here when the temple surrendered. Now he is among those captured," he said. Daniel was very careful about how loud he spoke and when. It took courage just to finish these two or three sentences.

No women or children were in the group assembled in the temple. They must have them somewhere else. It was a relief that they were not here, but not knowing about whether they were made captives or had escaped seemed harder than seeing them in captivity might have been.

About an hour later two more groups of palace leadership arrived. Just a few minutes later a group of men that were not from palace employees arrived. Among those were Benjamin and some other palace workers. Hadad and Daniel saw him right away and their eyes met, but nothing was said. Later that afternoon, in another general group, a face Benjamin had been seeking appeared. Mishael walked in with others who appeared to be prisoners rather than captives. He had shackles on and was badly beaten. They were kept in another spot in the temple. They did not catch his eye as he passed.

Back at the palace, the surrender was nearly complete. Before the time elapsed and with as much pomp as he could attain, Jehoiakim, Tigner, Baileen and Donolly exited the palace to go meet with the enemy king. They waited to be escorted to Nebuchadnezzar.

'What a scraggly crew of leaders,' Nebuchadnezzar thought. When Jehoiakim arrived in front of the King, he said, through an interpreter, "Are you Jehoiakim, king of the Jews?"

"I am."

"Are you ready to surrender to the great King of Babylon, Nebuchadnezzar, Conqueror of all of Israel?" asked Nebuchadnezzar.

"We choose to surrender to you rather than have our fair city and temple destroyed. Our people will cooperate fully, you have my word," Jehoiakim answered through his teeth. This was humiliating and embarrassing. Why couldn't we have enough of an army to meet the foe and win?

Jeremiah's words came into his mind unwillingly, "Because of your sin I will give you to the enemy. I will fight against you." That sounds like the God worshiped by the old Jews. 'Follow me or else' was God's attitude. Well, I am choosing 'or else.'

"Very well. We have agreed to spare your nobles and leaders. All will be moved to the temple, except you. I need you to give answers to questions that arise. You may stay in your palace under guard for the time being," Nebuchadnezzar told him.

Jehoiakim requested that he be able to keep Baileen with him. He was granted that courtesy. He was also told to keep his cooking staff and some other servants to help provide support to all the military outside. They were to prepare a supper for tonight to serve in the main banquet hall for the enemy leaders.

He, Tigner and Baileen returned to the main throne room and made themselves comfortable. The palace staff took care of him and they waited for further instructions.

The meal was served two hours later for about fifty of Nebuchadnezzar's generals and leaders. Jehoiakim was seated at the table in front of guards. He had no idea why they would want him there.

"I want to tell you what has been decided this afternoon," through Wakeem Nebuchadnezzar spoke to Jehoiakim. "We will be taking our captives with us in the next couple of days and moving on toward Egypt. A holding area will be made in the southern area to keep them until we return from Egypt on the return to Babylon. We need a ruler who knows the town and people, but is wise enough to know who will take care of him and who he should serve. Could you be that wise a leader?" Nebuchadnezzar asked Jehoiakim through a mouth full of quail. He took a long drink of wine from a fine gold goblet and tore a piece of bread from a loaf.

When Wakeem finished the question, the look on Jehoiakim's face was obvious. Jehoiakim was stunned. He was also very pleased, having been afraid that he would be moved to Babylon and of what life he would live there. This was an offer to continue things more or less as they are without much change for him. 'Could he be that man?' Nebuchadnezzar asked. Absolutely! And that is what he said, trying not to sound too eager.

"Good," said Nebuchadnezzar, "then it is settled. You will serve me here in Jerusalem. We will have emissaries living here that will give a full report and you will have to answer for any improprieties. But if you are wise and do as you are told, you will live here for a long time in good conditions."

"I am that man for you, sire. It would be my pleasure to work for you here and to maintain a somewhat normal existence here. I ask one favor, that I be allowed to keep my right hand man, Tigner and my servant, Baileen. I will be more effectual in your service with these two remaining." He paused for effect, "And," whispering, "I do not think my mother would help you at all. In fact, she would be a drain to your economy besides being too old to serve anyone well."

"Granted. But these two are the only ones close to you that can remain. Of course, some servants may also stay that we do not consider valuable to our cause. As for your mother, very few elders will be needed and certainly not the useless ones. We could kill her for you?" Nebuchadnezzar replied with a glint in his eye.

Jehoiakim thought about that for a full minute, before answering, "No, I think she can serve me well. It will bring joy to see her suffer and not get her every wish met after the way she has been so demanding of me. Let her live."

Nebuchadnezzar burst into laughter, slapping Jehoiakim on the shoulder, "A man who thinks like me. I think you will be of value to me here." The rest of the meal was uneventful. Jehoiakim returned to his relatively normal existence moving back into his room. He was so grateful to be king. It did have advantages.

CHAPTER 29

"You cannot do this, Meriel. It is foolish," were her mother's words of warning. Meriel was determined to leave the house and find her children.

"I must. How can I leave my children alone with these madmen who have stolen them away from me. No telling what would happen to them," she cried. She had been in tears most of the night. Her thinking was muddled by grief and lack of sleep. "I must try to find them. After that, I don't know what I will do. If I can find them and be with them, you know I will. Mother, I love you, but you have lived your life and can continue as an adult with or without me."

Mary broke into tears, when Meriel said those words, "Are saying that if you find them, you will go with them and not return to me?"

Meriel knew that her mother was fearful, but that is exactly what she was thinking, "Yes, I will go with them, if they are alive."

"No, no. I cannot live alone. I am afraid and I would mourn myself to death. Please don't leave me!" Mary begged. She fell on her daughter's shoulders.

Meriel held her away and looked at her, "Mother, I will always love you, but if you were me and I was taken captive by crazy men, what would you do?"

Mary finally gained control of her emotions and looked at Meriel. Then she pulled away and walked to the nearest chair. Meriel followed her and knelt at her knees, placing her head in Mary's lap. They sat quietly like that for a few minutes with Mary stroking her daughter's hair. They both knew the answer to Meriel's question.

"Mother, the longer I wait the more difficult it may be to find them," she stood and held her mother's hands for a few minutes. Then, she turned to go to her room and change clothes. This may be the last time she would be able to be in her own house, in her own room with things that belonged to her.

She dropped to her knees again and wept. How had it come to this point that God had forsaken them? That the city and people He loved were now captives of a brutal government? It was so.

Impossible to believe that everyone she loved had been at home and living a normal life just over one day ago and now they were all missing. How was it possible to survive with such a weight of grief? She didn't know for she had never faced anything so devastating.

And now, she was compounding her mother's grief by leaving her alone with no family at all. This is a choice that one should never need to make. She gathered what she could on her body, making use of a cloak and several layers. These may be helpful later, though, right now, she didn't need the warmth.

"Mother, I am ready," she said, arriving at the courtyard where her mother had prepared some food for her to eat and some to take along. Meriel ate quickly and prepared to leave.

Mary stood up and inspected her precious daughter, "You look lovely, my dear, though somehow overdressed." They both enjoyed a giggle together. Hugging her daughter for probably the last time, she prayed, "'God, grant her peace and put Jothal and Salme safe and sound in her arms by nightfall.' I love you more than life itself. I cannot imagine the future, but I know our God and somehow it will be bright again. Now, go, if you must," Mary pushed her free with tears streaming down her cheeks.

Meriel walked away looking back as she reached the courtyard door and waving. She was sick inside. Sick with grief and fear and longing for things like they had been just a day ago.

She stopped someone on the road and asked about captives. The rumor was that captives were being held somewhere near the palace. As she approached the side of the palace, she was stopped by an enemy guard. He held out his spear, blocking her advance.

"Sir, I am looking for my children. Do you know where the captives are being held?" she asked.

He continued holding the spear and did not respond. She tried again with the same question and got the same response. 'That was foolish,' she thought, 'he probably doesn't understand my language.'

In frustration she turned and went away from the palace. She walked south asking anyone she could find about the location of captives. "Do you know where the captives are being held?" she questioned an old man on the street.

"They are in the theatre. I saw them walking a couple of groups in the main gate," he replied. "Who did you lose?"

"My two children were taken. I have not seen my husband or older son either," she answered moving on down the road. She turned around and called back, "Thanks."

In a quarter-hour she had arrived outside the theatre. Other Hebrews were standing around probably asking for the same privilege—to see if there loved ones were inside. They were being turned away at spear-point, also. That approach was not going to work. The soldiers didn't understand Hebrew anyway, so there was little use in asking to look inside.

She knew she risked being killed, but that didn't matter to her. She had to find Salme and Jothal. She was worried about Daniel and Gideon, too, but they could handle themselves in most situations, so she worried less about them. The younger children were helpless. She would rather go along as a slave, too, than leave them uncared for. Or to not know what was happening to them. Watching from a distance, a plan began to form in her mind. It was radical, but these were desperate times and she was a desperate woman.

In minutes she had moved to the back of the theatre. She approached a small entrance that was fairly well concealed. No guards were visible so she sneaked to the door. It was locked, as she expected it would be. A minute of searching provided the necessary tool to break the latch. She took the large stone and knocked it against the lock. It was solid and did not move. After several more hits, she decided that the lock was not yielding to the rock, but she noticed that the latch itself was loosening.

So engrossed was she in her effort that she failed to notice the approaching guard. He watched from a distance with a smirk that implied how foolish he thought she was. She was free, but now she would be part of the captives she so desperately wanted to help escape. Too bad for her.

He walked up behind her quietly and grabbed her arm as she took a backward swing. She looked shocked and began to protest. She looked at him with anger and every emotion she could manufacture. She yelled every unpleasantry that came to her mind. He became more pleased as he saw her becoming upset. He would show her who was in control in Jerusalem. It took several minutes to maneuver her around the theatre with all of her fighting, screaming and protesting. After processing he took her inside to a clearing and said some incomprehensible words, leaving her alone.

She watched him leave, her face beaming. She was inside.

Meriel was shocked by the site of the people. Many lay wounded with dried blood on their faces. In the far corner some dead bodies had been laid in as reverent a fashion as their families could arrange them. The faces that turned toward her were filled with anguish and utter fear. Never before had she seen a picture like this. She hoped this was not an omen of things to come.

She put aside the situation and began working her way around the wall to the right asking people about Jothal and Salme. No one had seen them. Other children were in the area, but not hers. She was beginning to panic. What if she had allowed herself to be caught in order to get inside and they weren't here?

Abeetha is sitting against the wall by the main door of the theater watching Meriel interviewing captives. There is no doubt that this mother is looking for her children.

Speaking to a prostitute is not approved of among the women of town, but at this point Abeetha had nothing to lose. She got up and walked over to her, "Meriel, I am Abeetha. Are you a captive now, too?" she ventured a question to this respected woman.

Meriel is well aware of who this woman was and under other circumstances she might have ignored her, but these were extra-ordinary circumstances, "I am more of a volunteer than a true captive. My children are missing and I have reason to believe they were taken captive. Have you seen them here anywhere?"

"In the area under the seats there are several large rooms. I think some captives have been put in those areas. Let me show you," Abeetha walked toward the far wall and a large arched opening. "I think some are in these two areas, but the guards aren't likely to let you in," she whispered.

"Come with me, if you would like, and play along," Meriel whispered back. She hid out of sight and took a roll and some cheese from a wrapped cloth in her sash. If they saw that she had a stash of food hidden away, they might take it all. They walked forward with purpose to the first guard. She pointed her hand toward the door and then held out the food. He was a young man with quick eyes. He took in the situation and thought it looked safe enough, and besides, he was hungry. He grabbed the food and cocked his head toward the door.

"Do you see them?" Abeetha asked Meriel. "I am having a hard time seeing faces in this dim light," she added.

"Jothal. Salme." Meriel was walking along speaking their names out loud first to one group and then to another. Abeetha was right. Faces were hard to see, but she was sure if her children were here and alive, they would respond to her voice.

When they had made their way around the room, they returned to the door, hoping the guard who had let them in would still be on duty and would let them go to the other room. As they opened the door, he moved in front of it and crossed the spear over the exit. For a fleeting second he stood in their way until he recognized them. A smile crossed his face and then he let them pass.

They went to the next room. He nodded to the other guard who let them inside.

Meriel and Abeetha followed the same pattern working their way around the room. No faces or sweet voices of her children were seen or heard. Meriel was discouraged. She just sat down in the dust and began sobbed. Abeetha tried to comfort her, "No, no, Meriel. Don't give up yet. Maybe there are other rooms. Let's keep trying. Come along." She pulled Meriel back to her feet and they were again allowed to leave.

They went back to the first guard and gave the universal signal for, "Nothing, I don't know." Meriel hunched her shoulders lifting her hands up to the sides with her palms up and looked questioningly at him. He had done his duty in his mind. They had looked and found nothing. He shrugged his shoulders back again.

Meriel sighed and looked at Abeetha, "Now what?"

Abeetha pointed the other way down the hall and made signs asking if any other rooms had people in them. He nodded yes. When they started to go down that way, he stopped them. He obviously wasn't going to let them continue to search. They had used up their bribe.

Abeetha looked at Meriel's face and knew she had to do something. She moved to get near him and he stopped her. He wanted to be sure they didn't try to trick him. Abeetha smiled at him and moved a little closer. This time he understood what she was thinking. He took her shoulder and pulled her against him. They were both smiling.

"Stop that!" Meriel snapped, "How disgusting."

Abeetha flipped her head back toward Meriel, with pleading in her eyes for understanding, "Do you or don't you want to find your children? And how badly?" she said in a cooing voice, not to give away the real tone of the conversation. The whole time she was romancing the soldier.

Meriel was angry and appalled at her own willingness to sell this girl to this man for the privilege of finding for her children. "I want to find them, you know that, but I cannot do this to you. Please move back over here to me."

"You are not doing this to me. It is what I do and I do it well. Besides, I am volunteering to help in the only way I can." A second later, the soldier had called to the guard at the other door. He took Abeetha by the arm and they disappeared into the hallway around the corner.

"Oh, God. What have I done?" Meriel sat on the floor and wept. "How could I have come this far to use this woman for my own gains and to care about my needs more than I care about hers? I have, overnight, become selfish and crude. God, please don't let this captivity make me bitter and useless to you. And thank you for Abeetha," she prayed the whole time Abeetha was gone. She knew this was Abeetha's profession, but she never dreamed she would see a prostitute in action up close and very personal. And she never dreamed she would be thankful for her.

Abeetha called from down the hall, "Come with me. Hurry."

Meriel ran to her side. "Are you okay? Did he hurt you?" she asked looking at Abeetha carefully. She was amazed. She seemed absolutely the same as she had a few minutes earlier.

"What? Are you expecting warts or horns to grow out of my head? It is just work. Nothing more. Come on. I think they may be in the next room. With some sign language I was able to explain a little to him that we were looking for children and he implied there were many in this room," she was walking away toward the door he had indicated.

As far as Meriel was concerned, Abeetha didn't have horns. She had a halo around her head. Meriel said, "Thank you, Abeetha, but promise me you will never do that again. Please?" She looked pleadingly at her new friend as she followed her into the next room. "Jothal. Salme," Meriel called.

"Mother! Mother!" were the screams that they heard immediately. Jothal and Salme ran to her arms. Weeping was heard all around. Even Abeetha was in tears. To see this family reunited was thrilling when all thought the other might be dead.

"Come with me, children. Let's go out into the arena. It is more pleasant outside. Abeetha, you are one of us now. Come along, too, if you would like. I would count it a privilege to call you my friend," Meriel added.

Abeetha was really weeping now. Never had she dreamed that any respectable woman would ever again befriend her. It was more than she could have hoped for. The tiny group was allowed to leave and return to the open air after Abeetha had her guard do some negotiating with the other guard.

They sat together reliving what had happened to all of them in the past few hours. Salme and Jothal were unharmed. They had not seen Gideon or Daniel anywhere in the arena. It must be they were being held somewhere else. At least, that is what they all chose to believe.

From across the arena in the theater the little group was being watched. Dinah had found Lotta with the boys last night. Most of the captives had gone through the crowds yelling out names of loved ones and trying to find someone they knew. Some were reunited and other sat alone in their grief. Lotta was alone when Dinah was searching.

"Lotta, look. Isn't that Meriel over there?" Dinah asked. "I think she has the children. I didn't see her last night at all. I wander what has happened."

"Do you think the guards would notice if we moved over to join them. I would find it very comforting to be with as many friends right now as we can, wouldn't you?" Lotta asked.

"Let's just stand and move around some. I see other people moving. If we take it slow without appearing to have a destination in mind. Let's move into the sun, like we are too cool sitting in the shade of the wall. After a while we can relocated near the wall in a closer location in the shade again. That way we can work our way over gradually. What do you think?" suggested Dinah, "Besides, the boys are getting restless."

They stood up and stretched. They pointed to a place in the sun and the guard nodded. The group walked slowly out to the center of the arena and sat down. The sun did feel wonderful on their faces after spending a cold night in the open air. Neither of them had talked about their capture. The pain was too fresh for them to discuss any of the details now.

The guards came to the main entrance with several wagons filled with food. They choose captives to distribute it around the area. While that was going on, Dinah and Lotta moved back to the wall, but much closer to Meriel. After eating, they rested for a while and then motioned that they would like a bathroom break.

The guards had set up a latrine in the hallway to the south of the main entrance, which faced northeast. After the break they exited through a door closer to where Meriel had been. When they came out, they walked over to Meriel's area.

"Meriel, hello," Dinah said quietly, so as to not attract attention from the guards.

Meriel stood and hugged her, "All of you sit down by us, quickly. Your faces are such a welcomed sight to me. These last two days have brought grief and anguish of soul beyond my ability to put into words."

"Did you come here with the two children yesterday? I didn't see you, but then there are many people I did not find," Lotta said. "By the way, I am Lotta. I am not sure we have met officially. I am betrothed to Azariah, Dinah's brother. My parents are Abram and Myra. Do you know them?"

"Yes, my dear. I know your family. I have also kept up with your romance with Azariah through Daniel. He has been very pleased to have his friend marrying such a fine woman. I hope that someday things will work out and you can find each other again. This situation is so unsure, that I know we have no idea what our future may hold," her voice quivered slightly as her sentence ended. "Oh, I am sorry for being so rude. Let me introduce, my friend, Abeetha. She has helped me so much." Abeetha smiled shyly back to the other woman who acknowledged her presence with a nod. She did not expect more. They were likely confused by the association and would have to warm-up to the situation.

Dinah sat in wonder at Meriel's use of the word 'friend.' Since when does a respectable woman call one of the city's prostitutes a 'friend?' There must be something Dinah did not understand, but there would be time to find out what had caused this strange relationship later.

"You asked about me and the children. I was not taken captive with them. Chloe and I hid in our shop and the managed to escape to our homes last night. Well, at least I hope she reached her home. When I arrived, mother told me the children were made captive. I said my good-bye to her this morning and went in search of their whereabouts. I managed to get 'captured' and began my search for them once I was inside. With Abeetha's great assistance I found them this morning," she pulled them close, kissing their heads.

"Well, that is wonderful. At least none of us were killed. I was taken from my family. They were left there because they are too old to be taken as captives. I may never see them again," Lotta began to weep. Nathan came over and put his little arms around his mother's neck and held on to her. Mattan just looked at her and began to cry, too. "Oh dear, now I have made him cry. Sh-h-h. I am sorry. Mommie is okay." She kissed little Nathan and stroked Mattan's cheek. Lotta looked at Dinah, who took Nathan and held him in her lap. The comfort to him reminded Lotta how happy she was to have some family with her, "I am so grateful that Dinah found me last night. This horrid affair has been made easier by her presence."

Abeetha spoke for the first time, "My mother was also left and she is my only family. It will be hard to be alone."

Meriel turned to her, "You are no longer alone. You have us now as your family," she smiled at her and patted her arm.

'What on earth could happen that would cause such a comment like that to Abeetha?' It was amazing to Dinah, but she made no comment, only asked a question, "Do any of you have any idea about our brothers and fathers? I am very worried about them. And I have not seen my mother either." Now it was Dinah's turn to weep.

CHAPTER 30

Robron and Garridon had survived the ordeal. Many of their men had not been so fortunate. Marold was had died last night after suffering a severe stab wound and it did not look good for Ben-Zion, the clerk. Surviving Hebrew soldiers had been moved to a holding area outside of town. Robron was tied to a wagon wheel at the front and Garridon was tied at the back. The Babylonian soldiers had made the loading dock their headquarters, keeping these two leaders close by to answer questions that might arise.

Tied up with them were Oshiel and Donolly. All were here to provide any needed information. The spies who had killed so many Hebrew soldiers in the tribute raid are now Robron's captors. How that ate at him! Wakeem and Eddu, the two names he now knew and recognized as two of the spies, spoke Hebrew well enough to act as interpreters for the all information needed by the enemy. So these two were now the ones he had to deal with on a face to face basis. Nothing he could imagine could have been more galling.

Wakeem came to them, drawing his sword from its scabbard, "Up and on your feet. We are taking you outside the city with the other captives." He slapped the ropes with the sabre edge slicing through them like butter. The two soldiers untied their feet. Oshiel was ready to be moved. This area was too tense for his liking. Donolly was still sitting on the stone wall, trying to get his limbs awake after being tied for so long.

"Hurry, you idiot! You three turn around," Eddu had come over to the group bringing shackles with him. He cuffed the first three men and pushed them over toward the door. When Eddu returned to see Donolly still sitting with his feet tied, he was furious. He jerked the man to his feet and dragged him over to the door still tied.

"You three carry him or drag him or get him ready. We are leaving." A band of enemy soldiers surrounded the small group of Jews as they marched out the door with Donolly being dragged behind Garridon. After they were outside the city gates, Donolly was dropped on the pavement because Garridon could no longer pull him up the road. His feet and knees were bleeding. As quickly as he was dropped he dug his fingers into the ropes on his ankles and was free. He stood up and followed the group on his own two feet.

"You are a slow learner, old man. You had better catch on to other things faster if you want to survive," said Wakeem, as he trotted up from behind the group on Ibbisin.

Across town at the Temple decisions were being made about what to do with the other captives. Most of the leaders were being taken to Babylon. A few of the older men would be left here since the trip would be too hard for them. Nebuzaradan did not want to have stragglers on the trek. A dead leader was of no value to his king in Babylon. Only those who could make the trip would be taken. Some of those would also likely die during the harsh overland trek, but he could not control that. It was one of the hazards of being a captive. He hoped most would make it, since fresh laborers were always in need.

Pashhur was arguing with Eddu, who had been sent to interpret, "I am too old to make this trip. I would be useless to your government and to your religion." He was trying to stop Vicken from preparing him to march. He was getting all the captives ready for relocation.

Vicken pushed him toward the line of men that were going to Babylon, totally ignoring his babbling. He yelled, "Sir, you have made a mistake. I am to stay here and serve. I cannot go with you to your fair city." The group of men continued to push him along. His yelling did not stop. He was convinced they had just made an error. When they were fully aware of who he was and his position in the city, they would allow him, of all people, to stay.

Pashhur felt the tenseness and fearfulness for all the captives. All, but one, that is. Jeremiah, who was also being held at the temple, stood to his feet and began his prophesying in the midst of the turmoil. If anyone could make Pashhur even angrier, it would be him. Hearing Jeremiah preaching the same things he had been saying for years. Pashhur could not, would not, admit that this prophet had been correct in his warnings. It was just too much to bear.

"I have been warning you, but you have not listened. 'Repent, do not go after other gods, and I will not harm you.' I have said these words to you many times in many ways. Therefore the Lord of hosts says, 'I will send and take all the families of the north and Nebuchadnezzar the king of Babylon, My servant, will bring them against this land and its inhabitants.'"

"Shut up, you fool. That is not a prophecy. We can see he is here already. What do you know?" different ones yelled at him. Even now in their moment of grief, they refused to yield to their God, who could have delivered them.

"I will take from them mirth and marriage and gladness. The whole land shall be in desolation and astonishment, and these nations shall serve the king of Babylon seventy years," he continued. Yelling at him did not intimidate him in the least.

"Seventy years. We will escape and come back home before we are out of our own land. We will return within a year. No country can hold the Hebrews for 70 years." Again he heard the taunts from his listeners and failure to repent.

Pashhur spoke up, "We demand that your stop right now. You are not speaking God's words to our ears. We are listening to prophets who know what God wants to say to us."

Jeremiah continued the preaching. Eddu was fascinated by this man's words. He turned to the man sitting on the pavement beside him, "What is this man's name?" The man told him the name. He walked over to where Jeremiah was standing. From what Eddu had observed while he was spying and even how, this man had been telling the truth. Everything that he prophesied had come to pass.

Zaradan came over, too, to talk to Eddu, "What are you thinking about this one?" They spoke in Chaldean to avoid being understood.

"I have known about him for the months we were in town. He has always spoken the truth. Just now he said...." Eddu and Zaradan discussed what was said.

Zaradan smiled and said, "Release him to go. A man who knows and tells the truth like that in the face of condemnation deserves our respect. Let him go."

Eddu smiled, "That is exactly what I hoped we could do and I agree. It will be my pleasure to tell him." He turned to Jeremiah, "You have told the truth when others spoke against you. You have been right in your prophesies. We are impressed by your courage, even if your own people are fools and do not see it." Eddu released the shackles, handing them to Zaradan. Zaradan nodded his approved and moved toward the other group. "Go and keep telling the truth," said Eddu.

Jeremiah was stunned. He rubbed his wrists and stood looking around the group of quiet men. They heard what Eddu had told him and it cut them to the quick like the words of Jeremiah always had.

Pashhur spoke up, "Of all the people to let go, he is not the one. He must be sent to Babylon. He causes great turmoil in our city. I, on the other hand, am most valuable to our city. I am the chief religious leader here. I must be allowed to remain. Take Jeremiah in my place," he said, pleased with his convincing argument. Jeremiah would not get away that easily. It just wasn't right for him to be left in his own city.

Eddu walked over to Pashhur with Zaradan right behind. Eddu had heard enough of the demands of the priest. They stopped in front of him, smiling. Pashhur knew he had finally convinced them of the error of their ways in taking him to Babylon.

Zaradan took out the shackles, which had just been removed from Jeremiah. Eddu grabbed Pashhur and spun him around holding him while Zaradan snapped the shackles in place. Then Eddu took out a funny looking leather device with a one inch wooden nipple attached in the middle. He put it over the priest's head and slid it down, putting the nipple in his mouth. He buckled it behind Pashhur's head. Eddu tightened it so that the man could no longer speak. Then he turned him to face them.

"Well, priest, it seems you are the fool. This man," Zaradan pointed to Jeremiah, "has been telling you for years that we were coming and all of you had better repent. You should have listened. Now, you can only listen. No more talking for you. All of today and tomorrow, you will not talk and you will not eat. If a friend is willing they can pour some things through the nipple. It is hollow," he spun Pashhur in a circle a couple of times. Calling out in loud Hebrew, "Everyone look at him. This is what happens to people who talk too much, especially with stupid words." He turned Pashhur back to face him, "On the third day, I will have the device removed. If I hear more stupid words, or arguing, or anything I just don't like, I will cut out your tongue. Is that clear?" Eddu spoke all of these words loud enough that the entire group could hear.

Pashhur was livid. He had never been humiliated like this. He was special and always considered wise. His eyes flashed in a warning to Zaradan and

Eddu. They must understand who they were dealing with. This was all just a bad misunderstanding. He tried to speak, but all that was heard was a guttural mumble.

Zaradan caught on very quickly. He slapped Pashhur across the face first with his left hand, following immediately with his right hand. When Pashhur slipped slightly, Eddu stuck his foot out and tripped Pashhur, causing him to fall backwards to the floor, hitting his seat and then falling back further, hitting his head. He was knocked unconscious.

No one moved to help him. He just lay there until he awakened. He could not move at first. One finger was broken and something wet was behind his head. He waited for help, but none came. Wasn't someone going to come get him up and check on his wounds? He rolled his head from side to side, spreading the blood all over his hair and beard. He was looking for a helper, but none were allowed to move. After several minutes, he sat up and then rolled to his knees. With great effort he got up and moved back against the wall, waiting for sympathy or aid. But he stood there alone, until the group was moved.

"Eddu, move them all outside to the holding area by the sheep market. We should be ready to set up a permanent camp there until we are ready to move them north, which may be soon." Eddu's men had started the front of the group moving toward the back gate at the temple mount. It would lead out of the city wall come out very near the holding area.

Eddu took the end of the group. He looked around to make sure they hadn't missed anyone. Jeremiah, the prophet, was still standing under Solomon's porch. He nodded at him, as the final man passed out of the courtyard toward the gate with Eddu right behind him. It was the last sight of these people that this prophet would ever see. They were going to Babylon.

CHAPTER 31

The guard at the tower could see the riders coming at full speed toward the gate. As they drew closer, he could see that they were Babylonian. He called down to the men at the gate with information.

The two riders slowed down and walked carefully up to the gate. The horses were lathered up but seemed to be in good shape. It was apparent that both horses and riders had traveled some distance.

"Identify yourselves," said the guard, with his spear held at the ready.

"We have come from the base camp north of here in Megiddo. We have been riding since the morning with a message from the king in Babylon. We are here on most urgent business for the Prince personally."

"Do you have tablets of passage and identification?" he looked at the cuneiform writing and then said, "Wait here." The guard sent a man inside with the tablets. A few minutes later, the two riders were admitted and taken into the tent of Mongin, "Sirs, I have seen your identification tablets. What message is so urgent that you came in such haste?"

The first rider spoke, "Nabopolassar, as you remember was not feeling well, when his son left on this campaign. He has become more gravely ill. The doctors fear that although we have prayed to the god Marduk, the King may not live much longer. They are advising that Nebuchadnezzar return at once to be at his father's side."

Mongin was very concerned, saying, "I will go to his tent at once. If he is willing, you may come in and tell him what you have told me and answer any questions." Mongin went to the Prince.

He came to the area outside the tent and told the aid that he needed to speak to Nebuchadnezzar. A minute later he stood before him, "Sire, we have two riders that have come to us from the palace in Babylon. They have news of your father. Could they speak with you now?"

He was pleased to hear that there was news about his father. "Absolutely. Bring them right in." He awaited their arrival eagerly. It had been several months since he had seen him.

The riders had never been with Nebuchadnezzar. They were pleased to be able to speak with him personally, but were very worried about the message they were to deliver. What if he lost his temper at them for bring such bad news and had them killed? Sometimes messengers were killed. They bowed to the floor when they entered and waited to be heard.

"Rise, please, and give me news. I have great eagerness to know how my father is faring. Tell me of him," Nebuchadnezzar stood and moved toward them. "Get them some wine. You must be thirsty," he said to his aid who brought them wine.

After accepting a drink and taking a sip, the first man spoke, "Sire, we were sent to you over one week ago. We have ridden over eighty miles a day, stopping at your outposts to switch horses, eat and sleep only. We have taken the shortest route possible to arrive quickly to bring you news of your father. Your father's doctors have told us to hurry to your side and let you know that Nabopolassar is very ill."

"How bad is he? What do they think will be the outcome of his illness?" He encouraged them to continue.

The second rider spoke, "They are not sure of what the outcome might be. They are praying to Marduk for his recovery and good health. Sacrifices of many bulls are offered daily on his behalf."

"And why are you coming to me? If they hope he will get better, then what is the urgency?" he was reading between the lines. These two riders seemed to be having a hard time saying what needed to be said. "Tell me outright. Do they think my father is dying?"

The riders looked at other and then nodded yes.

"How long do they think I have to get back?"

"They do not know, sire. They told us to make haste and to recommend that you return immediately to be at his side," the first rider spoke.

Nebuchadnezzar knew the political climate in his city. He had been at his father's side for thirty of his thirty-five years. He had been trained for this moment, but he was not ready to face the world without his father, his mentor. When Nebuchadnezzar left Babylon in the early spring, his father was not feeling well, but it was assumed by all he would be feeling better soon. He had not considered his father's death as imminent.

He also considered that someone might try to usurp the throne, if he was not home when his father passed away. He had several brothers who would love the opportunity to rule. If they could be crowned king at their father's death, then Nebuchadnezzar would have to fight his way into power to overcome whoever was then king. He would rather take it by natural succession than have to fight for it.

"Get Zaradan and Mongin for me," he yelled, and the quietly, "You two may leave. Get what you need for travel and be ready to head out in the morning."

Mongin came immediately, "Sire, I am so sorry to hear of your father's poor health. I will do anything I can to aid you. Do you have a plan?"

"Yes. Get my armed guard ready for travel. We leave in the morning. Next, get the King of these people down here, so I can give him some instructions. Find Wakeem and get him in here to translate. Have the servants prepare a meal in the banquet hall so I can meet with everyone and give instructions for my absence. Hurry. We have much to do in a very short time," ordered Nebuchadnezzar.

For the next hour everyone worked to get the Prince ready to leave in the morning. Jehoiakim came to the tent surprised by the hubbub of activity. "Tell Nebuchadnezzar I have arrived at his request," he waited until he was admitted to the tent.

Nebuchadnezzar appeared somewhat upset. He said, "I have called for you to make some things clear before I leave."

Jehoiakim was surprised. Nebuchadnezzar had been in town such a short time and now he was leaving. What could possibly cause him to be leaving in such a rush? He made no comment.

"My wish is that you continue to run the city as you have previously. We will expect the same tribute payment from you on a yearly basis. It can be the same as the one you were paying to Necho, the one my men so craftily took from you," he nodded toward Wakeem, who was translating. Wakeem acknowledged the recognition the Prince had just given him.

"Sire, you have made our city poor and are taking all of its leaders with you to Babylon. I will not have any wealthy people left to call on for taxes or payments. How shall I raise such a great amount of money? It is not possible."

"I am not interested in your problems. You have my command. Mongin will remain with you until our emissaries arrive from Babylon. They will make sure you are adhering to my wishes. We will have dinner in one hour. Join us then and you will find out the other things you need to know. Leave," Nebuchadnezzar commanded.

Jehoiakim was very upset when he got back inside. He told Tigner what Nebuchadnezzar had said, "He is leaving. I hope to find out more details at the dinner in half an hour. And, he expects us to pay tribute. We have nothing left. They have taken our treasury, our livestock, or food stock. The leadership will have to be replaced with inadequate novices who have been left behind. They burned several fields and two orchards. And they have raided everything they could find from the temple."

Tigner agreed, "I do not see how it will be possible, but we will try to figure out what can be done later. For tonight, let's see what is happening that is causing this man to leave. Did he give you any hints?"

"No. Just that I was to come to dinner again. I hope it is informative. If he does not provide an interpreter, I will not have much of an idea of what is being said." He went upstairs to change for dinner. He at least would be presentable on the final time he hoped he would ever see this prince. Tomorrow the city would again be his. The army would remain for a while, but eventually, just that one general and a couple of emissaries would be around. He was not worried about them. He had handled worse in his reign.

When he arrived at dinner, the men were seating themselves around the table. He sat near Wakeem, hoping to have help from him to understand what was going on. This prince was living well from the riches of Jerusalem and his men were enjoying the fruit of the labor of the people. They had roast lamb, lentils, stewed cabbage, goat cheese, a bowl of dates and nuts, bread and olive oil and wine in abundance.

Nebuchadnezzar spoke to the men after they had been eating for less than half an hour, "I asked everyone at the beginning to eat a quick meal because of my plans. I want to discuss what is going to happen. Two riders came today from Babylon. It has been some time since we have had word of what is going on in our fair city. According to the men, my father, your great King Nabopolassar, is very ill, even unto death. I am being called to return to his side. His death is imminent and the leaders want me there to assume the throne when that sad day arrives. I will be leaving at dawn to ride a top speed to his side," he paused to have his goblet filled with wine. He stood and held his glass high, waiting for the rest of the table to follow his lead, "Long live King Nabopolassar."

"Long live Nabopolassar!" was repeated around the table as goblets clunked together in toast to their gravely ill king.

Jehoiakim stood and followed the prince's lead. He looked at Wakeem with a question, asking for an interpretation. Wakeem leaned over and gave Jehoiakim a quick summary while everyone was being seated.

"I will take the royal guard with me. We will ride hard stopping to rest the horses and meet our basic needs. You are to gather all of the captives that we have left across the countries and return to Babylon along the standard route home. There will be no further campaign at this time to any other peoples, including Egypt."

"How quickly do you want us to begin our return?" asked Zaradan.

"You may start when you feel everything here is ready. Send word ahead to the other camps. They can begin immediately at the same time you do. It is not necessary and actually may be wise, to not have the full group of captives from all the countries traveling along the route at one time. It is easier to provide for a smaller number. I will leave you in charge, Zaradan," said Nebuchadnezzar.

"Sire, I will serve you proudly. We will ask Marduk for your quick journey and your father's good health when you arrive," Zaradan filled his glass with wine and stood, again waiting for others to follow, "To our great general, Nebuchadnezzar. All hail!"

"All Hail!" was heard around the table.

"Thank you, gentlemen. I will see you again when you arrive in Babylon. Take whatever spoil you can along the way. Come back with great wealth and many hands that can serve us well in our great land. I say good night," Nebuchadnezzar stood and left the room.

Then rest of the men relaxed and finished their meal and drinking. Wakeem looked at Jehoiakim, "Well, you will be rid of us very soon. We are leaving in a day or two. The prince is leaving tomorrow at dawn. Don't get any ideas about rebelling against us. I would come back here before you could blink. If you do not send us our tribute, I will come back and steal it from each person who still lives here in this dusty city," he laughed drinking his fill of more wine.

Jehoiakim stood and excused himself from the meal. He was full of food and of words. Tomorrow could not come soon enough for him. He found Tigner to fill him in on what had happened. He would love this story.

The next morning Nebuchadnezzar was up early, eating breakfast by lamp light in his tent. Zaradan came in, "Sire, did you rest well? It is a long trip home and it will help to start with a good night's rest."

"I am fairly fit at this point. Sit and eat with me so we can talk," Nebuchadnezzar invited him to join him. "I want you to tell Wakeem to give the people the chance to go home and get their things. It will save us money, in the long run."

Zaradan listened. This was not always done, but it was not that unusual, "He will handle that well. I was thinking about our departure for Babylon. We have at least two more days to finish up here and be ready for travel. I will send a man this morning to the camps in Megiddo and Syria to tell them to head on to Babylon at their earliest convenience. We will not try to join them. That is what you suggested, right?"

"Yes, I think it makes sense," Nebuchadnezzar grew somber.

"Sire, I am so sorry that your father has taken a turn toward worse health. I know you are concerned about making it home to see him. Can I help you personally?"

"No. I appreciate your interest. It is a great distance home and we will make the best of it. I think I will go directly east from here and cross the desert by the caravan route. It will make us short for water. We will have to be careful. We can cut the distance in half by going this direction. We could never take the captive by this route. It is one thing to find water for a few men and quite another to try to water livestock and thousands of people, plus the army." He leaned back in his seat and drank his strong, black coffee. "How many captives do you think we have here?"

"We estimate just over 3, 000. With the army we will be moving over 8,000 back to Babylon. It will take some careful planning, but we have excellent leadership among the men. We will miss your wisdom, but we are up to the challenge."

"I trained you all well. I am sure all will be well handled." He stood and got a hand full of grapes from the side table, "Is Hammur ready?"

"He is stomping his feet in anticipation of the trip. You know Arabians. They love the long distance travel. He will drink the wind and eat the miles for enough days for you to be home in a week. The wrangler going with you has handled many long, distance trips for others. You can depend on him to take care of Hammur and the others."

"He is a strong horse and has served me well, but if he tires, we will either rest a day or trade him," he said hating even the thought of trading him. He would hate to do that. "I doubt that will be necessary. In the past he has shown his true Arabian nature, covering long distances without effort or without slowing him down the next day.

Zaradan nodded in agreement, "Hammur is a credit to his breed. You can tell he was desert bred for the tough conditions. He will make it home fine. Changing the subject, if you cover 50 or more miles a day, you should be home in a week. I think that is easily doable." Zaradan stood and prepared to leave, "Sire, is there anything else before you leave?"

"I will be out in a minute. See you then."

Zaradan walked over to check out the group of men and animals who had gathered for the trip. Normally, there would be a large entourage traveling with the prince, but this was a skeleton crew designed for fast travel rather than for creature comforts.

"Are the saddle bags packed and loaded? Good. How about water bags? Good. Horse feed sacks on the back? Yes. And blanket rolls for rest? Okay, I think all are in place."

Nebuchadnezzar joined the men. He was dressed for travel, looking more like a desert nomad than a prince. This prince was very familiar with the hardship of desert travel and knew the tricks of making it for many miles with harsh conditions. His head was covered with a linen scarf wrapped with turban. He had a loose-fitting smock over free-flowing trousers. He had sturdy sandals that wrapped up his calf. All of his men were dressed similarly, discarding the uniform for the more practical garb of the desert. They were well armed and ready for travel.

He mounted Hammur, named for the great Babylonian law-giver Hammurabi, who responded with a flip of his head and snort, "Easy boy. Just a couple more minutes," he said rubbing the side of his long neck. "Good luck, men. We will see you in Babylon."

The group took off just after the first rays of the sun were piercing the darkness. They moved directly east along the road to the Jordan River. They would be in Moab and into Syria before the night fell.

They rode steadily for two hours and took a break to drink at the ford in the river. There was a beautiful oasis there that was inviting to them all. They refilled their water bags and rode north and east away from their last major water source for many miles. They rode along the Jordan for as far as they could, to keep water close at hand.

Watching from their small camping area in the oasis were two young people. They stayed out of sight and watched quietly. This was a small band for men stopping for a drink, but it was clear they were on the move and in a hurry. Within half an hour they had moved on.

"I think I recognized one of the men. He was in the tent when dad was killed," said Ezekiel. He was recovering some from his wounds, but was still hurting. It took them all the previous day and part of the night to walk to the river from Jerusalem. He was not moving very quickly, so covering the fifteen miles was an effort. They crossed on the hilly footpath to the river from town. It was very dry and narrow, but had plenty of shade from the sycamore trees.

"I am so relieved that they didn't see us. I don't think they were a raiding party. It looked like they had a destination in mind," said Chloe. "You know the captives might be coming this way, too."

Ezekiel thought about that, "No, I think they will follow the water. That means up the Jordan on the west side and along the coast to the Euphrates. I doubt we see any soldiers or captives."

"That is fine with me. I have seen enough for a lifetime."

"I am tired. I'm going to rest for a while," Ezekiel laid back to rest and Chloe got up to gather some wood. It would be some time before they could return to Jerusalem. They would make do here for now.

CHAPTER 32

"You there, at the gate, open up! It is I, Nebuchadnezzar and my men." he called up to the wall above the gate. Sentries were always on duty. He had come to the back of the city to avoid notice. He would prefer being able to get to his father without fanfare or interruption. He had been gone for months and there would be great joy, under normal circumstances, at his return.

"Wait there, sir, for identification," the guard replied.

In just minutes a man arrived who can confirm whether or not this night visitor is indeed the king's son. He opened the small side gate and called, "Sire, please come to the light," and held the torch high to see the man's face. "Sire, we are so glad to have you back," he said as he bowed before Nebuchadnezzar.

"No time for that now, Phibeck. Get someone to take care of the men and then take me to father."

The two men passed back inside the wall with Hammur close behind. Nebuchadnezzar turned to his horse, patting his neck, "Good work on this long trip, friend. Take him and get him taken care of well. He has done a great service to his kingdom," said Nebuchadnezzar, handing the reigns to a young soldier on guard just inside the entrance.

The rest of the men and horses came inside and went to the stables behind the palace. "Men, come to the palace kitchen in half an hour and we will have something for you to eat," he said to them as they separated from him.

Since he entered from the back of the city, he was nearer the palace than he would have been had he entered the main front gate. Phibeck and he were walking quickly to the palace servant's entrance. "I want to avoid any discussions with people, until I have seen my father. Go ahead of me and clear the way. When you get to father's room, send Tojo to me and you come back to keep people away," Nebuchadnezzar told Phibeck. He went to a trough of water near the wall and splashed water on his face and hands. He took off his riding tunic and slapped away as much dust as he could, then he entered the kitchen.

"Any food to eat in this kitchen, or does a man have to cook for himself these days?" Nebuchadnezzar asks as he walks up behind the main cook, Saroxa.

She turned from kneading the dough for breakfast and looked at a man she hardly recognized. She analyzed the face. Recognition dawned, "Sire. It is so good to see you." She looked him over from head to toe. Speaking with the confidence borne of years of feeding this little boy in the palace kitchen and helping raise him like a great aunt, "Humph, you look a mess."

He hugged her and said, "What's to eat?"

She handed him a slice of beef with bread and a large bowl of yogurt. He sat at the cutting table and ate hungrily while awaiting the return of Tojo.

The door popped open and Tojo entered, "Sire, so good to have you return," he said walking over and bowing from the waist to him. "We really need you here. How did you manage to make the trip so quickly?"

"We went directly through the desert. It cut the time in half. I left the troops and the captives with Nebuzaradan to bring back," Nebuchadnezzar stood and put his hand on the eunuch's shoulder. "Take me to father," he said. They went up the back stairs and down the hall toward his room, "How is he? Prepare me for what to expect with him."

"He is failing fast. We were afraid you would not make it home in time. His doctors say he will live only hours or days. His breathing is ragged and his color is pale. He can only talk for short periods and often drifts off to sleep while talking. They are keeping him quiet as they can. He doesn't seem to be in pain, he is just wearing out." They were at the room door. Phibeck spoke to the guard who opened the door for them.

Nebuchadnezzar walked quietly into his father's room and stood by his bed, Phibeck following him with a lamp. He looked like he might already be dead. Nebuchadnezzar looked up at the eunuch, wondering if he was too late. Phibeck spoke, "Sire, sire. Can you open your eyes for me? I have a surprise for you." There was no movement. Phibeck sat on the edge of the bed and touched the arm of the king, shaking it gently. Such familiarity with the king could be cause for death. But this situation was not one to stand on propriety, but on a friendship of years, "Sire, can you wake for a few minutes. We have something important to say to you."

Nabopolassar's head turned slightly and he took a deep breath. His eyes opened and focused on his eunuch, "Okay, I am with you, Phibeck. What is happening?"

Phibeck stood and motioned for Nebuchadnezzar to sit where he had been sitting. "Father, I am home to see you," Nebuchadnezzar said.

Nabopolassar tried to sit up some and look at his son. "Bring more light," he said. He looked carefully at his son and then reached out to hug him. "It is you, come home from the wars. I didn't think I would make it until you go here." He lay back against his pillows with his son's aid.

"No need to sit up, father. I can hear you fine." They talked about each other and their health and Nebuchadnezzar's trip home.

Then Nabopolassar turned to Phibeck, "You had better get the governor up and get them over here tonight. Who knows how long I have? I do not war a battle for power and leadership after my death."

Those instructions got the palace in motion. By midnight all of the political leaders, though somewhat muddled, were in place in the still-King' bedchamber. Nabopolassar had been robed and was propped up high in h bed. He looked presentable and of sound mind. Nebuchadnezzar was sittin beside his father in an imposing chair, chosen to resemble a throne f semblance. He had clean-up and changed into his princely garb, robes ar crown.

"I will transfer power tonight, conditional to my death, to my sc Nebuchadnezzar. Nebuchadnezzar will sit on my throne beginning tomorro morning." While he was speaking, servants were handing out goblets of wi to all who were in the room. He looked to Tojo for his wine and then he lean up slightly and said, "Long live the new king, Nebuchadnezzar!"

The toast rang around the room. "Long live the king." called all w attended. Though there were some who would rather have said any oth words than those. To say otherwise tonight would have meant instant dea

CHAPTER 33

Zaradan had some of the men get with their sons. Those they thought the soldiers could manage without difficulty. They would send them home to get items to take along. The cheapest way to transport the captives was to allow them to take as much along as they could. If they had clothing, bedding, food or tents, it made it more likely that the people would arrive at their destination alive. It also meant the Nebuchadnezzar did not have to provide for the captives as much. They were sent with soldiers to return to their homes. They could take what they could carry on their shoulders or in their carts. The general provided a few horses or mules, so any man could take a cart. It was not for furniture or big items, but for basic needs. Many men used a cart provided by a neighbor.

Daniel and Gideon came into the courtyard. The first place they went was to find Mary. She was asleep. Gideon knelt beside his mother-in-law's bed, "Mary," he said quietly.

She jumped and gathered her covers around her. Could that actually be Gideon's voice? She never dreamed she would hear it again. The dim light of morning was filtering into the room. "Gideon, is that you?" she asked in disbelief.

"Yes, mother. Daniel and I are both here."

"Oh, my dear ones," she reached out her arms and they both dropped their packs and came over to her bed. After embracing she said, "It is so good to hear your voice and to see you. Oh, God is so good to let me see you both again." They spent some precious minutes together just saying they loved each other.

"Do you know what has happened to Meriel and the children?" asked Gideon.

"Meriel came home...," she told them what had happened. "She left a couple of mornings ago looking for the children. I guess she found them, since she didn't return." Her look was one of worry, "I hope you all find each other again when you are on the road or when you get there."

There was a great deal of weeping from all as she told the story.

"Mother, there is cash upstairs under the stone in the far corner. I think you should have enough to survive well. You might want to sell this home and buy a smaller one. We love you very much."

"I doubt if anyone will have the money to buy this home. I will close up the back part and the rooms that aren't needed. Or maybe I could open an inn and take in boarders. That would help me earn a living. I don't really know, but you needn't worry about me. The Lord has always been faithful to provide for me."

"We have to get busy and gather some supplies before the guard comes. Do you want to walk with us?"

"No, I will go to the kitchen and gather as much food and things that I think you can you use. I will wrap them up and meet you as you are leaving," she said as she grabbed a cape and wrapped it around her. She hurried to the kitchen by the back steps.

They went to their rooms and put on as many pieces of clothing as they could. Then they wrapped up food and some gold in a blanket, and packed more clothes. The gold could be valuable to buy their way out of a problem situation. They took large sashes and laced them together. These they used make straps to go over their shoulders. They hefted two bags each.

The guard appeared in the room and motioned for the two men to come with him. As they were leaving they stopped in the kitchen. Mary had prepared food for them and the guard as well. He allowed them time for breakfast with her and enjoyed his time as well.

They kissed Mary good-bye and put on their shoulder bags, then proceeded with him.

At their home, Hadad and Azariah had taken similar items in their make shift bags. They tied the bag to poles so they could be carried over the shoulders. A neighbor had a small cart which he agreed with share with them. Azariah was able to load several satchels and bedding. They also had two tents and extra canvas, which they took. Azariah walked around Dinah's room trying to decide what else would be of importance. He noticed her new lyre in the corner. They had found it in the market just last week. It would bring her comfort and her music would bless others. He took that to the cart.

When Hadad noticed that he was bringing the lyre along, he said, "Great idea, son. She will love that and so will the rest of us," and patted Azariah's arm.

Hadad nodded to his neighbor that they were ready. The men took up positions around the cart to help steady the cargo and to give them added support as the cart bounced along the rough streets and footpaths. They had only gone a few feet when Azariah heard a quiet, "meow" at his feet. He looked down to find Hagi rubbing against his leg. He wasn't sure what to do with her. Would it work to take a pet on a trip like this and what would the soldiers do? They might not care one way or the other. They might even eat cats, for all he knew. But for now, Hagi was part of the family. Azariah picked her up and settled her among the bedding. Hagi was so glad to be with her family that she purred loud enough for all to hear. That little bit of happiness on her part gave the group a moment of joy. The owner spoke to the mule and the cart moved ahead again. Three armed soldiers followed behind them.

Benjamin was allowed to return to his home, but Mishael was not. They considered him too combative and a risk. It was too bad, really, since that greatly limited what Benjamin could bring with them. He did, however, load three very large shoulder bundles and bring them with him. He knew he couldn't carry them alone for far, but he figured that eventually, they would release Misha, and then he could help him. Misha and Benjamin were both strong from their manual labor. Since Misha was young, they would have him doing some labor during the trip, anyway, so they would have to release him.

Benjamin thought ahead to what it might be like in Babylon. He assumed that is where they would be taken, but he had a hard time imagining what that might be like. He had been to very few places outside of his native country and even there, he had travel mostly near Jerusalem. His contact with foreigners came through business and they came to him with their wares, he didn't go to them.

Babylon was supposed to be a great, modern city. He had heard it was said to be very large with massive walls and a river running through the middle of town. What lay between here and Babylon might be just as amazing.

The guard kicked him on the thigh as he was kneeling down · just daydreaming. Benjamin lifted two packs on his back and put the third on a pole to carry. The guard laughed at the man, shaking his head. He knew no one could carry a load that heavy for very long, but, he admired the man's effort. They joined the others in the street and walked to the camp outside the Sheep Gate.

There were about fifteen hundred men and boys in this area with soldiers patrolling all around. Nebuchadnezzar's camp ground plus the area for the captives and the spoil of war had spread out over twenty acres of land. The wheat and barley grain fields were in this area, but it was so early in the season that they were not high yet. No harvest would be seen this season after the grains were trampled by thousands of people.

Hadad had arrived at camp before his friends because he had use of a cart. It allowed his little group to travel a little faster. He had been allowed to set up the two small tents he had and he gave the canvas to the neighbor who shared his cart with them. In exchange, they would be allowed to share the cart each day during the travel. He had a small camp area established by the time Gideon and Daniel arrived. The Hebrews were allowed to move around within the captive area freely, up to a point.

Hadad and Azariah were sitting outside their tent when Gideon and Daniel walked up. They were exhausted from carrying their bags all the way from town. Hadad caught their attention, motioning for them to set up next to his camp.

"It is a blessing from God to be allowed the freedom to choose something as simple as setting up your camp. I was afraid they would try to keep us all from seeing each other," said Gideon said to Hadad as he dropped the bags on the ground. He and Daniel both sat down to rest. At that moment Hagi came up and jumped in Daniel's lap.

"Well, this is a surprise. Dinah will be thrilled. I hope the cat makes it. I guess her chances are just a good as any of us here, as good as they would be if she was left in town," he said as he scratched under Hagi's chin.

"You are exactly right. The chances are that some of us will not survive the trip. It will be very difficult. I am very concerned for all of us," said Daniel.

Hadad brought out some bread and water for the men, who accepted gladly. After a brief rest, Daniel got up and began opening the bags to see what they had with them. He separated the food from the bedding. He made a stack of clothes and took off all the extra layers he was wearing. He helped his dad to do the same, adding those clothes to the pile.

"Okay, dad, how do you want to set things up here?" Daniel asked.

Hadad stepped in, "May I make a suggestion?"

"By all means," said Gideon.

"I have two tents. If our women survive, and I pray they do, then we could put them all in one tent and the men in the other. That would allow everyone to have a cover over their heads. What do you think?"

"That is very generous of you. Will that meet the needs of your family? They are your tents, after all," said Gideon.

Hadad smiled back at him, "Under these conditions, we must look beyond our own needs to the needs of others. I am blessed to have two tents, but I would be selfish to take only my own families' needs into account."

"Let's see. We have Abigail, Meriel, Salme, Dinah and possibly Jothal who would be in one tent," said Daniel.

Azariah spoke up, "Father, we have someone else to consider, my betrothed and two sons."

Hadad apologized, "Son, I am so sorry. Of course, we will include them. If we add Lotta and the two boys to that tent, we would definitely take Jothal into the men's' tent. That tent would have Gideon, Daniel, Jothal, Azariah and me and sometimes, Nathan. I think both of those would be just fine. What do you think, Gideon?"

Gideon was humbled, "Just to realize how God has provided for us through you humbles me. It would be wonderful to have the set up you suggested and I think it would work perfectly. We would use the tents mostly for sleeping anyway. If they happened to be crowded, it would be fine. We gladly accept your offer. Which tent should be the men's?"

"Let's have the men take the smaller tent. Since there are two little boys in the other tent, they will need some extra room. Daniel and Azariah go ahead and move your things into the right tent. When we set up each night, we will try to always put them with the ladies on the left and us on the right."

While the young men got their tent in order, the men observed what was happening around them. Other captives were coming with a variety of carts, wagons, and other push barrels. They were unloading and the fortunate were putting up tents. Others would have to sleep under the stars, which was not a problem unless the weather turned bad or it became very cold. There were a couple of central campfires burning and some smaller campsites with friends and neighbors pulling in together. Azariah came out with Daniel and they began putting clothes and bedding in the ladies' tent.

When Azariah picked up the lyre to put it inside, Daniel commented, "That was a great thing to bring. Music will help to heal our spirits."

Gideon stood up, "Benjamin, come over here and join our group. We have room for you."

Azariah came out about that time and could see Ben in the distance struggling to make it. He ran to meet him taking two of the packs Ben was carrying, "Sir, you have carried so much. Let me take the third one and you just walk over to the camp and rest. I will bring these on after you." Benjamin gladly accepted the help and transferred all three bags to Azariah's strong shoulders. They finished the walk together to camp.

"Thank you for inviting me to join you all. It would be most lonely without Mishael. I don't know if they will release him or not. Have you seen any of the prisoners since you set up camp? I wonder where they are keeping them," he said.

"I saw a small group at the north edge of the captive's campground. They were kept separate from the free captives," said Azariah.

"If I have time before dark, I would like to head up there to check on him. Maybe we could see him."

"We will go with you in a little while. We wanted to wait to see if maybe they would combine the other camps with us. We were hoping the ladies might join us," said Daniel.

All agreed with that statement and the conversation flow switched to wondering what the women were doing and who had survived. All were hoping their women were all safe. About mid-afternoon new arrivals began walking through the camp from the main entrance area situated to the south. Daniel and Azariah ran to the entrance along with many others to watch for their loved ones. They were not in this group. They returned to camp disappointed.

"We did not see any of our group. Maybe they will bring over the other groups tomorrow. Should we go see if we can find Mishael?" said Azariah.

Benjamin stood up, ready to go. He was rested and was mostly concerned about finding his son. The small group walked toward the north boundary. They passed hundreds of people. Many had nothing with them. They were there with just the clothes on their backs. Some were as fortunate as Hadad and Gideons groups. The soldiers were omnipresent on their horses walking around the edges and through the center of camp. Gideon had chosen a spot about 100 yards from the perimeter, but not on the main track through camp.

This location, he hoped, would avoid many direct contacts with the soldiers.

"There. See the group of men in shackles. I think they are all prisoners," said Azariah to Benjamin. The paced picked up as they neared the perimeter of their camp.

"What do you want?" said a soldier on horseback, standing between the group and the prisoners. It was said in broken Hebrew, but understandable.

"We wanted to see if my son is in the group of prisoners?" this sentence was said with a great amount of hand signals and pointing.

The soldier looked at the prisoners and then back at the men. He motioned for them to follow him. He walked the horse into the crowd of prisoners, sitting in rows with shackles and chains binding them together. They all walked along looking from side to side but they did not see Mishael. When they reached the end of the walk, they looked at each other with the question, 'If he wasn't there, where was he?'

The guard looked back at them and said, "Yes?" They shook their heads no. They were about to walk back to the campground, when he motioned for them to continue to follow him. They walked another 100 yards to a work site. Many men were packing up the things that had been taken from the Jews for the trip to the north. There at a large wagon working with another man was Mishael.

Benjamin motioned to the guard, pointing at Mishael, "Him!"

The guard went to him with the group following behind. Mishael saw the guard first and then the group of friends and his father not far behind. He stopped his work, but did not get out of the wagon. He was not shackled, but he had been beaten with a whip. His back and arms showed large red whelps where the whip done its damage. That must be the reason he was afraid to stop his work. The guard motioned from him to get off the wagon and come to the group.

He eagerly jumped down and went to see his father. Never before had enjoyed a hug and hated the pain it caused. He pulled away flinching. "What are you all doing together and doing here? How did you find me?"

They gave him the short version of the story. They filled him in on the fact that the women had not been seen yet. Now that they had visited for a while, they weren't really sure what he had to do next. They wondered if he could come with them or if he had to stay?

Their question was answered when the guard came over and motioned him back into the wagon to continue his work. The group was escorted back to their campsite. Although, they would glad to have seen him, they were disappointed he was not allowed to return with them. The evening was still good, though, because they had at least found each other for now. Tomorrow was another day when, maybe, the ladies would be found.

CHAPTER 34

The next day the spring morning dawned bright and clear. A trumpet sounded with a strange tone to the ears of the Hebrews, but a tone that over the next months would become familiar. It was a long blast, followed by two short blasts and another long. A few minutes after the sound soldiers came through camp making sure everyone was up and addressing the needs of the day—dressing, eating and preparing for whatever they were told to do.

Meriel said, "Okay, everyone up." She shook Jothal and said, "Jothal, get up and go with Abeetha to the main gate. The food wagon will be arriving soon. We may as well be ready today. Yesterday we got the remnants of food that were left because we waited too long to get in line."

Jothal was rubbing his tired eyes. It was just after sunrise when the trumpet blast woke him. He said, "You know, mom, I think that trumpet just means get up and get ready. It is the same as what happened yesterday when we heard it for the first time."

"And I think it may have something to do with food arriving, but I am not sure yet," added Lotta. "Dinah, if you will watch the boys, I will go with them to get the food."

"Sure will. Do you think the three of you can handle it?" They all laughed. Yesterday the food supplied had been pitiful. They were given day-old bread, cheese, water and some early-birds got yogurt.

"Very funny. Maybe today will be better, since we are going early," Lotta said, as she turned to go to the gate with Jothal and Abeetha. They had been in place just about five minutes when the gate opened and the wagons began to arrive. There were more wagons today. They were getting a little better organized. They waited their turn and were given a better selection today.

At the first wagon each individual or group was given bread in a basket and it was fresh. Lotta took Jothal with her to help and Abeetha went separately in order to get more food. At the second wagon they got a flask or skin of grape juice and at the third wagon cheese was added to the basket along with a couple of hands-full of figs.

When they got back everyone was excited. This was real food and they were starved. Not much had been given to them to eat since they had been made captives. Within half an hour all of the food was consumed. They could probably have eaten more, but at least they were satisfied for now. The gnawing hunger was stopped. They saved the flasks and baskets, hoping they would not be taken away from them. Every item was of great value when you own nothing at all, but the clothes on your back.

"Do you think they will let us have the baskets? It would be helpful carrying items when we travel...," said Jothal.

"...and we could gather wood in them for a fire," added Meriel.

"Maybe there will be berries or wild wheat on the roads that we could fill them with," imagined Abigail. "Umm, does that sound wonderful. Fresh berries?"

"Stop it. You will make me hungry again," warned Dinah.

"Looks like they are pulling all the wagons out. Breakfast must be finished and they didn't take the basket or flasks back. That is really good for us," said Abeetha. She was becoming more relaxed with the family unit she was a part of.

Just then the trumpet sounded again. This time it was a totally different sound. This was three equal tones with a fourth tone lower and longer. They had no idea what it meant, but again the soldiers appeared. They got everyone up and pointed at them to take their things with them. Then they forced the captives to more forward toward the main gate. They were actually leaving. But to where?

Salme started crying immediately. Meriel picked her up and held her close, "Honey, don't cry. We will go someplace new and I am sure it will be exciting" she tried to comfort her daughter.

"Mommy, I want to go to my house. Why can't we go home? I miss grandmother. Why can't we go home and see her?" the crying continued.

A soldier rode up beside them and reached down grabbing Salme from Meriel's arms. Meriel began screaming, "Oh, please, don't hurt her. She is just a baby. She is just a baby." He rode away with Salme on his saddle front. She was no longer crying; she was hysterical.

Abigail came over and held Meriel, "I am sure he is just trying to scare her into being quiet. He surely wouldn't harm her." She was trying to encourage her, but in truth, she was not so sure he wouldn't kill her. She had heard rumors about the dashing children against stone walls and streets, killing them or maiming them. She knew that was what Meriel was thinking.

They pushed ahead as quickly as they could trying to see the horse and soldier that had taken Salme. The crowd was so thick that they couldn't see anyone that looked like him. If she was crying, they would not have heard her. Her voice was just too small. Meriel was frantic. Running to one side and then the other.

The rest of the group tried to help look, but they were afraid to separate. They were not sure they would be able to find each other in this crowd or whether they would be allowed to move through the group that freely. Meriel asked, "Can we move to the outside edge of the crowd on the left. We can try to stand still or walk slowly. Then we can see if she is on that side. If a guard comes along to push us forward, we can walk across the people to the right and look there too."

They all agreed that was an excellent idea. They had just passed to the outside of the gate and were able to maneuver to the left side of the group.

"Do you see him or is she anywhere around? Call her name. Salme! Salme!" she was trying to look like she was moving so the guard wouldn't suspect anything. "Oh, God. Where is she?" she was losing it again. "You all just aren't trying hard enough. I know that you can find her. Look everywhere."

Abigail came to her, "Get hold of yourself, Meriel. This attitude isn't helping any of us. We are trying and looking. Let's move to the other side." They re-grouped.

"Abeetha, you take the lead fighting your way across the crowd. I am too overcome," she asked her friend.

Abeetha lead the way, weaving in and out of moms and children and old men. Finally, they were across. The soldier was not seen anywhere. They tried calling and looked while they were moving.

"I see a little spot against the wall over there. See?" said Dinah. "Do you want me to go look?"

Abigail said, "Yes, but be careful. The guards may stop you. Point to the spot, if they do." Dinah walked carefully, trying to not draw attention. She was about half-way to the wall when a guard rode up to see what she was doing out there by herself.

He moved between her and the wall pointing for her to return to the line. She smiled and pretended to not understand. She tried to walk around his horse and continue to the wall. He repositioned himself and pointed again, this time with anger. She smiled again and pointed at the small spot of color against the gray stone. He looked and then rode over to it. He motioned for her to come and see.

She shook her head 'no' and ran back to her group. "It was someone's old blanket. It looked like it had blood on it."

"Oh, why couldn't that have been her?" All the time they are moving away from the theatre and to the Jaffa Gate. The closer they got to the gate, the more upset Meriel became. She was sure they had left Salme somewhere near the theatre and she did not want to leave without finding her. Outside the walls she somehow thought Salme would never be seen again.

Once they were on the road walking north, Meriel became quiet. There was no further use, in her mind, of mourning. She was convinced that they had left Salme in the city somewhere, maybe alone, maybe injured and maybe dead. She became numb, just moving like the walking dead with no will to live.

At the men's camp the morning had started with a similar set of events except they were not traveling. Azariah said, "I am going down with Daniel to wait at the gate. Maybe they will move the other captives today. If you are here, then there will be someone to welcome them at either location." The men had already had breakfast and were ready to greet the day.

Azariah and Daniel got near the camp entrance which was set up with check-in system. Each of the men had already been registered yesterday. The second group that afternoon also had their names listed. The wagons that bordered each side were equipped with a scribe and an interpreter. Daniel and Azariah were seated about fifty feet from the wagons on the most likely track for all newcomers.

"I am really concerned. What if one of the ladies or children is not in the final group? I heard there were only three groups," asked Azariah.

"It is possible and some might say likely that all our families will not remain complete. We would be blessed indeed, if they were," Daniel stood look into the distance. They had been waiting about half an hour. "Do you see dust rising over to the south, there?"

Azariah stood, "I can't really tell. It might be fog." They continued to watch.

"No, it is dust rising, like when horses and people are walking along that highway. I think this might be our group coming. I am going to run back and tell dad. I will be back by the time the first of the group is processed," said Daniel. He took off running with the news.

Azariah continue to look into the distance. It was indeed dust, and it was getting closer by the minute. He was getting anxious. He would be thrilled to see his family, but he would be sick if one of them was not among the last group.

Daniel returned, "How close are they?"

"About ten minutes. What did the dads say?" asked Azariah.

"They are relieved, but somewhat afraid, too."

The soldiers arrived at the wagons giving the scribes an update in their native language. Then the first group who arrived at the wagons was processed and they began to straggle in. For some, it was a glad reunion. There were hugs and tears and weeping with joy. What was lost had been found!

The interpreters were calling out instructions, as the groups were processed, "You need to begin looking around the campground to see if any of your fathers, sons or husbands are here. If they are not, then they many be among the ones put into shackles in another area. You may travel together as a family."

Daniel noticed several more groups arrived and then a strange little group of soldiers surrounding a pitiful dozen children, who obviously, had lost parents or were just lost. They were terrified. It was like looking into the eyes of a stray dog, belonging to nobody.

Then two eyes caught his attention, "Salme!" he yelled at the top of his lungs and ran as close as he could get to where her little group was being processed. She did not hear him and she could not see him. He just had to wait.

After a few minutes the children were allowed to walk between the wagons. Most were holding hands with someone else, just for security. They probably had not known that person when they were living in town, but for this time, that person was very important to them.

When Salme finally came out from between the wagon, Daniel dropped to his knees in front of her and just smiled. He said nothing.

Salme did not smile, speak or cry. She looked at him as if he were a total stranger. "Sister, it is me, your brother, Daniel." He did not touch her. He was afraid he would frighten her further. He just waited. He motioned for the little boy she was holding hands with to follow him over to the side.

"What's your name, son?"

"I am Seth. Have you seen my mommy?" he asked with the sweetest voice. It nearly broke Daniel's heart.

"Honey, I have not seen her, but how about if you and Salme come home with me and we will look for her in a little while," asked Daniel. Seth agreed. "Azariah, I am taking these two to the tent. I will try to come back soon. Okay, kids, let's go to our tent." He tried to take Salme's hand, but she pulled it in against her and looked at the little boy, like he was her only friend. Daniel took his hand and they walk they few minutes to the tent.

When they got near the tent, Daniel saw the three fathers sitting on a log waiting. Gideon ran to them, when he saw it was Salme with Daniel. He picked her up and began hugging her and talking, "Hello, my lovely one. I am so glad to see you. Are you okay? Where is your mommy?"

She looked at him with those blank eyes and then tried to get down. He looked at Daniel and said, "What is going on? Why is she like this?"

"I don't know. She was with this little boy, Seth, who has lost his mommy, too. She did not know me either. She seems to be in a trance or something."

Gideon sat down with her on his lap, "Seth, come over here and sit beside us. Tell me about where you have been."

"Well, I was with my mommy and then a soldier took me away because I was crying so hard. They put me with lots of other children and I didn't see mommy again." He looked by at Gideon, "Will you help me find her?"

Gideon pulled him close, "You can depend on us to try very hard to find your mommy. We will start looking later. I am going to wait to see if our mommy comes to our tent. You can go back with Daniel and watch the ladies coming from the city. Would you like that? Maybe you can see your mommy."

He looked at Daniel. Daniel stood and held out his hand, "Let's go back and watch the people. We will look for her as they come in." Seth smiled for the first time as they began their walked back to join Azariah at the wagons. When they arrived, he asked Azariah, "Have you seen anyone else we know?"

"No, but look at all the people waiting to be processed. It will take many more hours. We have nothing else to do, anyway, but wait." They could see the crowd going back from the wagons about half a mile. Azariah turned to Daniel, "How is Salme? Did she respond to her father?"

"Azariah, she is so sad. I hope she snaps out of it after she gets some rest and is with us for a while. I cannot stand to see her like this," said Daniel.

They had been sitting an hour, faithfully watching everyone that went by. Every once in a while, they would look to Seth with a question, "See anyone you know?"

His sad little face and eyes told them she had not come in yet. It was getting near lunch and they were feeling hungry. Daniel looked down at Seth and he was sleeping in a little ball beside him. Daniel hated to wake him, but more ladies were coming in and maybe one of them was his mother, "Seth, there are some more captives coming in. Do you want to see them to see if your mother is here?" He touched his shoulder and tried to wake him. He did not stir.

"Azariah, why don't you go get us something to eat and I will keep watching while he sleeps. Maybe someone will know who his mother is." Daniel picked Seth up and set him in his lap with his little face resting against his shoulder, so that it could be clearly seen.

Azariah came back with dates and cheese and a flask of water, which he had just filled from a barrel in the center of camp.

"It is not much, but it will hold you over until later. He is still asleep, huh?" He looked at Seth, who was resting conformably in Daniel's lap.

"I wish I had asked Seth what his mommy's name was. That might have helped, if we had to call out to get her attention."

Many captives were just standing in the center of the camp looking around, not sure what to do next. A great number of these were ladies who could be Seth's mother. Daniel tried again to wake Seth, "Seth, wake up and look at the ladies standing here. They have just arrived. Also, I have some cheese and dates for you."

Seth stirred and looked up at Daniel, "I am hungry." He ate several dates and a big chunk of cheese. Daniel gave him the flask, which he tipped up and drank from. Before he had finished more than a few sips, he choked. Then he stood, dropping the flask and running away from Daniel toward the ladies. In the center of the group stood a woman of thirty who appeared to be alone. She was like the rest, standing still and just staring. By the time Seth reached her side he was crying and screaming at her, "Mommy."

It was a moment until he was close enough for her to hear, then her head

273

turned toward the direction of the call, "Mommy!" She scanned the crowd. She thought it sounded like Seth, but she was sure he must be dead by now. He had been missing for days. She had given up on him long ago.

Seth came into view about twenty feet from his mother. She began to tremble and wave her arms in no particular pattern. She was just so happy, she couldn't move. He ran all the way to her side where she scooped him into her arms. She sat down right there on the spot and held him, both weeping freely and rocking back and forth.

"Seth, oh, Seth. I thought you were gone for good. I thought the soldiers had hurt you. Mommy is so glad to see you. What happened?"

He told her his story up until today when the two kind men took care of him. He turned and pointed in Daniel and Azariah's direction. She came over, "I am Sarah. Thank you so much for helping Seth. I am so glad there was someone who cared in this crazy situation for my little boy."

"It was my privilege. I am glad you are here and he found you again. We are looking for our families. Have you seen Abigail, wife of Hadad, or Meriel, wife of Gideon?" Azariah asked.

"I don't know Abigail, but I know Meriel from her shop. She was in the theatre with several other ladies and some children. She was safe and healthy."

"Oh, that is indeed good news. Thank you for the encouragement. We will keep looking for them," said Daniel.

"And thank you. We are going to look for our families. Several of us have been helping each other and they are waiting." She bowed slightly indicating her gratefulness. She returned with Seth to the central area where she had been standing. The group moved to their right in camp.

Azariah returned to sit down with Daniel, "I have been watching while you were visiting. What did she say?"

"Nothing we didn't know, except that she saw your mother safe and healthy in the theatre," Azariah smiled at his friend's obvious relief.

"That is wonderful news. Then I should be looking carefully. We will be seeing her soon." They continued to watch into the afternoon. Mid-afternoon a group of ladies entered on the far side, away from where they were sitting. None of them looked familiar until Daniel remembered that they had been in those clothes and unwashed for days. They would all look more frazzled than he was used to seeing.

He stood up and looked more carefully. First he saw Abeetha, which meant nothing to him until he saw her talking to a little boy. It was Jothal. He poked Azariah, "Stand up and look at this group with me. See over there on the far side by the barrel, I think that is Abeetha talking with Jothal. Doesn't that look like her with my brother? How on earth did the city prostitute end up talking to him? That is amazing. Let's go over. Maybe the rest are not far behind."

They trotted across the space stopping in beside Abeetha. Azariah spoke to Abeetha, "Hello. I am Azariah. I see you are with Jothal. We were wondering if you have seen Abigail or Meriel or Lotta?"

Daniel knelt down to hug his squealing brother. They were rocking side to side and laughing, but he was still listening to Abeetha's response.

"Hello to you. Yes, they are all right behind me. See. Look coming just over there," she pointed about fifty feet behind her.

There was the most beautiful group of disheveled ladies they had ever seen. They all ran into a huddle hugging and crying, each talking as fast as they could about how the other was and what had been happening.

"Let's go to our camp. It is good, really. I think you will be happy," said Daniel to the ladies.

They all walked up together. Gideon went to his wife and they hugged and kissed, then she laid her head on his shoulder and wept. "Oh, Gideon, I am so glad to see you again and to know that Daniel is safe. But, I have lost our daughter. A soldier took her away and I cannot find her anywhere. We have looked and looked," she just couldn't stop crying.

Gideon put his finger under her chin and nodded, "I am so sorry you are suffering with this, but I have something to show you. This is the ladies' tent. You will be sleeping here with the children," when he said that word, her tears began to flow again. He stopped talking and took her hand.

"Gideon, it is wonderful to have a tent and I would like to see it sometime, but don't you think we should start searching to see if we can find Salme?" she asked her husband.

He did not speak, but continued walking as if he couldn't hear her. She was a little frustrated with his nonchalance, but followed him anyway. This would not take long, and then they could begin looking for her.

He pushed the tent flap back and motioned for her to proceed into the tent. There was a small bundle lying on a palette of blankets. Her eyes could not see inside clearly yet, but it looked like a child. The light in her mind dawned before any light ever reached her eyes. She ran to the palette and knelt beside her daughter, "Salme, darling, it is mommy. Salme, wake up honey. I want to talk with you." She did not respond. Meriel looked up at Gideon.

"She has been like this since we found her this afternoon. She was with a group of children and was holding the hand of a boy named Seth. We have no idea what happened. He just said they were all taken from their mothers and put with this group. I guess it was a form of punishment for children they didn't like. Was Salme doing something when they took her?"

She was still listening, but her eyes were on Salme, "She was hysterical with fear and was crying. He just rode up beside me and jerked her out of my arms. Then he rode off with her. That was this morning and I haven't seen her since. What is wrong with her? She hasn't talked to you or Daniel?"

"Not only has she not talked. She acts like she doesn't even know who we are. I wonder if she could be in a stupor from fear. I have heard of that happening before, haven't you?" he asked her.

"Yes, I have heard of that. It is just hard for me to imagine our vibrant Salme so silent and distant. What are we going to do?"

"Let's just let her sleep and when she wakes up, we will see how she responds. Maybe time will make things better." She agreed and they went back outside.

Over the next hour everyone got settled in their tents. The men had not asked yet what was going on with Abeetha. They were curious, but they assumed that they would find out soon what was going on. For now the men were waiting until the ladies could or would talk.

"Hadad, this is unbelievable. We can actually live our life almost in a normal fashion for nomads. And the tents are just an added blessing. I had forgotten we had these."

Dinah came in, "Dad, this is so wonderful. It seems unbelievable after not having anything over our heads for days," she said. She was going through her things and noticed a wooden object in the corner. She held her breath, "Is that my lyre in the corner?" she looked up at her father.

"You need to thank him for thinking of you," he said pointing to Azariah. "Of course, we will all be blessed by your music, too. So I think he may have had a selfish motive," he added.

They were about ready to step out of the tent when a little fur ball appeared beside Dinah. "Hagi, oh, I can't believe it. Dad, how did you do it, in this place? I just can't believe it." She picked her up and held her close. This was one of the most comforting things that could ever have happened to her. She lay back on the blanket and just rested with her beside her purring. Hadad and Abigail left her there, contentedly petting her cat.

Sitting on the log watching the boys, Azariah was in deep conversation

276

with Lotta, "But I think we should go ahead and get married while we are on the road. I am sure there are priests traveling with us."

"Azariah, let's be reasonable for just a minute. We don't have any idea what lay ahead for us. I am not opposed to getting married, but let's wait until we see how this all works. I still love you just as much, but love alone is not enough right now. If you would just be willing to see how things are going to go...," she suggested as he walked away from her and took off down one of the many corridors between the people.

Lotta looked up at Abigail, "Well, I didn't handle that very well, did I?"

"You did fine, my dear. He is just afraid of losing you again and thinks that if he marries you, he can protect you from harm. I wish that just marrying guaranteed safety, but it doesn't. Give him a chance to think through your suggestion. I think is made sense," said Abigail.

"Benjamin, where is Misahel?" asked Lotta.

"He is being held in a different area in shackles. We did get to see him, but they have not released him. I don't know whether or not they will let him go." He was resolved, but not unhappy. He could wait until that day came.

CHAPTER 35

The trumpet blast woke them as usual, but nothing about today was usual. Their families were together, but they were starting over. Life would never be the same. It didn't matter that they were living in a tent rather than their homes. In fact, they were so grateful for the tents that the houses seemed like unnecessary luxuries.

"Oh, I slept so well last night. Just having our family whole made me able to relax and sleep," said Meriel to Gideon when he joined her at the campfire.

"I feel the same way. Now if we can see an improvement in Salme, our reunion will be complete. Was she awake when you came out this morning?"

"No, she was still sleeping. Maybe being with us and having enough sleep will help her recover. Abigail, how can I help?" said Meriel.

"Could you go ahead and get water for the cooking? Use the flasks we have. We have some food, but I don't see any utensils. Hadad, did you put any pans in the cart when you took things from the house?" Abigail asked.

He came out of the men's tent, putting his arm through the other side of the tunic, "What did you say?" rubbing his beard and eyes.

"Pots and pans? I don't see any. How can a woman cook for the family without pots?" Abigail wanted to make breakfast and wasn't sure how to do so without pans.

"Sorry, honey. I wasn't thinking about cooking when I loaded the wagon. Let's see what we can do. What are you going to need?"

"I would like to make bread. I have flour and we can add some water and dates. It will be good."

Hadad disappeared and returned with a pan and some large stones. Abigail raised her eyebrows, "Where do you get that?"

"I bartered one of the baskets for a pan. The stones are to cook the bread either on or under as an oven," he said. He dug a hole and gathered some brush and dead wood. The fire was burning well by the time Abigail was ready. The stone was rather rounded and smooth. He balanced it over the coals on two lower rocks. Abigail took a handful of dough and rolled it into a ball and then tossed it into the air until it was flat and about the size of a spread out hand. Abigail took the small flat rounds and tossed them on the heated stone. When one side was finished, she took an edge and turned the bread. They were thrown into the basket when they were cooked.

Dinah was up and getting some more flasks of water and also cutting pieces of cheese and placing them at the other end of the bread basket. The baking bread smelled so good. It had been a while since anyone had the privilege of cooking a good, hot meal. She would enjoy the break so much. It wouldn't keep after today, but at least for this day, they would have good bread. Dinah also made some coffee in the washed pot that the bread dough had been made in.

By the time the bread was completed everyone had gathered around, sitting on the ground or squatting around the fire. The smell was so inviting. Before they ate, Hadad prayed for everyone and thanked God that all were here. He also prayed for Mishael's return to them.

They dug in to the communal basket. All were busy with their breakfast. Meriel reached into the basket for more bread, when she saw a small hand reach in with hers for a piece of cheese. When she looked down, Salme was squatting beside her. Meriel smiled, but did not rush to touch her. She was afraid she would frighten Salme.

"Good morning, sweetheart. It is good to see you up. Would you like some water?" she questioned calmly.

Salme looked at her with neutrality, but seemed to know her, "Yes, mommy."

When Meriel heard her speak again, it took all her will-power to not pick her up and weep. Instead, Meriel took a flask and handed it to Salme and then sat back from her haunches and rested on the ground. Salme got in her lap and lay back on her chest. She just sat there quietly. A tear rolled down Meriel's cheek as told God thank you for Salme's improvement.

A jolting trumpet blast shocked them out of the moment and sent tremors through Salme. Meriel did not move, she just waited until Salme grew calm again. The last time they had heard that blast was at the theatre. It was followed by the soldiers ushering them out of there and on to the road.

Daniel asked, "I haven't heard that call before. Anyone else heard it?"

Abigail spoke, "We heard it at the theatre. The guards came in and began moving us out to the road. I think it means we will be going soon."

Gideon added, "If we are leaving then it must be to head north. I don't think they will move us again to anywhere here in this area." He had a funny feeling in his stomach.

Azariah looked at Lotta, "It is hard to believe we may never be here again. I never thought about my home until it was gone. But to think it might not be possible to ever come back in my lifetime is very hard."

"I know, my dear. I feel the same way and I have one other reason to miss town. I am leaving my parents behind. I can't even...," she began to cry, "...imagine not seeing them again and that they will never see Nathan or Mattan. My two boys will not know their grandparents at all. It breaks my heart." She leaned her head on Azariah's shoulder. She did not weep, but silent tears trickled down her cheeks.

"We had better pack up. I don't want to get caught when it is time to go and have to leave things behind because we aren't ready. Let's get started."

He stood up and snuffed the fire out and went to the men's tent. Within a short time all of the items inside the tent were ready for travel. Azariah and Daniel took the tents down. The neighbor with the cart was camped just around the corner. They were loading the tents when the first soldiers arrived on horseback.

There were soldiers on the road to Shechem called the Patriarch's Highway. About horsemen lead the way with leaders and guests from Nebuchadnezzar's army coming right behind them. It was always wise to be at the head of the caravan. Those at the back ate the dust from the traffic and smelled the stench of animals and people ahead of them. After the leaders, came the shackled men and they were flanked by several soldiers. Then they moved the camp starting with those to the north and ending the camp that had originally been near the entrance where the wagons were set-up. Finally, the rest of the army moved behind them for miles along with wagons of booty, wagons of food, livestock and chariots. Soldiers were on foot, in chariots and on horseback. The caravan was strewn over about five miles of highway.

Just before the soldiers moved their group, Abeetha set Nathan on top of the cart and put Salme beside him. They made a sling that was large enough to hold Mattan on someone's back. He started the day with his step-mother. She would trade with others, when she got tired.

They had no idea what to expect. Walking around town or in the country would not compare to walking miles and miles day after day. It would take months of walking to reach their far off destination. They had no idea how far it really was.

It started easily. They were generally rested from the days of waiting. They had fairly clean clothes. Their feet had no blisters and their muscles didn't ache. The day held a great amount of anticipation mixed with grief.

As they walked north away from town weeping could be heard across the miles. The captives were leaving the land they loved, possibly forever. Dinah looked back, stopping among the throngs. She wanted to remember her land. She would tell her children about Jerusalem, her home.

THE END